FRONTIER

BAEN BOOKS
by PATRICK CHILES

Frozen Orbit
Frontier

FRONTIER

PATRICK CHILES

BAEN

FRONTIER

A Baen Books Original

Baen Publishing Enterprises
P.O. Box 1403
Riverdale, NY 10471
www.baen.com

ISBN: 978-1-9821-2541-7

Cover art by Bob Eggleton

First printing, June 2021

Distributed by Simon & Schuster
1230 Avenue of the Americas
New York, NY 10020

Library of Congress Cataloging-in-Publication Data

Names: Chiles, Patrick, author.
Title: Frontier / by Patrick Chiles.
Description: Riverdale, NY : Baen Books, [2021] | A Baen Books Original.
Identifiers: LCCN 2021011869 | ISBN 9781982125417 (trade paperback)
Classification: LCC PS3603.H5644 F756 2020 | DDC 813/.6—dc23
LC record available at https://lccn.loc.gov/2021011869

Printed in the United States of America

10 9 8 7 6 5 4 3 2 1

For my late grandfather, Joseph Gooch,
who patiently nurtured my early fascination
with astronomy and space exploration.
Hopefully this makes up for all those times
I disassembled his pocket watch.

◈ PROLOGUE ◈

Front Range Spaceport, Denver, CO

"A thousand things can happen when you light a rocket engine. Only one of them is good."

Marshall Hunter had heard that refrain from his old man and his extended family of spaceplane pilots so often that it had threatened to lose all meaning. As he'd learned to fly these powerful machines, it had become a mantra he repeated to himself before every flight.

As he approached his assigned plane, a westerly wind with a hint of vanilla from the nearby Ponderosa forests mixed with the odor of kerosene fuel into an aroma disturbingly similar to the floor cleaner from the junior officer's quarters. With an annoyed wrinkle of his nose, Marshall shook off the unwelcome reminder of barracks life and began his preflight inspection.

The Puma suborbital trainer was a squat, flat-nosed craft sporting twin vertical stabilizers at the tips of its clipped delta wing. The little spaceplane's cockpit had just enough room to seat two pilots in front of a pressure bulkhead that separated them from tanks of liquid oxygen and RP-1 rocket fuel.

Marshall moved methodically from nose to tail and wingtip to wingtip, measuring his progress against a checklist on the tablet he carried. He'd flown this little craft enough that the preflight routine was burned into his brain. Opening the checklist itself had become a rote formality—by now he could recite it from memory, but he didn't trust the training squadron to not slip in some minor change just to trip up an overconfident student.

Finally arriving at the tail—the rocket plane's business end—he opened an engine access panel to make sure all the plumbing was still in the right place and not leaking. The engine itself was sparkling clean but for the usual discoloration around the nozzle: the glazing of high-temperature alloys after repeated ignition cycles. If there were a fault hidden in there somewhere, there'd be precious little he could do here to detect it. If there were some dormant failure lurking in there with his name on it, then the gremlin would find him soon enough. That's what the "Dash-One" emergency memory items were for. And if those failed, there was always the ejection seat. He tried not to think about that.

Moving on, he went back to the wing and worked his way out to the oversized winglets at either end. He paid particular attention to the reinforced carbon heat shielding around its leading edge: of all the potential catastrophic failures, this was one of the few he could evaluate with his own eyes ahead of time.

Satisfied with their integrity, he tapped an icon on the tablet marking his preflight checklist complete. It would show up immediately in the training squadron's records and let his instructor pilot know that Ensign M. T. Hunter was ready to blast.

The IP, a newly-minted lieutenant named Wylie, hadn't needed the automated records to let him know as he'd been watching from a distance the whole time. This being the check ride for Marshall's "suborbital rocket vehicle" endorsement, he wasn't about to let any detail slip by that might potentially fail a candidate on his final exam.

"Let's go," the IP said abruptly as he passed Marshall from behind, bounding up the access ladder and tossing his flight bag behind the seat in one motion.

Show off. "Yes sir," Marshall said, dutifully climbing up the opposite ladder and carefully slipping his own bag beneath the restraining net behind his seat and securing his IP's wayward gear at the same time.

Lieutenant Wylie stared impatiently at him as he locked down his shoulder and lap restraints. If it was a ploy to throw him off, he was determined to keep it from working. This was supposed to be a final check ride, not an exercise in tripping up the student. But if that's how he wanted to play the game, so be it.

"Pre-departure briefing," Marshall recited with detached cool as he pulled up the next checklist, apparently satisfying the IP's unspoken demand. "Winds favor takeoff on three-four left, standard profile. V1 is 131 knots, if there's an engine failure after V1 we'll follow the emergency procedure. Otherwise we'll maintain centerline heading into the warning area and start our pitch-up maneuver at the entry waypoint, maintaining sixty-degree climb angle until engine cutoff at four minutes, fifty seconds."

"And is that time hack from launch or pitch up?"

"Pitch up," Marshall confirmed. *It always is.*

"Important to know," the IP said as if he were imparting hard-won wisdom.

Marshall nodded as if he'd learned something. "Predicted apogee is three hundred eighty thousand feet, max velocity seventeen hundred knots. MMO is Mach 3.6. Flight path will take us up along the front range, all inside the warning area."

"Winds aloft?"

At which level? Marshall wondered, and decided on the most impactful. He looked up, studying the rows of thin clouds high to the east. "Jet stream core's forecast a hundred knots out of the northwest, so I expect some mountain wave turbulence between flight levels three-six-zero to four-zero-zero."

"Will that be a problem for us?"

"By that point we'll be at Mach and blow through it fast on the climb," Marshall said. "We'll have to suck it up and ride out the bumps on our way down."

"You might consider extending west after reentry, get on the other side of that turbulence and then cross the ridgeline back to base."

Marshall felt his eyebrows lift and quickly changed expressions, hoping to hide his reaction. That was a dumbass idea if he'd ever heard one. "We'll be a glider at that point, sir. I'll have to see what our energy state is, but I'd prefer to avoid that scenario."

"We'll see about that," Wylie said in words pregnant with certitude. "Word is your old man taught you a thing or two about flying gliders."

And here we go, Marshall realized. *One more prick who wants to make sure I don't get any special favors.* "Yes sir, I learned all kinds of tricks from him."

✖   ✖   ✖

The lineup and takeoff were uneventful but for the merciless kick in the seat that always came from lighting a rocket motor with thirty thousand pounds of thrust. Even at partial power, the little spaceplane hurtled down the runway and leapt into the cobalt sky.

Marshall kept still against the headrest, not fighting the steady two-g pull as they accelerated away from the field. His eyes darted across the control panel, alternating his instrument scan with quick peeks outside for any conflicting traffic that ATC might have overlooked. "Passing ten thousand," he said for the IP's benefit. "Initial point in five, four . . ."

"No need to count down, Ensign. Just do it."

Arriving at "zero" in his head, Marshall silently pushed the throttle full forward and pulled back on the control stick until the nose settled at sixty degrees up: not vertical, but it sure felt like it.

Marshall watched the digital Mach meter tick upward as the little craft shot through the thick lower atmosphere. He could feel the high-frequency vibration building as they became transonic, the control stick buzzing against his hand as the shock wave crept along the wing and over the control surfaces. Even before his instruments gave him the cue, he could feel the spaceplane was ready for one final burst of power. "Max Q," he said, and moved the throttle lever to its forward detent, applying the last few thousand pounds of thrust and watching the fuel and oxidizer totals head for zero. He'd burn through most of it up through engine cutoff, hoarding a few hundred pounds in reserve for the return leg just in case.

As expected, wind shear buffeted them as they pierced the coursing jet stream, fast enough that it was no worse than driving over a rough patch of highway. It would feel a lot different on the way back down, with less speed and a lighter craft. He expected to get tossed around like a leaf on the wind.

The sky ahead had already turned a deep violet as they left a final layer of wispy cirrus behind. The ride became strikingly smoother, the only vibration coming from the rocket motor as it began to burn itself out. Passing one hundred thousand feet, nearly all meaningful atmosphere was now beneath them. Marshall compared the predicted vector on his vertical situation display against remaining fuel. Main engine cutoff at 180,000 feet would send them vaulting well above the Karman line, officially into space with a good four minutes of freefall as they coasted over the top of an almost seventy-mile-high parabola.

The press of gravity vanished as Marshall chopped the throttle and began their coast into the black sky above. With the g's subsided, he took a quick peek over his shoulder at the mottled brown and green hues of Colorado far below. A thin blue line outlined the curving horizon: the fragile shell of Earth's atmosphere they'd briefly left behind.

"You didn't call out main engine cutoff," Wylie noted. "Good to know."

I thought you didn't want . . . oh, whatever. "Yes sir," Marshall said. "That was MECO."

The ride over the top remained smooth and quiet if only for the lack of conversation. Normally, Marshall would've let out at least one whoop of joy but set that aside today in the hopes of passing his check ride with this unpredictable lieutenant. Now, the only sounds were the whir of cooling fans and the occasional puff of a reaction control jet.

The g's mounted rapidly as the plane fell back into the atmosphere belly first, aided by drag flaps which Marshall carefully manipulated in the thickening air.

"Extend to the west," Wylie ordered. "Get us around that clear-air turbulence."

It caught Marshall off guard. This was a check ride; the IP wasn't supposed to be giving instructions. He glanced at his airspeed and altitude, making a quick judgment of their energy state. They could do it, but . . .

"I don't like it, sir," he said, peering over the nose at the furrows of thin clouds racing below. "I'd rather take my chances with those rollers than double back over the ridgeline." He could fly through turbulence; granite was different.

"I need to see how you respond to contingencies, Ensign. Are you uncomfortable with diverting if necessary?"

Not when all of my alternates are surrounded by mountains, not really. "Depends on the definition of 'necessary,' sir. Stand by," he said, and thumbed the microphone switch on his stick. "Transition control, Puma Two-One requesting vectors to the west, changing reentry to descent corridor Bravo."

"Puma Two-One, Control copies. Turn to heading two-five-five and contact Denver center upon crossing sixty thousand."

Marshall looked over at his IP. "Guess we're heading west."

The turbulence was only marginally better on the windward side of the Rockies, forcing him to keep more speed and thus giving up precious altitude. "I don't like this," he said. "We're not going to be able to extend back to base from here."

"Diversion is always a possibility. Ultimately, you're the pilot in command."

Which means he's pushing to see how assertive I'll be, Marshall realized. He punched up a map on the center console and examined his options. Grand Junction was a good field but uncomfortably far. Aspen and Eagle airports were out of the question: surrounded by high terrain, they left no margin for error. Rifle wasn't much better, but at least it sat along a shallow river valley. He'd still have to cross some ridges to get there, but once he was in the pattern it'd be fine. Just as important, they could tank up and fly out later without taking a big hit on climb performance. He punched "KRIL" into the flight management computer and recalculated their descent.

"You're going to Rifle?" Wylie challenged him. "Any diversions are supposed to be to the nearest suitable airfield."

"And if I'm the pilot in command, then 'suitable' is whatever I decide it is. Sir." Marshall nudged the stick back, trading some speed for altitude, and reached down into his flight bag. He pulled up a monocular and peered through it, keeping its level bubble centered while he gauged the terrain ahead. He noticed his IP staring at him. "Trick I picked up flying gliders around here," he explained.

The sharp peaks grew closer as they whispered past mountain ridges, descending deeper into the valley. Marshall checked his fuel levels—there might be enough in the tanks for one short boost if he got into trouble.

"You're not going to clear that terrain. We can still make Eagle," Wylie said, reaching for the controls. "My aircraft."

Which meant he'd just busted his check ride. "*What?* We're not over the ridge yet!" He looked at the airspeed, altitude, and angle of attack indicators. "We've got plenty of energy so long as we don't do anything stupid."

"Too late for that." He began turning them away from the ridge.

Fuming, Marshall tightened his grip around the optical level in his hand. He looked back through it, judging the new terrain as it centered in the windscreen. "It's too far!"

"No it's not," Wylie protested. "I got this."

Which Marshall understood to mean he *didn't* have this. He couldn't take his eyes off the mountain ridges ahead of them: there was precious little time and few options to correct if this guy blew it. *He did say I was the pilot in command* . . .

Marshall grabbed the stick. "My aircraft!" he snapped, rolling them through the turn and back onto their original heading. They'd wasted a good thousand feet in this circle, which would put them below the ridgeline. He reached down to the control pedestal and armed the rocket motor.

"You'll bust your check ride." Wylie stabbed at the checklist strapped to his knee. "No relights on descent; right there on the test card."

"I already busted it when you took over a second ago," Marshall reminded him. "I'm just trying to keep from getting killed."

Wylie pointed an accusing finger at the engine instruments. "You're not going to be able to relight anyway. Chamber temps are still out of range."

"I'm not relighting," Marshall said as they continued down. "I'm dumping weight." He flipped a toggle switch and a cloud of kerosene and oxygen mist began trailing behind them. The craft eased up higher as it grew lighter; he hoped it would be enough. He noticed Wylie tugging at his harness and eyeing the eject lever. "Oh no," Marshall snapped. "You bail on me and I'll beat your ass as soon as we touch dirt. Hands in your lap!"

"You can't talk to me that way!"

"You said I'm the PIC." He eased back on the stick, sending them up higher as speed tapered off. The stall warning buzzed intermittently and he felt the nose grow mushy. He pushed down, carefully targeting their best lift-to-drag ratio as the final few pounds of propellant evaporated behind them.

The rocks were close but passed safely beneath them as they sailed over the last mesa and the Colorado River valley opened up beyond.

He began a shallow, circling descent and pressed the mic button. "Rifle approach, Puma Two One is five miles east of the field, declaring minimum fuel. Request priority handling."

With no other aircraft in the area, ATC's reply was as he'd hoped. "Puma Two One, Rifle copies. You're cleared to land runway two-five."

1

"I'm telling you, it'll be garbage detail."

One of Marshall's classmates, a petite brunette named Roberta McCall, hopped up from a well-used recliner to grab a pair of beers from the minifridge behind them. She wasn't much taller than when sitting down and wore her hair in tight curls that were almost as bouncy as she was, highlighting her round features. She was like a wound-up spring anxious to release its energy. "You worry too much, dude. Nothing is promised to us, not even the next sunrise," she said, tossing one of the longnecks into his lap.

Marshall jerked upright as it landed a little too close for comfort. "I busted my first check ride and threatened my IP," he argued. "I think I worry just about enough."

"You aced your second ride and he got reamed for painting you into a corner," she said. "Sounds like justice to me."

Marshall turned sour, still in a slow burn over a thought that wouldn't stop nagging at him. "He had to get in a dig about my dad, and I let it get to me."

Roberta blew out a frustrated sigh in sympathy. "Not something you want to hear on a check ride. That's supposed to be about *your* competence, not someone else's reputation. IP's will throw all kinds of curveballs to put you off balance. He was baiting you."

"If he was then I took it hook, line and sinker." He took an angry sip from his bottle.

"That's not the first time someone's brought it up," she continued. "We're about to head out into the fleet, so face facts. Your old man's a legit hero. He pulled off some epic feats with bleeding-edge spacecraft, *twice*. He stuck his neck out and saved lives."

He sat quietly, contemplating the unwelcome reminder of his childhood. What had started as a search for a missing colleague ended with his father in a desperate chase around the far side of the moon. While Ryan Hunter was fighting to stop a hijacked spacecraft from deflecting a shattered comet toward Earth, Marshall and his mother had to survive its aftermath at home. "Dad said he knew it was going to get sporty when the Marines reactivated his commission. He was happy to go back to civilian flying when it was over. If he'd stayed in, I'd have probably joined the Peace Corps in protest."

"Good thing you didn't. We have much better equipment. And get over Wylie, word is they sent him back to wherever his last duty posting was." Marshall had in fact gotten points for recovering the spaceplane, even if it had been out of service for three days.

"So I passed the makeup test. Now I've got a rep nobody's going to touch. How can you be so sanguine?"

"San-what?"

"Optimistic. Hopeful."

"I forgot you were the one who always paid attention in freshman Composition. You've got to stop throwing those fifty-dollar words at simple girls like me."

"I'm on a mission to get you cultured before we graduate, so at least one of us has a decent chance of getting a crew assignment."

Roberta grinned and took a pull from her bottle. "Then why create competition for yourself if you're so worried about getting stuck with the scut work? It's not like we're in the Navy cleaning bilges, or whatever they stick the new guys with. Anyway, we're officers."

"So we'll at least be in charge of the poor schlubs cleaning bilges?"

"That's my point," she said. "We won't be, no matter what. The worst job in the Space Force is still better than anything in the other branches. Launching rockets? Controlling satellites? Sign me up." She tapped her temple with a finger. "Adjust your attitude. *None* of this is boring."

Some of it is, Marshall thought. "I took this instead of the Air Force because I want to fly spacecraft."

"Which you knew was a gamble. There's a lot more slots for drone pilots and satellite jockeys than there are Starlifters or patrol cruisers. I'm cool with that."

Marshall was about to protest when the TV in the background

caught their attention: old video of a dramatic nighttime Falcon Heavy launch, followed by an animation of the orbits of Earth and Mars superimposed over the image of a middle-aged Asian couple. He turned up the volume.

"...Jasmine Jiang reports they 'feel great' and are enjoying their extended time away from the pressures of running their far-ranging business empire. *Prospector* mission control in Palmdale, California, reports the spacecraft remains on track for an extended encounter with the asteroid 2023 RQ39 next month, en route to the first human flyby of the Red Planet. NASA spokesmen..."

Roberta reached over and muted the newsfeed. "NASA spokesmen struggled valiantly to continue grasping at straws to appear relevant," she mocked. "They really got left in the dust this time."

"They did most of the trajectory work," Marshall said, taking the remote back from her.

"Only because Planetary Protection was crapping bricks that they'd screw up, crash into Mars and contaminate it with human cooties."

Marshall ignored her and turned the volume back up as a diagram of the spacecraft appeared. "Just zip it and let me indulge myself, then."

"...following what is known as a 'free return trajectory,' they will have limited course-correction ability. Other than their launch-and-entry capsule, the spacecraft is composed of an inflatable habitation module, over half of which is devoted to food storage and life-support equipment for the five hundred day journey. Before passing within one hundred kilometers of the Martian surface, their path will coincide with that of the asteroid 2023 RQ39. This is a particularly enticing target for the Jiangs given their already substantial investments in lunar mining technology. In an interview recorded before launch, Maleko 'Max' Jiang explained some of his reasons for embarking on such a hazardous journey."

The interviewer adopted a knowing grin for the camera. "Your given name, Maleko, roughly translated, means 'Pledged to Mars.' Do you somehow feel fated to undertake this journey?"

A slight man with a shock of jet-black hair appeared on screen. His words were measured, though his eyes flared with an energy which animated every gesture: "Only in that I have long held the conviction that it is well past time for someone to demonstrate serious long-duration spaceflight is possible. The journey we are undertaking now as civilian entrepreneurs could have been accomplished with Apollo technology in the 1970s." He held up a finger, eyes glinting mischievously. "But I will say this: Mars free returns of this sort only occur about every eighteen years—for it to share a common orbit with that of a promising new mineral resource only strengthens my conviction that humanity is meant to expand into the solar system."

The interviewer struck an inquisitive pose. "To preserve the species, perhaps?"

Jiang smiled patiently, no doubt having answered hundreds of variations of the same question. "In some ways, yes. It's better to extract valuable minerals from the space environment than to take them from our own environment on Earth." He paused, taking on a somber tone. "In other ways, I admit to a bit of raw survival instinct. No one can forget the destruction Comet Weatherby visited on the American East Coast. I want to improve our understanding of what's out here."

There it was again. Was that all anybody ever talked about? He ignored the sideways glance from Roberta; the billionaire explorer's offhand remark dredged up deep and unpleasant childhood memories. Standing with his mother on their rooftop, he'd never imagined water could roar like a freight train, that something so tranquil could bring such destruction.

"... but we are building a Space Guard fleet to deflect those kinds of threats," the interviewer contended.

"*Orbit* Guard," Roberta shouted at the screen, suddenly animated. "Geez, can't anybody get that right?"

"That is only one piece of the puzzle. I am a businessman," Jiang continued. "I improve lives by creating wealth, which provides people with jobs and the government with revenue. Ill-considered technological advances and uncontrolled debt are putting both of those in jeopardy. In fact I'd argue either of those threaten our civilization as much as any planet-killing rock."

The interviewer looked amused now. "And you believe mining asteroids will solve those problems?"

Jiang leaned into the camera with earnest. "We have to expand our economic sphere off-planet. That doesn't mean we can't also grow here; it just means I don't think we have time to waste. We must grow our economic base to avoid devaluing our currency."

"You've accumulated quite a bit of currency on your own since emigrating from mainland China."

Jiang adopted a lecturing tone, responding to the interviewer's subtle barb. "Some of America's most successful children are its adopted ones, because we appreciate that which we craved so badly. Think of America's westward expansion, the Transcontinental Railroad, transoceanic air travel . . . how much wealth did they create? Now think of how many rare-earth minerals are contained on a single average-sized Class-M asteroid, and how beneficial it would be to bring those metals back to Earth once we've solved the problem of getting there."

"Some speculate the value of a single asteroid could be in the trillions of dollars. You'd like to be the world's first trillionaire, wouldn't you?"

Another patient smile, ignoring the implication that he was motivated by greed. "Someone's going to be eventually. If I can do that while providing something of immense value to others, then sure. It might as well be me."

Roberta muted the television. "So there's gold in them thar 'roids," she drawled.

"You don't think they're serious?" Marshall asked. "Because closing yourself up in something the size of a Winnebago for a year and a half sounds pretty serious."

"Sure it is—seriously *messed up*. Look, it's not that I don't want people to go to Mars. I just think this is a publicity stunt while they're out staking claims."

"Publicity stunt, or proof of concept?"

She waved her now almost-empty longneck at the screen. "When this many people are watching, is there a difference?"

Marshall was about to argue when both of their tablets pinged with messages which were mirrored on screen: NOTICE: ASSIGNMENTS TO DUTY.

Space Launch Complex 37

Kennedy Space Center, Florida
Nicholas Lesko craned his neck upward, straining to take in the full

stature of the rocket he was about to board. It stretched in a spire two hundred feet overhead, creaking and groaning like a living thing as it vented excess liquid oxygen into the humid Florida sky. Even through the hiss of air in his helmet, he could sense the beast straining with the loads inside of it.

As his companions gathered around the base of the launch gantry, Lesko unconsciously tugged at the neck ring of his pressure suit, searching for relief from an itch that had developed almost as soon as they'd locked down their faceplates to begin acclimating to the spacecraft's environment. The suit insulated him from most of the outside world's noise, though it was impossible to ignore the cacophany from the north as a Polaris Clipper spaceplane thundered away from Kennedy Spaceport's runway on its way to low Earth orbit.

That's the way to do space travel, he thought. He'd have by far preferred the Clipper's first-class accommodations over being so much "Spam in a can" in one of these gumdrop-shaped Stardust passenger capsules. Launched by an old-fashioned Vulcan rocket, at present it remained the only way to reach the much higher geosynchronous orbit.

Nick studied his travel companions with carefully masked disdain. One, a young hacker named Billy Burns who insisted on being called by his handle, "Xenos," particularly annoyed him. Too pudgy, too chatty, and too full of himself. Did he truly not consider the fact that there were a thousand other black hats who could've been recruited for this op?

As if he'd been listening to Nick's own thoughts, Billy/Xenos caught his eye and gave a cocky thumbs-up. The kid had barely made it through the spaceflight participant training they'd been required to finish before taking this job. He'd soon find out if it had been worthwhile. Nick had his doubts, though it had been the only way to charter a Stardust all to themselves without having to rely on a safety pilot assigned by the launch company. The flying duties would be handled by their own pilot, Clint Whitman, who impatiently shifted his weight and flexed his arms as he waited for his moment to take control of their spacecraft.

So much had become automated now that they could almost completely rely on it with only occasional input from the company's control center, which didn't really matter since none of those dweebs would be onboard with them. He'd already worked out a way to get around the interior cameras, and all the real work was going to be either on the kid's laptops or outside during EVAs. The outside work would be handled by their fourth crewmember, Giselle Dumont, a former astronaut whose lithe frame and long legs gave her away despite the bulky pressure suit, thus her nickname "Gazelle."

An attendant tapped his shoulder, pointing him to the base of the gantry where another attendant recorded each of their names on a manifest before leading them one by one into an open elevator cab.

The elevator ride to the top was slow and clunky, drawing a sharp contrast between it and the ride they were about to take. As Nick allowed white-room technicians to strap him into his flight couch and hook him into Stardust's cabin systems, he knew the difference would be dramatic in ways his companions did not suspect.

◎ 2 ◎

"So?" Roberta prodded. "What'd you get?"

"You first," Marshall said.

She held up her tablet. "Looks like I'm staying local. Just down the road at Schriever Garrison. Satellite control and intel. Says I'll get my Delta assignment after I report."

If she was disappointed, she didn't show it. Roberta really believed her own B.S., Marshall thought as he stared at his own waiting message. *There were no bad jobs in the Space Force*, he thought, but some were undeniably better than others.

His heart raced as his finger hovered over the waiting notice. That a simple message could have such a hold over his life angered him at some level. He reflexively said a quick prayer, not even sure what part of his brain it came from, and tapped the mail icon:

ATTENTION TO ORDERS
FROM: G-1, USSF HQ
TO: ENSIGN M. T. HUNTER
SUBJ: DUTY STATION
    YOU ARE HEREBY DIRECTED TO REPORT TO COMMANDER, 30TH SPACE OPERATIONS WING, VANDENBERG SFB, CA, NO LATER THAN 0700 ON 14 JUN TO AWAIT FURTHER ASSIGNMENT.

His legs rubbery, Marshall slumped into his chair, unsure of how to process this news. Specific enough to know where he was going, but excruciatingly vague as to what he'd actually be doing. "The *Wing*?" he wondered. "Why would they send me to a headquarters command?" It wasn't drones, it wasn't Starlifter spaceplanes, it wasn't even suborbital trainers. If anything, it sounded like flying a desk.

For once, Roberta was stumped as well. "Forget everything I said a minute ago."

The chief instructor said much the same as Roberta had, not that Marshall had expected any different: "It's not garbage duty, Hunter. They could put you anywhere, and probably will at some point."

"Meaning garbage duty, sir."

His commander's eyes narrowed. "Not that I should have to remind you, but this is a fault on my part since I obviously haven't trained you well enough: You're a junior officer, Hunter. Being rotated between assignments and given the occasional shit job is part of learning the ropes. Just because you're a hot stick doesn't mean the service won't put you where they need you at the moment."

"'Hot stick'?" Marshall said. "Sir, I busted my final check ride."

"And you didn't bust your retest. In the meantime, HQ had to make duty assignments. That's just how the cookie turns and the screw crumbles. You'll make a good pilot, Hunter. Suck it up, get past this setback, and trust that your next IP out in the fleet won't have such a hard-on to bust you."

That was what he couldn't figure out: he hadn't flown with the guy before, and he wasn't aware he'd had that kind of reputation. "May I ask a question, sir?"

A nod.

"Is that normal IP behavior for a check ride? I mean, pressuring me to set myself up for failure just to see if I can pull it off at the last second? It all seems counterproductive, sir."

The commander straightened up, leaning forward. "My instructors can behave any way they see fit, within limits: no fraternization, and don't smack the students around. Otherwise they have latitude to do whatever they think is necessary to accomplish the mission, which is to make sure we are sending properly trained pilots upstairs to become fully qualified spacecraft operators. Period, full stop." He paused before continuing. "Having said that, sometimes the individual shows through and their agenda threatens to get in the way."

Marshall looked perplexed. "I don't understand, sir."

The commander drummed his fingers as he considered his words. "We don't pay you to understand yet, Ensign. There are machinations behind the scenes that would curl your hair, only because most of it is unintentional and it rarely makes sense. The only advice I can offer is to treat every assignment like it's the best deal you could imagine. It's like the grunts say: 'embrace the suck.'"

The ride to orbit had indeed been a good deal more exciting—and noisier—than the trip up that clunky gantry elevator. Stardust rattled and roared for nine straight minutes and seemed on the verge of shaking itself to pieces, when suddenly all became still. The spacecraft which had at first felt so crowded sitting atop its booster suddenly seemed to triple in size as they experienced the first liberating sensations of zero g. The floor was no longer the floor—it could be the ceiling or a sidewall if someone wanted it to be. Impossibly bright, unfiltered sunlight exploded through the windows along one side while the blue glow of Earth filled the other, turning their little spacecraft from a ride in a barrel over Niagara Falls into a kaleidoscope of novel sensations.

Of the group, only Giselle and Whitman had been here before. Experience had apparently done nothing to blunt her enthusiasm, as Nick noticed her turning to the nearest window every chance she had while stowing her pressure suit. It didn't seem to slow her down as she worked her way through checking out their spacewalk gear, a top priority before Whitman began the series of burns that would raise them into a geosynchronous transfer orbit. And for his part, the pilot's focus had not wavered since their rocket first roared to life. If the view outside threatened to distract him he'd yet to show it. Other than stowing his gloves and helmet beneath his seat after engine cutoff, the pilot had barely moved. Nick watched as his eyes darted around the control panel, scanning critical instruments as his hands barely touched the controls. An occasional tap on a control stick set thrusters to banging outside, otherwise the spacecraft was remarkably quiet.

It was therefore no surprise that Billy/Xenos would be the one to interrupt it. "Oh my God it's stuffy," he complained, and reflexively honked his nose against his hand.

"It's the fluids in your body stabilizing," Giselle said as she pushed away from the EVA locker. "Just like we are in this spacecraft, your insides float along with you."

That they'd all been warned about this in training didn't seem to matter. He tried blowing his nose again.

"That won't really work like you think it should," Giselle said. "Give it time, you'll get used to it."

The kid looked at her disdainfully. "Doubtful," he said. "Not if the conditions don't change until we're back in gravity. How can you enjoy this?"

That prompted a reaction from the stoic Whitman. He turned his head slowly—either for effect or for avoiding sudden movements that might upset his vestibular system—and stared. "You're kidding, right?" he finally said, and motioned to the nearest window. "You're in *space*, kid. Millionaires still spend big money for trips to orbit. Businesses invest all kinds of dough into training schlubs like us to work up here. You're in an exclusive club."

Billy/Xenos appeared uninterested and proceeded to begin checking over his own equipment stash. "I was in an exclusive club before this," he sniffed.

Whitman exchanged an amused look with Nick. "Very well, then. A reminder, people: we have one orbit to check out the spacecraft and our equipment before we start our first transfer burn. If you have any concerns or no-go calls, you have exactly"—he checked his watch—"eighty-nine minutes to tell me. Otherwise, enjoy the ride."

Nick Lesko's smile was less for the experience than for the satisfaction of seeing that the pilot they'd selected seemed more than willing to keep this gaggle of oddballs on task. After they reached GEO in another day, it would become life or death. And that was information he preferred to keep to himself.

◈ 3 ◈

Vandenberg Space Force Base
California

Despite advances in biometric security and artificial intelligence, the check-in process for a freshly minted officer in the newest and highest-tech service branch remained confoundingly byzantine and hopelessly bound to paperwork (in triplicate, of course). First the gate security police checked his ID, then waited for the base provost to confirm that he was, in fact, supposed to be there before being allowed to report to Wing headquarters in order to wait on some disinterested admin clerk who misplaced his orders before eventually uncovering them in last week's pile of onboarding paperwork—a good thing, because otherwise they'd have considered him AWOL—before finally arriving at the subordinate command to which he was assigned, where a slightly more interested admin clerk repeated the process until he was directed to report to the group commander's office in order to wait some more until, at last, a door opened.

"Hunter."

Startled, Marshall managed not to show it only because it was now getting on into midafternoon and he'd really been craving a cup of coffee. He was greeted by a stocky man with buzz-cut red hair that contrasted sharply with the blue-gray uniform of the Force's new Orbit Guard. The silver stripes on his epaulets signified he was indeed the group CO, Commodore Harlan Haynes. The old-style silver pilot wings on his chest signified he'd once been Air Force and

21

had jumped ship for the newer service along with the other space cadets.

Marshall snapped to attention. "Yes sir, Ensign Hunter, reporting as ordered."

The CO took Marshall's records and studied him for a moment. "Come in." He gestured to a chair by his desk. "Have a seat."

He made sure to sit up straight and not get too comfortable, becoming more awkward as the senior officer flipped through his training file and cross-referenced certain pages while scrolling through something on his desktop monitor. "Funny thing about the Pentagon never letting go of paper records—we out in the field have ways around that."

"I'm afraid I don't follow, sir."

The CO waved the folder. "There's a lot that paper just can't capture. For instance, this doesn't tell me squat about a man's attitude or work ethic unless you just plain failed. Which you mostly didn't."

Here it comes, Marshall thought.

"Anything you'd like to share with me about that busted check ride? Because I'm guessing you'd much rather be in a cockpit than down here pounding a keyboard."

"No sir. I have to accept the instructor's assessment. I failed to meet the test criteria." There. It felt like complete horseshit to him, but nothing about it was technically *false*.

The commodore's quizzical look indicated he wasn't buying it. "No contributing factors, then?"

Marshall swallowed hard and hoped it wasn't too noticeable. "Sir, I allowed myself to be pushed into a corner. That was my fault. It doesn't matter what the IP might have been trying to achieve, in the end I could've said no."

"You kind of did," the commodore said. "Albeit too late to salvage that hop. Startling your IP into not punching out let you keep the spaceplane intact and land safely."

"We lost the bird for three days, sir, between trucking out a tanker full of RP-1 and getting a temporary launch-site permit."

Haynes waved it off. "Bah. The more common these kind of hops become, the more that's going to happen to smaller airports. They'll get used to it. They're just going through the same growing pains the big air carrier hubs went through with your old man's company."

And here we go again. Marshall wondered if he'd ever grow out of his dad's shadow.

His reaction must have shown on his face. "So here's your first piece of your CO's Advice for Life: don't run away from your past, Ensign. Embrace it. Use it. I don't know your old man, but I know the type," he said, poking at his own chest. "He wasn't looking for notoriety when he took the job. He was just looking to challenge himself and fly something badass. The rest came after he got backed into a couple of bad corners and had to miracle his way out of them. That sound about right?"

Marshall had to chuckle at that. "Yes sir. That sounds about right."

"That's all any of us are doing. Anybody who's looking for fame in this business needs to stay out of the cockpit because he's just going to be dangerous. Now's the time to be honest: Is that what you're looking for?"

He didn't hesitate. "No sir. I just want to fly something badass."

A smile from the CO. "Then you'll do all right. Might even get you enough admin hops with the training squadron to keep your flight pay."

"That would be great, sir."

"You'd better believe it's great!" Haynes handed back his training records. "Take these to the S-1, he'll be your reporting officer while you wait for your permanent assignment."

If hope were a balloon slowly filling his soul, this was the pinprick that deflated it: S-1 was administration. He'd be flying a desk until they decided what to do with him.

After a day of steadily raising their orbit to geosynchronous altitude, Nick's crew hovered in space above South America. Stardust's velocity at this distance now matched that of Earth's rotation, keeping it locked in place over the same point on the globe.

Their target appeared as a bright blip in the crosshairs of a monitor on Whitman's control panel; over the past few hours it had grown from a point of light nearly indistinguishable from the background stars into a jagged white smudge.

Nick pushed away from behind the pilot and floated over to the other forward-facing window. Without the video, their nominally dead comsat was simply a luminous speck in the distance. He was surprised there weren't more; if this was the geosynchronous plane, he'd expected to see a long trail of communication and weather satellites. "Are you certain we're clear of interference?"

"We're in the graveyard orbit," Whitman confirmed, "three hundred klicks above GEO. Even down there we'd have plenty of separation. It's a big sky, we're not going to hit anything."

Nick was more concerned about their being seen but kept that to himself. He looked back toward Giselle and Billy. She didn't seem to be bothered by spending so much time in a cramped spacecraft with three men and their smelly bodily functions; if anything it was a testament to her experience and professionalism. Billy, on the other hand, had seemed mortified by the lack of privacy. Nick wondered at that—after their training with the zero-g toilet and all the other privations of spaceflight, how could anyone be surprised? Maybe it was being faced with the reality of not being able to open a window for some fresh air, maybe it was just the kid's prickly nature. In the end, Nick didn't care so long as everyone did their jobs.

Which they appeared to be doing. After struggling with setting up their private network in zero g, Billy had found something of a groove for himself. He floated among a nest of laptops and network cables, wearing a distant countenance though his eyes were intensely focused on the information before him.

"Billy?" Nick prodded. He was ignored. He sighed as he remembered, then finally: "Xenos."

"Yup."

"Are you satisfied with your level of control?"

"Test environment hasn't given me problems, but then it's my setup. Can't know until we get closer. If I boosted the signal enough to link from here, somebody on Earth would notice our EM emissions."

Nick understood but played along anyway. "You're right. We don't want to arouse suspicion."

He turned to Giselle, who was buried down to the waist in her pressure suit. He rapped on the helmet to get her attention, and her head popped up through the opening. "One moment," she chirped, at ease in her element. He wondered if she'd be this chipper once they were outside. "Yes?"

He gave her an intentionally disarming smile. "Just seeing if you're ready. Anticipating any problems?"

"If I did, rest assured we wouldn't go," she said flatly. "Both suits are pressure checked. Right now I'm checking the coolant and hydration lines. Trust me, you wouldn't want a pinched drinking tube on an eight-hour spacewalk."

"Then I defer to your judgment," he said solemnly, and checked his watch. "Twelve hours from now we'll open the hatch, correct? An hour to suit up, another two hours to pre-breathe"—he looked back toward Whitman, who held up two fingers in anticipation of his question—"and two hours until we're on station with our first job. That leaves us just enough time to rest before getting to work. If anyone thinks they're going to have trouble meeting those timelines, let me know now."

The hacker and the spacewalker silently shook their heads no, and Whitman's two fingers turned into a thumbs up. Without another word, they each turned back to their work, the cabin silent but for the hum of circulation fans and the occasional thump of a thruster.

Schriever Space Force Base
Colorado

Roberta McCall had navigated a nearly identical administrative labyrinth as her old classmate and now stood in front of the 9th Space Delta's S-3, or Operations officer, an Air Force light colonel on loan to the Space Force. His pilot wings and missileer's badge suggested someone who'd lost his flight rating at some point and moved on to manning ICBM silos. He pointed Roberta to a nondescript government-issue synthetic wood desk. "You'll work here when you're not on shift in the SOC."

She looked around for any clues as to what her actual role might be. A foot-high stack of folders sitting by the desktop monitor hinted at it. "Are those training files, sir?"

"They said you were bright," he said, clapping her on the shoulder. "You're our new training officer. Haven't had one for about a month now and the turds are starting to pile up accordingly. Got a lot of junior enlisteds who need to finish NCO school before we can promote them, they'll be waiting on you to get their quals back up to speed. And we've got to put on a physical fitness test next month, that'll be up to you."

Sounds fascinating, she thought, keeping a straight face. "Understood, sir. And when will I be on shift?"

"Had lunch yet?" The lieutenant colonel looked at his watch for effect. "Never mind, doesn't matter. How about right now?" He walked away, turning down the hall and not waiting for her to follow.

"Yes sir," Roberta mumbled, and hurried after him while trying to not look like she was in *too* much of a hurry.

The Space Operations Center was decidedly less high tech than she'd expected. The setup was familiar enough: a dimly lit amphitheater room filled with rows of multiscreen computer consoles, each occupied by clean-cut young people in charcoal Space Force jumpsuits. A couple of serious-looking senior officers stalked the back of the room, occasionally looking over someone's shoulder and giving commands. At the front of the room were the kind of floor-to-ceiling monitors that had become signature features of control centers since the early days of the space program: a "god's-eye view" of whatever they were tasked with controlling.

What surprised her was the age of the equipment: some newer curved screens, but very few of the holographic projections that made managing objects in 3-D space so much easier to visualize. Half of the telephones looked to be older stand-alone units, not integrated into the network comms. She'd seen the same in the training squadron and had assumed it was intended to not make things too easy for the students. But now, seeing her country's Space Force still mired in tech that had been old when she was a kid was startling. It must get the job done, but she wondered how much more they could do if they could just upgrade their systems.

She forgot to notice the Ops officer was still talking to her while pointing to the various rows of consoles.

"...and over there is Space Weather. These guys," he said, pointing to the row behind them, "coordinate with FAA's launch-and-entry traffic control. You'll notice they're on the phone a lot. It's old school, but it gets the job done. Kind of like that stack of training records," the lieutenant colonel said, apparently reading her mind. He walked down another row and stopped behind a young man. "This is Lieutenant Ivey. He's our intel liaison and your section lead," he said, and walked away.

Roberta wasn't even sure which section they were in; she was looking for a sign atop the consoles when a gangly young man with a brush of sandy blond hair unfolded himself from his seat and seemed to tower over her. "Jacob Ivey," he said, and extended his hand.

"Roberta McCall," she said, taking his hand.

"I'm Poison."

"Excuse me?"

"That's my call sign. Kind of obvious, I know."

"Oh," she said, slightly embarrassed. "Sorry, Lieutenant. I should've caught that. I'm still used to the IPs keeping it formal with students. Rank, last name, you know."

He eyed her up and down but not in an obviously leering way. She decided this was probably how he sized up every newbie, gender be damned. "No call sign yet," he muttered around what looked like a wad of chewing tobacco. Interesting, as that was supposed to be prohibited on duty. "Well, you'll do something to earn one soon enough. Roberta, eh? For now we'll just call you Roboto."

Didn't see that *one coming.* She smiled to herself and looked around the control room. "Didn't realize we needed call signs in here, sir."

"Does anybody really need them?" he said. "Pilots just like it because it's one more way to indulge their arrested development."

She noticed the spacecraft operator wings on his name patch. "Doesn't look like it stopped you."

"I only act mature when I have to," he said, at which the enlisted technicians on his console row smirked. "And that'll be enough out of the peanut gallery," he added over his shoulder.

Roberta suspected she was being rude but couldn't stop looking past him to study their monitors, trying to get a sense of what they were doing. She hadn't seen any placards like the other sections had.

Ivey smiled around the wad of whatever it was in his mouth. "You're wondering what we do here."

She turned back to him. "Sorry, Lieutenant. That obvious?"

"Don't apologize." He motioned her off to the side. "And you're an officer, not a cadet anymore, okay? I only made full L-T last month, so you can drop the rank when it's just us talking." He eyed her once more, apparently deciding how much to trust her. "Traditionally we'd waste the new guy's time for a day or so, maybe send you down to S-2 for a box of grid squares."

"Intel shop ... that's down by the flight line isn't it?" she asked seriously. "Will you need me to bring back a bucket of prop wash too? And is that before or after I stop by admin for the ID.10.T form?"

He stared at her coldly for a second, then broke into another goofy smile. "You're savvy. Good. I don't have much patience for newbs, and the naïve ones just piss me off." He pointed her back to his console, which is when she finally noticed the aircraft-style control column mounted to it.

"So you work in the intel shop?" Roberta wondered. "I thought this was all Ops."

He motioned for her to take a seat beside him. "You'll find a lot of overlap in what we do here."

She noticed his monitors were configured differently than the others too. They looked more like an aircraft's multifunction displays, including an eight-ball attitude indicator in the center screen. "Is that what I think it is?"

"That depends. What do you think it is?"

She didn't want to get her hopes up, but ... "It looks like a drone pilot's station."

"We have a winner," he said. "Welcome to the X-37C Remote Orbital Vehicle control team."

4

Max and Jasmine Jiang floated side by side, smiling for the camera. Centered in *Prospector*'s habitation module, they were surrounded by meticulously wrapped packages of freeze-dried food and the other dry goods needed for almost a year and a half in space.

"It looks crowded in there." The observation came from a news anchor, off camera and with the nearly six-minute signal delay edited out.

Jasmine's face beamed, framed by black hair which flowed around her in zero g. "It gets a little better with each passing week. As we dig into our supplies, it frees up more room." She gestured toward a small porthole at the back of the hab. "We couldn't see that bulkhead a month ago. Getting access to another window was a nice incentive."

Max Jiang interjected. "We still have to stow our garbage, though, so waste is always a challenge. It makes us creative."

The video skipped and they were positioned differently, a byproduct of the editing as the announcer moved on to his next scripted question. "You're now less than two weeks out from your asteroid rendezvous. Are you able to make out any details yet?"

Another video skip, now Max and Jasmine were giving a lesson in orbital mechanics. He held up a sugar cube; she held a bulb of fruit juice. "Not without assistance," Max said. "RQ39 is still only a point of light in our window, but it's showing some variation now and is obviously not just another background star." He pushed the cube away, she soon followed with the drinking bulb. "We're essentially pulling up alongside it for the next several million miles." Max worked a remote and the camera tracked the cube and bulb as they approached and crossed paths, then refocused on himself and his wife. "It will be a few days until we can make out features with the naked eye. Until then, we still have to rely on our telescope and binoculars."

"Binoculars," the interviewer chuckled. "You can make out details with only binoculars?"

"You'd be surprised," came Max's time-edited reply. "Plenty of amateur astronomers on Earth use them for deep-sky viewing. Out here, this much closer to the objective and with no atmosphere to sully the view, it's amazing what you can make out."

"Though he prefers the telescope," Jasmine cut in with a laugh. "The binoculars are there for whichever of us couldn't get to the eyepiece first. Here, I'll show you." She reached out for the camera and the hab appeared to spin about with her movement. It stabilized and settled in on the eyepiece of a compact commercial telescope on a fork mount in front of a porthole. "Because the spacecraft is in a slow roll to control our solar heating, we don't get the same view from the same windows all the time. It should be coming up here in a second." Off camera, Max turned down the cabin lights.

The video went black but began to brighten as a pale gray, oblate shape appeared in one corner and began to slowly transit the screen. "This is a low-power, wide-field eyepiece. We sometimes use higher-power eyepieces, but it's harder to track that way."

Another time-edited remark from the announcer. "And there is your target, the asteroid . . ." He paused for effect as if checking his notes and not responding to a producer's cue in his ear. "2023 RQ39?" A self-effacing chuckle. "It's quite a mouthful. Are you planning give it a different name?"

The camera was back on Max now. "We thought about 'Mine 39' but the International Astronomical Union frowns on commercializing celestial bodies." He turned to his wife with a smile. "I've just taken to calling it 'Malati.'"

The interviewer's production staff had taken advantage of the time lag to look up the word and its translation from Mandarin Chinese. "Jasmine Flower," he said appreciatively. "I'm sure Mrs. Jiang is flattered."

⚹ ⚹ ⚹

"You watch that crap?" Ivey leaned over Roberta's shoulder in the SOC's breakroom.

She put her tablet away. "A friend of mine in primary flight was obsessed with them. Wants to go to Mars himself." Even if it was only for a quick look as they flew by, Marshall had been captivated by their adventure. "I was too focused on not washing out at the time, but what they're doing is dramatic and dangerous as hell. I have to admire them."

Ivey nodded. "And true to form, we found a way to turn it into reality TV garbage. Seriously, at this point I'll bet half the country's just waiting to see if they crash into the planet."

Her eyes widened. "Okay, now that's just sick. Seriously?"

"Didn't say *I* hope so. It's simply an observation of our hopeless train-wreck culture." He glanced at his watch and spun a finger in a hurry-up gesture. "Break's almost over. We've got real work coming up soon."

Roberta nodded and gathered her things, grabbing a paper coffee cup as she followed him back into the Ops center. He'd promised a big day.

She settled into a drone control station identical to the one Ivey occupied next to her. "Best way to learn aero-grav assists is to follow my lead," he explained. "We can program the Orbital Maneuvering System ahead of time and the bird will take care of itself, but when it's time to bite into atmo we have to do our pilot thing."

Her eyes danced over the multifunction displays. A camera mounted between the drone's v-tail stabilizers provided a view outside the spacecraft, but it was the instrument panel that demanded most of her attention. Where was the spacecraft right now, where was it heading, and were any critical systems hinting at an unpleasant surprise?

The yellow and green bands on the digital gauges made the "systems" part easy. The hard part, as always, was interpolating between the differences to anticipate problems: Was a rise in fuel pressure just due to solar heating or a sign that a tank was about to fail? For now she could leave that to Ivey. She focused on the flight path indicators instead, as that was the intent of today's lesson. The drone was set to intercept a maneuver node they'd programmed to begin over the South Pacific near Chile. The effect of whatever action they took there would manifest itself on the opposite side of the globe over China.

A sudden dissonant, grinding noise distracted her. "What the hell is that?"

"'Seek and Destroy,'" he said. "Metallica. Gets me in the mood."

"Seriously? That was old when my grandparents were listening to it."

"You get to pick the music when it's your turn in the box," he said. "Until then, let me enjoy my golden oldies." He pointed to a cascade of numbers scrolling down one display. "Watch here. The fun's about to start." He kept his hands free of the controls while the spacecraft followed its programmed burn schedule. "Orbital maneuvers 101. A retro burn at perigee does what?"

"Lowers apogee," she said. Easy.

"How?"

"Subtracting velocity reduces the orbital period," she said. "Burn just long enough and you circularize the orbit. Burn too long and you re-enter."

"Correct, and neither of which we're here for today," he said with a mischievous grin. "Today we are faking out the spooks who are expecting us to show up over Beijing in forty-five minutes."

"If satellite spotters are looking for us, then they can work backwards and figure out when and where we'd have to do a burn to avoid them."

His grin didn't change; he was clearly enjoying the lesson. "That's what makes this so much fun, besides the actual flying. Anybody can do back-of-the-envelope math to figure out how much we can change orbits with the OMS. What they can't do yet is predict our atmospheric skips, and by the time they figure it out we'll be in position to do another."

She pointed at the upcoming burn sequence. "So the retro fire is to get us into the atmosphere?"

"Just enough to use it. That's where we come in. We can program the drone to do a lot, but it takes a pilot's feel to fly through this. Dig too deep and we're re-entering. Don't dig far enough and we're skipping off in the wrong direction." He pointed her to the control sticks. "Haptic feedback; you can feel what the spacecraft's feeling as it starts biting into the air. Today you're just gonna follow me through the maneuver. You'll be able to feel the air build up and what I do in response."

"It'll lose too much energy to just skip back into orbit, won't it?"

"Correct," he said. "We'll still have to do an OMS burn at the top of the bounce. This is more about using the aerodynamics to give us a plane change instead of burning propellant."

Plane changes—that is, changing the orbit's inclination from Earth's equator—required the spacecraft to overcome its considerable momentum in one direction to end up on a tangent to it, which took equally considerable of energy. Using aerodynamic forces to change directions still required fuel to remain in orbit after dipping into the atmosphere, but more importantly it made the X-37 wildly unpredictable.

The chief petty officer monitoring the drone's health spoke up from the workstation next to them. "Coming up on PC minus one. Setting your countdown to start at thirty seconds from node entry. She's your spacecraft, Lieutenant."

Ivey threw a cutover switch transferring control to his flight station. "My spacecraft. Thanks, Chief." He placed one hand lightly on the sidestick controller on his armrest and gestured for her to do the same. "Thirty seconds."

She mimicked his motions, just barely touching the sidestick. As the countdown reached zero, she felt it jump slightly and press back against her palm.

"Retro thrusters firing," Ivey said, "right on cue. Feel that?"

"Yeah," she said, if a bit uneasily. The stick vibrated against her fingertips. Was he certain she couldn't give this thing any inputs from here?

"Don't worry, you can't do anything to this bird," he said, as if anticipating her reaction. "Just get a feel for it. I'm only following along right now myself."

As he'd warned her, the real work began when the X-37 began its tentative descent into the upper atmosphere. "This is where the fun starts," he said as the digital altimeter unwound along one side of their main display. "Entry interface at four hundred and twenty thousand feet, but that's just tapeline height. I want to know where the air really is."

"So the pitot-static system isn't enough?"

"Sure, once we're too low for it to matter. The air data computer can't always keep up." He pointed to the sidestick. "Get your hand around it. Can you feel anything?"

Roberta wrapped her hand gently around the controller and closed her eyes. A slight wobble here, a bit of pressure there . . . "Yeah, I can. Barely. What's our altitude?" she asked, not wanting to lose focus.

"Four hundred thousand even," he said. They'd lost twenty thousand feet just in the last minute. "I'm going to ease back and shallow us out."

She felt the stick press into her palm as Ivey pulled the nose up ever so slightly. She opened her eyes and noticed the altimeter wasn't unwinding quite so rapidly. On the main display the drone's forward camera showed the view ahead. Superimposed above Earth's horizon were animated attitude and direction indicators, scrolling speed and altitude counters, and an ever-changing array of numbers beneath a column of Greek letters. Sigma, delta, and theta each represented atmospheric pressure, density, and temperature, which were more important than the spacecraft's geometric height above Earth.

"Watch outside pressure and density for me," Ivey said, more for her benefit than his. He'd done this enough to sense when they'd hit the sweet spot.

"Kind of high for this altitude," she said.

"Exactly. Even in the ionosphere, the air doesn't always behave the way you think it should. We haven't studied it enough."

"Are we gathering data then too?"

"Sure," he laughed. "We just can't share it with NOAA. Classified."

That sounded too ridiculous, even for the military. "The upper atmosphere is classified?"

"Of course not. But the way we get the data is." She noticed his hand tighten around the stick. "Here we go. Watch this."

Not as subtly this time, the stick pressed against the side of her palm as Ivey put the spacecraft into a shallow turn. Ahead, the horizon tilted onscreen. "Ten degree bank. How long at this rate?"

"Not quite twenty seconds. Doesn't take much at this end for a big change at the other end." He turned to his senior technician. "How's it looking on your side, Chief?"

"Solid. You're on target to be about four minutes early and three degrees south of where they'll be looking. New inclination will be twenty-eight point four."

"Sweetness. I'll hand her back off to you after the OMS burn."

"Yes sir," the chief said. "Ready whenever you are."

Three degrees of inclination change? Roberta watched as a diamond target appeared ahead. As it crept across the screen, Ivey eased up on the stick until it sat neutral as the diamond centered in the attitude and direction indicator. The T-handled translation controller, dormant beneath her left hand until now, startled her when it jumped.

"OMS relight," Ivey announced. "We hit our target and are burning back into our new orbit. Not a bad day's work."

Nick felt an overwhelming urge to scratch his nose almost as soon as Giselle locked his helmet in place, making it impossible. The suit techs had helpfully placed strips of Velcro inside, along the edges of his visor, which he had been repeatedly taking advantage of during their seemingly interminable pre-breathing period.

"It's purely psychological," Giselle tried to explain as the compartment depressurized. "You know that, right?"

"It's no less real," Nick said testily, not letting on that his snout now felt raw as well. It didn't help that their confinement to Stardust's cramped nose-mounted airlock had kept him mostly immobile.

"I guarantee you wouldn't feel it if you had the option of taking your helmet off."

"Then I'd be able to do something about it."

She reached for the outer door and pushed it open. "Trust me, you're about to forget all that." She pulled herself up and out, apparently in as much of a hurry to get outside as he was to get out of his suit.

Nick made a final check of his safety tether, just as they'd rehearsed, and pushed off for the opening and the empty black ahead.

It was a sensation that abruptly ended as he emerged from the airlock tunnel.

"Something else, isn't it?"

He was speechless. In the midst of the nothingness he'd dreaded hung Earth in full sunlight, sparkling and glorious and distant enough that he could see its entirety as if he could spread out his arms and embrace the whole planet. The Sun exploded out of the blackness behind him. "Um ... yes," he stammered.

"It's called the overview effect." Did he hear her chuckle? Her voice seemed distant now, after two hours of being almost nose to nose in the airlock. He was acutely aware of the cool air around his face and the crisp, sanitized scent of a fresh EVA suit. "Welcome to space. Your perspective will be forever changed from now on."

He turned to face the disabled satellite they'd come to revive and thought of the money they stood to make if they were successful. That was one perspective he knew wouldn't change. "Yeah, wonderful," he said. "Let's do what we came here for."

◎ 5 ◎

Marshall balanced himself atop a rickety chair behind a worn desk in an empty corner of the Group Admin office, a spot that looked to be a well-traveled waystation for incoming junior officers while the CO found useful work for them.

The S-1 officer had sent him a file, password protected and marked for his use only, which had seemed interesting at first but had turned out to be the personnel records of a mix of flight-rated officers and enlisted specialists currently assigned to orbital patrol duties. That put them in one place, because as of now the Orbit Guard fleet consisted of only one spacecraft: the USS *Borman*.

He studied the files, scrolling through in alphabetical order, the whole time wondering why they'd been given to him with no further instruction. Was there some paperwork error he was supposed to be looking for? Maybe an IG inspection coming up? Because that sounded exactly like the kind of drudgery they'd assign to a new guy...

He was nearing the end of the alphabet when he recognized a name. Wylie, Travis J., call sign "Coyote." Cute.

Wylie.

It couldn't be, could it? The recent promotion photo appended to his file confirmed that indeed it could. The sonofabitch looked like a recruiting poster: green eyes, hair light brown to blond with just enough curl to keep it interesting, a small, upturned nose which the girls probably thought was cute . . . Marshall contrasted that to his own unruly thatch of black hair, rounded nose, and a persistent five-o'clock shadow inherited from his father. But for the piercing blue eyes he got from his mother, most days he felt decidedly plain.

He shook his head, clearing the cobwebs and wondering why he was wasting brain cells worrying about this when he looked up from the government-issue PC to find an uncomfortably familiar face standing above him. An annoyingly perfect-looking, familiar face.

"Good afternoon, Ensign Hunter."

Marshall's mouth fell agape like a hooked fish before he collected himself. "Umm...afternoon, Lieutenant Wylie. What can I do for you?" he asked, nearly choking on the words.

A peculiar smirk creased his otherwise flawless visage. "I'm afraid you have that backwards, Ensign." He motioned for him to get up and follow him into an empty meeting room nearby.

"There has to be a mistake, sir," Marshall said. Meanwhile the voice in the back of his mind screamed *Why are you protesting, dumbass?*

"No mistake," Wylie said patiently. "You've been selected to train on the *Specter* shuttle."

"But you busted me on my final check ride."

"Tsk-tsk," Wylie tutted through that same peculiar smirk; Marshall couldn't be sure whether it was playfully sincere or just smarmy. "There's failure, and there's *creative* failure. You were being tested in more ways than one. We weren't concerned about your piloting skills. We already knew you were a good stick."

"We?" Marshall asked. "You mean, the group CO?"

"Negative," Wylie said, circling his finger. "Group doesn't control this assignment."

Marshall only became more confused with each question. "I don't understand, sir. Who would be assigning me here if the group CO didn't approve?"

"Some things they leave up to individual component commanders. And this is *definitely* one of those things." He swiped at his tablet, pushing a new file to Marshall's.

For the first time, Marshall noticed the subtle differences in Wylie's charcoal-gray flight suit. The mission patches showed he'd seen orbital duty. A lot of it, judging by the worn Nomex flap that covered the biomonitor umbilical opening above his waist. Nobody used those things unless they spent an awful lot of time hanging out in zero g.

He read the message. "I'm being assigned as secondary pilot on a

Specter shuttle," he read aloud, and stopped. "Aboard the USS *Borman*." He looked up in disbelief. "But junior officers don't get Orbit Guard billets," Marshall said.

"You're right. They don't. Maybe you should think about that," Wylie said with an upturned eyebrow. "Captain Poole is used to getting his way. Sometimes we have to work extra hard to clear the path for him." He rose from the table and rapped his knuckles on it impatiently. "Come on, we're running late."

"Late? For what?"

"Life Support," Wylie said. "We've got to get you fitted for a new pressure suit."

After six hours of work, the ache in Nick's forearms and fingers was like fire shooting into his bones. Neutral buoyancy tanks and complex high-wire contraptions could only prepare one so much for the reality of working inside a pressurized suit in hard vacuum. It had quickly made him forget about his raw, itchy nose.

Their first task had been the most hazardous: Refilling the satellite's hydrazine tanks, for if its kick motor couldn't produce any thrust then everything else would be for nothing. They'd removed a spare bottle from a bay in Stardust's service module and aligned it with a filler port on the sat's lower propulsion section. "Careful," Giselle warned. Meticulous by nature, she'd been especially so during this part of the job. "You get so much as a drop of that stuff on your suit, and you're staying out here until your air runs out."

"Relax, I got this," he'd said, disabling its quantity sensors and connecting the filler ports just as they'd practiced. "I thought all the DOT regulations for these tanks made them idiot proof."

Giselle had been cautious to the point of acting superstitious about handling the toxic propellant. "Nature always has a way of finding a better idiot. You're chill because you have no idea how evil that stuff really is."

Already prepared to do most of the grunt work under her expert direction, it was no wonder she'd been so willing to let him handle this. Once Nick felt the tank's probe lock into place, he'd started the refilling process and moved away to a safe distance, again just as rehearsed. Inside, a secondary bottle of helium discharged into the tank, forcing the hydrazine through the filler port and into the satellite. A gauge mounted on the bottle's base began falling, invisible to the ground control station. "Hydrazine's topping off. Twenty percent, on the way up to thirty," Billy/Xenos reported from his makeshift satellite control station aboard Stardust. "Good job not killing yourselves."

Nick lifted his sun visor and looked to Giselle: How dangerous was it that even that hacker nerd seemed to know better?

"I told you—it's evil stuff."

Nick had done his homework for this job like no other before, but clearly there was more to learn. As a "fixer" for his patrons, he'd been a supremely confident jack-of-all-trades in every job they'd hired him for. Out here he'd thought the biggest threat would be burning up during a launch or reentry accident.

Arduous as that work had been, the main event was yet to come.

The comsat, built around a housing and electrical bus common to many satellites in GEO, had been brought back to life one component at a time. What made this one different, and therefore useful to his patrons, was the vacant port on its payload bay. With the components they'd come to install designed around it, the physical connections had been as straightforward as they could've expected on a spacewalk. The hard part had been waiting for Billy/Xenos to activate them through the satellite's command and control network without attracting attention. That had required opening up the instrument compartment and replacing the satellite's communications array: transponder, antenna, and control units all swapped out in favor of new gear brought up with them in Stardust's service bay. The touchiest work had involved wiring all those new gadgets into the electrical bus. The avionics bay hadn't necessarily been designed for easy access—who would've anticipated that someone might someday send a repair crew all the way up to GEO?

Nick had to remind himself it was by similar thinking that the question of salvage rights in orbit had yet to be seriously tested and would be left unresolved until someone arrived to challenge the status quo. This was a stupendously expensive dead satellite whose owners had already been recompensed by an equally stupendous insurance policy. If someone else was willing to come up here and breathe new life into it, then why should anyone stop them?

"I've got good uplink," Billy said in their headsets. "Ready for the test sequence whenever you're clear."

Giselle pulled on her tether, reeling herself in towards Stardust. "On my way in." She looked back at Nick expectantly. "Nick is right behind me."

He waited for her to arrive at the opening, not looking forward to being cramped in there again. He hauled on the tether and floated toward the opening. "I'm coming."

Safely cocooned back inside, he felt thrusters kick as Whitman moved them away from the satellite. Nick wanted to watch their computer wizard work his magic, but Giselle had convinced him it was better to remain ready to head back out immediately if there was a glitch.

"We're clear," the pilot reported.

"Initiating," Billy/Xenos said. Nick waited nervously through the intervening silence. "Okay, the microwave emitter is working. That makes test card item one A-OK."

The kid was already starting to act like he was a real astronaut. "And the manipulator arm?" Nick asked impatiently.

"Slow down," the hacker replied, just as impatient.

Not willing to idly wait, Nick pulled himself back to the airlock opening to see the results of their work. Though Whitman had put another hundred meters of distance between them, the big comsat still loomed large against the Earth beyond. Now midafternoon at their longitude, he could see the shadow of night creeping toward them across the Atlantic. If there was any more work to be done, they'd have to do it under floodlights in the dark.

To his great relief, four mechanical arms unfolded from their mounts and began to move about their articulated joints. He thought it ironic the revived satellite now resembled a bacteriophage virus, with its insectile arms seeking a host.

Billy/Xenos confirmed what Nick could see. "Test card item two is good. I've got full control authority through each axis and the grapplers are responsive. We're ready to go try it on our test subject."

"We're at min safe distance," Whitman said. "Bird is clear to maneuver." At that, Nick felt Giselle grab his feet to yank him back inside. They weren't wasting any time. The EVA had been timed to end near the opening of their first maneuver window.

"Stand by," Billy/Xenos said. "Ignition in three . . . two . . ."

Outside, there was a flash of white fire as the comsat's previously dead kick stage flared to life for the first time in months. It would have been a wild surprise back at its ground station had it still been connected to its owner's control net.

It was almost a full twenty-four hours before the reanimated satellite arrived at its next stop. With a final puff of control jets, it settled into its new orbit alongside a still-functioning comsat below Stardust's position in the graveyard band. "Bird is in position and stable," Whitman said. "On station at Z plus one hundred meters. Reaction wheels are holding orientation. Drift is negligible."

Nick let out a satisfied grunt and pushed away from the flight station. He was slowly getting accustomed to the pilot's practical, minimalist way of conveying information. No emotion, no hyperbole, no enthusiasm: here's where they stood, where they were going, and what might get in the way. The anodyne *nominal* was apparently the highest expression of confidence one could utter in the spaceflight business.

He settled into the lower equipment bay, careful to avoid entangling himself in the patchwork of cables and monitors that made up their makeshift satellite control station. It already dominated most of the lower bay and what would normally have been their sleeping area, and the empty squeeze bottles and food wrappers carelessly left to float about only added to the clutter. Nick imagined a floor cluttered with empty pizza boxes and energy drinks back on Earth. He pulled himself to a stop and floated above Billy's shoulder. As the hacker took over control of the satellite from the pilot, he paid no attention to Nick's exasperated efforts to clean up his mess.

"We do have trash receptacles, you know," Nick said.

"This is how I work, man," Billy/Xenos said without apology. "A job like this takes ninja-like focus."

"It also takes functioning equipment," Nick said as he waved an empty wrapper, surprised at himself. He was starting to sound like an old hand. "If this stuff fouls an air exchanger or a cooling fan, this could all end up being a very expensive sightseeing trip." One that his paymasters would be most unhappy about and unwilling to accept excuses for.

"Okay. Here." Billy sighed and reached for an empty squeeze bottle by his head in a perfunctory gesture. "Now would you like to know how Necromancer is doing?"

"Necro-what?"

"Necromancer. A magic being able to control the dead."

Did this really have to turn into a Dungeons & Dragons metaphor? Though he had to admit the name was in fact appropriate. Nick bit off his rising irritation. "Please," he said. "Indulge me."

Billy/Xenos pointed to his center screen, which showed another satellite overlaid with intercept data from their revived comsat. "That's our target, SAMCOM-3. In service for ten years, scheduled for disposal in eight months. It won't be missed."

"And you're sure we've not been detected?"

The hacker shrugged. "There's no way to be certain. It's not like it'll broadcast a warning or turn around and blast us like a milsat would."

Nick smiled to himself. The kid held a lot of baseless assumptions about just how capable the military supposedly was up here. He'd remained stubbornly unconvinced that precious few satellites were armed even with cursory defensive weapons, a fact Nick knew their patrons were counting on. "So we're close enough to test?"

"Yes," Billy said too patiently. "It hasn't budged, which tells me its operators are completely unaware we've tucked in right next to it." He pointed at a digital map of South America studded with overlapping circles. "This is their network coverage of Paraguay and Brazil. We'll be able to see the effects in real time once we neutralize SAMCOM-3."

The kid really was going native up here. "Neutralize" sounded so much more astronautically professional than "cripple" or "take out."

Whitman turned and caught Nick's eye. "Spoken like a steely-eyed missile man," the pilot joked.

Of course, there was no doubt that both he and their EVA specialist had noticed plenty of other details, if not already figured out the purpose of their mission. Nick would deal with that variable later, after reentry. For now they still had tests to conduct and two more satellites to modify if this worked.

Billy was otherwise oblivious to them, hyperfocused on his work and in full character as the notorious hacker Xenos. "Capacitors have a full charge from the solar cells. The microwave emitter's self-test routine came back clean, no squawks. We can proceed whenever you're ready."

Nick made a grand gesture of deferring to the kid. "You may proceed."

It was as simple as Billy/Xenos selecting a password-protected item on his control menu. He entered a six-digit code and watched a status bar change color. "It's emitting. SAMCOM's getting cooked right now."

"You're certain?"

"Again, no. Not without directly hacking the satellite. But the whole point of this is to not leave a trail, right?" He pointed at the network map.

Nick watched it for any clues. "Nothing's happening."

"Give it a second."

Soon one of the overlapping circles, labeled SMCM-3, flickered before disappearing completely. Adjacent circles soon began flickering as well, changing radii as ground controllers scrambled to compensate.

"And there you go. SAMCOM-3 is cooked like a microwave burrito. Paraguay and northern Argentina just lost whatever passes for the internet down there."

No great loss, Nick thought to himself. Still, this was encouraging. "No signs of life from the satellite?"

Billy pointed at a status window. "EM spectrum's quiet. You can see they're pinging the crap out of it, but it's not transmitting."

So they'd just passed the first test. Nick noticed Whitman looking back over his shoulder expectantly. "Ready when you are."

"The bird's all yours," Billy said, lifting his hands from the keyboard.

At that, Whitman pushed up from his seat and floated back to join them. He opened up a hard-shell case that held a set of simple controls: numeric keypad, a few covered switches, and two small joysticks. "This'll take a bit of a fine touch," Whitman said, slaving one of Billy's monitors to his control box. After scrolling through an activation menu, he tapped one of the joysticks and the image in his monitor shifted with it as he pulsed Necromancer's thrusters. "I've got control authority." He turned to Billy. "Can you confirm our range?"

"Fifty meters," the kid said.

"Give me callouts every ten meters. Thrusting forward." He tapped against the other joystick and SAMCOM-3 soon began to grow onscreen.

"Forty." The satellite grew steadily larger.

"Thirty." It began to fill the screen. Nick was surprised at how steadily everything moved, as if he'd anticipated wind or waves to nudge them about as they might on Earth.

"Twenty." Whitman tapped back against the joystick and the image slowed.

"Ten." One more tap and the image stopped cold.

"Stable at four meters," Whitman said. "Ready for the claw." He looked to Giselle, who had stayed in the copilot seat. Without a word, she floated down to them and took over the control box as Whitman went back to his seat. If what came next didn't work, their trip would be for nothing.

She threw over a mode selector, and the same joysticks used to maneuver the satellite now controlled the grappling arms. It limited what they could do at any one time—fly the satellite or use the grappler—but it saved precious mass and volume aboard their small orbiting workshop. She activated a camera mounted alongside the claw and another window appeared on-screen, filled with SAMCOM's frame. It grew as she moved the claw closer until ending with a shudder.

"Capture."

◎ 6 ◎

In his limited flying career, Marshall Hunter had yet to succumb to airsickness. Not during instrument training, not while learning aerobatics and upset recovery; not once had he felt the urge to tear off his mask and lunge for a barf bag.

All of that had occurred while he'd been in the pilot's seat, behind a windscreen or beneath a bubble canopy with his instruments to lean on instead of his own vestibular vicissitudes. The rolling and shaking of launch might have been otherwise tolerable if he'd had some kind of outside reference. Here, strapped into the back of an S-21 *Specter* spaceplane, its lifting-body fuselage enclosed behind a clamshell fairing, he had no view of the window or even the pilot's instruments. For the first time in his flying experience, he was a helpless passenger.

The rattles and roars of ignition hadn't bothered him at all; it was the roll and pitchover after clearing the tower at Vandenberg's Space Launch Complex 6 which had sent his inner ear spinning. There'd been a brief respite as the Vulcan booster's first stage burned out, but the rumbling and shaking had returned immediately when the second stage ignited. The ride smoothed out once they'd climbed above the atmosphere, when he eyed the chronograph strapped to the cuff of his orange pressure suit: one minute until second-stage cutoff. They'd jettison the protective shroud soon after.

The vibrations finally ended. "SECO," Wylie announced over the intercom. Though he'd never been in orbit, Marshall had flown enough suborbital hops that he anticipated that sudden sense of speeding over the crest of a hill into infinite freefall. He felt freedom even as his body floated against the five-point harness.

"Shroud jett," Wylie announced, and the upper stage's clamshell doors sprang open to fall away behind them. The darkness that had surrounded them disappeared in a blaze of sunlight, dazzling and disorienting him even further. His ears had gotten used to their new normal and now Earth was all of a sudden not where he'd expected it to be. Up was down, left was right, and now the rising bile in his gut wasn't just from being in freefall. He tore an airsick bag from the leg pocket of his suit and snapped open his visor just in time to avoid fouling his helmet.

The passenger beside him silently offered a package of wet wipes which were clearly not government issue. Marshall took them, embarrassed and hoping Wylie hadn't noticed from his perch up front. The smell in such a confined space would've been unmistakable if their visors were up. "Thanks."

"Don't mention it, Ensign. This ride's a bit like climbing into a paint mixer and getting thrown off a building."

He watched his fellow passenger slip the package back into one of his cargo pockets. "That part of your personal gear, Master Chief?"

"Never leave home without them," the older petty officer said. "After the first couple of times, I figured this was just how it was going to be."

Marshall finished cleaning himself up and stuffed the wipes into a waste bag by his seat. "You seem okay with it."

The chief held up a hand and spread his fingers apart. "Five. This is the first time I haven't blown chunks. Guess that means I'm acclimated."

Wylie gave them the all clear to unbuckle, and that was the first time Marshall had gotten a good look at the chief's ID patch on his chest. Besides his name and rank—GARVER, MCPO—it showed both the wings of an enlisted space crewman and the dolphins of a former submariner. The Force's Orbit Guard hadn't been around long enough yet for anyone to reach senior rank who hadn't first spent time in one of the other branches.

He nodded at the chief. "It takes that long to get your space legs?"

The older man floated up from his seat and braced himself against a handhold in the ceiling. "Wouldn't know," he said. "Everybody's different. I always do fine once I'm aboard. It's getting up here's the bitch of it."

Satisfied he was clean, Marshall hit the quick release on his waist and floated free. He grabbed hold of a cargo container behind them. "I figured it'd hit me after we were in orbit."

"I'd heard the same thing when I cut over from the Navy." Garver pointed at the cockpit. "Maybe if you got up here on a different ride, one with windows. Those damn clamshell doors guarantee it'll be disorienting."

He followed the chief's gesture. Earth rolled by above them as they climbed toward apogee. There, another engine burn would begin phasing their orbit to eventually match their target, the USS *Borman*.

Marshall blinked and fought the urge to shake his head—that would just make the zero-g disorientation worse. "I knew we were inverted, but my body thought otherwise. It felt like we were right-side up."

The chief laughed. "Always does. First cruises are for learning; about yourself as much as how things work in the fleet. You'll find the skipper will never let you forget that you don't know squat."

"You worked with Captain Poole before, then?"

The chief nodded. "During the shakedown cruise, and a long time ago before that."

Marshall took another look at the submariner's dolphins on his chest and realized they must have gone very way back, indeed. "You cruised with him in the Navy?"

"You figured that out yourself? Good. Skipper doesn't like having to spoon-feed his officers." He smiled. "But yeah, I was a reactor tech with him on the *West Virginia*, right before he first got into the astronaut program."

He was impressed. "Any advice for a nugget like me, then?"

Chief Garver put a steadying hand on his shoulder. "Don't be afraid to make mistakes. Learn from them. If it feels like you're having the worst day of your life, just remember it's only the worst day of your life *so far*."

They spent the next day catching up, Wylie and his copilot precisely timing burns until their orbits were co-elliptical. They approached from below and slightly behind, affording Marshall the opportunity to check out his home for the next six months as the

Borman's crew inspected their new shuttlecraft. With a puff of control jets the shuttle pitched up perpendicular, momentarily taking the bigger ship out of view. Soon enough, it began to slowly fill their windows.

The first thing he noticed were a pair of rocket nozzles, each mounted to a bottle-shaped fission engine. Just ahead of them, coolant panels formed a cluster of right triangles that fanned out around the base, angled to shield the forward section of the spacecraft from radiation. Two crewmen in saffron-yellow EVA suits were working on the next module, just ahead of the engines and radiator panels. One waved as they passed by while the other remained turned away, apparently focused on an exposed access panel. The module was covered by domes and square hatches, which he recognized as protective covers for long-range interceptor missiles.

"That's the primary weapons and sensor module," Chief Garver explained, anticipating Marshall's question. "Some of that equipment's pretty sensitive, so this mod gets a lot of TLC. It needs outside work almost every week. The yellow suits are for working in high-radiation environments. Like, you know, nuclear reactors."

Marshall remembered some mention of them back at the academy, developed specifically for the *Borman* as it was being outfitted. "Those suits are externally mounted, right?"

"Very good, Ensign. Yep, we can't have them bringing contaminated gear into the airlocks. Wouldn't do to give the whole crew cancer."

As the shuttle continued its drift along *Borman's* long axis, more of it came into view: long, cylindrical tanks wrapped with insulating fabric and reflective panels; those were the hydrogen and oxygen that fed the engines and pressurized the crew modules. The tanks were mounted along a truss that served as the vessel's spine, its length covered in handrails and tracks for mobile service platforms. On its forward end was mounted a squat, hexagonal module. Two long booms extended from it in opposite directions, each topped with parabolic antennas. Four bulbous, fork-mounted turrets were placed between them on adjacent sides.

"That's the comm suite," the Chief explained, "and those are the Phalanx pods."

"Point-defense guns," Marshall said, letting the chief know he'd done his homework. "Ten-millimeter, caseless depleted-uranium slugs, useful against hostile satellites or wayward space junk."

"Correct, sir. We keep those things on an especially short leash. The first time we have to use them, the debris field and stray slugs will make that whole orbital plane unnavigable for years."

"The Kessler cascade. Yeah, they did mention that in school once or twice." It made one wonder what the whole purpose of a spaceborne patrol vessel could be, but the sad fact was that the more people had access to orbit, the more bad actors would arrive to screw it up for everybody else.

He heard one of the pilots call over the radio. "*Borman*, *Specter* one-one; coming up on Waypoint One."

They arrived at the forward end of the ship, a cluster of six cylinders mounted along opposite sides of a central core with an observation dome in its center, which Marshall knew would be the control deck. The others were crew quarters and logistics. In the center module, a floodlight came to life above the open docking port in the nose.

A controller on *Borman* answered. "*Specter* one-one, we have you in sight. Call the ball."

More completely unnecessary Navy lingo, but the pilots played along so seamlessly that he realized it had become custom— something they didn't get in training.

"Roger ball. *Specter* one-one holding at Waypoint One with four souls onboard, three point three thousand kilos cargo, five point two thousand kilos propellant."

"'Call the ball'? That's carrier slang."

"That it is," the chief said. "Up here, it means we confirm they've got lidar lock."

Marshall was feeling comfortable enough to get some digs in. "They let a few squids into the program and you just took over, didn't you?"

"Somebody had to. Think we'd leave all this up to the Air Force? They can't build anything without first figuring out where to put the golf course. That didn't work out so well up here."

With another ripple of control jets the shuttle pitched over once more, turning its tail to face *Borman*. After several minutes, a final kick from its nose thrusters slowed them down enough for the big ship to drift into the shuttle's tail-mounted docking port. The little spaceplane shuddered as they made contact. Amber lights flashed above the portal and on the pilot's control panel.

"That's a good capture," one of the pilots said.

A second passed before the *Borman*'s controller answered. "Confirm hard dock. Stand by while we equalize pressure in the tunnel."

The hatch creaked unnervingly as air moved behind it. He heard shuffling from the other side, which he knew were crewmembers connecting umbilicals between the two ships. Within minutes, the amber lights turned green and they had the all clear to open. With a nod from the pilot, the chief pulled on a lever and heaved the lock open. The hatch opened with a faint hiss. Marshall watched as he floated into the tunnel and saluted an officer in dark gray coveralls on the other side of the vestibule.

"Master Chief Petty Officer Garver, Anton A., request permission to come aboard."

The officer rang a ship's bell mounted above the entry. "Welcome back, Chief."

The introductory tour was remarkably short; being a new officer, Marshall had been expected to memorize the ship's layout. It shouldn't have been complicated, as the interior volume was equivalent to a 737 airliner. The problem was that it was all broken up among compartments in modules arranged along the core tunnel, so turning into any one of them was like entering a different spacecraft. Two-dimensional diagrams, even a 3-D virtual tour, could not prepare him for the confusing experience of floating through *Borman*'s innards for the first time in zero g. Even with every deck and overhead in every compartment having clear labels to keep him oriented, it was a dizzying maze of hatchways and corridors all set against a monochrome background of white and gray.

After getting himself hopelessly turned around for the third time, he found Chief Garver floating patiently nearby.

"Something I can help you with, Ensign?"

"Maybe," he admitted. "I seem to have gotten myself disoriented."

"Layout's a little screwy," Garver said, "what with all those different modules plugged in like my kid's Legos." He looked around. "They were originally going to build it with a couple of big inflatables to save mass. The skipper wouldn't have it. He doesn't trust the things."

Marshall was pretty sure he knew why. "The Navy wouldn't have built subs out of ballistic fabrics, either."

"Exactly. Though you may have noticed the outer skin's the same material, just not pressurized. Inner hulls are titanium-aluminum alloy."

"Standard construction materials. Seems risky for a warship."

The chief nodded. "Hard to think of her that way sometimes. We're a patrol vessel; our job is to protect US assets, keep the cislunar supply lanes clear, and provide on-orbit rescue. All of which would be cheaper and easier to do with satellites except for that last part."

"Rescue," Marshall said. "That takes up a lot of our bandwidth, doesn't it?"

"We have twelve crew, fully half of whom are EVA specialists. The other half are dual qualified."

"And how many rescues?"

Garver held up a finger. "One. Last year. Tourist vessel in LEO got holed by a micrometeoroid. Fortunately the pax were still in their pressure suits, otherwise it would've all been over before we got there."

"I read about it. That was the only one?"

"World's full of people with more money than sense, sir. The more civilians have access to space, the more knuckleheads are going to get themselves into trouble up here. It won't be the last."

"What about the rest—protecting the space lanes, showing the flag?"

"That's the part that doesn't make the papers." The chief eyed him. "You got your threat briefing with your assignment here, right? About all of the foreign military birds up here?"

Marshall nodded. "LEO and GEO are chock full of comm and spy sats."

"They're not all spies," the chief said ominously. "More than a few are what we like to call 'dual-purpose' birds."

"Hunter-killers? Isn't that a treaty violation?"

Garver laughed. "You have to understand that our Eastern friends regard treaties to be valid only as long as the ink's still wet. After that, everything's up for grabs."

"Good thing we're up here then. Nobody else has a deterrent like us."

The chief nodded toward a porthole that looked out into space in the direction of the Moon. "Some of us have our suspicions about that Chinese station at L1, Peng Fei. They're being awfully damned cagey about it."

"They're secretive about everything. Isn't it supposed to be a propellant depot for their lunar ops?"

"That's the official story, but they'll have to really pick up the pace for that explanation to make sense."

"They do like to appear inscrutable."

"Screwing the inscrutable, effing the ineffable," the chief drawled. "Whatever they say they're doing, you can be sure they're actually doing something else." He waved Marshall ahead. "Come on, I'll give you the nickel tour."

"The modules are all oriented longitudinally," Garver explained as he pushed off for the tail end of the connecting tunnel. Marshall only knew this because of the arrows labeled "Forward" and "Aft" along the sidewalls, otherwise there was nothing to distinguish one direction from another. A ladder was embedded in the ceiling along its length.

"Each deck is along the aft side of the module, then? How much time do we spend under thrust?"

"Enough for it to be a nuisance if we hadn't paid attention to that. Those NERVA engines can burn for a couple hours before we have to cool them down. Not good for your deck to become your sidewall for that amount of time."

Marshall did the math in his head. Though he'd seen the numbers before, being on the ship made them real. Each engine produced eight hundred seconds of specific impulse, thrust-to-weight ratio of almost point five ... take it down by another half for the ship's mass, and they were capable of a quarter-g burn. For two hours. He looked up and down the compartment's length and whistled.

Garver read his expression. "Puts it in a different perspective being up here, doesn't it?"

"It does. I'm just trying to think of what we'd need to burn that long for."

"Only if the skipper was taking us to Jupiter for a couple of years, but I'm not signing up for that cruise. Mars, sure. Plug in a couple extra supply modules, get rid of some nonessentials, upload new nav software . . . we could do it. Out and back in about six months. Nine, tops."

Which told him they'd been thinking about it. "Are they thinking about a 'show the flag' mission?" *Please please please . . .*

"Above my paygrade, Ensign. Yours too, I'm afraid. But it is fun to think about."

"That was my senior thesis in astrodynamics," Marshall volunteered, a bit too eagerly. "Adapting a *Borman*-class vessel for interplanetary flight. The delta-v budget's not too far off from what we already use getting around cislunar space. Biggest hurdle would be consumables and life support."

Garver nodded. "We know. Skipper and the XO have read it. They were amused."

"Oh."

"I read it too. You made a powerful case for a national Exploration Corps. But there's a lot that can go sideways up here. Biggest problem with long-duration spaceflight is the 'duration' part."

Marshall felt himself blush. "Maybe I let my enthusiasm get the better of me. Now that I'm here, it's hard to look around a ship like this and not want to take it somewhere."

"Don't be too hard on yourself, Ensign. Your job as a cadet was to learn how to think about outside-the-box concepts like that. Now you just have a different set of boxes. Come on." He led them into the farthest aft module, the engineering compartment. The space was uniformly gray, one side filled with circuit breakers and access panels festooned with warning labels. The other side held racks of air and water filtration beds fed by clusters of ductwork and plumbing fed into the module's entrance from all directions.

"Electrical, environmental, and comm are all in here," he explained. "We can run everything from the control deck, but if something needs fixing this is your first stop. If it can't be fixed here, your next stop is outside."

It seemed as patched together as the old International Space

Station every new flight officer had been familiarized with. "All that plumbing's internal for a reason. They need too much work to keep the feed lines outside. Every other compartment can be sealed off if there's an emergency depress. It's not perfect but they couldn't come up with a better layout," the chief said. He pointed back to the entrance, across the connecting corridor. "Over there is reactor control, computer network, sensors and weapons. Other than the server racks, there's not much that can be fixed in there." He floated past, back into the gangway.

Marshall poked his head in and saw a much tidier version of the module they'd just left. Almost immediately, the chief's feet disappeared into the next adjacent portal. "This is medical and suit maintenance."

Pulling himself inside, it was clear that the space was as much about suit maintenance than any medicine. Racks of EVA suits and helmets lined an entire half of the module; work benches and supply cabinets took up much of the other half. "Where's the medical gear?"

Garver pulled on a white panel with a Red Cross symbol to unfold an exam table out of one wall. As he locked it in place and unstrapped its zero-g restraints, a rack of patient vital-sign monitors and intravenous pumps embedded in the wall behind it switched themselves on. "All here," he said, "including idiot-proof EKG leads and an auto-defibrillator. Theoretically any one of us can use these. I don't pretend to understand what they do, but the rescue spacers can explain that better anyway."

"You're not one?" Marshall asked, surprised. He noticed three more tables just like it folded up along the aft wall—realizing it was in case they had patients to work on while under thrust. Another panel embedded in the ceiling was labeled "IV Meds." So that's where they kept it all. Yet another access panel in the floor was labeled "First Aid."

"Oh, I'm cross qualified in three different areas," Garver said. "Doesn't mean I understand them all. My primary rating is propulsion and reactor systems." He pointed to the massive inner door of the emergency airlock at the far end of the module, beyond the racks of EVA suits. "My medical training is just enough to get a person through that 'lock and plugged into one of these beds without making matters worse. The rescue spacers are the real docs." He floated back into the connecting tunnel. "We're headed for their berth next. You can see for yourself."

They briefly popped into a module filled with exercise equipment. Two men pounded away on treadmills embedded in the wall, each strapped to it with elastic cords. On the opposite wall were resistance machines. A large HD television screen dominated the far corner. "Rec deck," Garver said. "Crew recreation and wardroom." He pointed to a long table whose surface was embedded in the floor. "Double or triple use, just like everything else up here. We also use it for cards. Movie night's on Saturday, otherwise you're likely to find people in here running video game tournaments when they're off duty."

Moving next door, Garver led him into the first crew berthing module. Three retractable fabric doors lined either sidewall, each decorated with personal photos, flags, and mostly profane messages. One featured an action-movie poster with someone else's head cropped over the hero's face. "Back on the boat, those would've been centerfolds and tool-calendar pinups," Garver said.

"Was that back when Noah was still a sailor?"

"Seems longer than that," the chief lamented. "You should've seen it back when they banned tobacco aboard ship. That was the only thing that kept a lot of us sane." He pirouetted and headed back out, turning right. "Your quarters are next door."

The only difference between the officer and crew berthing was a larger compartment at the end of the module, which he guessed were the captain's quarters. If the others weren't much bigger than a closet on Earth, the skipper's was at least walk-in sized.

Marshall pulled open the folding door to his own compartment. On the ground it would've felt claustrophobic, but you could make more use of the same living space in zero g. Any surface could be a wall, as orientation didn't matter except under thrust. To that end, he noticed his bunk (really a light sleeping bag) was along the aft wall, just as the chief had mentioned. So if he were in it during a burn, he'd be pressed into the padded sidewall behind him. The whole thing in fact looked like a padded cell.

If the room wasn't any bigger than a closet, then it wasn't furnished much more than one either. Small drawers were embedded into one wall, mounting brackets for a tablet computer and keyboard faced his "bunk," while the adjacent wall was bare. From what he'd seen, most crewmembers filled that blank wall with personal photos. He realized he hadn't brought any and wondered if he'd have enough time to spend in here for it to matter. He imagined the guys with families back on Earth probably had. Would that make a stint up here harder or easier? He wondered.

It wasn't long after connecting to the ship's network that his tablet and phone began pinging him with backlogged messages. Most were anodyne administrative notices from Fleet HQ, thrice-sent confirmations of his duty assignment, forwarding addresses, generic safety briefings, though it was the next-of-kin designation form that got his attention. A formality, but still . . .

He was grateful for the distraction when his phone buzzed with a raft of incoming texts from Roberta, starting two days ago. Her hyper-staccato texting perfectly mirrored her bouncy personality.

U wont believe this. They got me operating X37s!

Hope ur job at the Wing isnt too boring.

DUDE where r u?

U ghosting me? SRSLY?

OK man, now u got me worried. Its been 2 days. Where u b?

Had it really been that long? Things had happened fast. How to answer her? There wasn't anything in his assignment notice or onboarding brief about secrecy. Coming here was unexpected, but it wasn't classified either.

Hope your job at the Wing isn't too boring. Yeah, about that . . .

He began thumb typing and almost sent his phone flying away with a screen full of garbled text. His usual light grip wouldn't work up here; one more minor adjustment he'd have to make in zero g. This time he made sure it was wrapped firmly in his hands and tried again.

Not ghosting u. Sorry. Been a busy week.

And it was only Wednesday, he realized. He kept typing.

Got my assignment. Not what I expected at all.

The familiar incoming message bubble appeared on screen. It hadn't taken long for her to reply.

Its all good. Hope ur well. Remember the worst job in the SF is still better than the other branches. So what r u doing?

That was Roberta, always trying to lift his spirits, but in this case not really necessary. How to answer that? He found it was always best to get to the point...

Nothing much. Hanging out on the Borman. Rode a Specter shuttle up here yesterday.

Marshall sent it, checked the time and wondered exactly how much her eyeballs must have been popping out of her skull at that moment.

U @$$hole!

So, about that much. He stuffed his small pouch of personal effects into a drawer and secured his duffel bag inside the sleep restraint. He could unpack later. The chief was giving him a tour of the ship because that's what was customary, but now he was expected to report to Captain Poole.

The control deck felt cramped compared to the layout he'd studied so much. The diagrams and virtual models had looked so much more spacious, but Marshall soon realized that was because they weren't occupied with people.

Half the crew was on duty at any one time, and most of them were in here. Two pilots floated above the flight station, one stood in front of the reactor systems panel with his feet hooked into restraints in the deck. Another hovered in front of what Marshall assumed to be the EVA management station, watching a monitor which showed the two crewmen in yellow spacesuits still working on the sensor suite. Two sets of legs dangled out of the observation cupola mounted in the overhead. One of them belonged to Captain Simon Poole.

A voice boomed from the cupola. "That you, Chief?"

"It is, sir." Garver straightened perceptibly. Marshall strove to do the same.

"Got our new nugget in tow, do you?"

"Aye, Skipper. Just finished giving him the ship's tour."

"That should've taken all of five minutes," Poole said, not moving from his spot in the dome. "What'd you do, fold his clothes for him?"

Garver checked his watch. "Five minutes, twenty seconds, sir. And the young ensign stowed his own gear."

Hands reached around the lip of the cupola, and a stocky form in a gray flight suit floated down into the control deck. A black ballcap embroidered with the spacecraft's logo and captain's scrambled eggs on its brim covered Simon Poole's bald head.

Marshall pulled himself to attention to the extent possible in zero g and saluted. "Ensign Hunter reporting for duty, sir."

Simon—*Captain Poole*, Marshall had to remind himself—made a show of looking him over before returning the salute. "Welcome aboard, Mister Hunter." He waved a hand dismissively. "And *at ease*, for God's sake. Got your service record?"

That Poole could've just as easily pulled it up on the tablet in his hip pocket signaled that he still preferred to go about this the old-fashioned way. Marshall handed over his own tablet, his service record already displayed. He shot a glance over at Chief Garver, silently thanking him for the heads-up, and realized this was no doubt a standing routine between the two. He wondered if that was behind the chief's many trips to and from Earth—suiting up and flying into orbit with each new crewmember, with an introduction to the *Borman* following naturally—and made a mental note to find out. If he was right, five launches seemed like an awfully low count.

It was obvious Poole leaned hard on his senior NCO to break in new crew, especially officers. *Especially* extremely junior officers he'd known since they were children.

"So you got the chief's tour—think you can find your way around my ship without breaking anything?"

"I'll do my best, Captain."

"I'm sure you will. And if you don't, I'll be busting both of your asses."

"I'll keep him out of trouble, Skipper," Garver said. Marshall laughed nervously.

Poole swiped through the pages in his records. "Aced your suborbital pilot quals, good scores in space ops concepts—so you might have a decent chance at orbital quals." He continued. "Double majors in Astro and Mech E," he read aloud, though he already knew that story. "So if you break something, you have some idea how to fix it." Poole closed the file. "Mister Hunter, know this: there's no way to learn this business without doing it. You've had a good start, but you're about to find out how little they teach in school."

"I had a taste of that in orbital mechanics, sir," he said, hoping he wasn't digging himself a hole. "I didn't really get it until I played a couple of PC games."

"That old one with the little green men who build rockets?" Poole laughed. "The crew runs a tournament on Thursday nights. Best way to learn until you get up here to actually do it. I'd rather you blow up something you built online instead of my ship."

"I will endeavor to not blow up your ship, sir."

"Don't crap where you eat. Always a good idea." He swiped across another page. "Mister Hunter, you'll be the division officer for the EVA specialists. Finish stowing your gear and report down to their spaces."

"Yes sir," Marshall said, silently eyeing the pilot's flight station over Poole's shoulder.

Poole followed his gaze. "Looking for something?"

"No sir."

The captain arched an eyebrow. "Do you understand the mission of this vessel, Mister Hunter?"

He tried not to sound like he was repeating the stock answer that had been drilled into him during basic officer school. "Sir, the *Borman* is a spaceborne medium-endurance patrol vessel analogous to a US Coast Guard national security cutter. Our mission is to protect US assets in orbit, ensure freedom of navigation in cislunar space, and rescue spacecraft of any nationality in peril. Sir."

Poole smiled. "Congratulations, you paid attention in class. What that means in real life is that we're one ship with an overly broad mission and a small crew. Everybody here is dual or triple qualified, Mister Hunter, including pilots. Outside work is one area they can't train you for on the ground, I don't care how much time you spend in the tank." He pointed to the crewman at the EVA control station with a headset jacked into the panel, intently focused on the video from the spacewalkers' helmet cameras. "Petty Officer Riley here is their NCO in charge." Poole looked up into the cupola at the pair of feet jutting out from its opening. "Lieutenant Flynn had been their division officer until now, but he's rotating back into engineering. He'll show you the ropes." Poole gestured for Marshall to join him.

Even with one crewman inside, the cupola swirled with activity. The dome was less than two meters across, ringed with six trapezoidal windows around a central round window. Laptops jacked into the ship's network were strapped beneath the windows with Velcro. Flynn, short with a close-cropped head of red hair, watched the spacewalking crew outside. He spied them through a pair of binoculars on the rare instances when he thumbed the mic on his headset to speak with them, apparently choosing to leave the running commentary to Riley down at the control station. He nodded, silently acknowledging Marshall before turning back to watch his men.

Marshall floated behind him to watch the two spacers still working around the sensor module. Now over Earth's night side, their yellow suits shone brilliantly under the ship's floodlights. Beneath them, the planet sparkled with the lights of cities passing by. Ahead, the sky along Earth's limb glowed with their reflection.

"Must be hard to stay focused out there," he offered, hoping it didn't sound too lame.

"You get used to it," Flynn said, "and plans get filled up quick. Too much work to waste time looking around." He lifted the binoculars and clicked his mic. "Rosie, how's that P2 harness? Continuity's intermittent."

A female voice crackled on the radio, frustration cutting through. "One of the cannon plugs isn't seating. I'm about to disconnect and try again."

Flynn poked his head down into the control cabin. "Riley?"

The petty officer at the EVA station answered. "It's from that same batch that gave us trouble last month, sir. She'll get it, it'll just take some time."

Flynn checked his watch against an exposure table taped beneath a window. "Not too much time," he said. "They're going to be pushing their rad limits being that close to the reactors."

They couldn't have illustrated Flynn's point better if they'd tried: limited time, and every task outside seemed to be twice as hard as on Earth—or so he'd been told repeatedly. Panels stuck in place, cold welded to each other. Wire harnesses and coolant lines frayed from unexpected torque. Drop a tool or component in the training tank and it'd float to the bottom of the pool. Here, it'd go off in whatever direction it had been inadvertently pushed, forever.

"Lowest bidder," Flynn muttered.

"Pardon?"

"Before John Glenn flew into orbit, he supposedly said he couldn't help but think that every single part of his spacecraft had been assembled by the lowest bidder. Some things never change."

Marshall tried to sound savvy. "So you've got a set of spares giving you trouble?"

"More than one. You can take an aircraft component that does the same job up here, but as soon as you put it in space it won't work. I don't think all of our suppliers understand that yet. Sometimes it's as simple as gas flow not working the same in zero g. Sometimes it's the radiation environment, sometimes it's thermal. Sometimes the thing just gets shaken up too much on the ride uphill and shits the bed. You'll save yourself a lot of frustration if you just assume nothing works right out of the box."

Back in the EVA/medical module, Marshall watched as the two spacewalkers emerged, exhausted, from their external suit ports. Despite the already stringent exposure protocols—keeping their rad-hardened spacesuits outside the spacecraft in a dedicated shelter—the pair still had to go through a decontamination shower as one final step before entering the module. The complications of having even one normal shower functioning in space were daunting enough, having two sealed behind plastic screens just for deconning spacewalkers must have been a huge mass penalty.

He averted his eyes when he discovered both were women, and not unattractive ones either. It didn't help that they seemed to be getting a good laugh at his expense as they vacuumed away globules of water and patted themselves dry.

Chief Garver had tagged along and tried not to look amused. "Everything okay, Ensign?"

"Great, Master Chief. Awesome." He shot a glance over at Flynn, who just shrugged and began making introductions. He was going to have to develop thick skin, and quickly.

One dark-haired crewman—woman, he corrected himself—who seemed to be enjoying it the most made a halfhearted effort to cover herself up. "Petty Officer First Class Ana Rosado," she said, and gestured to her partner. "And that there is Petty Officer Second Class Nikki Harper."

"Heard a lot about you guys but haven't met any yet," Marshall said. There were tall tales about the Rescue Spacers, their service's equivalent to Air Force pararescue or Coast Guard rescue swimmers, "special operators" on par with the SEALs or Rangers.

Harper pulled on a clean jumpsuit. "Guess there aren't many of us to meet yet, sir." She looked to her partner. "There's what, a couple dozen of us?"

Rosado had made no such effort to get presentable yet, which made Marshall increasingly uncomfortable. "That's total for the whole force, yeah." She looked at Marshall. "A third of us are up here in orbit now, the rest are either training for their own cruise or on leave. There's more in the pipeline but the training footprint is huge."

"I've heard," Marshall said, forcing himself to look at her face. "Tough school?"

"Like BUD/S, just with a lot more math," she said with a shrug. "There's a few more differences, like learning how not to die in vacuum instead of by drowning."

"Zero-g combat training too?"

"Wish there wasn't, but yeah," she said with an edge to her voice, and jerked a thumb at the emergency medical packs Velcroed to a sidewall. That they were in such close proximity to the small-arms locker seemed to grate on her. "That's what we're about. I get why Pararescue has to—downed pilots are being hunted by the bad guys and you may have to shoot your way out. But us? Up here? No idea . . . sir."

"You'll have to pardon us, sir," Harper interjected. "We were all medics before becoming spacers. Combatants run a distant third to us, at least until hordes of marauding space aliens show up."

Marshall shrugged it off. "I appreciate your candor. I've got a lot to learn here."

Rosado stifled a laugh. "It never stops, sir. Soon as you think you've got it all locked down, that's when everything comes unglued."

"I'll try and remember that, Petty Officer."

Flynn helpfully interjected himself back into the conversation. "Everyone calls her Rosie," he explained. "Also, ranks and ratings get complicated compared to the ground forces so it's easier to just call them spacers."

Marshall wondered about that. "So new officers would be . . . ?"

"Space Cadets." Flynn smiled. "What, you thought we were gonna make this easy on you?"

After just a few weeks on the job, Roberta was starting to understand how people became coffee snobs. She'd never touched the stuff as a cadet and had barely tolerated it in fleet officer's basic, but pulling regular shifts in the Ops center was teaching her to avoid the nasty government-issue stuff in favor of their team's private stash.

She rubbed the sleep from her eyes and lifted a mug of the hot black liquid as she flipped through the day's intel brief on a monitor. The drone work with the X-37 was interesting stuff, but in the end they were still just moving unmanned birds around, avoiding traffic, and keeping tabs on what other countries were up to. Even the occasional debris-removal ops promised more of a challenge, as it involved maneuvering one satellite in close proximity to a chunk of orbiting flotsam. But still, she found an odd satisfaction in getting the god's-eye view of orbital space.

The Russians had almost pancaked another Soyuz the day before, and its upper stage was tumbling in a barely stable low orbit that would bring it down some time over the next few days. *Where* was the million-dollar question. There was a range of uncertainty that depended greatly on perturbations of the upper atmosphere. It might come down in the Pacific, it might come down in Alaska. Roscosmos claimed to have everything under control but the techs here seemed to think otherwise.

SpaceX had just put up another string of broadband-internet satellites, constantly replacing its old constellation in medium orbit. Astronomers would be pissed as usual as the string of artificial stars took their places in the sky. That was the downside to space commerce: the people who paid attention to the night sky were having their views obstructed on a regular basis.

Up in geosynchronous orbit, yet another comsat had gone dark: SAMCOM-3, a South American bird already near the end of its service life, which was weird. Most of those comsats were built around common frames and network buses. Once they reached orbit they were famously reliable, most lasting well beyond their design life. Yet this was the third one to go dark this week, just shy of its sell-by date.

She scrolled back through the week's database updates: the SAMCOM bird, GULFSAT 10-A, and a Japanese bird, NSTAR-G. All in GEO, and all near the end of their service lives. So maybe common frames and buses hadn't been such a good idea after all? Not if it led to a single point of failure.

Nothing a rookie officer could do about it except note the updates to their database and warn other operators about them. As she swiped over to the next page in the daily briefing, an alert popped up from Space Weather that made her forget about it.

After the first few lines, she put her coffee mug down slowly and looked across the room to their consoles. "Hey, Met," she called across the room. "What's up with this CME warning?"

"It's big and fast," the lieutenant responded. "The filament we observed is a solid six degrees across and doesn't look to be dissipating. Solar wind speed clocked over a thousand kilometers per second."

After being quiet for months, the Sun had just burped up a major coronal mass ejection, a solar storm that would impact Earth in less than a day. The stream of charged particles hitting Earth's magnetic field carried the potential for widespread power and communication outages, not to mention the radiation hazard to anyone in orbit.

"And what about this K-index . . . eight?" Roberta whistled. "You really think it'll be that high?" That portended a severe geomagnetic storm. She scrolled through the details. The leading edge of the filament would hit in sixteen hours; it would take another two for the bulk of the CME to strike.

"Wouldn't be there if I didn't think so. Batten down the hatches," the lieutenant said. "It'll be a real show. When the lights go out, they'll be able to see auroras all the way into Arkansas."

She wondered what kind of sight that would be from orbit, then thought of Marshall up there on the *Borman*. The lucky bastard. Yes, she decided, he deserved a good ribbing.

The handheld on Marshall's hip had been buzzing incessantly ever since the first warning came across the message board, with one cryptic message from Roberta kicking it off: Heads up - hope u brought ur lead underwear. He stopped wondering what she was talking about when the space weather brief showed up soon after.

As he floated through *Borman*'s core module, headed for the rec area, his watch chimed with its friendly reminder that he was once again running late. He'd already not been looking forward to the hours they'd be spending in the hardened shelter, which was the entire central hub of the spacecraft. It would seem a lot less roomy with all twelve crew in it.

That was until the all-hands meeting had been called in the now even more crowded rec module. As Marshall scrambled into the module, Captain Poole began his announcements.

"I know your private message folders are filling up quicker than the official traffic, so I won't waste time on the obvious. There is one big-ass solar flare headed our way, folks, and it promises to play hell on anything in its path. So we're not going to stay in its path."

The gathered crew exchanged curious looks. What he was describing sounded like the opposite of easy.

"If you don't want to get slimed when the shit hits the fan, then you move out of the way." He nodded toward Riley and his team. "Your people have already spent too much time outside keeping the sensor suite up. I'm not about to throw all that work away while we wait inside for the storm to pass."

Poole looked over the gathered crew. "So here's what we're gonna do. Commander Wicklund and Chief Garver have worked out a burn sequence to change our orbital period and put us on the back side of Earth when this thing hits." He read their surprise. "This should be no big deal for us, we just haven't done it yet. This is the whole point of nuclear engines, people. They can burn hard enough, long enough, to get us where we need to be. We'll raise our orbit and put Earth between us and the storm."

He continued. "The trick is we have to act fast. It'll take several burns to get the phase changes we'll need, so we have to start at the next ascending node. That's in forty minutes. If you're not already on duty, start securing all loose gear by division modules and get them oriented for some long burns."

After giving them a minute to process that, he added: "One last thing. There is a civilian Stardust spacecraft in orbit right now that will be in the path if they don't move quickly. Once the ship's secured for burn, I want all hands getting the shuttle and medical bay prepped for possible rescue ops."

Harper raised her hand. "Sir, do we know if they need assistance now? Can we go get them and move them with us?"

"Not that simple," Poole said. "They're up in GEO and our orbits don't converge. We're already going to have to do a transverse burn to rotate our plane, and we can't do both maneuvers in time. The Stardust-class vehicle has a docking tunnel that can double as a rad shelter. It'll be cramped as all hell but they'll survive."

Nick Lesko struggled to stay awake while the others slept in the darkened capsule. It was his turn to stay on comms watch with their tracking center, but another very full day of exhausting EVAs had left him drained. He cracked open another cold gel pack and pressed it against his aching hands, aware they were running short on them and not caring. They were done with spacewalks and he didn't much care if Giselle needed them or not. She was the pro, and so he assumed was therefore better conditioned against the physical toll. She was cocooned in her bag, sleeping soundly in the cabin's lower bay with Whitman and Billy/Xenos, though it was a sign of her exertion that he could easily pick out the heavy rise and fall of her breathing above the others. Not quite snoring, but the deep slumber of a person at the edge of exhaustion. He had to grudgingly admire her for not showing it while awake.

He examined his bruised fingertips, wondering how she did it. Experienced walkers must develop calluses harder than farmers, he decided. Well, this would be his last—his only—excursion beyond Earth if he had anything to say about it.

Hopefully his patrons would feel the same way. He did not look forward to talking with them despite their success up here.

Nick reached for the radio panel and made sure all their telemetry was isolated to the primary high-gain antenna. There would be no interruption in their feed to the ground, and he could still nominally stay on comms watch. But he had other, more urgent, matters to relay to another group: his patrons had their own priorities beyond that of the company they'd hired Stardust from.

He looked down at his sleeping companions, making one last check that they were fully asleep, and opened an access panel beneath the radio controls. He found the secondary antenna relays just as he'd practiced on the ground, disconnected them, and jacked his own laptop into its signal path. He opened up an encrypted message app and began typing.

ALL OBJECTIVES ACHIEVED. SUCCESSFULLY EXERCISED LOCAL CONTROL. DATA PACKET TO FOLLOW.

With that, he sent a compressed file that held each satellite's encryption codes as planted by Billy. It took longer using the frequency-hopping algorithm built into his message program, but someone would have to know what they were looking for to find it.

The reply came much sooner than he'd expected, thankfully. He didn't want to risk having this hack laid out in the open for the others to wake up and see.

ACKNOWLEDGED. PROCEED WITH CLEANUP PLAN UPON RETURN.

"Cleanup." A typically anodyne euphemism for some very nasty work. Nick quietly disconnected his laptop and replaced the antenna cables. When he switched his headset back to the company frequency, the alert tone startled him. They were demanding he acknowledge something impossibly urgent. When he read the message in the comms window, he understood. His initial fright soon gave way to a sense of focused calm—he knew the contingency plan for a CME. It wouldn't be pleasant, but the experience would be survivable.

There were many opportunities for tragic accidents in space, some more believable than others. He checked the time and began moving supplies into the tunnel while the others slept.

❀ 7 ❀

"There is no need to worry about us. We are quite well protected," Max Jiang said to the camera. He'd become well practiced enough by now to anticipate certain questions and work around the increasing signal delay. He'd also become more camera savvy, always knowing where the live one was and taking care to not look directly at it, giving the illusion of a sit-down interview with the itinerant astronaut.

"Our command and service module is radiation hardened, and we are shutting down all nonessential systems before the coronal mass reaches us," he explained. Behind him, his wife could be seen moving packages from their inflatable habitat module through the docking tunnel.

"We see Jasmine back there," the interviewer said, and she waved as if on cue. "What is she doing?"

Jiang looked over his shoulder. "She's bringing food and water from the hab into the CM. We don't know for certain how long we'll have to stay in here, but our control center thought it best to plan for an extended stay," he said with a hint of amusement at the expense of their overly cautious control team. "As you may know, water is an excellent insulator against particle radiation and we plan to have every square inch of panel space covered with water bladders."

The interviewer had no such idea but nodded along as if he did. "Yes, of course. But is there enough aboard?"

A self-effacing laugh from Jiang. "It's complicated. The environmental recycler filters and recirculates nearly all of our air and water, the rest is made up for with onboard supplies. We have enough stored for a sixty-day contingency." He made a sweeping gesture around the cabin. "Part of which is intended for situations just like this." He moved briefly off camera and returned with an undulating blue bladder, about a half-meter square. "Five liters of fresh water right here. Notice the Velcro strips and corner grommets?" He fastened one to an empty side panel, then grabbed another to place next to it, then another. "There. Instant rad shielding."

"It looks as if you still have some work to do," the interviewer said as the floating camera bot spun about in midair, showing off the cabin's cramped quarters and mostly bare walls. "You're only a week away from your first destination, asteroid RQ39." Which wasn't the proper name, but the media had been running with it long enough that it had stuck. "Are you concerned about this solar storm interrupting your exploration plans?"

"Not at all," Jiang said. "It will be over with well before we begin our rendezvous. On the contrary, our confinement will make us all the more eager to get outside for a walk." He reached out for the camera and placed it in front of a nearby window. "You can see it from here already. It's just a bright spot in the sky right now, but our destination is literally in sight and we're quite excited."

Preparations aboard the *Borman* were much more hectic, and being a brand-new division officer only made it that much harder. Lieutenant Flynn already had his hands full as their newly appointed engineer, which left Marshall completely reliant on his senior NCO. This was much as it had been in military organizations throughout history.

Chief Riley's patience with him was admirable, no doubt helped along by the fact that the spacers on their team had apparently drilled for this to the point where they could do it blindfolded. His biggest challenge was staying out of their way, not an easy task in a module already full of equipment.

After fumbling around in a storage compartment that held exactly all of the wrong items, Riley handed him a pair of clear wraparound goggles. "Augmented reality glasses," he explained. "Tap the right hinge and a menu bar will show up. Navigating it's pretty self-explanatory."

Marshall turned them over in his hands. "Can't help but notice no one else is wearing them."

"You're the only one who needs them, sir. Nothing to be ashamed of. It'll be asses to elbows around here for a while and this'll help you find your way around. Every piece of gear on this boat has an RFID tag, but not all of it ended up where Fleet Ops thought it should go. What makes sense on the ground ain't always so up here."

"So I'm finding out."

"Just the way things are, sir. Like I said, nothing to be ashamed of." Riley looked around the compartment, appearing satisfied with their preparations. Of the seven enlisted crew aboard *Borman*, four worked here. It was a plum job and they knew it—there would be no slackers for him to worry about on this crew.

"Coming through. Make a hole—sir." Rosie swam past them, trailing a net bag filled with medical packs.

"Anti-radiation prophylactics," Riley explained. "She's taking them down to the core module. If anyone starts feeling funny or sees any light flashes, we'll all be taking them." He motioned for Marshall to put the AR goggles on and tapped the hinge for him. "You should be seeing an inventory list scrolling down the right side of your field of view."

Floating tables of alphanumeric characters appeared, rolling over and changing wherever he looked as green outlines appeared over his constantly changing focus points. "So it's telling me what's in each compartment I look at?"

"Yessir. We all know what's stored where because we're the ones who set up the spaces. You'll pick it up soon enough. Where you will see these glasses used is when we take inventory for resupply missions. Easier than working off a tablet and it updates in real time."

Everywhere he looked, new outlines and rosters appeared. He tapped the hinge and they disappeared. This would be useful. He noticed a countdown timer in the opposite corner of his view. "Is that time to ignition?" he asked, realizing it was a stupid question as he said it. *What else would it be, a self-destruct timer?*

"That it is, sir. All major shipboard events will show up on the left side." He made a sweeping gesture around the medical cabin. "You can see the module's prepped for a burn. We only had to make sure any loose items were secured, and I can promise you there were none. Loose gear turns into projectiles as soon as those engines light, so the skipper takes a hard line on it."

He searched his memory for anything he might have left floating loose in his quarters. He'd find out in a couple of minutes. "Thanks. Good to know."

"Wouldn't worry too much, sir," Riley said, reading his mind. "Unless you left a socket wrench or cutting tool loose somewhere. Which I'm sure you didn't."

So they're checking up on me, he realized, not sure whether he should be reassured or irritated. Maybe they just wanted to make sure the new ensign was settled in, but he now realized he and his personal space were being sized up. He shook it off. They lived in close quarters and there were any number of ways for a stupid mistake to get lots of people killed.

Riley must have known he was processing that very thought. "Come on, sir," he said, pointing him toward a seat embedded in the aft sidewall. "We need to get secured. That first burn's going to be a long one."

Molecular hydrogen flowed through twin solid-core fission reactors to be flashed into plasma and expelled through a pair of rocket nozzles. The reaction was immediate and intense—Marshall could feel the ship move beneath him, and a quick glance through a nearby porthole showed Earth falling away from them.

With less thrust than the chemical rockets which had brought *Borman*'s various pieces to orbit, nuclear-thermal's advantage was its efficiency: they could get more impulse from of each gram of propellant than even the best chemical engine, almost twice as much. This meant they could burn for a long time and use a lot less propellant for the same work. It was what enabled the *Borman* to move freely between Earth orbit and cislunar space with only occasional refueling. Though after this episode, Fleet Ops would already be planning to send a tanker mission up to them.

The scuttlebutt among the crew was to expect a lot of postflare cleanup work. There were certain to be a lot of damaged satellites to clear out of their orbits, not to mention a possible rescue of that civilian Stardust vessel. That had really set the EVA team abuzz. His spacers—and Marshall was still learning to think of them as "his"— were chomping at the bit to get out and apply the skills they endlessly trained for. They wouldn't admit to it, but everybody wanted that first Space Lifesaving medal.

Nick Lesko kept the radios off and the shades down, keeping the cabin quiet and dark as the Sun emerged from behind Earth. He'd stayed up well beyond the end of his watch, driven by urgency and adrenaline. It was a testament to how hard they'd worked that they'd all managed to sleep through it without stirring, but the time had come to wake them.

He turned the cabin lights up slowly, not wanting to unnecessarily startle them. They had only a few hours until the first waves of the CME would hit, and Nick had scrambled to engineer one last spacewalk while they slept.

"Wakey wakey," he said as they stirred. "A lot has happened while you guys were sleeping."

"Like what?" Whitman asked, rubbing his eyes.

"Necromancer was acting squirrely," Nick said, a tad overconfident. "Some servo calibration errors came up in its daily diagnostic routine."

Billy looked at his watch. "And you didn't wake me up?"

Nick looked away sheepishly. "Didn't want to bug you. It wasn't control related, so I thought it could wait."

"Servo problems are enough," Billy said, annoyed as usual but now with good reason. "If the manipulator arms don't work, then this whole trip was for nothing." He snatched a tablet from his personal kit by his sleeping bag, opened up a window, and began scrolling.

Giselle peeked out of her sleeping bag. "You didn't wake any of us. Your watch ended four hours ago."

"You guys were all sleeping hard, and I was wide awake," Nick said, mostly truthfully. "Too amped up, I guess. Figured I could sleep later."

"You may have figured wrong, then," she said. "If we have to work in another EVA, we'll have to get cracking on it right now."

He was counting on that. "I know, at least I do now." He yawned. "Don't worry, I'll be good."

Giselle regarded him. If he looked as tired as he truly felt, this might work as the others would have to pick up his slack. "No, you won't. If it's a simple matter of recalibrating a drive motor..." she said, looking expectantly at Billy.

The hacker swiped through the report. "Wrist roll joint alignment. It's not off by much, just enough to make it harder to control if you're not looking right at your target. The latching effectors won't go precisely where the operator's aiming."

She sighed. "Yeah, that's a problem. We'll have to get out there." She looked at Whitman. "When's our first deorbit burn?"

The pilot checked the master display on his control panel. "Twenty-six hours to leave GEO, then another day before entry interface. We're already using our consumable reserves."

"So we have to get on this fast." She cursed, rubbing her temples. "Here's what we'll do. Nick and I will do a hasty suit checkout and start pre-breathing now."

"Wait a minute," Whitman protested. "He's not rested, and you can't go solo."

"We don't have time to keep this by the book," Giselle said. "I'll do the outside work. I won't be solo. All Nick has to do is hang out in the 'lock and send me tools if I need them." She looked to Nick. "Think you can handle that?"

"Absolutely," he said, stifling a yawn that wasn't entirely for show. He stole a glance at the comm access panel and secured an equipment box in front of it as he helped them stow their sleeping bags.

Whitman's voice sounded surprisingly remote for just being on the other side of the hatch. Static hissed and popped in the background. "I'm having trouble with the ground," he said. "Looks like telemetry's being transmitted but voice comms are crap. It's like I'm talking into thin air."

"We'll have to work on that later," Giselle said, already secured to their pirated satellite. "Radios sound lousy out here too."

"Do you need to wave off?"

"Negative," she said tersely. "Negative. So long as Nick can hear me when I need something. You still awake back there?"

"Affirm," he called back helpfully, though he was starting to feel the fatigue wash over him. "I'm—"

He winced as a flash of light in the corner of his eye snapped him awake, a pinprick from the Sun passing through his skull. "What was that?" Despite knowing what to expect, it was still a shock.

"What was what?" she asked, then, "Oh. Cosmic ray; just zapped me too. It happens occasionally . . . *oh shit.*"

"What's happen—?" but Giselle was already barking commands over their frequency before he could finish.

"Whitman, you seeing this too?" she snapped.

"We are," he said through a crashing wave of static. "Like a damned fireworks show in here. I can't raise the ground. Stand by . . . no space weather alerts . . . what the hell?"

"Report."

"It hasn't just been quiet—we lost data uplink six hours ago. Nothing since." Staying professional, Whitman flicked off his mic just as he was unleashing a torrent of curses.

Giselle finished his thought. "If we've missed a flare warning . . ." He watched her suddenly double over, gloved hands cradling her helmet. "Nick!" she shouted. "Get me—"

Her voice disappeared beneath a crescendo of static, accompanied by another explosion of light like flashbulbs going off in his head. And he was in a shielded compartment—what was it like being exposed?

"I don't feel very good . . ." Billy said weakly. Nick thought he could hear retching through the rising fuzz before he dropped off the frequency. He reached for the outer door and pulled it shut, sealing himself inside their storm shelter. He turned off his radio so as not to hear them shouting his name.

8

From the Global News Network

"Yesterday's solar flare proved to be an almost unprecedented astronomical event. The closest analogy occurred back in 1859 in a geomagnetic storm known as the Carrington Event, named for the astronomer who first observed the solar eruption that sparked it. It caused worldwide disruption of the telegraph system and caused auroras to be visible as far south as Mexico.

"Today, we are seeing widespread failures of electrical grids from the northern US deep into Central America. Besides our society being so dependent on electricity, another feature of life today markedly different from 1859 is the advent of space travel, where human beings now risk being in the direct path of these deadly solar flares.

"Most notable of this group are the explorers Max and Jasmine Jiang, who are well beyond Earth's protective magnetic field. We were able to speak with them after the flare had safely passed and they could emerge from their spacecraft's radiation-hardened shelter. The interview has been edited to remove the light delay due to their extreme distance."

The picture transitioned to the interviewer posed in front of a stylized starfield. "Mr. and Mrs. Jiang, it's good to see you both again. Let me begin by saying it was difficult for us to appreciate how much danger you were in until the solar flare hit Earth. I believe now we understand."

Jasmine Jiang smiled in the gentle manner that had endeared her to millions. "We have been perfectly fine," she said. "Our home up here is well prepared for emergencies like this. All we had to do was stay in the designated safe zone."

Max Jiang spoke up. "Yes, we managed quite well. We're just relieved that it didn't happen a week from now."

"You mean during your rendezvous with the asteroid?" the announcer asked rhetorically, as he already knew the answer. "That would have been unfortunate indeed. Several commercial satellites in Earth orbit have been damaged, and apparently even the military has suffered some losses. Did you notice anything unusual aboard your spacecraft during the flare?"

"Nothing of importance, thank goodness. Our ground control had us shut off everything that wasn't absolutely necessary. We've had to reset a few circuit breakers but that's it."

"It was to our advantage to be so far beyond Earth's magnetic field," Jasmine explained. "It channeled and amplified the stream of charged particles. We were more concerned with everyone back home."

The camera cut to the interviewer, now wearing a grim expression. "I'm afraid you were right to be concerned. Much of Central and South America is still without power and a large number of communications satellites are out of commission." The camera cut away to an illustration of a Stardust spacecraft. "Perhaps most concerning is the report of a manned capsule on some sort of maintenance mission in geosynchronous orbit; they have not been heard from since the flare hit."

The Jiangs traded looks of surprise and genuine concern. "That is . . . that's quite disturbing. We will be praying for them."

"Skipper says the ship's in good condition, but we're going to have our work cut out for us," Chief Garver said when he visited the rescuer's workspaces. "There's a lot of fried satellites on the other side of GEO, and it looks like their operators want to cut their losses and just move them to the graveyard with service drones. But there's a couple in LEO we might get tasked to deorbit."

Marshall noticed his crewmen looking fidgety, if such a thing were possible in zero g. It wasn't like they could shuffle their feet.

"Anything else, Chief?" Rosie asked hopefully.

"There is," he said, with a dire look that suggested he'd wished for better news. "We received a mayday call from Stardust's ops center. That civilian expedition was still in GEO at 83 West when the flare hit, and they've been out of contact with it ever since. They lost telemetry and voice comm."

Rosie and the other spacers exchanged pessimistic looks. That position put it almost dead center in the CME's impact zone.

"So it's a recovery op, then."

Garver looked at Marshall, deferring to his position as their officer in charge and thus throwing his weight with the enlisted crew behind him. "Sir, I know the captain said to have your people be prepared for rescue ops." He paused for effect. "But no voice comm suggests otherwise."

It was a breach in protocol Marshall couldn't help but notice—if the boss needed to relay orders to a junior officer, he'd have the XO or another officer do it, not the senior NCO. That told him they were getting swamped back on the control deck. "How's it going forward, Chief?"

Garver lifted an eyebrow, the most expression he typically allowed. "It was already asses to bellybuttons, sir, when they got the mayday call. Now it's all hands on deck," he said, answering the unspoken question. "We suddenly went from moving dead satellites out of the way, to, well . . ."

"Dead people?"

They were startled by the buzz of the maneuver alarm, quickly followed by a distant rumble as the engines lit and built up to full thrust. The floor moved up to meet them. With barely a warning, they were burning for a new orbit already.

"Like I said, sir. Asses to bellybuttons."

"New frag order," Ivey announced as he breezed past Roberta at the watch officer's console, just returning from group command's morning meeting. He swiped at his tablet and a tasking order appeared on the main screen. Dozens of lines of text in coded shorthand he was only beginning to understand scrolled past.

"That's a lot of dead birds to move around," Roberta said as she studied the growing list of problem satellites. Between their lone X-37 in orbit and the half-dozen maintenance sats they controlled, it was going to take a lot of time and propellant to deorbit or reposition crippled satellites. "Wasn't the *Borman* supposed to clear some of these lanes?"

"They were," he said, "but things just got worse up in GEO and they're the only game in town." He pushed another file onto her screen. "They just got underway on a rescue op."

She read through it quickly and let out a low whistle. "Civilians are stuck up there?" Nobody ever went to geosynch orbit, there was just no need to take the risk. It in fact took more propellant to park a human-rated vehicle into an orbit that far uphill than it would to send it on a loop around the Moon.

Ivey shook his head. "Some kind of satellite recovery proving flight." He sighed. "Everybody thinks they've got a better idea to save money. Those big comm birds aren't cheap, but geez . . . people aren't cheap, either, y'know?"

"Says here the spacecraft operator declared the emergency, not the crew. So nobody's heard from them?"

"They're all civilian contractors. I think only a couple of them had any time in the seat. Ship's still sending telemetry but they haven't heard squat from the passengers. Maybe they're stuck in its storm shelter. Maybe not."

Roberta nodded grimly. The "maybe not" part wasn't something she wanted to think about.

He could see it in her face, and squeezed her shoulder. "Don't do that to yourself." He pointed to a prominent listing in the Ops order—tasking to put another X-37 in orbit. "They're prepping the alert bird for launch right now. This time tomorrow we'll each be flying our own drones up there."

"Attention on deck!"

It was a command that in space was more about getting everyone quiet and focused than it was for them to snap to and stand straight. Nevertheless they each drew themselves upright and stiff, heels together with hands clenched and thumbs along the seams of their trousers. Those who could first slipped their feet into restraints along the deck. That some crewmembers floated at odd angles to each other in zero g was a reality of spaceflight that military courtesies still had to adjust for.

The multipurpose module that served as the *Borman*'s rec

room/galley was crowded with the dozen crewmembers. The sharp odor of antiseptic cleaning wipes, mixed with the normal background scent of recycled air, signaled that someone had made sure the space was squared away before the skipper showed up. No doubt it was some of the NCO's who were already crammed with work. Marshall made a mental note to do a better job of cleaning up after himself.

Poole descended into the module feet first, grabbed an overhead handhold, and somersaulted into place at the head of the table. "As you were," he said, adjusting his ball cap. "And can everyone please try to get oriented heads up? You're giving me vertigo."

A few snickered quietly while others pulled themselves upright, or rather had their feet and heads oriented in the same general direction.

"That's better," Poole said, and noticed a few smirks. "Do I look like I'm joking?" The smirks disappeared. "Captain's privilege. Consider it a professional courtesy to have all your sorry asses pointed in the same direction."

He continued. "About that short notice burn earlier, it couldn't be helped. Time was not on our side. You're all pros so I'm taking it on faith that nobody had any unstowed gear to worry about," he said with a caustic tone and knowing look.

Marshall noticed a few crewmembers stealing glances at each other: Who'd been guilty of leaving something out that had made an embarrassing mess? It hadn't been in the EVA section, of that he was certain, while Rosie and the other spacers weren't showing him any reasons to worry. Maybe it was just his way of keeping them on their toes?

Poole tapped a remote control and flicked on the widescreen monitor behind him. Earth was at the center of a polar graph, surrounded by looping ellipses illustrating their maneuver plan. "We got the warning order for this op without a flight plan, so this was all on us. Soon as Garver figured out the burn sequence, we were already coming up on the first maneuver window."

There were some understanding nods from the crew and he pressed on. He highlighted a series of cotangent ellipses. A blinking dot representing the *Borman* slowly moved along the innermost loop. "We've lowered our orbit to rephase and will begin raising it back to GEO when we cross opposite their latitude. These are going to be hard burns—this is time-critical and we can top off propellant later. Vandenberg's prepping two rapid-reaction launches right now; the alert X-37 and a tanker stage to replenish our H_2 after we're done here." He eyed the crew gravely. "We're going to need it."

It was an aggressive plan, only three burns before they intercepted the stranded Stardust with one hard deceleration to rendezvous. That was still a full day and a half's journey. A dashed curve appeared between the middle ellipse and the circle of their target's orbit. Poole moved on without waiting for the obvious questions. "As I said, time is critical. So we're going about this a little creatively."

Marshall tried not to gulp—*was he looking at me?*

The chief caught his eye—*yes, he's looking at you.*

"Mister Hunter, you and your spacers are going to freelance this one," Poole said, and zoomed in on the dashed line. "On our second phasing orbit, we'll pass within six thousand kilometers of the Stardust. We can't get the whole ship there soon enough, but we can get part of it there. Lieutenant Wylie will pilot the shuttle with you, Chief Riley, and two EVA specialists into a transfer orbit, rendezvous with Stardust and start rescue ops. Clear?"

"Aye, sir," Wylie answered. "That'll take a lot of propellant, though." Marshall thought he did an admirable job of hiding his trepidation.

"Just about all of it," Poole said. "It won't be going anywhere until we meet you back there after we've matched orbits. We'll top off the shuttle from the tanker stage meeting us down in LEO."

Marshall stole a glance over at Riley and the spacers. That was a full day they'd be on their own, separated from the mother ship but with no fuel left to maneuver. Rosie spoke up. "Question, sir."

"Shoot."

"Do we have any reason to believe there are survivors? Or is this strictly going to be a recovery op?"

If Wylie had been good at hiding his concern, Poole was even better. "No way to know, Rosado. Its operator was getting a data stream up until the flare hit, but that's all they were getting. For some reason there was no voice comm and no acknowledgment of their storm warnings. It's like they weren't listening."

The crew traded some exasperated looks and murmurs between

them. A group of civilians had probably overextended themselves, become overconfident, and gotten themselves good and dead. Nobody on board had bothered talking to the ground—had they even been aware they were out of touch?

"It gets better," Poole said. "It looks like they cycled the airlock as the storm was starting to hit."

That sparked concern among them: There could have been spacewalkers out there, exposed in the middle of a flare and ignorant of their fate. "They went outside? Were they *trying* to commit suicide?"

Poole responded firmly, squelching any speculation. "We're not going to play that game, people. It's a mayday call, and we're answering it." He paused for effect. "And I will remind you that it'll take a few more days for this to dissipate in the Van Allen belts, so I expect everyone to observe strict exposure precautions and dosage limits. If you're not on duty, stay in the core module." He pointed at Marshall. "Shuttle crew, start taking your preventatives now. I don't want anyone going back home with extra limbs growing out of their skulls."

He brought up a graphic of Stardust. It was a large, truncated cone with a cylindrical airlock portal mounted in its nose. "Their control center was able to see from telemetry that two passengers were prepped for an EVA while the other two remained inside." He zoomed in on the cylinder. "The airlock in its nose doubles as their radiation shelter. It can hold four people in shirtsleeves or two in suits. It's possible that we have survivors stuck in that airlock who are unable to communicate. I can promise you that is not a pleasant place to be." He surveyed the room with a look that told of hard-earned experience. "Snap to it, I want the shuttle prepped for departure before our next phasing burn."

Nick took a sip from his suit's hydration bladder and could barely swallow. His throat felt swollen and raw—was that a symptom of radiation sickness, or was he just growing paranoid? His mind exaggerated every itch, ache and twitch into looming disaster. Every creak was a seam about to rupture into vacuum, every pop was a dying crewmember trying to get into the airlock with him.

After what he'd heard from their final hours, he could hardly be blamed. It was hard to know who'd had the worst of it—Giselle had been outside, completely exposed, and had received the full force of the flare. She'd succumbed quickly, or at least had been quiet about it. As a professional spacewalker, she must have known it was a unique occupational hazard—right? Her last word while still in control of her own body, trapped outside the closed airlock, had been a single accusation: "Bastard."

The others, having somewhat better protection inside the capsule's pressure vessel, had taken considerably longer to succumb. He'd had to turn up his headset volume until the waves of static drowned out their bangs and shouts from the other side of the locked hatch. Billy literally hadn't known what hit them, but Whitman had of course figured it out quickly. Perhaps Nick's silence had fooled them into thinking he'd suffered the same fate as Giselle, perhaps not. Whitman was a seasoned pilot and had probably figured it out. Given the sketchy nature of their work, there was no way they could all be allowed to continue existing with such knowledge. It was going to happen up here or down there; you throw your dice and you take your chances.

Lesko had never taken a human life, though he'd been surrounded by others who had. It was always "business" to them, and a side of it he'd preferred to avoid.

What happened next? In his fatigue, he hadn't thought that part through. He was safe from the flare now, in fact was probably safe to go back down into the cabin, but that was the thought which paralyzed him. His only ride back to Earth was going to be inside a cramped spacecraft full of dead people, and he'd be trusting the automation and ground support to fly him home.

The thought would not leave his mind: Inside a cramped spacecraft, full of dead people.

That was his best option, which only worked if the spacecraft worked. And right now, it appeared that much of the spacecraft wasn't working. He hadn't counted on the electromagnetic surges overwhelming its avionics—weren't they supposed to be designed to handle this stuff? The lights wouldn't come on and the airlock's environmental panel was dead. He had no idea how or if air was circulating, so he'd kept his suit plugged in to the spacecraft's air supply. He would occasionally open his visor for a bite from a protein bar; when he did the air felt close. Stale. He took another sip of water, cringing at its chlorinated taste. After all this time, why was he only now noticing every little irritant?

Perhaps because he knew that nearly every action from now on could be among his last. As he'd reached for the lever that would unlock the inner hatch, he'd found it wouldn't budge. Whitman—it had to be—had somehow locked him out. He'd known, and he'd taken his revenge in the only way he had left.

Lesko stared at the locked inner hatch, imagining his dead companions on the other side and wondering how long it would be before he joined them.

◎ 9 ◎

The shuttle's cabin was roughly the size of a private jet's, with seats for two pilots and eight passengers. Of those, the pilots' seats were the only permanently mounted fixtures. Any passenger seat could be swapped out for an equipment rack or cargo container. Even when mated to a mobile airlock as it was now—which really served as an orbital ambulance bay—their bulky pressure suits made it feel cramped inside.

Following along as Wylie prepped the shuttle for departure, Marshall looked for analogies with the Puma suborbital trainers he'd qualified on. *Specter* looked similar on the outside, if considerably larger: bulbous nose, thin rectangular windshield, its lifting-body fuselage tapered into a pair of stubby, upturned winglets. Its tail was a universal docking adapter mounted between two maneuvering engines, each canted outward so as not to damage the mobile airlock now mated to it.

"Most of the preflight checks are automated," the senior pilot explained. "I had it start the onboard diagnostics as soon as the skipper gave the order." He traced a gloved finger from the overhead switch panel down to the cluster of engine controls on a pedestal between their seats. "Just follow the flow and it'll tell you right away if it's going to work. But this baby hardly ever has any squawks."

"So not as intense as prepping for a launch from the ground?"

Wylie nodded inside of his helmet. "You don't have all the booster interface and abort modes to worry about. That's half of what can go wrong. Getting around up here is simple by comparison." He tapped a small screen above the control pedestal to show their propellant

89

load. "This is what we'll have to keep an eye on. We haven't been able to top off tanks since we got here last week and the OMS has just enough delta-v to reach Stardust after they throw us at it. All we have after that are maneuvering thrusters, and we'll be using those a lot just for station-keeping until they come back for us tomorrow."

Marshall was about to ask about that when a radio call interrupted him. "*Specter*, this is home plate. Comm check, over."

"*Specter* reads you five by five, preflight complete," Wylie said. He turned to Riley, who gave him a thumbs-up. "EVA team is secure. Pressure is equalized and we are on internal power."

"Copy that. We're on pitch for release in thirty." A countdown clock came to life atop the instrument panel. "You're go for undock at zero."

Wylie reached up for his open visor. "Faceplates down, people," he announced for everyone aboard. "Stand by for release." He pointed to a lever above the throttle quadrant and motioned for Marshall to pull it as the timer reached zero.

My first duty as an actual pilot, he thought. *Retract the gear and don't touch anything else.* So flying the right seat in space wasn't much different than on Earth. At zero, he pulled the release handle out and down and felt the spacecraft detach. A gentle kick from the spring-loaded docking collar pushed them away slowly.

Another call came after several minutes of drifting apart. "*Specter*, you're at Waypoint Zero, on vector to intercept Stardust. Clear to maneuver."

"That's what I was waiting for." Wylie tapped the sidestick controller and brought the nose around quickly. Attitude indicators in front of each pilot rolled and pitched in unison until he stopped them on the preprogrammed heading. "*Specter* is burning in three," he said, and did a short count to ignition. There was a firm kick as the tail-mounted orbital maneuvering thrusters lit off.

Just as Marshall was thinking this was all happening awfully fast, Wylie explained himself. "I'm normally a lot smoother than this, but we're in kind of a hurry," he said, again eyeing the propellant gauges. "We have to use all the free momentum we can get, so every second matters. Planned or not, I don't want to get there with empty tanks."

"Got it." It made sense—unlike atmospheric flying there would be no winds to take advantage of, no managing power to improve range. Once you were pointed in the right direction, reaching your destination in space was all about delta-v: changing velocity. There were ways to leverage a planet's gravity in your favor but in the end you either had enough fuel, or you didn't. Every launch, every change in orbit, required adding velocity—even "reducing" it was simply adding velocity in the opposite direction. Coming up short by even a few meters per second was the difference between making orbit or returning to Earth—or if already in orbit, *not* returning at all.

The press of acceleration subsided quickly and they were back in zero g. It was a short burn, just enough to put them on a tangent from *Borman*'s trajectory that intercepted Stardust's orbit. As they approached the stricken craft, they'd turn around and make a longer burn to slow down and meet it.

Through the overhead window Marshall could see their mother ship falling behind, a graphic reminder of how quickly things could happen up here. Ahead of them was nothing but black space with a string of distant lights, like a diamond necklace in a velvet case—geostationary satellites, their target somewhere among those false jewels.

Bastard.

The accusation would not leave his mind. It was as if he'd been stung in his soul and couldn't remove the barb, still alive and pumping its venom into him.

He'd done a lot in his life to have deserved such a slur but no one who knew him had ever dared utter it, no one who knew what kind of retribution he could bring. Even as one of the low-level hangers-on around the New Jersey mob, he could inspire fear in those even farther down the ladder. After he'd gone to Nevada and embedded himself in the casino business, his reputation had garnered an invitation into an even more secretive—and lucrative—foreign concern. Not only had his "family" not objected, they'd encouraged it, which told him he was just valuable enough for them to let go so as to garner some kind of favor from whoever it was that had brought him into this new organization—and after five years with them, he still wasn't sure who that was.

There were all kinds of "fixers" in this world, each with their own specialty. In the old days, that had meant someone who could manipulate others into doing the bosses' bidding without looking like it. Nick, however, had become skilled in manipulating electronics into doing his bidding without it looking as if they were. A valuable skill set in Vegas, apparently it was even more valuable in other parts of the world—east Asia, in particular. He'd spent a great deal of time shuttling between casinos all around the Pacific Rim and collecting increasingly handsome payouts.

When the call had come for this job, he'd had to hide his surprise: *Sure, boss, it's just another job, only the scenery is different.* A lot different. Plus he'd had to spend six weeks of intense training just to qualify for the ride, with another six weeks learning how to be a spacewalker. That part had mostly consisted of showing him how not to get himself killed.

Truth be told, Nick had taken a liking to this astronaut stuff. If his life had gone differently, maybe it was something he could've done legitimately. Math had always come naturally to him—one doesn't run numbers in Jersey without it being second nature—from which his affinity for electronics and control systems had sprung. That he'd applied those skills in the manner he'd chosen had as much to do with his environment than any conscious decision. He'd just never conceived of it being very lucrative in the "legit" world. Every successful person he'd met had been playing some kind of angle; it was just how stuff got done. You did what was necessary to get ahead. You didn't wait for fortune to arrive—that was a sucker's game. You *made* it happen. If that involved cutting corners—or worse—then it was only business. Growing up, the nuns had tried to teach him it was because we were all sinful creatures in a fallen world. Whatever. Business was business.

This had been the first time he'd experienced anyone committed to a job because they *wanted* to do it. From the Stardust interns fitting them for suits, to the eggheads back in ground support, to the experienced spacers like Giselle and Whitman, he'd never seen devotion to a cause just for the thrill of it.

He wished he could look outside. The tiny porthole centered in the outer door was just big enough to let in sunlight; not enough to see outside as long as he had his helmet on. He could take it off and rely on the compartment air, but staying in his suit and plugged directly into its supply kept the voices at bay.

He needed to move, to get out of this suit. His throat was parched, and soon there would be no more water. He'd hidden plenty of water and rations inside the 'lock for just this reason—he knew he couldn't stay encased in this suit for two or three days. He had to be able to get out, move around, eat and breathe normally. Not living in a cocoon and surviving off distilled water and protein shakes.

But that meant taking off his helmet, and that was when the voices came.

Inside its protective cocoon, the only sounds came from circulation fans and his own breathing. Without it, his mind was pummeled by a barrage of accusations: *Psycho. Lunatic. Murderer.*

At this point Nick wasn't sure and no longer cared if he'd truly heard—was hearing—any of them. Yesterday, the voices behind the inner door had become muffled and indistinct before trailing off to nothing. He thought he'd heard an occasional retching sound. Nothing like Giselle's last, clear as crystal, breaking through the roaring static from the solar flare that had killed her: *Bastard.*

"Stand by for retro fire in three . . . two . . ."

Marshall waited by the second flight station in back of the cabin, bracing himself against the bulkhead as the engines came to life once more. This was going to be a long burn, cancelling their excess velocity to match Stardust's orbit. The little craft shuddered as the twin rockets pushed hard against them. He watched their target grow in the crosshairs of the docking monitor, figuring he must have been doing something right for Wylie to have trusted him to be near any set of controls.

The pilot had been obsessive about their approach vector and propellant load, with good reason—if he missed, they'd zip by the stranded spacecraft and would need to be rescued themselves the next time *Borman*'s orbit brought them in proximity. That would mean another day in a spaceplane that was feeling increasingly confined.

Rosie and the other spacers had been jovial, almost boisterous, during the transit here. Now that they were close, they'd grown quiet and serious. They were professionals who trained constantly for exceedingly rare "live" missions—it was common to pull a six-month tour in orbit without a single mayday call. They were eager to get outside on a real spaceborne rescue and not just do a dock-and-extract, the preferred and safest method.

As they drew closer, Marshall's job was to monitor their target for any outside damage that might prevent docking. The image had been fuzzy in the distance, bouncing in the crosshairs as they shuddered under the OMS rocket's thrust. When the first burn was finished and the image stabilized, Marshall began zooming in. "I've got visual."

It looked bigger than he expected from this distance—maybe his perspective was skewed? When he dialed back the magnification, its shape was still off. "Stand by," he said. Something wasn't right.

His hesitation caught Chief Riley's attention, who pulled up behind him. At normal magnification, their target slowly grew larger as they drifted closer. Riley said, "I think there's more than the one vehicle out there, sir."

"Anything blocking our approach?" Wylie asked from up front.

"Not that I can see, at least up until your final hold." Riley gestured at the panel controls. "May I?"

Marshall lifted his hands. "Have at it, Chief."

Riley zoomed back in slowly until the spacecraft was at the edge of resolution. He panned the image left, then right. "See that?" He pointed at a blocky shape just ahead of the cylindrical nose-mounted airlock. "That's a comsat, standard Model 1400 frame. It's gonna be in our way, for sure." He zoomed in closer, right up to the point where the image threatened to blur out of usefulness. "But this is what I was really curious about." He pointed out a figure floating nearby.

Marshall leaned in closer. He felt a stab of dread, like an icicle in the gut. "Is that—?"

Riley nodded somberly. "Afraid so, sir." He turned back to face their small team. "Saddle up, gang. Looks like we're going to earn our pay."

With a stray satellite and an unresponsive astronaut inside their maneuvering bubble, docking with Stardust was impossible. With a determination suitable for their grim task, the spacers took to it with quiet professionalism.

"Watch your dosimeters," Rosie admonished her team as they drifted clear of *Specter*, crossing space toward the stricken capsule.

"Any debris out there?" Marshall asked from inside the bay, he and Riley both suited up to go outside if necessary.

"Negative," she said. "All clear except for, you know." The crackling frequency hinted that here in GEO, closer to the outer Van Allen belts, electromagnetic and radiation spikes were still a risk. It was going to put a strict time limit on them.

"Ahoy, Stardust," she called over UHF 243.0, the universal emergency frequency. "We are a launch from the US orbital vessel *Borman*. What is your condition, over?"

They eyed the spacewalker ahead and waited for any hint of a response. Even encased in a suit and maneuvering pack, whoever it was looked lifeless.

Rosie waited a few seconds and repeated her call. "Ahoy, Stardust—"

A faint voice cut through the static. "My name is Nick Lesko. I hear you. Please help."

"We've got a live one!" she said over their private channel, then switched back to the emergency freq. "Nick, my name is Ana Rosado. I'm with the Space Force orbit guard. We're going to get you out, okay? Is that you we see outside, or are you inside the spacecraft?"

"I'm inside," he said, his voice cracking with emotion now instead of radio interference. "In the airlock. That's Giselle outside. She's . . ."

"It's okay," Rosie said, and motioned to one of her team to retrieve Giselle's lifeless form. "We'll take care of you. Your manifest had four people listed on board. Are the others with you?"

"No . . . I mean, negative. They're in the control cabin. I haven't heard from them since yesterday."

Rosie turned to signal her companions: *Later*. There was one person still left to save. "What is your condition, Nick?" she asked as they approached the airlock. "How are you feeling?"

"Okay, I guess. A little shaky."

"Any nausea or vision problems?" She held out her hands. Almost there.

"I saw a couple of flashes when the storm hit," he said, his voice faltering. "It happened so fast. When Giselle got sick, I . . . I couldn't—"

"Couldn't what?" With a quick burst from her suit thrusters, she stopped right in front of the hatch. It was closed and locked, with both outside indicators "barber-poled."

"—get her back," he finished. "I couldn't."

"It's okay, Nick." She reached out and grabbed the frame. "I'm here, okay? We're gonna get you out of there. Are you sealed off from the cabin?"

"Yeah...yeah, I am."

"Do you have access to an EVA suit?"

"I'm wearing it."

That was unexpected, but this Nick fellow didn't sound like much of a spacer either. Maybe he'd just been afraid to take it off. "Good. Are you sealed up then, pressurized?"

"I am," he said. "I've been drawing air from the main cabin supply."

Also unexpected. She raised her eyebrows. So his suit bottles had run out and instead of letting the 'lock do its thing, he just plugged in to the cabin tanks?

She shrugged it off. People did all kinds of dumb things under stress, especially greenhorn civilians. "Good. Nick, I'm going to vent your airlock so I can open it up from out here, okay?"

"Okay. Please hurry." His voice cracked.

"Don't worry, we're on it. You just hang in there." She tried to keep him talking as she hand-walked down the hull. "So where you from, Nick?"

"Jersey."

"Which exit?" She stopped at the main hatch.

"Funny," he said weakly. "East Orange. Outside Newark."

"I know where it is." Not really, but it kept him talking. She peered through a nearby window into the darkened cabin. "When's the last time you heard from your crewmates?"

He was silent.

"Nick? You still with me?" She took a detachable lamp and positioned it against the hatch's porthole, illuminating the cabin while she looked through the nearest window. A pair of legs floated lifelessly. She moved across to the window on the opposite side of the capsule.

"Yeah. It's been, I don't know...a while? I can't be sure," he said, questioning his own recollection.

She stopped at the next window and moved the light. As she cast its beam about, random bits of detritus fell under its dusty glow: An empty drink pouch, scraps of note paper, random globules of food... no, probably vomit. A lot of it. *Ugh.* This didn't look good. "We got the mayday call from your operator yesterday. Can you remember?"

"It's all kind of a blur. Maybe a day."

"Okay. Thanks. That helps." The radiation burst had hit them hard and fast, amplified by the magnetic fields. She looked down at her own dosimeter, then back through the window. A pale figure drifted into her beam—a face, contorted, staring back at her with glassy eyes. It might have been the light, but it looked pale. He was— had been—young, with an uneven beard and unkempt, curly hair. The oatmeal-like crust around his mouth and matching stains on his jumpsuit screamed "radiation sickness" to her.

She dipped her head sadly. They would've moved through each stage quickly, though she suspected the latent stage—where symptoms seemed to disappear—would have passed almost unnoticed. They'd gotten real sick, real fast. "Did they say anything to you?"

"I don't want to talk about it." His voice was firm now.

"Fair enough." He'd been in the airlock, the others had been outside or in the cabin . . . had it really hit that hard, that they hadn't tried to hunker down in the 'lock's safe zone with him? That the woman outside hadn't been able to get inside? Had he panicked and shut himself in?

"I . . . couldn't open the hatch," he finally began to explain. "If they locked me in, then what does that mean?"

It was either profoundly selfless or profoundly stupid, she thought. Those questions would have to wait. Her spacewalk partner pointed at his dosimeter and circled a finger in a "hurry up" gesture. She answered him with a thumbs-up. *Right. Let's get on with it.*

They moved, hand over hand, back up the hull and came to a rest on opposite sides of the airlock. "Nick, I need you to sit tight. We're coming in now." Rosie motioned for her partner to open the airlock's outflow valve. A cloud of ice crystals erupted behind them as the chamber vented its air into space. She cranked on the latch and the outer hatch opened easily.

Peering down into the tunnel, a lone figure cowered—to such an extent possible in a pressure suit—by the inner hatch. She lifted her gold sun visor so he could see her face. "You must be Nick," she said in a cheerful, no-worries voice. "Ready to get out of here?"

The face inside the bubble helmet turned up to see her and squinted. He held up a hand to block the sudden burst of sunlight she'd let in. "Yes. Please." He was back to sounding exhausted.

She reached in and grasped his hand, pulling him up and out of the chamber until his umbilical hose went taut. The first thing she did was check the dosimeter clipped to his chest: Yellow with a hint of orange, so no immediate risk of radiation sickness. Good. "Let's get you unhooked. We're going to buddy breathe, okay?" His suit was one of the sleeker lightweight models, not nearly as cumbersome as her government-issued garment. This was partly because it wasn't as rad-hardened, so she worked quickly. She closed his intake valve, unplugged his hose from the environment panel, and plugged it into the emergency port on her chest pack. "And there you go," she said. "We're breathing the same air. Hope you haven't been eating anything too funky."

The face behind the bubble smiled weakly. "Nothing but water and protein shakes since yesterday."

She made an exaggerated grimace. "That'll do a number on your digestive tract. Let's make this quick. C'mon." She grasped his arms and pulled him out, clipping a pair of carabiners to his waist to keep him firmly secured in front of her.

She folded out the control arms for her maneuvering pack and gave the translation controller a push. With a puff of cold gas jets, they were headed back to the nearby shuttle where another spacer hovered outside.

"Hector," she called, "head back to Stardust and help Mikey with the others. Be prepared to force the latch." She made a slashing motion across her neck, signaling him that they'd be recovering bodies but not wanting to say so in front of their survivor. "I'll be back as soon as we get Nick here settled aboard."

Hector patted a pair of dark, heavy pouches clipped to his utility harness—he'd already figured as much. "You'll have to make it fast, Rosie. We're already bumping up against our limit."

She looked down at her dosimeter. *Damn.* She was already at the edge of the orange band. By the time she got this kid aboard and back over to the Stardust . . . "Roger that. I'll stand by here, then."

"No sweat, boss. We got this."

"Madre de Dios."

Hector recoiled after tentatively poking his head into the cabin. No matter how realistic, no amount of training drills or virtual-reality simulations could prepare them for confronting the real thing for the first time. He was grateful to be encased in their suits, as he didn't want to imagine what the smell would be like otherwise.

Not especially roomy to begin with, the Stardust crew cabin was a tangle of floating debris and human waste. Hector made his way inside, pushing aside random bits and pieces, flinching in disgust when blobs of what he hoped was only vomit attached to his suit. Surface tension became the dominant force in fluids under no gravity, so when a random globule of any liquid touched any surface, it attached itself fully. By the time he gave Mikey the all clear, he was covered in it.

"Damn, bro, you're a sight," Mikey said as he followed Hector inside. "Thanks for cleaning up for me."

"Very funny. There's gonna be more where this came from." Though from the looks of the two remaining crewmen, there'd be no more added to the already frightful mess.

"Should've vented the cabin before entry," Mikey thought out loud. "That would've at least sucked the liquids into the vents."

"Can't go changing protocols for our convenience," Hector reminded him. "If someone had been alive and unresponsive ..."

"I know, I know." The spacer wiped at a glob of something foul that had just attached itself to his chest pace, his face a mask of disgust. "Aw hell. It's all over my control pack. That's gonna be a bitch to clean."

"Save it for the debrief," Hector said, and meant it. There would be a lot of lessons to pass on to the others after this. "Let's remember why we're here."

They'd allowed the cloud of detritus to obscure what they had come here for. This was no longer a rescue—it had become a recovery operation, the bland euphemism for the grisly act of clearing out dead bodies. There would be time to deal with the remains of this mess once they were safely back inside their own spacecraft.

Hector pushed aside a stray laptop floating in front of him to reach the first victim. He began reciting what he saw for the event record now streaming from his helmet camera. "Caucasian, middle-aged male. Brown hair, brown eyes. Average height, estimate mass about ninety kilos." He looked down at the nametape on the man's jumpsuit. "Name 'C. Whitman' matches the pilot listed on the manifest."

"I have the other one," Mikey said. "Young guy, also Caucasian, maybe midtwenties. Neckbeard. Nametape only says 'Xenos.'"

Rosie's voice cut in on their channel. "Stand by." There was a pause as she went off-freq. "Yeah, Nick here says that was the kid's gamer handle. He insisted on using it."

"Let's start getting these guys out of here." Hector unsnapped the pouch from his utility belt and handed it to Mikey, motioning for him to move back into the airlock. "Keep it open over the hatchway. I'll push them up to you one at a time, you bag and tag." It was a grisly task and being the senior man on site, he'd decided to take on the worst part for himself. His partner nodded his assent and pushed off into the tunnel.

They worked quickly once the path was cleared of trash. It was only when the two crewmen were gone did Hector begin to notice what they'd left behind: a jungle of conduits, cables, and laptops. It looked like a perfectly horrible work environment.

He was used to Poole running a tight ship, and knowing they might want to dock this thing to *Borman* when it swung back by here tomorrow, he'd reflexively begun stowing loose gear when Rosie interrupted him.

"Hector, what's your exposure?"

He checked the dosimeter clipped to his chest and cursed at his carelessness. She probably already knew the answer from her own meter. He was well into the orange band. "Yeah, I'm about medium-well here. Tell the chief they'll need to come over here to clean up."

Marshall's first live spacewalk was not what he'd expected it to be. They'd jetted over from the shuttle so quickly that he could focus on nothing but his closing rate with the spacecraft ahead as he followed Riley's lead. No time to look back at Earth behind them, certainly no time to contemplate the depthless black surrounding them. It was all just background, there but not there.

And as Hector had warned them, the spacecraft was a wreck inside. As they shone their helmet lamps down the tunnel, the cabin was a cloud of floating garbage. A stray bit would occasionally bounce off the sidewall and into the tunnel. Riley caught one as it floated toward them; it looked to be someone's notepad. It occurred to Marshall that as much as he'd wanted to avoid "garbage duty" in a satellite control room, he was getting it good and hard up here in orbit.

"I've got an idea to make this a little more palatable, sir."

Marshall reached in and caught another piece of loose gear before it could float into space. "Cycle the cabin pressure?"

Riley smiled. "Roger that. Let the air returns do the messy work."

They moved quickly, Marshall first pushing himself into the airlock and waiting for Riley to come in behind. "I'm at the ECS panel," he said. "Ready when you are."

Riley dogged down the hatch. "Sealed."

Marshall stabbed at the panel. "Pressurizing." The environmental panel was childishly simple: A small touchscreen with a green button to pressurize, a red button to depressurize, and a rotary dial above to manually control it if either failed.

He heard a dull hiss of air through his helmet as the pressure climbed. The cloud of trash swirled on fresh air currents. He watched digits on the panel climb quickly until the counter leveled off at a little over six pounds per square inch. "Six point two psi," Riley noted. "That's low."

"They don't normally take these all the way to GEO," Marshall said. He watched the gas mixture ratios on screen. "They kept a mostly pure oxygen environment to save mass. It's maybe ten percent nitrogen."

"Just enough to keep everything from spontaneously combusting," Riley noted. "But it still makes me nervous."

"Me too. Good thing we're dumping it." Marshall tapped the "depress" button on screen. The clouds of floating waste spiraled away, following the escaping air currents to attach themselves to the nearest circulation grate. It had the effect of pulling the messier stuff aside.

"There," Riley said with satisfaction. "Now we can get to work."

Marshall gripped the rim of the tunnel and pulled up with his fingers to slowly float into the cabin. Mostly clear of debris, it was deceptively spacious. He reached out for a passing binder, with several pages dog-eared while others were more carefully marked with flags of colored tape. "Some kind of reference manual," he said, "but not for the spacecraft."

"Looks bulky," Riley observed as he drifted down behind him. If they were saving mass to get here, it was an odd thing to bring along. "Must have been important."

Marshall tried flipping through its pages but his thick gloves made such finesse impossible. He ended up pawing at a few at random. "Satellite specs. Schematics. Lots of handwritten notes."

Riley paused at a computer workstation in the lower bay, beneath the crew seats. "Check this out, sir. It's like my son's gaming setup."

Marshall pushed away to meet him on the other side of the cabin. It held two racks of monitors over some kind of control box with a keyboard and a pair of joysticks. He whistled. "Your son must be a serious gamer, Chief."

Riley shook his head. "Okay, so maybe it's his dream setup. You could just about fly your own spaceship with this rig."

"This was supposed to be a maintenance hop." All of the screens and switch backlights were dark. Marshall found the workstation's master switch was on, just no power. "Must've gotten cooked in the flare. This is first-rate gear but it's still off the shelf. None of it looks space rated."

"Mighty unusual for up here," Riley said. "If this was for controlling repair drones . . ."

"They would've needed a higher-power transmitter. A whole antenna farm. But yeah, they could've done that from the ground with this same gear." It in fact looked a lot like the control consoles he'd become familiar with as a cadet.

"Apparently not." Riley looked about and shook his head sadly. "Who knows what they were doing, sir. New businesses are popping up in orbit like weeds in my backyard, and every one of them is looking for an edge over the other. They must have figured out something to turn to their advantage." He began reaching out for more loose gear, bulky items that hadn't been pulled into the vents by escaping air. "We'd better get a move on if we're going to recover this thing, sir. Skipper's going to want it squared away before he lets us plug it into his ship."

Marshall looked around the cabin once more, not wanting to imagine what their final hours must have been like. "Can't blame him. It's like the aftermath of a frat party in here. I'm getting a hangover just looking at it."

"Thought the academy didn't have fraternities, sir."

"Doesn't mean the other schools didn't," he grinned. "Not that I'd know anything about that."

☼ 10 ☼

Nick Lesko seemed anxious. He wasn't a professional spacer; he was just a project manager for some conglomerate they'd never heard of, hired to oversee a crew of odd characters sent to geosynch to try out some new satellite recovery techniques. Something about making it cost effective to repair expensive comm and remote-sensing birds using quick-response launch services.

"There isn't much 'quick' about this," Marshall said. "Not if you spent nearly six months preparing for it." Even the two experienced spacers on their team had endured weeks of training just to satisfy the insurance underwriters.

"First time for everything," Lesko explained. "If we could prove the concept, then we'd only have to train up a few teams and keep them on standby for when the call comes."

"Space plumbers, then?"

A slow nod from Lesko. "Plumbers, yeah. That works."

Marshall wondered at the possibilities, and if any of them made sense. Somebody had to have run the numbers and decided that yes, it did make sense. It wasn't hard to imagine—these birds cost a small fortune. In fact they cost almost as much to insure as to build them in the first place. He didn't pretend to understand the marketplace beyond the major players, and whoever this was didn't sound like a major player. They were trying to break out with a hot new idea, trying to achieve the impossible on a shoestring budget and hoping for lightning to strike.

Maybe that's why their patient seemed so *im*patient. Like he dearly wanted to be anywhere else. Marshall had to remind himself that Mr. Lesko was just some guy on a job, out of his element and eager to get back to something familiar after a brush with death.

"We can't just fly back to Earth?" Lesko asked insistently. "Isn't that what the wings are for?"

Chief Riley looked over to Marshall before answering. "They are, but it's not that simple. We don't have the delta-v to deorbit from up here."

"Delta...oh yeah. Fuel." Lesko's eyes widened. "Wait a minute. You mean we don't have enough fuel to go home?"

"It took most of what we had to get to you," Riley explained. "We have enough left for station-keeping and rendezvous with the *Borman* tomorrow."

Lesko's eyes widened. "That's where you came from? Isn't that some kind of orbiting battleship?"

Riley exchanged muted smirks with Marshall, and gestured for him to join in.

"It's not a battleship," Marshall said. "It's a patrol vessel. We're up here to protect assets in orbit, ensure free navigation of space lanes, and provide search and rescue." He realized he was repeating the service's standard PR mantra. "Kind of like the Coast Guard," he offered.

"So that's where we're going?"

"More like they're coming to us," Marshall said. "We looked up your flight plan. Remember how it took you about three days of burns to raise your orbit to GEO?"

"Not that I was flying it, but yeah. Whit kept having to make small boosts to get us up here, a little at a time."

"*Borman*'s nuclear powered," Marshall explained. "It can do more with less, but it's not unlimited. The choice was to take another day to reach you, or fling us off in the shuttle on a tangent to intersect your orbit. We used their velocity to get here, but it took most of what we had to slow down to match orbits with you." He checked his watch. "They'll be on station here in about fourteen hours. All we can do is sit tight until then."

"So you guys voluntarily stranded yourselves out here with me?"

"I guess you could see it like that." Marshall had tried not to think of it that way. If something happened to *Borman*, the shuttle only offered a few days' worth of life support with a full cabin.

"It's what we do," Rosie interjected. She glanced over at Marshall. "Sorry, sir. Didn't mean to interrupt."

He waved it away, looking up and down the length of the cramped cabin. "It's okay. Not exactly a private conversation anyway. How's your team?"

"All of us were out too long, sir. We're going to need anti-rad treatments as soon as we get settled back onboard. Might even need to rotate a couple people back home."

Marshall raised an eyebrow. That would be a big deal. He turned back to Lesko. "You might have a ride home sooner than you thought if that happens. They'll have to bring up another shuttle."

"We had enough fuel left to—what is it—deorbit?" Nick said. "Any chance you can use that?"

Marshall looked over his shoulder, forward, to Wylie up at the pilot's station. He knew the answer but waited for the senior officer to turn that one down. "Negative."

"Why can't you dock with our capsule, use our engines like a booster or something?"

"Couple of things working against that." Marshall hated to keep shooting the guy down, if out of nothing more than sympathy. "We have common berthing ports but that's it. We can't just plug in to your spacecraft and take over. If we can't aim precisely or time the burns, we'd all end up much worse off."

"Don't forget why we're here," Riley said. "Looks like your guidance platform—hell, most of your avionics—might be cooked."

Nick Lesko's eyes darted back and forth. "So . . . do we just leave it up here?"

Riley shook his head. "Can't do that either. It's a navigation hazard. Pushing it up to the graveyard orbit might've been an option if there weren't people involved." He deferred to Marshall, not wanting to speak up too much for a new officer. "Am I correct, sir?"

Marshall had a lot more confidence in the chief's expertise than his own, but part of learning to lead was knowing when to take up the baton. "Chief Riley's right. Injuries or fatalities means the National Transportation Safety Board will claim jurisdiction. By law they have to investigate, which means we have to recover the vehicle if able."

"I see." Lesko's lips drew tight as he thought through the

implications. "But what is there to investigate? We got cooked by a solar flare. Done, right?"

Riley shot a look at Marshall. "It must've hit you guys hard and fast," he said, turning back to Lesko. "Were you in the 'lock the whole time?"

"Yeah. Giselle brought me along because we couldn't do a solo EVA. I was just there to hand her tools." He scratched angrily at his mane of black hair. "I was tired. I'd stayed up on comms all night."

"A worldwide alert went out for that storm. That's something your ground control should've advised you of," Marshall said. "You don't remember any kind of warning?"

Lesko shrugged. "Whitman was our pilot. He and Giselle took care of all of that stuff. They were the real pros, not me or Billy. We were just up here to fix stuff. We were supposed to go home tomorrow..." He paused, as if to collect himself. "The satellite we'd been working on started throwing out error codes. Servos. Stuff we couldn't fix with a software patch, you know?"

"So Billy was your computer engineer. And you are—?"

"Project manager. You could call me a handyman," Lesko said. "I fix stuff."

Marshall exchanged looks with Chief Riley. "Kind of specialized work for an earthbound handyman. Are you an engineer?"

Lesko waved the idea away. "Who has time for that crap? All that math? Like I said, I fix stuff." He eyed them both. "Look, our sponsors trust me to get stuff done. I'm the guy they came to with this project. Biggest job they've ever handed me, plus I got to go into space." His laugh was dark and hollow. "Some deal, eh?"

"So not like any other job then?"

Lesko stared at him blankly. *Really?*

Marshall decided they'd asked enough questions. He changed the subject. "It'll take time for the NTSB to send a go-team up here. We're probably going to bring your spacecraft down to LEO in the meantime." He looked to the pilot's station. "Is that about right, Lieutenant Wylie?"

"Right-o," the senior officer said. "If this were on Earth, even the Moon, we'd preserve the site in place. In this case, we need to bring the vehicle down for them to examine in low orbit. Keep everything else as is but make it as easy to get to as possible."

"Then why not send it back to Earth?"

"Reentry's a big deal," the pilot explained. "That's a lot of stress on a vehicle that's already been put through the wringer. And if your guidance platform's fried, it might not even make it back in one piece."

Lesko didn't seem bothered by that idea. Chief Riley nudged Marshall and pointed to a row of sleep restraints mounted along the bulkhead. "This young man's been through a lot, sir. Maybe we should let him get some rest."

Roberta waded through a growing roster of crippled satellites, filtering between those which were disabled, unresponsive, or simply waiting to come out of safe mode. Most were of the latter category—as they'd been designed to withstand exactly this kind of event—but a surprising number weren't.

She compared this newest tally to a separate list she'd already been compiling on her own. Seeing so many go dark in such a short time had gotten her attention, and having a CME spike the sample size by nearly a whole order of magnitude wasn't helping her make sense of it. If someone had been making mischief in GEO, that storm was an unbelievable stroke of luck for them.

Still . . . it hadn't made sense before the flare, and it didn't make any more sense now. What had been a most unusual series of events threatened to be lost in the background noise of a region that had become cluttered with disabled and expensive hardware. While operators all over the world were scrambling to put their networks back together, some were figuring out they were beyond recovery and so had begun asking for help clearing the deadwood. She was going to have to sort through a lot of garbage to pick out the few points of useful data.

The apparent lack of interest from anyone else was striking—or was it understandable with so many individual crises erupting overnight? Surely someone had to be trying to connect the same dots?

Ivey would be the one to ask. He was their official conduit to the intel weenies, and seemed trustworthy enough to tell her if she was just a rookie with a too-active imagination.

She looked over at the empty ROV control station. The

Vandenberg alert crew was prepping the standby X-37 for launch; it was already stacked and going through vehicle integration. Tomorrow they'd have two of them to manage in orbit; meanwhile *Borman* had just finished its last phasing burn to intercept that civvie with the mayday call. That had been a weird one, too: What the hell were a bunch of civilian wrench monkeys doing all the way up in GEO anyway?

Roberta shook her head. Too much data to process, plus a new drone on the way. She'd just have to wait for the good birds to come out of safe mode and the dead ones to be cleared out of the way. The graveyard was about to get a lot more residents.

✲ 11 ✲

Max Jiang had spent most of the last day incessantly humming to himself. No matter his task—whether pulling rations out of the storm shelter and repacking the log module, checking in with Palmdale, or servicing the waste recycler—the constant almost-melodies emanating from him would have ordinarily driven his wife to distraction.

For her part, Jasmine Jiang was so preoccupied as to barely notice and was just as giddy. Whatever she put her hands to, she did with newfound enthusiasm. They had long ago learned to arrange their daily activities so that neither of them would become bogged down in mundane housekeeping or become overwhelmed with the mental gymnastics of managing a spacecraft, but after emerging from the safety of their storm shelter the timeline had become compressed to the point where load sharing was pointless.

A day and a half cocooned inside the tunnel had left them both swamped with work, as their destination was relentlessly drawing close. Physics didn't care if fragile humans needed protection, as time and motion carried on regardless.

If anything, the compressed timeline excited them even more. After a short braking burn to match orbits, asteroid RQ39 emerged into full view. As their spacecraft turned about its long axis to distribute solar heat, the oblong body moved from one row of windows to the next, its color palette shifting subtly between shades of brown and gray as it slowly rotated in the sunlight.

Besides having something to look at other than empty space, tomorrow they would finally be able to get outside after weeks of confinement. "It's been like driving an RV around the world," Max had said during their storm quarantine, "except you can't stop to get out and the only other place you can go is the passenger seat."

It was too soon yet for direct exploration of RQ39's—Malati's— surface. That would come after another few days, when *Prospector* would draw close enough for them to safely jet across. For now they would have to be satisfied with tomorrow's short jaunt outside to prep their survey equipment, currently mounted to a pallet on the hab's utility port.

It would be enough for now. Perhaps on Earth the journey itself was half the fun, but space was different. There was remarkably little to see along the way; for as many weeks as they'd spent in transit, on a cosmic scale they'd not traveled far at all, though it was enough for Earth to appear painfully small and distant. From their vantage point it did look like the proverbial blue marble, and the lack of any atmospheric haze eliminated all sense of perspective. Suspended in depthless black, their home planet could very well have been a pebble at arm's length—or a world the size of Jupiter, millions of kilometers distant.

That every single person they had ever known was on that tiny blue marble filled Jasmine with both longing and dread: longing to be back among the familiar, with trees and water and blue skies, dread for the inescapable realization of just how fragile it all was.

Was this how God saw the world—like an anthill? Enormously complex, indescribably beautiful, but in cosmic terms still just an anthill. Is this what omniscience felt like?

She decided it couldn't be. For even as humans might regard the entirety of an anthill, they could never perceive the individual perspective of every creature in the colony. That was the difference between the Creator and the created: We might be temporarily privileged to be given a taste of the Creator's perspective, but it was only the smallest sliver of its totality. Barely a peek through a keyhole.

As *Prospector* continued rotating, RQ39 once again passed out of view. It would reappear soon enough in the opposite window, but its absence was enough to make her acutely aware of Max's atonal droning.

"What is that tune?"

His humming abruptly stopped, as did his work. He left a tablet floating in midair, plugged into a data port on his spacesuit. "What was that?"

"My question exactly. Was that a song, or simply whatever random notes come to mind?"

He shoved his hands in his pockets with a sheepish grin. "The latter. You know I was never much of a musician."

She pushed away from the sidewall with her fingertips to float closer. "That I do know," she said. She stopped just in front of him with another gentle push from her fingers. "At least not in the West. You never quite shook off our homeland's musical styles."

"Some things were too ingrained in me, I suppose." He kissed her forehead. "I will endeavor to be more melodic, my dear."

She tapped her watch, and soon symphonic movements were emanating from speakers embedded in the overhead. "Or we can just put on actual music and hum along to it."

"Even better." His eyes widened as he looked beyond her. He pointed to the porthole over her shoulder. "There it is again."

Malati drifted back into view, brilliant in full sunlight. From this angle its pebbled surface shone white.

"What do you think it is?" she wondered. "Do you think we'll be able to stand on it?"

"It appears dense enough." They both considered the asteroid's surface. "Japanese and European probes at similar asteroids were able to maintain direct contact. I don't think we'll find ourselves sinking into an aggregate if that's what you mean. There won't be enough gravity to sink into anything."

"I suppose you're right. Forgive me, but now that we're here I'm having second thoughts. This is rather dangerous, you know."

Concern darkened his eyes. "Are you nervous about leaving the spacecraft?"

"I'm nervous about everything," she said. "Assuming all goes well tomorrow, we'll each have done exactly one spacewalk in our entire lives before we attempt to stand on an asteroid."

Max tried to humor her. "As they say, there's a first time for everything."

"I was hoping for a wildly inappropriate pun."

"I've not had enough time to read other people's jokes lately. You should know by now I'm not that original," Max said. He gestured at the tablet running diagnostics on his EVA suit. "I've checked our maneuvering units three times. Their gyro stabilizers are working perfectly, we have the asteroid for spatial reference, and our little home here will be less than half a kilometer away. You could practically jump to it from there."

"Please don't mistake my reticence for anxiety."

"I would never do that, my dear. I suppose fear of the unknown is to be expected, though I've been too excited to think about it. Excited and busy," he finished with a beaming smile.

"Fear of the unknown," she repeated, chewing a fingernail as she watched the asteroid drift across the window. "That's it, of course. I had hoped we would have been able to collect more spectral data by now but there's some odd electromagnetic background interference. The closer we get, the stronger it becomes."

"Faulty spectroscope, perhaps?"

"I thought there might be a coolant problem but the ground team agrees with the onboard diagnostics. It's transient, as if it's external interference. Very odd."

"That is odd," he agreed, "but not entirely bad news. If it has a magnetic field strong enough to affect passive instruments then it must have a dense iron core. That suggests even more valuable metals could be present. Literal 'rare earth' minerals, just as we hoped. If that's the case, then we were right to come here." He smiled and caressed her cheek. "And I'm now absolutely confident we'll be able to stand on it."

"Still," she sighed, "it would be nice to know what we're about to set foot on."

Lesko was surprisingly adept at manipulating playing cards in zero g. Shuffling was always a challenge for rookies, as the cards tended to shoot off in all directions, but he'd handled them masterfully. His control over the deck seemed effortless as he pitched them with a flick of his thumb, each flying across face down and arrow-straight.

"Smooth," Hector said as he caught his in midair. "Probably a good thing we're not playing for real money." After five hands, he'd amassed an impressive pile of digital chips on the tablet Velcroed to the small table between them.

Lesko shrugged. "It's a pastime." He turned and deftly began flicking a fresh hand in Rosie's direction. "So where are you from?" he asked, admiring her dark features.

"New Mexico," she said. "Santa Fe."

"So when was the last time you were in Jersey?"

She fanned out her cards and studied her hand, not lifting her eyes from them. "Never been there."

"But you said—"

"Yeah, about that," she said. "I had to keep you talking so I knew you weren't gonna freak out or die on me. No offense."

Lesko pursed his lips, now admiring her in a different way. "None taken." Though he would pay extra attention to how she played her next hand.

Despite being more commonplace with each passing year, spaceflight still carried the aura of grand adventure into the unknown. That it could sometimes be deadly dull was really only known to those who had spent more than a day in orbit.

Marshall had been warned, and he'd had no reason to doubt those who'd gone before him. Sometimes the workload was steady, but often as not it ended up compressed into times of near-overwhelming demands in an environment that had multiple ways of killing a man.

The intervals between were a battle to keep from dying of boredom, the struggle his team now found themselves in aboard the cramped and adrift shuttle. As he watched Rosie, Hector, and Mikey engage Lesko in another round of poker, he noticed their rescued civilian had already played enough rounds to look almost comfortable again. He had to admire the spacers' resourcefulness. They'd expected a lot of down time and had come prepared.

He pulled his tablet from a cargo pocket, swiped through its menu, and made a mental note to populate it with some music and e-books just in case. He'd spent enough time paging through system diagrams and fleet directives; it was all starting to run together and he needed a distraction.

Moving forward, Earth's blue glow in the window drew him like a moth to a flame. He'd forced himself to stay away from the cockpit, if only to avoid giving his team the impression that he'd rather be up there than working in the mid-deck with them. The word had to have gone out that the skipper was a family friend, and he couldn't afford to let that taint him.

The shuttle was set up as a two-pilot vehicle for launch and landing, but could easily be operated by one in orbit. Chief Riley sat in the second pilot's seat, Lieutenant Wylie in the left-side command seat—which he'd been in since departing *Borman* yesterday.

Riley cocked his head back as Marshall approached, and pushed himself up out of the seat.

"No need to get up, Chief. I'm good here."

"Begging your pardon, sir, but don't blow sunshine up my ass. Being polite will get you nowhere."

"My mother's a southern aristocrat, Chief. Politeness was bred into me. You might as well try to untrain a dog."

"Point taken." Riley floated up and away from the open seat. "But I'm getting up anyway, sir. You haven't been up here since we arrived."

"Didn't see the necessity." Marshall looked to Wylie—it was his ship, after all—who gestured for him to take the copilot's seat. He used a handgrip in the overhead to twist himself into the narrow opening and settled in, keeping his hands clear of the controls.

Wylie appreciatively noted his caution. "Nothing you could mess up right now," he said. "I've closed the RCS valves and the OMS tanks are almost dry. I'm using the gyros for station keeping." He had the craft pointed nose down, so that Earth filled the windows.

"Saving propellant for rendezvous later?" *Borman* was climbing their way, due on station in another ten hours.

"Bingo. Just in case they overshoot. Which they won't, but we've got to be ready to cover some distance on the off chance they do."

Marshall eyed the propellant and power gauges. "More draw on the fuel cells, isn't it?" Not keeping the craft in a thermal-control roll to even out solar heating put more load on the radiator panels as well.

"It is," Wylie agreed, "but we weren't pulling that many amps anyway. I wouldn't want to do this all on battery power. It'd start getting uncomfortable in here."

Riley pulled himself between them and lowered his voice. "Speaking of uncomfortable, gentlemen . . . now that both of you are up here, I have some thoughts."

Wylie flashed a knowing smile. "Thoughts, Chief? I've learned those frequently end up with something that looks like actual work."

"As it should, sir." He glanced behind them. "I'm sure I don't have to explain how unusual of a situation we find ourselves in here."

Marshall was silent. Besides deferring to the senior officer, he wasn't entirely sure where Riley was going and wanted to gauge Wylie's reaction.

"We haven't had a live rescue in almost a year," Wylie said. "And never one in GEO."

Riley nodded. "Because nobody ever comes up here, and with good reason. It's an expensive trip with almost no benefit and considerably more risk."

"You mean exposure to the Van Allen belts?" Marshall asked.

"That's part of it. Not to mention it's just harder to get to, which our predicament illustrates. Even if we had full OMS tanks, deorbiting from here isn't cheap."

Wylie glanced over his shoulder at the card game in back of the mid-deck. Marshall followed his gaze and realized that Rosie had arranged things so that her team was between Lesko and the officers, keeping their charge distracted and unable to overhear. She either had her own suspicions or had been reading the chief's mind. Either one was just as likely. "So what's your thinking, Chief?"

"Lots of hacker gear in that little ship, sir. I think Mister Hunter would agree it looked like they were ready to compete in a gamer tournament."

Marshall agreed. "That was one serious rig. Looked like they could've piloted the thing from there."

"Piloted something for sure," Riley said. "It's some kind of remote TT&C setup, for what I don't know."

"Tracking's one thing. But telemetry and control?" Wylie pulled up specs for the Stardust on a monitor. "How familiar are you with that model? Because I only see one high-gain antenna. If they're staying in touch with the ground, they wouldn't have bandwidth for much else."

"Might not need anything that powerful if they're close in," Riley said.

Marshall's eyebrows rose. He'd noticed some cables snaking across the space between the consoles and an open access panel. "What were they plugged into? I didn't get a good look."

"Neither did I, sir." Riley frowned. "The cabin was a wreck and our suits weren't meant to absorb that much dosing for long."

"No need to explain," Wylie said. "I would've sent Rosie to pull you guys out of there if you hadn't come on your own." He paged through a diagram of the spacecraft's command module. "All the Ka- and S-band stuff's on the service module. Command module has VHF for launch-and-entry comms. Low power, but they'd be able to jack directly into it from the crew cabin."

Marshall followed his reasoning. "So they were controlling that satellite? That's why they were so close to it?"

Riley agreed. "Makes sense. I still can't figure out why. It was dead."

"Only because no one was willing to spend the money to come up here and work on it," Wylie said. "Look, I'm no lawyer. They very well might have been exercising salvage rights. Or young Mr. Lesko back there might have been up to no good. The evidence could go either way. We advise the skipper, and he'll pitch it to the brass back on the ground. I'm guessing they won't see four people in a chartered spacecraft as much of a threat, especially since most of them died in the CME."

Marshall took one last look aft. "And a lone survivor who learned some hard lessons about spaceflight."

❂ 12 ❂

Only half a kilometer distant now, the gray edifice of asteroid RQ39 loomed above the Jiangs like a mountain. Still confined to their spacecraft, the Jiangs could only see what their portholes' limited fields of view allowed. Two pairs of "panoramic" windows on opposite sides of their inflatable hab module—each sixteen inches square, practically picture windows for their purposes—offered better viewing angles. With their craft parked at one end of the oblong object, Max and Jasmine each hovered by one of the big windows but not so far apart that they couldn't still hold hands. Each squeezed the other's excitedly. When Max turned to his wife, her face was beaming.

"Do you see that cliff face?" she asked, an apt if not a strictly accurate description for such a feature. Along one side of the asteroid, nearly a third of its surface was scalloped with deep grooves.

Max pressed his face against the window, looking up to where his wife was pointing. "Spectacular! It's like Half Dome in Yosemite."

"It looks more recent than the other features," she said, remembering that they were recording their observations for posterity. "Less impact erosion."

"You're right. For whatever meaning 'recent' might have here," he agreed. "This body could easily be five billion years old. Part of it must have broken off."

"My body feels almost that old sometimes," she joked, "but I haven't broken off any parts yet."

"Very funny, my dear. It could be promising. If this was once a larger body that somehow sheared in two, then it could give us a better sense of what's inside than any of our other instruments."

"That would be fortunate," she said. "Other than our magnetometer, I still can't get anything useful beyond visible spectrum. Even the CubeSats we deployed are sending back nothing but static."

"Still nothing from Palmdale?"

"They can't find anything wrong with our onboard sensing equipment or the CubeSats. Frustrating." She pointed at the window. "It's something environmental out there. There's no ionizing radiation, no decay that would account for it. Perhaps it is a very dense iron core as you suspected, a giant magnet."

"With a large piece of the asteroid cleaved away, exposing more of the core? That might explain it." He continued to stare outside. "It is indeed a strange universe God has made for us. Ready to go see a piece of it?"

"It feels like I'm staring at the heights of Everest from base camp," Max said, standing atop the sled that housed their in situ resource experiment. Free of their spacecraft and able to take in its totality up close, he felt remarkably small.

"Perhaps you will be able to do that one day as well." His love of geology and mineral exploration, besides making them wealthy, had created opportunities they'd never anticipated. Whether climbing rock faces or descending into caves, he had learned to embrace risks others wouldn't. And she was steadfastly at his side for all of it. But this was a particularly sore subject with them—Everest's summit straddled Nepal's border with China, exposing them to an entirely different kind of peril.

"One day, perhaps," he sighed. "Coming here was easier, I think."

The asteroid looked like a mountain, untethered from Earth and floating free in the void. Eroded outlines of impact craters beneath a loosely pebbled crust hinted at eons of bombardment from other, smaller bodies it had encountered through its endless voyage around the Sun.

After they each clipped their maneuvering units to opposite sides of the sled, Max reached down for its release lever. He glanced across at his wife. "Ready?"

Jasmine nodded nervously from behind her visor.

"We will be fine, my dear. Let the computer do the work, just like we practiced."

He tapped a command into a wrist-mounted computer. After a five-second count, compressed-gas jets in their backpacks fired in unison to pull them free of *Prospector*. Concentric circles appeared in each of their visors, projecting the path Max's guidance computer had calculated to take them to their desired landing spot on RQ39, a bright region where subsurface water ice was suspected. He tapped in another command to execute, and their backpacks fired once more. The computer guided their way across the half-kilometer divide, adjusting their path with coordinated bursts of control jets.

The floating mountain grew as they approached, showing more surface detail with each passing minute. It had a grainy texture, like a layer of gravel. Some areas had been scoured away by long-ago impacts, revealing smooth rock beneath.

Closer they drew, until rock was all they could see. As their shadows seemed to converge, the computer fired a final, forward burst to slow them just a meter shy of the surface. They descended slowly, the barest hint of gravity pulling them the rest of the way. He could feel the thud of the heavy ISRU sled through his boots as they touched down as one, a thin cloud of gravel scattering in all directions.

They absorbed the gentle impact through their knees before reaction could send them back into space. Grapplers from the sled automatically deployed when they sensed the sudden change in inertia, securing it to the surface.

As the dust settled, Max looked across at his wife, beaming just as she had when they first saw Malati up close yesterday. Neither spoke, and by the look on her face he could tell she was just as amazed that they'd made it. Her hand reached for his, clumsily gripping it through pressurized gloves.

Max drew in a breath to calm himself before speaking to the world. "Palmdale," he said, "we have arrived on Malati."

Transcript from the Global News Network
"Today's spacewalk on asteroid 2023 RQ39, now informally named Malati, will be the first and shortest of three planned extravehicular activities, or EVAs, over the next week while the *Prospector* spacecraft remains in close proximity. After that time, they will perform a short correction burn and their orbits will begin to diverge as *Prospector* continues on to its flyby of Mars.

"GNN is privileged to be the first to interview civilian astronauts Max and Jasmine Jiang on the surface of Malati from the Prospector Foundation's mission control in Palmdale, California. Light delays have been edited for time.

"Mr. and Mrs. Jiang, how are you? Could you describe your experience so far?"

Max: "We're doing quite well, thank you, Kevin. I suppose the best way to describe our experience is 'alien,' not to put too fine a point on it. It's surreal. If I turn one way I'm staring into deep space at so many stars it makes me dizzy. Eventually I'm able to pick out the blue Earth, even though we are several million kilometers from home. But then if I turn the opposite way, facing Malati's surface, it all seems familiar. If you've ever been climbing, it's not unlike the scree you might find on the slope of a mountain. The ground beneath us is bedrock with a fairly thick coating of loose gravel, though it doesn't behave like gravel would on Earth."

Jasmine: "If you follow my helmet camera, you'll see static electricity causes the smaller bits to cling to our boots. That's because this asteroid's gravity is perhaps a hundredth of Earth's. It's really not enough to stand on."

"We can see that. Moving around on a body that small must be challenging. Are you afraid of falling off?"

Jasmine: "It feels as if we could fall off with every turn. Whichever direction you look, you're seeing the edge of Malati. It's not like a horizon in the sense you would think of it on Earth, or even the Moon. Here, we could fly out into space if we pushed hard enough. We have to keep ourselves tethered to pitons we drove into the surface in the same way one might use them mountain climbing." [Pauses] "But mountains are more of my husband's area of expertise."

"And what about your experiment package? Does it need to be lashed to the surface as well?"

Max: "The In Situ Resource Unit is on a maneuvering sled with pneumatic bolts that secure it to the surface. Once it begins drilling, the shaft will be more than enough to keep it anchored."

"What do you expect to find there?"

Max: "King Solomon's Gold. Maybe D. B. Cooper's money." [Laughs] "Seriously, that's an interesting question. Malati is an interesting place. It has characteristics of both Class-C and Class-M asteroids. We have already detected water ice below the surface, as we're finding is more common on carbonaceous Class-C bodies. But there is a large area that appears to have been cleaved off in the past, which may have exposed a number of Class-M rare-earth minerals."

"Does that make Malati a good candidate for an asteroid-capture mission? Somehow bring it to Earth?"

Max: [Laughs] "Not in our lifetimes, it's far too big. It's ten miles across at its widest point. By the time we've developed the technology to do something like that, we probably wouldn't need it."

"I don't know how you do it, love," Jasmine said back aboard *Prospector*. They had just finished watching the replay of their interview after stowing their suits and cleaning up. "I don't have the patience for those inane questions. I have an easier time talking to grade schoolers."

"You are, in a sense," Max said as he hovered over the ISRU display. "They'll probably rebroadcast that to classrooms. And you were splendid demonstrating the low gravity, by the way."

"I didn't feel splendid," she said. "I'm not good at aiming for the lowest common denominator. Its awkward."

"Yet that's precisely the right tactic. Remember, statistically half the population is by definition of below-average intelligence."

She closed her eyes and smiled. "How can such a cynic be so good at handling interviews?"

"Precisely because I *am* a cynic, dear. Now, look at these preliminaries." He moved aside to let her see the returns from Malati's surface.

She slipped on a pair of reading glasses that had been pushed back on her head. "That's—amazing. Is that what I think it is?"

"Hydrogen and oxygen," he said, triumphantly folding his arms. "Water ice extracted from just beneath the surface and electrolyzed into its component elements."

"How much already?" she said, squinting at the figures. They looked impossibly good.

"It's already filled one O_2 bottle," he said. "The hydrogen is taking longer. Haven't really solved the boiloff problem but we can see the process works."

"Still, that's an excellent start." She beamed at her husband. "It makes the trip worth it."

"It wasn't already?"

She was about to level him with a cutting rejoinder when the master alarm began blaring. "What was that?"

13

Long before *Borman* had registered on their docking radar, they spotted it by the cherry-red glow of dual nuclear engines pointed directly at them as it decelerated into their orbit. The plasma exhaust itself was invisible, but their white heat shone like beacons in the distance. Marshall understood the chemistry but was still disappointed—that much power deserved a mile-long incandescent pillar of flame.

"This is the tricky part," Wylie explained as the glowing cluster turned away. The ship was rotating about its vertical axis to finish its approach nose first. "They have to brake to match orbits, but they can't keep pointing the main engines at us. We'd be staring down the mouths of open reactors." When Marshall first arrived for duty, *Borman* had been in a parking orbit with idle engines. They were still a radiation hazard, but nothing compared to when the control rods were removed and burning hydrogen.

Borman's slender alloy truss and stark white propellant tanks glistened as it turned beneath silent bursts of maneuvering jets. One final cloud of gas erupted from its nose as it faced them head-on.

"*Specter*, this is home plate. We're stable on approach, closing at five meters per second. What's your status?"

"We have one medevac aboard, three casualties in the logistics pod. Evac patient is stable, being treated for dehydration and mild radiation exposure." Marshall looked over his shoulder to confirm everyone was buckled into their seats and gave Wylie a thumbs up. "Evac team is secure aboard. RCS is pressurized and we are ready to maneuver."

"*Specter*, you're in the bubble. Cleared to approach."

"Copy. Underway." Wylie looked to Marshall expectantly. "Well?"

"You want me to fly us in?"

"Got to learn some time," Wylie said, motioning for him to take the controls.

Marshall kept a light touch, needing to feel how the spacecraft responded to his inputs. He gave the sidestick a gentle tap and Earth slipped silently out of view. After having it fill their windows for so long, its abrupt disappearance was unsettling. It underscored the emptiness facing them.

"Now, give us one second retrograde," Wylie said. When Marshall pushed the translation controller, there was a burst of vapor outside and they momentarily rose against the shoulder straps. They were flying backward, approaching tail first. *Borman*'s forward node appeared on screen, steadily growing larger as the two ships closed.

"Flies easier from up here, even when we're tail first," Wylie said. "Right?"

"Feels more natural," Marshall said. "Didn't expect that."

Wylie watched the docking target dance in their crosshairs. "Watch your closing rate," he cautioned. "Use smaller inputs the closer we get. Resist the urge to overcorrect, otherwise you'll scratch paint."

Marshall suspected "scratch paint" meant something much worse, as nothing that innocuous happened out here.

Poole was waiting for them at the far end of the docking tunnel. "Report."

Wylie spoke for them. "Evac team healthy and accounted for, sir. One live evacuee and three casualties. Survivor is named Nicholas Lesko. Chief Riley's team started treatment protocols for dehydration and low-level radiation exposure."

"What about their vehicle?"

Wylie turned to Marshall, as he'd been the officer on site. Marshall cleared his throat. "I don't know that I'd call it a derelict yet but it's in bad shape, sir. Loose debris all over the cabin. Mr. Lesko was safe in their shelter, stayed in his suit and plugged in to the ship's supply tanks. Most of their E and E systems were offline, most of the breakers were popped. We don't have enough information to know if they can be safely reset, so I wouldn't recommend maneuvering it under its own power."

"Yeah, that's not happening." Poole crossed his arms. "There's no safe approach vector for us to grab it being so close to another dead satellite. We'll leave it in place and declare it a navigational hazard. Ops will record its position and put out a notice to operators. NTSB will throw a fit but they can get up here themselves if they want it bad enough."

A voice piped up from behind them. "You're leaving it alone up here? Not taking it back to Earth?"

Poole looked over their shoulders. "Mr. Lesko, I presume?"

Marshall and Wylie moved aside. "Yeah, that's me." He seemed unsure of what to say next.

Poole prompted him. "Were you in charge of this expedition?"

"I guess," he said warily. "You could say I was the prime contractor."

"Somebody else hired you, then?"

"Yeah. I recruited the others."

"Then your crew wasn't working directly for one of the satellite operators?"

His eyes darted about. "What do you mean?"

Poole smiled disarmingly. "I meant that your mission up here was very unusual. I don't think we've ever seen a crewed repair mission in geosynch."

"I wouldn't know nothing about that. They give me jobs where things need fixing, and I fix them. If I can't do it myself, I find people who can. They trust me like that."

"So are you an engineer, then? A&P technician?"

"Sort of. Like I said, I fix things."

Poole decided that line of questioning was going nowhere. "What can you tell us about the event?"

Lesko looked away. When he turned back, his words came slowly. "I had the overnight watch and a problem showed up with one of the servos we'd installed on that satellite. I couldn't do nothin' remotely, so I knew that meant one more spacewalk. It was supposed to be our last day up here so I got in a hurry planning repairs before the others woke up."

"That's a lot to figure out on your own."

"Yeah, it was," he said with some pride. "And the damn constant chatter from the ground was just too much, so I shut the radios off."

Poole's eyebrows jumped. "You shut off your uplink?"

Lesko shrugged his shoulders.

Poole was flummoxed. "And your crewmates didn't have a problem with that?"

"I think they were all too busy to notice. And once I got my head into the repair plan, I just—forgot, I guess."

That's why we have checklists, Poole thought. He wondered what the scene must have been like inside that thing, especially when it became obvious they'd neglected basic space survival skills: if the Sun burps, shelter in place. Period. End of story. With a dismayed shake of his head, he gestured for Marshall to escort their survivor down to the med module. "Mr. Hunter, secure our passenger. Get him some chow and a fresh set of clothes. We're getting back underway as soon as your team's aboard. There's still a lot of fried satellites for us to deal with."

"Getting tired yet, sir?"

Marshall looked down from the satellite frame he had been hanging on to for the last half hour while Rosie worked on a stuck fitting. "Tired? Not me." Marshall wasn't sure that "tired" was the best choice of words: drained, maybe. Exasperated. They'd been back aboard for barely a day and were already outside again.

To the untrained and uninitiated, spacewalks looked as effortless as floating in a swimming pool—after all, that was how they trained for them. What could be easier?

A lot, he'd decided. Like running a marathon or playing football without a helmet. Maybe dentistry without anesthesia. He hadn't noticed on his first walk, being overwhelmed by the newness of it, and most recently by their haste to secure Lesko's spacecraft. It had only been well afterward that he'd noticed how sore and drenched in perspiration he'd been. The regular EVA crew looked like they'd had a workout too, but had still managed to carry on like champions.

Weightless or not, objects like this satellite still had mass, which meant they still had the same momentum as if sitting on the ground—it was just all very apparent now that it was up to his own body to counteract it instead of relying on gravity. He could easily push a large object in any direction, but it became much harder if he needed to stop said object. Here, stuck in a footrest at the end of *Borman*'s manipulator arm, he was essentially working as a human shock absorber.

When every single movement creates a countermovement, simply unsealing a sticky panel or moving a piece of equipment means you have to brace and absorb it yourself. Every single movement, every time. It was easy to overcorrect, which created more work. Rosie and her spacers seemed to breeze through their tasks like professional dancers with an economy of motion that he was still learning to adopt.

Details like suit fit mattered a lot—they were one size fits all, which really meant one size fit none. Legs and arms could be adjusted so joints were mostly in the right spots, but the gloves were what gave him fits. If he'd been a permanent spacer instead of "just" their officer in charge, the quartermaster might have taken the time and expense to outfit him with a custom set.

He wondered how much of a difference it made, as his hands burned from the exertion of movement compounding upon movement. For every torqueing moment Rosie imparted on the satellite, he had to counteract it using only his fingers and forearms. Just moving around outside was more of the same—the combined mass of his body and spacesuit was ultimately controlled by his fingertips, which had by now gone numb. That probably wasn't a good thing, but at least they didn't hurt anymore. He hoped the view would help take his mind off his discomfort, though it only worked for a short while between Rosie's occasional curses.

"Shit. Another one cold welded in place. It's almost like they didn't plan on anyone coming up here to work on this thing."

"You're being sarcastic, right?"

"You've known me long enough to understand that's kind of my default setting, sir."

"I've known you for all of two weeks, Rosie."

"Yes sir. That ought to be just about long enough."

"I like to think you're more complex than that." He felt the surveillance sat move as Rosie tugged at a locking lever.

"Our business is complicated enough on its own, sir. I like to keep everything else simple."

"So what do you do when you're not out here working?" He changed his grip for what felt like the hundredth time to keep the bird in place and blood flowing through his fingers.

"I'm inside working," she said with a grunt. "Suit maintenance, mostly, but the skipper uses us for a lot of the environmental systems work. Suit and ship life support kind of go hand in hand."

The satellite tried to turn away from him as it reacted to her movement. He considered the amount of force she was having to impart and realized he needed to spend more time on the resistance machine. No wonder there was always a wait for it. "Not a lot of time off up here," he said absentmindedly.

"Don't know what I'd do with it if there were. Not like we're making port calls anywhere."

"Ever wish we could?" Even if they could, where would they go? He looked in the direction of the ecliptic, the plane on which all of the Sun's planets orbited. Jupiter was over his right shoulder, which right now meant Mars was . . . there. In another couple of months they'd be in conjunction. Venus was behind him, hidden in the Sun's brilliance. To his left was Saturn. It intrigued him how the solar system had been arranged, almost geometrically. Jupiter was roughly twice as far from Earth as Mars, Saturn in turn was almost twice as far again. Thinking about it in those terms made the gas giant seem a lot closer than it really was, like it was the gateway to the outer system.

"Nowhere I'd want to go, sir. At least not for long."

"Not even Mars? Moons of Jupiter?"

She gave another tug and the satellite jerked in response. "I guess if all we're doing is looking, I can do that from here."

Marshall was about to press her on what would be fantastic vistas if they were ever to get up the gumption to do it—the thought of seeing Jupiter and its moons up close, in a sense its own miniature solar system, was an idea he was becoming more obsessed with. Patrol ships like theirs were a necessary step, which they'd just demonstrated with the Stardust rescue. He thought about a point Garver had made on his first day here: The more the civilian economy expanded outward, the more people would inevitably get themselves into trouble and need help getting out of it. Such had always been the case in seafaring, and spacefaring was just starting to catch up.

What he really wanted to see was something along the lines of an exploration corps, which is maybe what NASA should've been doing all along before it metastasized into one more self-preserving bureaucracy—the post office with rockets, he'd heard more than once.

His radio crackled. "Repeat, EVA One acknowledge."

Someone was calling—*had been* calling—over the command net. How badly had he just spaced out? He chinned the frequency selector inside his helmet. "This is EVA One. Go ahead."

"Hunter, this is the XO. The skipper is terminating your activity for an all-hands call. You and Rosie get back in the barn ASAP. Buster."

The XO's "Buster" call was shorthand for "get inside, get out of your suits, and grab the PBE masks." Normally they'd stay in the airlock, using it like a dive chamber to bring their bodies into equilibrium after being in the suit's pure oxygen environment. Marshall and Rosie stood out like sore thumbs in the makeshift ready room, each wearing a portable breathing mask as they readjusted their oxygen levels.

They were the last ones to make it in, just ahead of Poole. He sailed in behind them and pulled himself upright, slipping his feet into a pair of foot restraints at the head of the table. He wiped his bald head once with his cap and crossed his arms, a common position in zero g which nevertheless made him look perpetually displeased. Marshall wondered if that was intentional today.

Poole looked them over. "Hunter. Rosado. Glad to see you're not dying of the bends."

The day is young, Marshall thought to himself. "She's keeping me out of trouble, sir."

Poole nodded and carried on as if their exchange had never occurred. "We have new orders," he announced, and turned to a widescreen monitor on the bulkhead above him. A news program was frozen in midbroadcast. He tapped a remote to restart the feed.

The announcer appeared grim. "There has been no contact with the *Prospector* spacecraft since last night," he intoned over an illustration of the spacecraft. "The expedition's ground control director confirmed they have two-way signals with the vehicle, but there has been no response from either Max or Jasmine Jiang."

A middle-aged woman in glasses, her hair pulled into a tight bun, appeared on screen in front of a *Prospector* logo. Marshall guessed she was some kind of corporate communications type. "We have no information beyond what has already been provided," she said firmly. "Our mission control teams are poring over the available data and will continue attempting to establish contact with Mr. and Mrs. Jiang."

Poole froze the video on a depiction of *Prospector*'s position in orbit, adjacent to asteroid RQ39. "Here's the skinny," he said. "Last contact over eighteen hours ago, at 2314 Zulu. Here's what they won't tell you on the news: vehicle telemetry registered a temperature and pressure spike in their number one hydrogen tank before the whole platform dropped offline."

The room erupted in groans. Poole patted the air with his hand in a gesture for quiet. "They lost all data for almost an hour before they could reacquire signal through one of the Ka-band antennas. The Jiang's wrist biomonitors were still transmitting through the downlink, but those signals have gone weak to the point of being almost undetectable."

"What's their hab status, sir?" Flynn asked. "Is it pressurized, maybe cut off from the CSM?"

"Unknown, but possible. If a meteoroid holed the service module and they sealed themselves off in the hab, they'd still have limited comms," Poole said. "It gets better."

The crew exchanged glances, knowing "better" surely meant "worse." "Here's the fun part," Poole said. "I don't have to explain to you all what happens if a tank exploded: action, reaction, all that good stuff. Bottom line is it imparted enough radial velocity to bend their trajectory in the wrong direction." He paused. "Without a course correction, *Prospector* will impact Mars in three months."

He gave the crew a moment to digest that and turned to the XO to explain their mission. "We've been ordered to get underway immediately to intercept *Prospector*," Wicklund explained. "First mission objective is successful rescue or recovery of the spacecraft's occupants. Second objective is to change its course, either move it back onto a free-return trajectory to Earth or into a safe Mars-crossing orbit." He looked at Nick Lesko, who Marshall had just noticed was in a corner wearing a generic crew jumpsuit. "First pass at our delta-v budget is on the order of fifteen kilometers a second, so we're headed down to LEO to top off our tanks and shed any unnecessary mass. That means Mr. Lesko here will return to Earth, along with anything else we don't absolutely need."

There were no protests beyond wide-eyed surprise. Poole swiped at the controller and a plot of their orbits appeared. "Thank you, XO." He took the time to meet the gaze of each crewmember. "We're under serious time pressure, people. It took *Prospector* eight weeks to reach RQ39 with chemical engines and coasting on a free return. We're going to do it in eight *days*." He gave that a moment to sink in. "It'll take a maximum endurance burn. Longest duration these engines demonstrated on Earth was an hour and forty, and that was because the test cell ran out of cryogenic hydrogen. I think they can do better, and I want every last second of that impulse. Got it?"

"Aye sir!" came their roaring reply.

"Good." It was time to begin making assignments, and he looked at Marshall. "Mr. Hunter, you wanted to go somewhere? We're going all right, into interplanetary space with our hair on fire. You're going to work with Commander Wicklund and Chief Garver on our mass budget."

"Aye, sir," he said from behind his O_2 mask. *Mass budget*, he thought. In this case, that no doubt meant deciding who got left behind.

❀ 14 ❀

Marshall rubbed at his eyes, chasing away mounting fatigue. How long had he been at this? Stupid question, he decided, and counterproductive as well: The only question that mattered was how long had the Jiangs been out of contact with Earth? Their lives now came with fixed expiration dates.

Of the many cold, hard truths about working in space they'd tried to teach him in school, the crush of time was the one he now felt firsthand. Of all the esoteric and sometimes confounding displays aboard a spacecraft, one of the simplest and most indispensable was the master mission clock.

It governed every aspect of shipboard life. Every maneuver, which simply put was burning the engines for a specific amount of time at a specific power setting along a specific vector, was defined by time: when, and for how long, measured to the fraction of a second. If they needed the ship in a specific point in space, its arrival had to be worked backward to the second where they could begin burning engines. There would always be some point on the clock where they had to take action or miss the opportunity entirely. If it were a simple matter of changing their orbit around Earth, then missing a window meant waiting ninety minutes for it to come around again.

Leaving Earth entirely was a bit more complicated.

Which made Marshall wonder why the skipper had put him on it. Were the more senior officers that overwhelmed? Because this was way too important to just be some make-work exercise for the new guy.

Ours is not to reason why, he told himself. *Ours is but to do or die.* And please do try to avoid that last part.

The XO had given him a hard deadline, essentially twelve hours from Poole's briefing, when they were to rendezvous with the propellant depot in LEO. By the time they had tanked up and the evac shuttle had left with Lesko and the others, they were expected to get underway and Commander Wicklund wanted hard figures for Poole long before they arrived. The XO had made it clear that he and the master chief were going to be neck deep in logistics planning with the other division officers, and he was relying on Marshall's recency of training to carry the day.

"You just had this stuff in the last six months," he'd said. "For the rest of us, it might as well be theoretical. We've been too busy working up here to even think about doing a run like this, whereas you've devoted some time to the idea. So get to it, mister." Nobody at the academy had warned him that cadet research papers could come back to bite so hard in the ass once they were out in the fleet.

The XO had been just as unsparing in his critique of Marshall's first-pass calculations. "Too conservative," he'd said. "The first critical event comes in ten days when their hab's internal air supply runs out. We do not want to get there a day late. This ship can do a lot, but she has her limits. Find them, then find me a way to move them."

Find the limits, like it was a first-semester calculus problem. Marshall ran a tense hand through his bushy black hair and wished he could've had an actual desk to sit behind. Working these problems with a tablet and notepad Velcroed to the wall of his sleeping berth was not conducive to concentration.

Prospector should have been on a free-return trajectory, taking advantage of RQ39's current proximity to take some pictures and measurements, then continue on an ellipse that ended back on Earth.

The cold truth was a satellite could have done the same thing for a lot less money but the Jiangs had bigger dreams. They wanted to show it could be done, see it for themselves, and explore it. Exploit it, really, but the exploration had to come first. If it was as full of rare-earth minerals (and what could be more rare-earth than something not from Earth) as they believed, then it was worth the risk of matching its orbit to stop and look around it for a while.

The opportunity came roughly every four years, which in their minds made it all the more urgent—for what if they missed this opportunity, who else might come out four years hence to stake a claim? RQ39's synodic period put it within relatively easy reach on a cycle that could conceivably be exploited by humans, so the Jiangs had been out to prove an operating concept as much as to explore a near-Earth asteroid.

That wasn't making his current job any easier. *Borman*'s nuclear-thermal powerplants gave them options that *Prospector*'s chemical engines didn't, but it didn't change the fact that the optimal departure window had closed three weeks ago. They were going to have to expel a lot of energy to get there before that "first critical event," in order to reach a target that was flying farther away with each passing day. Then they'd have to burn again to slow down for a rendezvous, burn once more to accelerate back to Earth, then *again* to decelerate. There were some elegant tricks he could play that took advantage of Earth's gravity to bend their trajectory, but in the end they'd have to slow this beast down enough for the planet to catch them—otherwise they'd be flung back out on a long ellipse that might as well have been as remote as RQ39's.

It was just too much mass to move around. If time was the indispensable measurement, mass was the inescapable limitation.

What if it wasn't? Poole had said they were going downhill to refuel and shed mass. So how much was he willing to shed? The XO hadn't given him any insight. What about Garver?

Marshall opened up a message window on his tablet: HEY MASTER CHIEF. YOU UP?

He replied after a moment: IS THAT SUPPOSED TO BE A JOKE, SIR? COB IS THE ONLY BILLET ON THIS TUB THAT GETS LESS SLEEP THAN THE SKIPPER.

Point taken, he thought. JUST TRYING TO BE POLITE. I HAVE QUESTIONS. GOT A MINUTE?

Garver must have been thinking along the same lines: YOUR PLACE OR MINE?

The master chief's sleeping compartment, which was still too small for Marshall to seriously consider calling "quarters," felt lived-in to the point where he wondered if he would ever be that comfortable aboard. Every square inch of the wall opposite Garver's sleeping bag was covered with photos arranged in a deliberate pattern. In the center were pictures of his family: his wife and sons, who appeared to be budding teenagers. Surrounding it were images from his time both above Earth and beneath the sea: submarines and spacecraft, dive suits and space suits.

Marshall tried not to be distracted by the panoply of colors; if he didn't focus on them the hues and patterns came to resemble a quilt hanging above his bed. He realized that was precisely why Garver had arranged them so.

"So what's troubling you, Ensign?"

Marshall found an empty area of sidewall for his tablet and notes, deciding to not waste his time with pleasantries. "I can't make the numbers add up. We have the delta-v to get there in eight days, but not if we want to rendezvous and return."

Garver rubbed his nose as he scrolled through the results. He paused at a graph of velocity change versus time: a series of irregular, concentric shapes bisected by diagonals, each representing a different period of days and total energy needed. "I see your point. Had a feeling that's what you'd get hung up on. So you're wondering about our mass budget."

"I am."

"As you should be," Garver said. "As am I. As the skipper is, though he's smart enough to not show that in front of the crew."

"Would he want you telling me that?"

Garver smiled. "You're assuming he told me that. I'm only guessing based on his actions and body language. HQ wrote a very large check and it's up to him to figure out how to cash it."

"Up to us, you mean."

"Yes, that's precisely what I mean." He tapped at the graph's eight-day line. "So this is our target, nonnegotiable. We have to figure out how to fit the mission inside of that energy budget." He eyed Marshall. "You believe you've run out of ideas."

"I don't know how many I had to begin with, Master Chief." Marshall sounded defeated.

"Good thing you came to me and not one of the other officers," he said. "Because I, sir, do not care one whit about who gets credit for what. At least not among the officers. So what are your mass assumptions?"

"I started with standard loadout, but it became obvious that wasn't going to work."

"Could've told you that without even sharpening my pencil, sir. Only way we're getting there with a full boat is on a Hohmann transfer, which would take too long, and we've missed the window anyway."

"Right," Marshall said. "So then I looked at limiting consumables to the expected trip duration. That has its own drawbacks."

"You mean the part where if we have to stay longer, we run out of air or starve? It's still viable, though. If we stay out there too long, at some point we're not coming back within any kind of realistic timeframe. There's your upper limit on consumables."

"I thought about that. It still doesn't move the ball far enough."

"So you've trimmed all the fat. Now you've got to figure out which cuts of meat we can do without."

"I was hoping that's where you'd come in."

"I have some thoughts." Garver smiled, and pulled out his own notes. "We draw down to a skeleton crew. Not only does that save a hundred-ish kilos per body, it's a big cut out of our ration budget."

"You read my mind, Master Chief. But I'm not savvy enough to know how many crewmembers we actually need." It would be about much more than raw numbers: *who* stayed on mattered.

"Don't worry about that part, Mr. Hunter. I've already worked up a proposed roster." He tapped Marshall's graph, adjusting it for the new entry. "It still doesn't get us far enough, though."

Marshall scratched at his head, exasperated. "And this is where I hit the wall, Chief. I don't see what else we can shed."

Garver's eyes glinted with the satisfied look of a tutor leading his student to a revelation. "What's the mission, sir?"

"The mission? Intercept *Prospector*, rescue the Jiangs, and bring them back to Earth."

"Any threats we should be worried about?"

"Another coronal mass ejection. Getting holed by a micrometeoroid. Major system failure . . ."

"All true, sir, and all wrong. I'm talking about hostiles. Do we expect to encounter any?"

Marshall's eyes widened. That had been so far down his priority list as to put it out of his mind entirely, and Garver's question was a stark reminder to not let that happen. "Well . . . no. All the potential threats are milsats in Earth orbit, not that we've ever had to engage any. There's nothing out there but some stray boulders and a lot more nothing."

"And is that something we need a full weapons loadout for?" Garver prodded further. "Vaporizing any rocks that might get in our way?"

The light went on in his head. "That's a lot of mass we're lugging around."

"Indeed it is. Nearly all of it is for self-defense, and I'm not seeing what's out there to defend against."

Marshall thought about that. "We'd want some point-defense rounds for asteroid deflection in case we run across something uncharted. Say half a load. Maybe keep a couple of the ASAT interceptors in case we need to make something big disappear." He paused. "Would Captain Poole be good with that?"

Garver stretched and stared at his wall of photos, eyes focusing on one in particular as if it held the key. It was an old one, of him and Poole from their Navy days with a group of others Marshall didn't recognize, some of whom looked to be kitted out like SEALs. "It won't be an easy sell, but if it accomplishes the mission, then yes."

"A skeleton crew in an unarmed ship, taking it farther than it's ever been," Marshall deadpanned. "Where do I sign up?"

The reality was that in being the most junior officer, Marshall was likely to be the first in line to get cut, but not the only. He'd realized this, but now that they were presenting their findings to Poole he felt the press of the other officers' eyes at his back for the first time. Not only was the new guy sticking his neck out, he was exposing others to the same fate.

"What does cutting this much of the crew do for our consumables?" Poole asked, though Marshall suspected he knew the answer.

"Over six and a half kilos per person, per day," Marshall said.

Commander Wicklund approximated standing by Poole, his feet in a set of restraints and hands clasped behind his back. "Exact numbers, please."

"Six point five-five-four," Marshall said. "Apologies, sir. I thought it best to be conservative."

As was his way, the XO was unsparing in his critique. "This is not the time for padding figures, Mister Hunter. Tell us *precisely* what conditions we need to meet, and *precisely* what we can do to meet them. The captain will decide the rest."

Poole went a little easier on him. "Normally I'd say you're right to be conservative, but first let's work it down to the gnat's ass like the XO said. Then maybe we can start adding back mass." He rubbed his ball cap across his bald head as he looked for holes in their plan. "So we're eight days out, assume two days on station, maybe ten back?"

"We can save propellant on the return leg using a lower-energy trajectory," Chief Garver noted, "but then we're trading off consumables again."

"More time in transit equals more food and water," Poole agreed. "Especially if we have survivors to feed. We're not going to assume they've reached room temperature yet." He eyed them both. "Is that clear?"

Marshall spoke for them. "Aye, sir."

Poole pulled his cap back on, smoothing out the brim. "And by that logic, we can't plan on shaving propellant mass to take the scenic route home. If they're alive then they're probably going to need medical attention, so we plan to expedite."

"Our plan assumed the same, sir. We hadn't looked to save weight in medical stores." Marshall pointed to another equipment roster.

"We may have to consider that," Wicklund noted. "How many units of blood plasma do we need for two evacuees? How many liters of saline?" He was fixed on Marshall. "If you haven't looked to cut mass out of medical, then you haven't spent enough time with Flynn or Riley. Your plan is incomplete, Mister Hunter."

Marshall forced himself to keep his eyes fixed on the plotting board. "Understood, sir."

If Poole was concerned about that, he wasn't showing it. He tapped at his chin as he thought. There were other aspects he found more troubling. "Talk to me about the weapons loadout."

Marshall shot a nervous glance at Chief Garver. "We keep the two ASAT interceptors already in their tubes and offload the rest," he said. "We strip the magazines for the point-defense guns down by half. We can remove the small-arms locker but their mass ends up being so far inside the margin of error, Chief Garver convinced me it wasn't worth the hassle."

Poole nodded. "He's right. It's not. The fuel farm has racks for the big stuff so we can park it all in orbit until we get back. Side arms and carbines have to be signed for individually, packed away in a locked container, sent back to Earth on the shuttle, and secured in the armory at Vandenberg. Biggest pain in the ass over absolutely nothing..." he trailed off. They were meant for potential survival or escape situations in the event of an emergency return to Earth, which now was beside the point. "So yeah, those stay aboard. Never know when we might run into space pirates," he deadpanned.

"We didn't think you'd want to head out completely unarmed, sir." Marshall drew his fingers across the plotting board, zooming out to their destination. "We're concerned about uncatalogued NEOs in the vicinity, and as fast as we'll be going—"

"If we detect one in our path, our only choice will be to blast it," Poole agreed. "Instead of flying headlong into one big rock, we fly into a bunch of little rocks."

"Our recommended tactical plan is to keep one of the ASATs hot at all times," Marshall said, "with a continuous radar and lidar sweep along our vector. If we detect a collision threat, we destroy it with one of the interceptors and clean up any remains with the PDCs."

"Creating even more little rocks," the XO noted dryly. "We'd be trading one big hit for hundreds of little hits." He turned to Poole.

Poole rubbed the bridge of his nose as he studied the images of asteroid RQ39. Could there be more like it nearby which just hadn't been spotted yet? Hitting even a small one at over forty thousand kilometers an hour would be disastrous. "If it comes to that, it'll be good gunnery practice."

"That it will, sir," Garver said with a grin.

Poole drew a breath. "Very well. Half magazines on the PDCs," he said, "*if* you can make up the mass budget elsewhere."

As Garver adjusted the mass estimate, it began to reach the threshold they needed. "That puts our C_3 just over forty-six kps. It gets us there and back, sir, just barely."

Poole frowned. "Yeah, I don't like these margins. What else can you give me?"

Marshall searched his mind. He wasn't sure how to answer that. What else could they possibly lose and still remain effective? "Maybe one or two more crewmembers, sir, but that only saves about three hundred kilos each. Offload one more ASAT, maybe strip one more belt of point-defense ammo . . ."

"Unacceptable," Wicklund said. "We can't break orbit with that thin of a loadout. The inertia reels feeding the cannons become unreliable if there's not enough mass behind them to counterbalance. Even an empty belt on the other side is better than nothing."

"Aye, sir," was all Marshall could say, and made a mental note of it—one more example of exactly how much he still had to learn about this ship.

Poole swiped at the plotting board, his eyes following their elliptical orbit to intercept *Prospector*. "Where's the Moon in this scenario?"

"Sir?"

"You raced gliders cross-country, right?" It was a subtle reminder to the others that young Ensign Hunter wasn't exactly an unknown quantity to the CO. "You learned a lot about where to look for lift, I'll bet."

"Yes sir," Marshall said warily, wondering where Poole was going with this. "Sometimes you have to be creative to get where you're going." It was better to ride a column of warm air as high as possible before getting in a hurry to cover distance with unknown sources of lift.

Poole tapped the plot of their orbit and began dragging it in a different direction. "And a sailboat captain learns how to read the seas and tack into the wind, so he can get where he's going even if the wind's against him. We both use the environment to our advantage. If there's a gravity well anywhere on our way out, we can exploit that. And we've got two right here." He tapped on the Earth and the Moon.

"You mean a slingshot—er, gravity assist, sir?"

The XO corrected him. "He means an Oberth maneuver. Similar, but different."

Poole arched an eyebrow in Marshall's direction. "Your old man showed me what a good spacecraft driver does a long time ago, Mr. Hunter. Took us around the Moon hell-for-leather, he did. By the time we reached periapsis he had me closing my eyes and hoping we didn't scrape lunar dirt."

He did? "Begging your pardon, sir. I knew you were with him at the Gateway incident." Marshall swallowed. "He just never shared any of the details." He grew quiet. He didn't notice the looks Poole exchanged with the XO and chief, patting the air with his hand to dissuade their concern.

Poole laid a hand on the young man's shoulder. "Maybe later, when we're back on the beach." He looked up at the XO and chief. "It's a hell of a story, gents." He decided it was time to take the pressure off their newest officer. "Good work, Mr. Hunter. Not perfect, but a good start." He pointed at the plotting board. "The trick with a gravity assist is the gravity part. The deeper the well, the bigger the multiple. And the closer you can get to the bottom of that well, the greater your mass effect."

Their path was an ellipse beginning at Earth and curving tightly around RQ39, with arrows at numerous points along the way to mark critical events. "Sometimes when nature doesn't cooperate, the fastest route to your destination is to start in the wrong direction." He pulled the ellipse out toward the Moon, then back to Earth. "We climb up the well to the edge of Earth's Hill sphere, then let ourselves fall back. We're picking up velocity on the way down. We do a gravity-assist burn at the bottom and whip around Earth's backside, outbound to RQ39." The path from there grew straighter, reflecting their increased speed. "The other thing we can do is burn one hydrogen tank at a time instead of drawing from all three equally."

The XO leaned in. "I think I see where you're going, sir. Punching empty tanks will create some trim problems."

Poole waved it away. "Nothing we can't handle. You guys are smart enough, I think."

"Begging your pardon, sir, but I'm not following," Marshall said.

Poole explained. "We have too much mass to move quickly without having to expend just as much energy when we arrive. The lighter we are, the less we have to expend. So we're going to burn the outboard tanks first and jettison them when they're empty."

"The bean counters will scream bloody murder," the XO warned. "That's a heavy-lift launcher to replace each tank."

"Good thing Logistics isn't running this op," Poole said. "If we don't reach *Prospector* before the first critical event, Ops will be pissed. Either way, some staff officer's going to be pissed which means we're doing something right." Poole eyed the chief. "Garver, just make sure we don't do anything stupid like bomb rural Nebraska with an empty hydrogen tank."

"I'm from North Platte, sir. It's *all* rural," the chief reminded him. "I'll make sure we time it just right, Skipper."

Poole adjusted for their new mass estimate, which now landed squarely within their energy budget. "We'll drop the other outboard tank after our braking burn." They had too much mass to move so quickly without needing to expend just as much energy when they arrived on station—they wouldn't be doing the Jiangs any good if they shot past without slowing down enough to match orbits. "Not like we can tie a life preserver to a line and throw it out there."

"Would that it was true, sir," Garver said.

"And since tractor beams don't exist yet . . ." Poole mused, cheerful and satisfied that the pieces had come together. "Very well, gentlemen. This is a solid plan." He turned to Wicklund and Garver. "XO, put it into action. Give me sitreps every four hours. Chief, I'm assuming you already have a roster for me?"

"Affirmative, sir," he said, and swiped at his tablet to send the crew manifest to Poole's.

He studied it silently, his face a mask of impartiality. The CO was not giving up any clues as to whether the chief's recommendations made him feel anything. After a minute of contemplation, he looked up at them. "I'd only change one thing: take your own name off the cut list. You're going, Chief."

Before Garver could offer an alternative, Poole cut him off. "Spare me any bromides about avoiding the appearance of self-dealing. The only swinging Richard with more time on this tub than you, is me." He stabbed at the tablet. "If we're drawing down crew by half, then the remaining half had better be *locked on*."

That led him to Marshall. "I'm sorry, son. That means you're on the cut list."

❁ 15 ❁

Knowing he was the newest crewman aboard, officer or not, did not make being cut from the mission any easier. Marshall's fellow officers and the spacers under him were consumed with preparing for their ship's first voyage beyond Earth's influence and a first-of-its-kind rescue. It was analogous to the Coast Guard having only one cutter at sea, always within a day or two from shore, and suddenly sending it clear out to answer a mayday call in the middle of the North Atlantic with no resupply or refueling. Everything they needed to get there and back would have to be brought with them.

He understood it, yet the disappointment still stung. In addition to packing up his own gear to take with him, he'd been made responsible for offloading all the other nonessential gear. After only a couple of weeks aboard, he was working himself out of a job.

It was only temporary, he kept assuring himself. Probably. "Needs of the service" were constantly changing. In the end, they could send him wherever they needed and there were any number of officers who would jump at the chance to replace him.

He and the five others going Earthside with him would be assigned temporary duty probably doing something menial, as they wouldn't be around long enough to become useful to anyone. Yet he'd be expected to do his best at whatever he was assigned. It would be a balancing act of doing just enough to not get noticed, either good or ill. Do too good of a job and whoever was in charge down there just might want to keep him around. Screw up and they'd keep him from coming back out of spite.

He wondered how long he'd been staring into space like a moron when the XO appeared in his doorway. "Away Team meeting in twenty minutes, P-1 module. Bring your latest manifest and mass estimates. We've still got to find three hundred kilos to trim."

"Is that exact, sir?" he asked, immediately wishing he hadn't.

"You've been here long enough to know that I don't speak in round numbers unless they're actual round numbers, Mister Hunter."

"Aye, sir." Marshall made a note on his tablet to find precisely three hundred kilos their shipmates could live without.

Wicklund remained hovering in Marshall's doorway. "You're pissed."

"Sir?"

The XO had been unsparing in his critiques before, as he was in apparently every other regard. "No need to try and hide it. Skipper's taking our ship out on its first trip into interplanetary space. Might as well be going to Mars if you ask me. You figured out how to get us there, and now you're being kicked to the curb."

Marshall lifted his chin. "I understood that as soon as I realized we needed to cut head count, sir. Captain Poole needs experienced crew."

"Just doing your job, then?"

"Yes sir. That's how I see it. Doesn't mean I have to like the results."

A grin crept across Wicklund's face, ending at his eyes. "Sure you do. At least in front of the crew."

"Begging your pardon, sir, but I don't follow."

"No, I don't think you do." Wicklund came inside and pulled the privacy curtain behind him. "You've been dog-faced ever since leaving that meeting. You feel like the universe has dealt you a bad hand and you're the guy who shuffled the deck. The proverbial turd rolled downhill and landed on you. Whatever metaphor you prefer, I'm telling you to *get over it*."

"I didn't realize I'd said anything, sir."

"Did I say you had?" Wicklund leaned in. "It's all over your face, son. You look like somebody just ran over your favorite puppy with a dump truck. These spacers are smart people, Hunter. They pick up on body language and tics like you wouldn't believe."

He was right: Marshall didn't believe it. How could people so constantly busy even *want* to take the time to read him? What did they even care if he was about to be sent back down the well anyway?

"You grabbed a fiercely competitive billet and now that you're leaving, you think the knives are coming out for you."

Marshall looked up to meet his eyes. "Someone is bound to try and take advantage of the situation, sir."

"Maybe. Maybe not. Don't forget, the skipper has final say in who comes aboard his ship. How do you think you got here?"

At last, there it was. He felt his face flush with heat. "I listed this ship as my first preference for duty, sir, just like everyone else in my class. None of us thought we'd get it. I didn't ask for any favors and I didn't pull any strings." He laughed at himself. "I don't *have* any strings to pull. My family's not military."

Wicklund's cold eyes pierced him. "Sure you do. Maybe not blood, but they might as well be. You don't go through what your old man went through with the skipper without having ties that can't be broken. Signing your name to that request was pulling a string whether you think so or not. And you'd already strong-armed our check pilot into passing you."

Now the anger boiled up. "Just one minute, *sir*." He practically spat the word. "You can't tell me that was a normal check ride! Wylie was sent to evaluate me for duty here. I get it. But all I knew at the time was some IP I'd never met was about to bust me after setting me up for failure in the first place. I worked my ass off for that flight rating and he was in my way. I didn't give a damn why."

"You've got balls, I'll give you that."

"And you've been busting them since I arrived. Sir." *Should've kept that to myself*, he thought.

Another cold smile from the XO. "That's my job, Mister Hunter. If the captain played hard-ass every time it was needed, crew morale would be shot to hell. That's what executive officers are for. Haven't you watched any war movies?"

Marshall struggled with the question before finally spitting it out. "Why did you bring me aboard, sir?"

Wicklund studied him, considering his words. "You're a guinea pig."

Marshall cocked his head. "How?"

"Don't be dense, son. You're smarter than that. Right now the

Orbit Guard fleet has exactly one ship and it's treated like a career-pinnacle assignment," he said. "Which it is. But as they build more, we have to start grooming junior officers for duty up here." He tapped his chest. "That falls on us to make it happen. Skipper figured it's better to take that chance with a known quantity than some kid fresh out of the training squadron."

"I *am* a kid fresh out of the training squadron," Marshall reminded him. "Sir."

"Maybe to the rest of the crew, but not to the skipper. That's why he had Wylie put you through the ringer. He told us you could hack it, but you had to prove yourself."

Marshall did a silent double take. A part of him knew that, remembered it from the academy. But being in the middle of the barely controlled bedlam of adjusting to life in orbit, he'd never realized it.

Wicklund's cool demeanor warmed, if only a little. "It's my job to push the crew and make them worthy of being here. You did good, Hunter. But I'm telling you there's *always* one more step you can take, one more mile to go. We are expected to always do the right thing, particularly when it's not in our personal interest."

"I thought that's what I did, sir."

A hoarse laugh. "I'm not talking about *you*, numbnuts. Have you looked at the manifest lately?"

He hadn't. Marshall pulled up the cut roster and was shocked at the latest name atop the list. Master Chief Garver's name had been removed, and replaced with: CDR WICKLUND, JONAH B.

"See you at the meeting. And don't forget that manifest."

Moving down the cut roster from its senior (and only) officer meant that a lot of responsibility had just been lifted from his shoulders. He'd convinced himself to embrace the chance to be in charge of a ship's detachment, even if for temporary duty back on Earth.

The responsibility might be gone, but the work remained. With all the work just delegated to him by Wicklund, he was sure that none of the departure prep had simply been removed from the XO's purview. Poole would use him to ride herd on the crew right up until the moment they undocked to make their way downhill.

Being the detachment's junior officer, a twenty-minute warning from the XO meant he actually had ten minutes to make everything ready.

He sailed down the connecting corridor and pulled himself to a stop at the multi-mod hatch. When he floated inside, he found two crewmen sweating over the resistance machines. "Workout's over, guys. Sorry but the XO needs the space in ten."

One of the men, who hid an impressive physique beneath his usual coveralls, sent a glob of moisture flying from his shaved head when he looked up. "We know, sir. We're on the roster."

Marshall's eyes widened and he checked the roster again. Powers and Jefferson—of course they were. "Sorry fellas. I've got too much stuff competing for space in my brain."

"No need to keep apologizing, sir."

"Sorry, didn't know I—"

They both laughed. "There you go again, sir." Each moved to dry themselves off and stow the workout machines. "No worries, we'll help you set up. We were already down here when we got the notice."

"Appreciate that, guys." He tapped their names on his tablet to bring up a list of tasks they'd been assigned. "You two are already done with your inventory?" It felt like micromanaging, but the XO was certain to ask at some point and it would not pay for the new guy to come up short. The best way to avoid uncomfortable questions was to already have the answers at hand.

The other crewman, lanky and easygoing, folded an armature into the sidewall and locked it down. "Honestly, sir, it wasn't hard. We probably have a better idea of what's in the ship's stores than our own personal lockers. Otherwise stuff gets lost up here in ways you wouldn't dream of in gravity."

Marshall gave him a *you got that right* nod as he opened up the wardroom table. He tried not to think about what he'd lost himself just after a couple of weeks. "Has anybody figured out where everything ends up?" he asked, not hiding his frustration.

"It's space," Powers shrugged. "A black hole."

"There you go again," Jefferson said. "Gotta be black, don't it?"

Powers rolled his eyes. "Really, dude? Does everything have to go that way with you?"

"Only if it gets you riled up." He turned to Marshall. "My

shipmate's decidedly unscientific opinion notwithstanding, sir, it's a dilemma as old as spaceflight. Stuff floating loose finds its way into every unreachable nook and cranny. You'd think everything would just gravitate toward the air returns, but I've found missing gear in places you wouldn't believe."

That was the part that troubled him. How much mass was left aboard that they couldn't account for? He'd just have to make doubly certain they had every single piece of gear on their manifest. On the ground it would've been straightforward, up here it felt like herding cats. Cats that could fly.

The other two crewmen, Mikey Malone and Hector Navarro from Marshall's own section, soon floated into the compartment and watched as the four traded the kinds of fist bumps, high fives, and trash talking of people who'd spent a lot of time working in close quarters together.

"Ready to go downhill, Hector?"

His already dark face turned dour. "Hell, no. Think I want to miss this?" He waved his thumb between himself and Malone. "How is it that Mikey and I hit our dosage limits when you two are the ones working in the reactor spaces all the time?"

"There's more shielding in those compartments than anywhere but the storm shelter," Powers said. "You're the ones hanging your asses overboard every chance you get."

"It's what spacers do," Malone said, patting Hector's shoulder. "Being Earthside for a couple weeks won't be that bad, brother. Maybe do us some good."

"That's because you've got a wife and kids down there," Hector said. "Don't get all magnanimous on me. We've known each other too long."

"Then you can come over and grill some burgers with us. Maybe have a couple beers."

The four of them nodded approvingly. A little time on the beach wouldn't be so bad. "Now that's a plan," Hector said, turning back to Marshall. "That is, if Mister Hunter doesn't have our activities already planned full."

Marshall shook his head. "Not up to me," he said, just as the XO glided into the compartment and stopped at the head of the table.

"Gentlemen. You don't have time to listen to me drone on and I don't have time to listen to you bellyache," Wicklund said. "But here we are nonetheless."

So had he intended to have Marshall here early to get a feel for the NCOs' morale? Having to constantly think four-dimensionally was becoming exhausting.

The XO continued. "Based on our mass budget and available delta-v, our departure window closes in less than twenty-four hours. The skipper wants to get underway yesterday. If you're not feeling a sense of extreme urgency at this moment, you're wrong." He turned to Marshall. "Mister Hunter. What's the detachment's status?"

Marshall swiped at his tablet, glad that he'd had the time to question the others. "Ahead of schedule, sir. First two blocks on the list have been cleared and the third is underway. Inventory shows us under mass budget by one hundred eighty-four kilos," he said, remembering the XO liked precise numbers.

"And personal gear?"

Marshall hadn't expected that. He eyed the four NCOs, looking for any clues from them. A couple nodded their heads that they were okay. "Still being packed and catalogued for return, sir." It was all he could offer, and he hoped it was right.

"That won't be necessary," Wicklund said, eyeing Marshall, "*if* your inventory is correct. So let's all applaud Mr. Hunter for preventing us from having to completely remove our presence. Bring any personal gear you want to have Earthside, but it won't be necessary to bring everything."

Marshall sensed a wave of relief from the others, something he felt himself. It seemed like a small thing, but it would be a lot harder for HQ to reassign them back on the beach if their gear was still in orbit. Was that another angle the XO was working, by chance?

"Good thing you're ahead of schedule," Wicklund continued, "because we've just had a task added and our little group will have to pick up the slack."

The NCOs traded unmistakable *we're about to get screwed* looks.

"Nobody's about to get screwed," the XO said. So he was a mind reader, too. "But the skipper wasn't happy with some tests we ran on the outboard tank couplers. We're going to have to send another team out there to inspect the links and fittings."

Mikey Malone spoke up. "Begging your pardon, sir, but Hector and I are already off the EVA roster until we finish our course of treatment."

"Exactly," Wicklund said. "Which reminds me—don't spend too much time outside, gents, and load up on sunblock." His stony face gave no hint as to whether he might be joking. "Chief Riley and Rosado will go outside, Mr. Hunter here will back them up. So our detachment is down one man while Malone and Navarro do whatever Rosie and Riley were supposed to be doing." He checked his watch. "Report to the command deck in thirty minutes."

Simon Poole hovered above a diagram of *Borman*'s tanks and plumbing, while Rosado and Riley floated on either side of the plotting table. Marshall tried to follow along as best he could, needing to see what Poole described but not wanting to get in the way of the two people who'd be doing the work.

"We ran an end-to-end control simulation, jettisoning each outboard tank after running them dry," Poole explained. "The engine cutoff sensors didn't play along."

Chief Riley swiped at a spot on the diagram and zoomed in on it. "The sensors are upstream of the intake manifolds," he said. "Aren't they just feeding data to the flight computers?"

"Yes, but they're based on the same principle of the old space shuttle tanks," Poole said. "So they also have direct input to the manifolds. They'll command an engine shutdown if they think the tanks are dry."

"Which they will be," Riley frowned. "And we can't just rewrite the control logic, can we sir?"

"It'll take less time to send you and Rosie out there to disable them." Poole moved the diagram downstream of the sensors. "The ECO umbilicals are here, alongside the propellant crossfeeds. They're meant to keep us from over-speeding the engine turbopumps if the tanks run dry before we think they should. Each one can be disconnected separately."

Marshall raised his hand. "The flight data computers also use the cutoff sensors to update mass totals when we're burning, sir. Won't that create interference with the rest of the system?"

"Not if we do it right," Poole said. "If it's a hard disconnect, the FDCs will see the sensors are offline and ask us if we want to continue. In which case the answer is *yes*. It'll rely on the propellant quantity sensors and our ability to shut down the pumps once we reach dry tanks."

"Which we're not really doing," Marshall said, warming to the idea. "They'll still be drawing hydrogen from the center tank."

"Exactly," Poole said. "The ECO sensors are just doing their job, but that creates a failure mode that the control logic doesn't recognize."

Rosado understood now as well. "And we never simmed jettisoning the tanks before because they're too expensive to replace. We always burn evenly from each tank, not one at a time, don't we?"

"Easier to keep the ship trimmed that way," Poole acknowledged, "plus we're too busy getting actual work done to putz around with the what ifs." He turned to Riley. "Right, Chief?"

Riley smiled. "Kind of staring us in the face now, isn't it, sir?"

"That it is, Chief." Poole slapped him on the shoulder; it would've sent them both spinning away if they hadn't braced themselves. Marshall noted how they'd both picked up on the signals from each other's body language. Poole turned to him. "So how soon can you three get out there?"

"I'm going to defer to the chief on that one, sir. It's his show right now."

Riley nodded. "We'll need you as our safety spotter, sir. There's a lot that can go sideways on an excursion like this. If we get hung up on a task, we may need you to help us muscle through it. Those crossfeeds have been out there a long time and they're not going to give up too easily."

Marshall laughed to himself. "Got it. I'm your hired muscle. So how long to prep?"

"Four hours," Riley said. "We'll target another four for the EVA but it could easily go to eight. We can start pre-breathing while we're inspecting our suits. If you can do that with Rosie, I'll put the tool kits together."

Poole tapped his watch and started a countdown timer. "That's twelve hours from start to finish. That leaves you less than twelve to stow your gear and get ready for the ride home. Get cracking, people."

❀ 16 ❀

Marshall noticed the difference in his suit as soon as he pulled on his cooling garment, a set of long johns covered with loops of tubing that circulated water around his body. Gone was the "new car" smell of synthetic fabric blends, half of them coated in urethane. It now carried a distinct odor of old perspiration that wet wipes couldn't fully cleanse.

The rest of the suit, officially known as an Extravehicular Mobility Unit because no government agency could bear using simple English that couldn't also be distilled into an acronym, had fared better since it was mostly protected from direct contact with him by his cooling garment. Antimicrobial underwear notwithstanding, spacewalks were strenuous and all of that perspiration had to go somewhere.

Watching Rosie and Riley inspecting each other, he marveled at how they managed their own gear and workload. If they weren't out doing "hard hat" work on the spacecraft, they were running rescue drills. Did they like having something they relied on so completely to have that lived-in feeling? Was it reassuring? Did it create a sense of familiarity, and was that a good thing? It simultaneously made discrepancies easier to find while becoming complacent about them.

He found the internal bellows of the elbow and shoulder joints had more play, though the gloves hadn't improved. His fingertips were still raw from the other day's jaunt, so he was content to remain a "safety observer" instead of doing any actual work.

Just as well, he decided as he watched them climb hand over hand down the service railing. Officer or not, he was still a greenhorn and they were in a hurry.

They stopped at the first tank, a bright white barrel with ellipsoid domes at each end. Its brilliance struck him as not being tactically sound—but then, what was there to camouflage against? With no atmosphere to blur light or absorb heat, everything in space stuck out like a sore thumb. A ship painted flat black might be harder to see but there'd be no avoiding the heat signature, not without absurdly large radiators. And everything gave off electromagnetic radiation as well, though EM signatures could be easier to mask.

The *Borman* was not technically a warship, though classifying its weapons as "defensive" was an exercise in absurdity—that depended entirely on which end you were facing. Their loadout was meant as a last resort, either for clearing the space lanes of dangerous debris, or for deterring "bad actors" from controlling them. Either way meant directing fire on a target that would then be turned into more debris—exchanging fire with another ship threatened to create a cascade of shrapnel which could make whatever orbital plane it occurred in unusable for years.

That all was of course still hypothetical. In the same configuration, *Borman* could've been commissioned as something akin to a naval frigate and other spacefaring nations would've lost their minds. Make it a "safety patrol" ship for Orbit Guard, up here in full view for everybody's protection, and they mostly kept quiet. It seemed to him like a distinction without a difference.

Riley's voice crackled in his headset, interrupting Marshall's wandering thoughts. "We're on station at tank one's interlink. Can you take up our slack?"

"Roger that." He followed their umbilical lines as they snaked out of the open airlock, into space and along the length of the ship to disappear amongst the hydrogen tanks. The two spacers would've been difficult to spot were it not for their high-visibility saffron-yellow suits. Marshall grabbed one line and methodically coiled up its excess before securing it with a Velcro strap. He repeated it for the second line. "How's that?"

"Peachy," Rosie said. "Thanks."

Standing in the hatch atop the spacecraft's dorsal spine gave him an unobstructed view of their work area and the two pale yellow figures, over fifty meters away, bouncing and hovering over the gaps between three enormous tanks. They would be passing into darkness soon and their helmet lamps switched on, dazzling against the tank's already brilliant white skin. "How's your access?" he asked them.

He could hear the grunts behind Riley's voice. "It's a tight fit, that's for sure. I don't think they planned on anyone working around these things in orbit."

"We can see the crossfeed lines and bellows, but it limits our reach to the sensor conduits. Might be doing some of this by feel," Rosie said, which he assumed was a joke. They wouldn't be "feeling" much of anything.

Simon Poole's attention was spread thin between monitoring the EVA, coordinating with fleet control, keeping up with their departure prep, and running the ship in general. He didn't notice the chime of an incoming message packet from the flight station behind him.

"New software uplink from Ops, skipper," Flynn reported from the pilot's station. "It's the navigation plan we were waiting for."

"About time," Poole said. "How long to QC it?"

"Ran a checksum as it was loading, sir. Bits and bytes are all accounted for." Which was one, but not the only, indication that the new guidance package was ready to run.

Poole eyed the chronometer as it counted down the hours and minutes to their departure. "Program the primary FDC, but keep the others out of the loop until it's validated."

"Aye, sir."

Riley waved at Marshall as he emerged from between the tanks. "First inspection complete," he said. "Moving across to outboard two now."

"Rosie handling this next one?"

"You'd better believe it, sir. This was a little too claustrophobic for me."

"Can you unsnap my line, sir?" Rosie called. "I'm about to head over."

He pulled her coiled umbilical free. "You're all set. Go for it."

Marshall watched her deftly move along the handholds to the outer edge of the tank, then push off to fly across the spine of the ship and come to a stop at the opposite tank. Looking back down to where she'd started, Riley was fussing with his own line. "Need a minute on mine, sir. It's tangled up near this thruster quad."

"Uplink complete," Flynn said.

Poole pulled up behind him. "That was quick. Sure you got the whole package?"

The engineer tapped the screen, as if coaxing it to offer more information. "About the normal upload time, skipper. Maybe the nav solutions aren't as complicated as we thought."

"You're forgetting the first rule of spaceflight," Poole cautioned. "*Everything* is more complicated than we thought."

The skipper had lots of "first rules," Flynn thought, every single one of them being the most important at that moment. There were too many ways to get seriously dead out here. "The initial state vectors agree with ours."

Poole looked over his shoulder. "The big question is what happens next. That's going to be a long burn. Blow a trim angle, and we end up half a million miles off target."

"I still need to let the FMC run the program and plot it."

"Agreed," Poole said. "See where it takes us."

"Aye, sir." Flynn's fingers danced around the menu buttons embedded in the screen bezel, selected the PREFLIGHT-SIMULATE menu, then punched EXECUTE. There was a rattle of thrusters and the deck pitched up abruptly.

Marshall bounced hard off the lip of the airlock as the ship moved beneath him, knocking the wind out of him. A fountain of gas erupted from a thruster quad off to his left.

"What the *hell*?" Rosie exclaimed. "Why are we maneuvering?" she shouted into the intercom. A major safety precaution to protect spacers during an EVA was to limit controls to the reaction wheels so as not to have thrusters firing off around vulnerable spacewalkers.

Marshall caught his breath and reflexively patted down his suit, checking for any tears. "No idea!" he said, and felt a stabbing pain in his ribs. That would have to wait. The ship pitched again, this time falling away from him. He grabbed a handhold.

"Control, EVA One!" Riley called. "Cease maneuvering! We are still outside. Repeat, team is still on structure!"

Flynn's voice shot back. "We know! Overriding—"

There was a shout from Riley, and he disappeared behind a cloud of gas from a nearby thruster quad. When it cleared, a sinking feeling overtook Marshall as Riley tumbled away into space, his severed umbilical trailing behind him in a cloud of escaping oxygen.

"*Off structure!*" Rosie shouted. "Control, EVA One is off structure!" She was moving to go after him even though she was bracketed between active thruster quads.

"Stay there, I've got him!" Marshall said. "Control, EVA Three is in pursuit. Hang on, Chief!" He activated his emergency maneuvering and life-support pack, unhooked his umbilical and squared off to face Riley. He crouched down, took a deep breath, and jumped out of the airlock.

The ship fell away, disappearing behind him as he focused on the writhing figure dead ahead: a yellow mass thrashing against the depthless black. His visor's field of view, previously so much more expansive than the tiny portholes on *Borman*, now felt hopelessly limited—if he were experiencing tunnel vision, how would he tell the difference? There was no sense of depth perception: Riley could've been a child's toy he could simply reach out and grab. The sudden sense of isolation was beyond his experience; he was keenly aware of his now-heightened senses. The sound of his own breathing pushed the cacophony of voices in his earphones to the background. He fought the reflex to turn and find the ship for reference, desperate to not lose his bearings.

Riley's form grew larger as Marshall rapidly closed the distance between them. "Almost there, Chief!"

Why wasn't he answering? These guys practically drilled safety protocols in their sleep. If an umbilical somehow became disconnected, the suit fittings had redundant backflow valves that would stop any venting. His suit should've held pressure long enough for his emergency air supply and SAFER pack to guide him back to the spacecraft. Come to think of it, his suit looked awfully loose . . .

Oh.

Marshall swallowed. "Control, EVA Three. Have you been able to contact Riley?"

"Negative, Three. EVA One has not responded."

"Yeah . . . looks like he may have lost pressure. Stand by—"

He was suddenly on top of Riley. Marshall held his arms out to catch him just as they collided, the jolt from his rib cage signaling that something was torn or broken in there.

"Got you!"

Marshall pawed at Riley's suit and hastily clipped a D-ring onto his harness, lashing them together before he could bounce away. The tether went taut and snapped them back toward each other, bringing them face to face. He reached out to lift the chief's sun visor, finally getting a look at him.

His eyes were closed, his mouth hanging open. His breath had condensed and frozen inside of the visor.

Marshall's eyes widened. He mentally went down each step of the emergency assessment checklist he'd been drilled on—victim unresponsive. Okay, check suit condition.

Step one: check his chest pack. Pressure was low. Real low—the needle hovered around one pound per square inch. They normally breathed pure O_2 at five psi instead of an oxygen-nitrogen mixture at normal pressure. The lower pressure made the suits more flexible but that required pure oxygen to breathe.

This was close to vacuum. He had a breach somewhere. Step two, check for signs of leaks. The shredded umbilical was a big hint, but again, at least one of the backflow valves should've plugged that hole right away. It was a passive safety feature, no human intervention required at all: if a hose were somehow disconnected, the negative pressure would slam the valves shut. They couldn't *not* work.

So there was a tear in his suit somewhere. Okay, torso and upper body first . . . Marshall turned him over quickly, looking for holes. It'd have to be fairly big.

Nothing. He moved down to his waist, then his legs . . .

There.

"Control, this is Three. One's suit is breached in two places. Right upper thigh, each one about an inch around." He pulled out an emergency sealant kit from his utility harness and began opening the patch.

A firm voice answered, Poole himself. "Three, this is Actual. Stand by on that seal. Any signs of burn-through?"

What? They wanted him to *wait*? Marshall's instinct to keep it clipped and professional kicked in with the boss on the other end of the radio. "Actual, Three . . . burn-through. Please advise. What am I looking for?"

"It won't look scorched, like from a flame. Look for blistering."

"Copy blistering. Checking now." The outer layer of yellow ballistic fibers did look like a couple of bubbles that had burst, as did the inner pressure layers of latex-coated fabric. The severed end of his umbilical had numerous blisters. "That's affirmative, sir. Immediately surrounding the two holes, and all over the umbilical."

"Did it burn through his cooling garment?"

Marshall focused his helmet lamps on the two holes and pulled at them carefully. He could see the white elastic fabric and the edge of a cooling hose. "Looks intact, sir. Can I tape him up now?"

"Affirmative, Three. That's good news. He's not completely screwed, but that's exhaust residue. It burned through his umbilical and tagged his pressure suit, too."

"Understood, sir." Fear gnawed at him as he wrapped sealant tape over the holes. The thrusters burned hydrazine, an exceptionally toxic and corrosive compound. Breathing in a few droplets of the stuff could destroy a person's lungs, something he tried not to think about as he plugged Riley's suit into his own life-support pack and began sharing air. How much residue did he now have on his own suit? Could either one of them come aboard now without contaminating the airlock?

"Here's what you're going to do," Poole said calmly. "First, are you stable?"

Marshall closed his eyes and took a breath. When he opened them, he was looking at the heads-up projection in his visor. The horizon reference was motionless, no drift. Relative velocity was zero. The SAFER maneuvering pack had worked while he took care of Riley. "Affirmative. We're stable, and Riley's suit is patched. I've got him plugged into my air supply."

"Good. You're not coming back to the utility airlock. I need you to head for the emergency lock, straight to medical."

"Understand medical." Marshall unfolded control arms from either side of his backpack. Puffs of compressed gas surrounded him as he spun about to face *Borman*. It looked a lot farther away than he thought it would be. How far had they tumbled together? He tapped both controllers forward. "Three is Oscar Mike." On the move.

There was another unnerving jolt, this time at his back when Riley's mass pulled against the tether joining them. He goosed the thrusters again to keep them moving, steering them toward a yellow beacon that had begun flashing atop one of the forward modules. That would be the emergency airlock, a massive door two meters square meant for the rescue spacers to move incapacitated passengers aboard in a hurry—not unlike what he was doing right now.

There was a weak groan over the radio. "Good, you're up," Marshall said. "Stay with me, Chief. We're on our way back to the barn."

"Closing—" A cough. "—too fast."

"I know. Trust me." As they closed the distance, Marshall caught movement in his peripheral vision: Rosie, scrambling hand over hand along the length of *Borman*'s central truss.

"Rosie, I could've sworn I told you to stay put."

"No disrespect, but get bent. Sir. Ship's stable. I'm no spectator. See you at the med bay."

"Copy that." He let the sideways rebuke go. She was definitely not one to stay on the sidelines. And now that she'd pointed it out, he realized the RCS quads had stopped pulsing. No doubt there'd been an epic screwup somewhere and Captain Poole would be looking for somebody's head on a plate later, especially if it had harmed one of his crew.

As they drew closer, he watched her brace against the end of the truss and push off for the medical module. She flew across the last ten meters or so and absorbed the impact with her arms, her body swinging about as she pulled herself to a stop against a handrail. Her umbilical looped and coiled around her, which she scrambled to gather and get out of the way. He could sense the frustration in her movements despite the cumbersome suit encasing her. "From now on I think we stick with the MMUs," she grumbled. They'd saved time prepping for this spacewalk by not having to prep the self-contained maneuvering and life-support units, but the cost of being tied to the ship was now painfully apparent.

Marshall tapped back against the hand controllers, which brought him to a stop. Without a word, he unhooked the tether connecting him as Riley's form went sailing by. Rosie reached out to stop him as he flew into the open hatch. "How's your O_2, sir?"

Marshall looked down at his chest pack, confirming its gauge against the display projected in his visor. "Fifty percent."

"Good. You might need it."

"For how long?"

She clipped Riley to a restraint. "Depends on how much hydrazine residue I find, sir. Hold the chief still for me, please." He heard a sharp whistle in the background as she unhooked the lead for her umbilical. As she plugged the hose into a nearby port, he took the loose umbilical line and pushed it out of the way. They could gather it up from the airlock later.

Rosie punched the quick-release latch to open up a small orange locker marked HAZMAT RESPONSE and took out a testing kit. She activated its chemical sniffer and began sweeping it over Riley's still form. She then went to remove a pair of heavy shears from a nearby first-aid cabinet.

Marshall was alarmed. "You're cutting him out of his suit? We're still in vacuum!"

"Have to, sir. Gotta get the contaminated bits out of here first."

"He could lose his leg!"

"That damage is done, sir," she said calmly. "If he breathes in hydrazine residue, he'll lose a lot more than that. Now keep him still, please." She jammed the open shears into the outer shell just above the patch Marshall had applied, then moved to cut completely around his thigh. "Okay, now you pull away." She grabbed his boot and tugged in the opposite direction. Dual layers of the outer shell came free which she tossed outside in one smooth motion. Riley's leg, now in his exposed inner pressure and cooling garment, hung free. She circled him at arm's length, searching for any other signs of blistered fabric and making one more sweep with the chemical sniffer.

She then turned to Marshall, looking him up and down. "You're next, sir. Spin for me."

Marshall pushed against a wall with his fingertips and turned about, holding his breath as she swept a fresh testing kit over him.

"I think you're good." She reached for the big hatch and slid it into place, then spun down the latch. "Barn door secure. Pressurizing."

The next day, Marshall checked up on Riley in the med bay. He'd thought it impossible to make the area any cleaner than it already was, yet his spacers had somehow managed. Its ever-present antiseptic aroma seemed especially sharp now, and he wondered how they'd found time to scrub the place down with all of the other activity going on. Had some crewmembers come in here to prep the compartment while they'd been scrambling after Riley outside? One of their own—their chief, no less—was about to become a patient. Of course they'd wanted the space squared away.

Riley floated in a sleep restraint mounted along a wall, a tangle of hoses and leads snaking around him in zero g. The thin line of a nasal cannula looped around his head and beneath his nose while an inflated sleeve encased his injured leg: oxygen therapy for his vacuum- and chemical-damaged tissue.

His violaceous leg ballooned against the transparent therapy sleeve, a result of burst capillaries from exposure to vacuum. Marshall deliberately averted his gaze from Riley's swollen limb, focusing on the chief's tired face instead. The chief's eyes were bleary from either sedation or exhaustion; Marshall decided the distinction didn't matter.

"How are you feeling, Chief?" A stupid question, and the only one that came to mind.

"My lungs feel like sandpaper and my leg's one giant bruise but other than that I'm good, sir."

Marshall eyed his leg and grimaced. "No marathons for you for a while, I think."

"I hate running anyway. Only reason I do it is 'cause they make me. I keep hoping they'll add fishing to the annual fitness test, but it never happens." He looked Marshall square in the eye. "You shouldn't have come after me, sir. At least not until they got those thrusters isolated. That was foolhardy."

"I didn't have much choice," Marshall said. "You didn't activate your SAFER pack."

"I would have, just as soon as I got my suit patched."

"You were passing out, Chief."

Riley closed his eyes in submission. "Okay, so there's that. Still, we could've lost two people out there, sir."

"Three, sir. I had to stop Rosie from going after you while that quad was still firing." The Chief looked alarmed. Before he could say anything, Marshall held up a hand to stop him. "Would you have done any different?"

"You got me again." Riley stretched against his restraints and winced. He took a labored breath. "Do they know what happened yet?"

Marshall shook his head, wincing at his freshly wrapped ribs. Bruised, though he couldn't imagine how they'd feel if broken. "They're still troubleshooting, but obviously some fail-safes were missed in the ground sims. The guidance routine took over, tried to orient the ship as if it were executing the program live instead of running a QC check."

Riley lowered his voice. "Skipper's got to be pissed."

"Epically pissed," Marshall said. "He's going to have someone's ass for sure when we get back. Flynn was in the seat when it happened, and word is he's being sent back to oversee the beatdown."

"About that, sir . . ." Riley patted the sleeve around his leg. "If he's going, you realize this means you're staying. I sure can't, especially if we're expecting rescue sorties."

Marshall's eyes widened. "Nobody said anything to me," he demurred. "I just figured Commander Wicklund would end up back on the crew roster."

"The XO's a good fleet officer," Riley said, "but they'll need EVA specialists on this mission."

"I'm not one of those either."

"You are now, sir. That was some real Hollywood shit you did out there."

"Captain Poole's going to want more experienced officers. I'm not getting my hopes up," he said, embarrassed to admit it had been something he hoped for. Between Riley's injury and Flynn's misfortune it was a huge opening, and why wouldn't he want to go in either man's place? It would be their first mission into interplanetary space, sent to rescue a couple he'd been following near obsessively since they'd left Earth nearly two months ago. Yet this wasn't about what he wanted—it was deadly serious work, as he'd just experienced firsthand.

As if reading his mind, Riley gave him an equally serious look. "What's more important is the other spacers like you, and you're earning their respect. Have you checked the manifest lately?"

Marshall pulled out his tablet and looked up the latest mission plan. When he tapped the manifest icon, his name appeared at the top of the list.

He was going.

❁ 17 ❁

Special Aerospace Mission Twelve-Zero-Five, a chartered Clipper from Polaris Aerospace Lines, was almost invisible as it approached the *Borman* while still in Earth's night side. Its black and gray color scheme was a product of necessity, the spaceplane's belly being covered with carbon composite heat shielding and its upper fuselage skinned with titanium alloys. The curves of its lifting-body fuselage blended into clipped delta wings, and the company's swooping blue and white logo on its twin tails stood out against the plane's dark silhouette, prominently illuminated by its position lights.

Poole was in the dome, personally guiding them in. "SAM 1205, we have you in sight. Still ugly as ever."

"On the contrary," the pilot replied, "this has to be the prettiest bird in the sky."

"I wasn't talking about the plane."

"Nice to see you too, Simon. Keeping busy?"

"The new guy's giving me fits," he said wearily. "Just can't find good junior officers anymore."

"Sometimes you have to wish they'd bring back the old naval traditions, like public floggings."

"Sounds like something a jarhead would say."

"And here I thought a squid would appreciate the sentiment."

"I'll let you see for yourself." Simon switched tones, signaling it was time to get back to being professional. "SAM 1205, you're inside the bubble at Waypoint One. Cleared to approach."

"SAM 1205 has the ball. See you in a few."

❈ ❈ ❈

When Marshall opened the airlock door, he was greeted by a familiar face: puffier than he remembered thanks to the fluid rebalancing of zero gravity, but the piercing gray eyes and unruly black hair they shared (though a good bit thinner and shot through with streaks of white) was like looking in a mirror.

"Permission to come aboard, Ensign Hunter?"

"*Dad?*"

"I'll take that as a yes, then." Ryan Hunter pulled himself through the hatch and looked up to find the ship's bell. He gave the lanyard two firm tugs, announcing his arrival. He gave Marshall a knowing wink. "Somehow I knew Simon would put one of these up here."

"What are you doing here?"

"Just another government evac charter. They contracted us to come pick up your crewmates and those solar flare victims. You thought I'd pass this trip up?"

"I guess I hadn't thought . . ." Marshall stammered.

Ryan put a steady hand on his son's shoulder. "So I've heard. That was quite a stunt you pulled off yesterday."

Had it only been yesterday? It felt like at least a week. "Had to be done. The other spacer was pinned between two active thrusters and the chief wasn't responding."

"So you just leapt into the void, hell for leather?" The twinkle in his eyes signaled that he wasn't that upset. "Never mind. You can tell me the details later, and I promise it stays between us. Your mother doesn't need to know."

Marshall heaved out a relieved sigh. "I appreciate that." He waited for Ryan's copilot and loadmaster to follow him through the airlock. "Come on, I'll show you around."

Rumors, valid or otherwise, spread quickly among such a small crew and in fact Marshall was beginning to wonder if he'd been the only person aboard who hadn't known his father would be piloting the Clipper that was taking Riley and the others back to Earth. By the time they'd made their rounds, everyone aboard had met their civilian guests and heard at least one threat to relate embarrassing stories from his childhood. That didn't end when they arrived at their last stop, the command deck. "Skipper's in the cupola," Marshall said, pointing to a pair of feet clad in sneakers dangling out of the opening.

"I can tell," Ryan said, and raised his voice. "He's still the only astro I know who wears shoes in orbit."

The sneakers disappeared as Poole tucked and rolled, his ballcap-covered head emerging from the dome. "I'm a clumsy S.O.B. and it hurts less when I bang my toes against a bulkhead." He flew down from the cupola to give Ryan a firm handshake and a slap on the shoulder. "Good to see you." He looked past him to Marshall and handed him a slip of paper from the command deck's small thermal printer. "That'll be all, Mister Hunter. I'll take it from here. I believe you're needed back in medical."

Marshall quickly read the message. "Aye, sir, that I am," he said, and headed back down into the gangway tunnel after giving his dad a wink.

Ryan inclined his head back in his son's direction. "I was telling your young ensign here there was no way I wasn't going to take this trip." He lowered his voice, keeping the rest between them. "How's he handling not being in a flight billet?"

"Somehow I just knew you'd ask that." Simon looked away, turning pensive. "You know, I once had a former aviator assigned to my boat. Lost his medical and thought submarines sounded interesting. Aced the school, but he never could break his old habits when he got to the fleet. Too used to being in charge of his own machine, I guess. That doesn't work on a crewed vessel, under water or in space." He turned back to Ryan. "I haven't seen that so far, maybe because he hasn't been on his own yet. If he's bitching, he's keeping it to himself. No less than I'd expect from any of my officers."

Ryan beamed. "Appreciate that, Simon. And thanks for looking out for him."

"Oh, I'm not done. Clearly there's been a parenting failure," Simon taunted. "The kid keeps trying to get himself killed."

Ryan sighed. "He's always been like that. His mother didn't think he'd make it to first grade."

"And how is Marcy?"

"Excited. Worried sick. Everything in between." His tone suggested she wasn't alone. "You guys are going an awfully long way, you know. On really short notice."

Simon shrugged. "Part of the job. We expected something like this would happen eventually. Hell, I started running mission scenarios as soon as the Jiangs announced their wild-ass expedition. Already had a plan in my back pocket that Fleet HQ approved because they didn't have anything better."

"Sounds like they're swamped down there. There's already talk of Congress funding more ships like this one."

Simon nodded. If that was news to him, he didn't show it. "We have to be prepared. It's only a matter of time before somebody thinks it's in their interest to get aggressive up here. There's already enough people with plenty of money and big ideas, and trouble seems to always follow." His eyes bored in on Ryan's. "Speaking of which, have you met your passenger yet?"

Ryan knew he wasn't talking about the crewmembers he was taking earthward. "Lesko? Saw him in the med module, along with that spacer Marshall went after."

Simon arched an eyebrow, looking for a reaction: *And?*

"Little squirrely, isn't he? I mean, he went through some pretty hairy times up here." He gave Simon a knowing look. "But then, so have we."

"We're trained for it, though. You know their story, right? This kid got a few weeks of total-immersion training, then he's strapped into a capsule and shot up into GEO to revive a dead satellite. Ended up getting three other people killed and nearly did himself in, too."

"GEO sats still aren't cheap," Ryan said. "A lot of awfully expensive birds have been going dark lately. If they've found a way to bring some of them back, there could be a lot of money in it."

"I always thought that most of the dead ones could be serviced remotely by other satellites. Getting to geosynch takes almost as much delta-v as going to the Moon. Plus you have more exposure to the nasty parts of the Van Allen belts, which they just had a hard lesson in." Simon crossed his arms. "You know the commercial side of this better than I. Who the hell takes that kind of risk?"

"That's the downside of all *this* becoming part of the landscape," Ryan said, circling his hands for emphasis. "More people come up here thinking they've invented the next killer app. Some of them are occasionally right."

"Not everyone is an Elon Musk or Art Hammond," Simon agreed. "But there's a boatload of P. T. Barnums."

⁂

Floating down the connecting tunnel, Marshall stopped at the medical module and began to pull himself inside when he saw Garver hovering in front of their passenger, Nick Lesko, in what appeared to be a tense conversation.

Lesko was agitated, turning his body back and forth in an awkward imitation of pacing in zero g. "You've already been giving me radiation meds. I'm telling you, I can't spend two weeks in the hospital! That's not going to happen!"

Garver waved his hands in a "calm down" motion. "Petty Officer Rosado already explained, Mr. Lesko. The potassium iodide treatments were precautionary, and your body may react differently once you're back in gravity. We're not equipped to provide a full assessment of your exposure, particularly your bone marrow."

"I'll worry about that with my own doctor when I'm back on Earth and have time."

"You need testing and treatment right away, Mr. Lesko, by the same protocols our spacewalkers will have to go through. You need to make time. Schriever's base hospital has access to all kinds of specialists in radiation sickness."

"Lots of people do lots of things, like me. My ... sponsors ... need me back on the job as soon as my feet touch dirt. Why should I listen to you?"

"Because you really don't want leukemia," Marshall interjected. "Before you closed up your storm shelter, you were exposed to dangerously high doses of ionizing radiation, as was our crewmen who went after you."

"I'm not sick," he protested.

"Of course you're not. Yet. Let's see how you feel when you're back in gravity. If you start feeling dizzy or nauseated, then let the medics take you to the base hospital. Until we can treat you for radiation exposure, you're potentially a hazard to others." Which wasn't exactly true, but he was banking on Lesko's ignorance.

"What, are you saying I'm radioactive?"

"Just your stool," Marshall said. "That's how the treatments will pass contaminants out of your body. The docs will want to check that to see how you're progressing."

"I'm supposed to believe they're going to test my turds?"

"You can believe whatever you want," Marshall shrugged. "I'm just telling you how this is going to go. Now, you have one choice: you ride back to Earth on that Clipper, or you're stuck with us for the next couple of months."

"You mean back to a military base," Lesko sneered.

"I also meant it wasn't really a choice. We won't have the resources to keep a passenger onboard with us for that long. You'll be a literal waste of oxygen while you just sit here dying, either of boredom or cancer."

"So where does that leave me?"

"It leaves you in the first-class cabin of a chartered Clipper back to Earth, which is pretty much *all* first class. Uncle Sam just bought you a six-figure ticket home, and you're taking it. If that comes with strings attached, then I suggest you remember how you got here." He paused to let that sink in. "So let me break this down for you, Mr. Lesko: You're going back to Earth on the ride we're providing. You can either do that willingly, or we will sedate you right now and strap you in. Personally, I'd rather be able to look out the window instead of drooling all over myself."

Lesko steamed, his eyes darting between Marshall and the master chief. "Damned sailors...spacers...whatever, I don't even know what to call you people."

"*Rescuers* would be a good start," Marshall said. "You could still be stuck in that docking tunnel up in GEO instead of getting ready to go home."

Lesko chewed on his bottom lip as he thought it over. "Yeah, okay. You've got a deal."

Marshall looked him in the eye. "Good. Now, follow our people down to the forward node and get yourself seated. You guys are leaving within the hour."

Lesko gathered what few items he had and clumsily pushed his way into the corridor.

"Well done, sir," Garver said quietly after Lesko made his way forward. "He's been in space for three weeks. He's going to feel dizzy and nauseous no matter what." That he would think it was from radiation poisoning and not simply his body reacquainting itself with gravity would ensure he ended up in a secure wing of the base hospital. "I was wondering how we'd coerce him to not feeling, well, coerced."

"You already got the order from the captain, then?"

Garver waved his tablet. "Skipper texted me a couple of minutes before you got here, sir. They'll have that young man buttoned up nice and tight once he's dirt-side."

"Did he really have that much radiation exposure?" Marshall wondered, unsure himself but it was the best card to play at the time. Lesko still seemed to have no idea of what he'd gotten himself into up here.

Garver shook his head. "Judging by his dosimeter and what he told us, most of it came at the very beginning. He got zapped a little while their airlock was open to space and picked up some more while he was camped out with you guys on *Specter*. He's at a higher risk of cancer but it's not enough to get anyone's panties in a twist. The powers that be just want us to keep an eye on him."

"Nothing came up in his background when we brought him aboard," Marshall said. "But how deep do those manifest checks go?"

"Not very," Garver said. "Nothing came up on his dead crewmates with one exception. Two of them are former commercial astronauts, hired for their expertise. The pilot lost his first-class medical a few years ago so he could only fly private clients like this one. The spacewalker was a freelance contractor, former ESA astronaut."

"So who's the exception?"

"The young guy you found in Stardust, William Burns. He apparently liked to go by the hacker handle 'Xenos.' He had a few run-ins with cybercrime units in college, mostly nuisance stuff. Looks like he wanted legit work so Lesko's people brought him on as a programmer."

"Lesko's an odd duck," Marshall said. "Even for this type of work."

"*Especially* for this type of work, sir. I've seen every variation of nerd there is, but he's a different animal. Like he ought to be running a casino, not a space mission."

"On-orbit satellite repair isn't something I'd expect for a mob front operation."

Marshall met his father back in the forward docking node where his Clipper was berthed. His loadmaster was finishing the grim task of placing Nick Lesko's companions in the spaceplane's aft cargo bay.

"Is this a first?" Marshall asked. "Transporting human remains, I mean."

Ryan's eyes grew distant, sorrowful. He shook his head. "Not at all. That's one reason I took the trip. The precautions we follow are the ones I developed."

From experience, Marshall realized. As he'd grown up, he'd found his father open to answering nearly any question, but much remained unspoken. As he watched his father inspect their manifest and reentry plan, Marshall noticed his demeanor change. The gleam in his eyes when he'd first arrived was gone. His eyes turned dark, focused and intent. Already on a tight schedule, Marshall was beginning to see how working in space seemed to compress time itself—not from any weird relativistic physics, it was all just how much *work* even simple tasks could take. While perhaps a leftover from NASA days, activities in orbit were planned down to the minute because they'd learned whatever they did would eat up just about every minute assigned to them.

The passengers—Marshall's crewmates—had quietly made their way through the airlock and into the cabin. He'd expected nothing less from professionals, though he also knew none of them wanted to be rotated home right now. Even Lesko seemed more reserved than before. Had Garver or Rosie managed to sedate him somehow? He acknowledged Marshall with a curt nod and floated through the open hatchway and into his seat without protest.

After conferring with the Clipper's loadmaster and flight attendant, Commander Wicklund was the last to board. He swiped at his tablet, sending a file to Ryan's. "There's some last-minute cargo," he explained. "Will that be a problem?"

"Doubtful. We're pretty light." Ryan added up the additional mass. "A few extra boxes and bags are no big deal. We just need time to secure the load." He pulled up the passenger manifest. "Looks like all your people are accounted for."

"I lined 'em up and did a head count before they boarded. I'll do another once I'm seated just to make sure there's no stowaways left back here," he said, only half joking. "There's not a single person on your plane who wants to be there." He shot a knowing glance at Marshall. "Except one." And with that, he floated through the hatch, pushed off the ceiling, and twirled into the half-full cabin to land in an open seat directly behind Lesko. After a quick head count, he pulled on his shoulder and lap belts and closed his eyes, patiently awaiting their departure.

Ryan turned back to his son. "Not very subtle."

"I'm still learning to read him," Marshall said under his breath. "I'm never sure how much of it is intentional."

Ryan laughed. "If he's even a halfway decent XO, it's *all* intentional. But you didn't hear that from me."

An awkward silence passed between them, as happens when final goodbyes are imminent. There could be no putting it off; the strictures of orbital mechanics were more pitiless than any airline schedule. Ryan Hunter and his Clipper could stay up here for days, but if *Borman* were to meet its schedule then they had to separate on this orbit.

Ryan spoke first. "I was telling Simon—excuse me, the captain— your mother's worried sick."

"She's been up here enough to understand the risks, Dad."

"Exactly."

That took Marshall by surprise. "You're worried too?"

"Your mom's worried. I'm *apprehensive*. There's a difference. When it comes to your kids, some things stick with you forever." Ryan looked away for a moment, as if searching for something in the distant past he could grasp to better explain the here and now. "You were still little, not long after we moved to Colorado. We were looking through that old telescope of mine, and you asked me if you could go to the Moon like I did."

"There's a lot from back then I try not to remember." Marshall had never been able to fully bury his memories of the Comet Weatherby impact off Florida. A therapist might call that healthy, but neither he nor his mother had voluntarily been back to the ocean since then. "But I do remember that scope."

"I was still raw from that little escapade myself," Ryan admitted, thinking he'd lost his young family while in a fight for his own life on the far side of the Moon. He locked eyes with his son. "I didn't want you going anywhere near there, not like I did. Now you're going even farther, into who knows what."

"That was different," Marshall said with the bravado of inexperienced youth. "We're on a rescue mission. It's what we do."

"I know," Ryan said. "That's how it started out with me, too." He put his hands on Marshall's shoulders. "Just keep your wits about you and listen to Simon."

"I kind of have to, Dad," Marshall said glibly. "He's the captain."

"I don't mean follow orders. Pay attention to him. That man has forgotten more about spacefaring than most career astronauts *think* they know." And with that, Ryan gave his son a tight hug. When he pulled away, Marshall noticed him wipe at an eye and give a silent *you got this* nod before pushing away for his own spacecraft.

Marshall watched as his father curled around a corner to disappear down the tunnel. "Bye, Dad," he whispered to himself.

❂ 18 ❂

Try as she might, Roberta could not stay focused on her new tasks in ROV control despite—or because of—the recent crushing workload. She kept glancing over her shoulder at the row of consoles at the opposite end of the room: Fleet Operations, which as of now worked exclusively as the *Borman*'s mission control team. The ship was designed to be mostly autonomous, in anticipation of a small fleet of them to eventually be in service keeping the space lanes between Earth and Moon safe. Having only one such ship in orbit allowed the team to pay an inordinate amount of attention to every detail aboard, which she suspected was steadily driving the crew nuts.

"Something funny?" Ivey asked from behind her. "Because you're grinning like an idiot."

Roberta snapped out of it, making her distraction even more obvious. "Nothing. Sorry. Let myself get sidetracked."

He looked past her to Fleet Ops. "Could be worse. You could be riding a console over there and imagining what it's like aboard ship. At least here you're getting real work done."

"Am I?" she wondered aloud, immediately regretting it. Marshall's kvetching about "garbage duty" was starting to gain traction in her mind. "Sorry, Lieutenant."

He flopped into an empty chair beside her. "Look at it this way— if we don't keep these orbits clear, we're eventually going to end up with such a mess that nobody's going anywhere for a long time."

"That's what sidetracked me," she said, deciding that it was time to share her concerns. She unwrapped a stick of gum and began chewing, helping her concentration. "It's the big picture I don't think

179

anyone's put together yet. Check this out." She grabbed the trackpad by his keyboard and began slewing the view on a monitor, zooming out to a wide view of Earth. It appeared to be blanketed with satellites and orbital debris, an exaggerated but accurate depiction of the threat. "There was already enough junk in orbit to keep us busy for years, then that CME came along and created a real mess."

"Sure. More debris to move around or deorbit. But that's just a better view of how big the problem is. We'll be at this for weeks."

"That's the forest. Let me show you a few trees." Roberta began popping her gum more rapidly as she grew animated. She filtered the graphic for specific dates. "Look at this, three weeks ago. Random distribution, as you'd expect." It was the usual cloud of discarded rocket parts and disabled satellites. "Compare it to right now." When she scrolled ahead, more red dots appeared in the cloud of pixels around Earth.

"Back where we started," Ivey said. "Less random distribution because half of them were shielded behind Earth. It's just a bigger mess."

"And that's where I think people are losing the thread of the story. All you see is the mess. Look at this." She filtered the data once more and the cloud changed. Suddenly two clusters of disabled satellites appeared in geosynchronous orbit.

"Okay, that's weird. So this is before the CME?"

"Negatory," she said, popping her gum again for effect as she grew more confident. "This was *yesterday*." She scrolled back some more, and the angry red dots started to disappear one by one. "And this was three days ago."

"Wait a sec..." he said. "It's expanding geometrically. One dead bird, then two, then four."

"All centered around specific bands of longitude," Roberta noted. "No way this is random."

"Okay, maybe you've found something. So what's common about those regions?" Jacob wondered. "Any ground stations report being hacked?"

"Not a one," she said dejectedly, and pointed to a catalog of satellite data along one side of the graphic. "These are the only commonalities I've found."

He studied the roster of dead equipment. "All commercial birds.

Geospatial or communications. Only a couple weather sats, certainly nothing military. We'd have heard about it."

"I'll bet that's how it's escaped anyone's notice," she said triumphantly. "Especially with the cover from that solar storm."

"Really good cover." He realized they'd crossed a logical threshold by assuming these were deliberate events and not random chance. There could be a benign cause, but that grew less likely as more satellites went offline.

"That's what makes me question my own judgment. You can't engineer a CME. We can barely predict them."

Ivey seemed to stare through her, thinking. "True, but a good tactician knows how to take advantage of the weather. That goes for on Earth or in space. My guess is the flare created enough chaos that whoever is doing this decided they were safe to ramp up their schedule. I'll run this up the chain. Maybe the S-2 can make some sense of it." He unfolded himself from the chair and clapped her on the shoulder. "Welcome to spook world."

With half of the ship's complement gone, what was left of the crew had assembled in the control deck for departure. It hadn't been ordered, or even suggested, it had only felt like the proper place to be for their first Earth departure burn.

Being one of only three officers remaining aboard, Marshall had become keenly aware of the single task that had seemed to eat up most of Captain Poole's and Lieutenant Wylie's attention: recalibrating the guidance platform after their near-disastrous test run. It might not have been fair, but it had, by necessity, left Marshall in charge of most of the remaining pre-departure work with the NCOs.

The only reason they were still proceeding was that, in truth, the nav program had performed exactly as it was supposed to *if* they'd in fact meant to execute it. That it hadn't recognized it was in test mode, instead thinking it was supposed to orient the ship for an actual burn, was suspected to be the fault of an overworked programmer in a hurry. Flynn was no doubt turning over every rock in HQ, if only to find the moron ultimately responsible for getting him taken off the mission roster.

If Poole hadn't already gamed out this particular scenario ahead of time, he would have been rightly suspicious of the guidance upload from Ops. That the beginning and end state vectors almost precisely matched what he'd worked out on his own forced him to trust it, though he was wary of letting it run his ship on autopilot again. Time was never really on their side, and it was even less so now. Their departure was calculated for maximum efficiency, and each additional revolution around Earth spent troubleshooting software represented time not spent en route to their objective.

It highlighted the risks of such a hurried mission in a way that had left a bad taste in his mouth. Simon Poole's hand had been forced, a position he never enjoyed being in. Hovering at the computer-animated navigation and maneuvering board, Marshall could feel the tension emanating from him like heat from a radiator. He'd turned quiet, and when he did speak his words were clipped, his tone abrupt.

"Mister Wylie, I show five minutes until EDI. Do we have final approval from Fleet Ops?"

"That's affirmative, sir. Control says we're go."

"Any gripes with the ship?"

"Negative. Board is green, sir."

"Very well. Chief Garver?"

"Reactors and turbopumps are warmed up to operating temperature, Captain. Control rods checked nominal."

He looked up at Marshall. "Mister Hunter?"

"All modules are secure, sir. I checked each one myself."

"Very well." He checked his watch against the countdown timer and looked for the others to do the same. "Time hack at four minutes... and *hack*." If all else failed, they could time their maneuvers using their own watches—highly unlikely, but an old habit he'd long ago insisted his crew adopt. If anything, it kept them ever mindful of critical events.

Simon directed Marshall's attention to the "Mo Board" with an affability in his voice that Marshall hadn't heard in days. "I already assume everyone's got their shit together, I just need to hear it one more time since the XO's not here to bust your balls." A thin smile crept across his face. "Now, look here." He pointed at the circle of their orbit around Earth and the point where a long, graceful curve pulled away from it on a tangent: their path to asteroid RQ39. "This is where things get dicey. It might be a big sky up there, but it's awfully crowded down here in low orbit. We're going to be burning for almost two hours and I don't want us inadvertently running into anything." The white curve representing their trajectory was notably wider than their current orbit. "That's our zone of uncertainty. It'll get smaller as we burn and get our final plot nailed down." He circled a finger above it. "For the time being, we could be anywhere in that path so we don't want any space junk or wayward satellites crossing it. That's why timing is everything—we put this off until the next orbit, the whole picture changes." Poole looked up at him to make sure he understood.

"I believe I get it, sir."

Poole smiled. "Good. You're manning the board, Mr. Hunter. I'll be up in the dome. Captain's privilege."

Marshall went slack-jawed as he watched Poole disappear into the cupola. Behind him, he heard a chuckle from Wylie. Soon after, the ship began to rumble with the ignition of its nuclear engines.

The hunter had laid in wait, careful to keep any movement within its prey's blind spot as it drew closer. It was now in position to strike, near enough to close in for its killing stroke in a single swift move.

After perfecting its techniques on more obscure victims, the revived SAMCOM-3—now known as "Necromancer" to its new operators—had stalked its most prized trophy for days. Just as big-game hunters might exhaust themselves chasing pronghorns or mule deer up and down mountain slopes, so had Necromancer nearly exhausted itself chasing the American KH-13 Keyhole satellite uphill.

While there were no physical mountains to be scaled in orbit, being inclined to a different plane on Earth presented a similar challenge: Necromancer had begun as a communications satellite, spent and left for dead in the graveyard orbit, out of the way above Earth's equator. Its prey was much higher, being inclined nearly seventy degrees to the equator: three-fourths of the way to the North Pole. Thanks to Earth's rotation, it took considerably more energy to launch a large satellite into such a highly inclined orbit compared to just going to the equator. Already being parked above the equator, it had taken a considerable amount of energy to move Necromancer into position. Its new operators on Earth had known this and planned its maneuvers carefully—its prior kills had been necessary practice, while they had hoarded its precious new propellant for this final, great hunt.

Keyhole-13 would be quite the trophy. In essence a giant Earth-observing telescope like Hubble in reverse, its location in sun-synchronous orbit put it in a position to gather detailed images of any desired target on Earth with a massive three-meter primary mirror and electro-optical compensation for atmospheric distortions.

The hunt's goal was to do much more than disable the nuisance Keyhole. This prey was too valuable to simply kill and keep for a trophy. Killing satellites was easy, if messy, whereas disabling them undetected took more finesse and a lot of electromagnetic energy. Both were easily traceable to their source, which would not do outside of an actual shooting war.

Repurposing a complex, billion-dollar spy satellite was an entirely different matter. It was far better to let your opponent do the work if in the end you could benefit from it instead of remaining its target. Rope-a-dope, as the Americans liked to say.

Necromancer, of course, wasn't doing this on its own. Its controllers had carefully planned every maneuver to bring it to this point, hovering fifty meters above its prey, away from the line of sight of its powerful cameras and massive primary mirror. Necromancer had gone completely passive, emitting no electromagnetic energy that might give it away, drawing as close as its operators had dared bring it without activating its own cameras and sensors.

For two days it had stalked Keyhole from its orbital perch, watching its prey carry on completely unaware, like an unsuspecting buck at a poacher's feed trough. Its giant solar wings constantly rotated to catch sunlight, and occasionally its dish antenna would turn to maintain datalinks, or the telescope's large trap-door protective cover would open and shut as it engaged a target on the ground. And Necromancer sat and waited.

That signal came as *Borman* left Earth orbit. Clear of any potential interference, Necromancer's controllers began to bring the satellite back to life.

Its operators turned on a forward-looking video feed. If KH-13 sniffed out this new electromagnetic smell, it didn't show. No movement about the flywheels on its rotation axis, no puffs of maneuvering jets or reorienting of antenna. No doubt its controllers would notice the nearby EM emissions, but they would be barely distinguishable from random background noise. They would be slow to figure out there was a nearby threat, because how could there be? What they were attempting was impossible.

Yet not according to the months of carefully executed rehearsals. In fact, the video feed from Necromancer was remarkably close to the computer-generated imagery they'd practiced with.

With a gentle pulse of its thrusters, Necromancer moved from its perch. Its controller, an experienced spacecraft pilot, gingerly tapped a pair of joysticks at his station on Earth, watching the target grow on his screen. He waited until the last second to activate a lidar unit that Nick Lesko's crew had attached to the former SAMCOM satellite, needing the laser-ranging data for what they called the "terminal" phase.

Stopping at precisely two meters from the Keyhole's support bus, Necromancer's skeletal manipulator arms unfolded silently. Each grasped service railings mounted along opposite sides of the satellite, positioning it squarely in front of the Keyhole's comm antenna. Soon it began emitting its own modulating signal centered on 60 gigahertz, ensuring it overwhelmed any competing traffic with the network of relay satellites used to control it.

Necromancer's operators were now in control of a KH-13 spy satellite.

Roberta had been resisting the temptation to eavesdrop on the Borman's control team, as she was becoming swamped with her own work. They could take care of their own problems without her shoving her nose in their business, she figured. It was dramatic, it was no doubt exciting for the people involved, but in the end this was why the ship had been commissioned in the first place: A couple of high rollers had gotten themselves into a fix, and ultimately it was up to the US taxpayer to come to their rescue. She wondered if they'd get a bill, like for an ambulance ride.

It was an amusing mental diversion, but her concerns had been more numerous if not quite as dramatic. There were now fully one dozen ridiculously expensive satellites out of action in geosynchronous orbit, concentrated on two fairly narrow bands of longitude over both Western and Eastern hemispheres. All of them civilian, mostly communications with a few remote-sensing birds in the mix. While not leaving their customers completely blind, it still represented a loss of capability not easily replaced.

Yet other than the comm angle, she hadn't been able to determine a pattern. And she was becoming increasingly convinced there *was* a pattern. This was too much, concentrated in locations that were too specific. Somebody was disrupting GEO, and the solar flare event had created enough chaos to cover their tracks.

Nobody could plan for that, she knew. They'd gotten lucky. If anything, maybe it had led them to overplaying their hand. Whatever their goal was, they'd gotten greedy.

That was reflected by the latest satellite to go dark, which had finally gotten the brass's attention: they'd lost control of a major asset over Asia, a KH-13 bird in a high inclination orbit that gave them access to high-resolution visuals of much of the world's more interesting locales, at least from a military-intelligence perspective.

They'd lost its telemetry, and it had not responded to repeated tasking orders. The Keyhole was, for all they could tell, dead in space. Roberta suspected it had not died of natural causes.

Of course, she knew none of this through official channels. It had all been compartmentalized to the point of absurdity, as she could watch the reactions of the Keyhole control team and see that 13 had been lined out of the tasking order as if it were simply down for maintenance, like a software upload.

Ivey pulled up next to her. "I don't think we're going to be getting any help from S-2," he said, as if reading her mind. "It's all hands on deck in there right now, trying to find out what happened to that Keyhole."

"So we're supposed to stick with cleaning up trash in orbit and not ask too many questions," she said, her irritation mounting.

"You hear anything from your friend on the *Borman*?"

Funny you should ask, she thought. "No, and I haven't wanted to bother him. I was thinking about wandering over by their control team just to see what I can pick up."

"I'll save you the trouble. Apparently their XO and half the crew are being sent back here so they can make weight for the sprint out to RQ39. Landing at Denver on a chartered Polaris Clipper. They're keeping them down here on temporary duty until next month."

"Interesting," Roberta said, "but not very."

Ivey grinned, about to get one up on her. "You're getting tunnel vision. Remember that rescue mission they did up in GEO? They're putting the survivor in our base hospital. Something about treating him for radiation poisoning."

Her mouth twisted with skepticism. "That sounds like a load of crap."

"Exactly," Ivey said. "Lone survivor of a GEO satellite repair gone bad."

Her eyes widened. "You're right. I did have tunnel vision. What's this guy's name?"

Ivey pulled up the mission manifest from the day's tasking order. "Lesko. Nicholas Lesko."

Nick Lesko tugged at the tape around his IV, more annoyed by the adhesive's effect on his skin than the 18-gauge needle in his arm. How much fluid could they pump into him anyway before he started looking like a puffer fish? They'd poked and prodded him enough to feel like one.

A nurse covered in a thick paper gown, her face visible behind a plastic shield, had come in with more needles. Another round of blood samples, and another injection into his IV line. "Potassium iodide," she said, "to help your recovery."

"Couldn't I just eat a banana?" Lesko asked. "Don't those have potassium?"

She smiled with the bland condescension reserved for people who couldn't know better. "Potassium *iodide*," she emphasized, "to help your thyroid." Finished, she pulled out another injector and plunged it into the port. "And this is a protein compound to stimulate white blood cell growth."

He saw the tray of tubes beside her and winced. "Maybe if you wouldn't take so much of my blood, I wouldn't need to stimulate growth."

"I'm afraid we have to, Mr. Lesko. It's the only way we can monitor your white count. That will tell us a lot about how your bone marrow is functioning." Her friendly grin disappeared. "The alternative is a marrow aspiration, where we have to drill into your bone."

His eyes widened. He had no interest in some barbarian boring a hole in his leg and sucking out his marrow through a straw. That sounded like the kind of thing the sharks did if you owed them money. "I think I get it."

"That's good," she said pleasantly, probing the crook of his elbow for a vein. "Now this won't hurt a bit."

That's what they all say, he thought, as the cold needle plunged in. She hummed some nonmelody as she swapped out tubes. He had to admit this one didn't hurt as much, never appreciating technique before now. But then he'd never spent this much time in a hospital, at least not as a patient. It was a wonder anyone made it out these places alive and in one piece, after all the poking and prodding and bad food and even worse sleep. What was with that, anyway? Didn't anyone appreciate a sick person's need for a good night's sleep? Couldn't they find a way to *not* wake him up every couple of hours?

The longer he was here, the more bored he got with the paltry TV offerings and utter lack of internet access. No 6G coverage, not even a Wi-Fi signal. His phone and laptop had both been rendered useless, probably because of all the radiation precautions—the damned walls were probably lined with lead for all he knew.

More troublesome to him was the creeping paranoia that stalked him daily. With each sniffle or passing stomach burble, he wondered if *that was it*—was that going to be the telltale sign he'd taken a fatal dose? Every time he scratched his head, he pulled his hand away warily to see if any hair had come off with it.

"All done," the nurse said, interrupting his train of thought. She held up five vials of crimson fluid. "We'll get these to the lab right away."

"Good for you," he said absentmindedly. It wasn't like they were going to come running to him with results. Nobody had told him much of anything and he didn't see any signs of that changing. He grabbed the remote and stabbed at the menu. "But I'd like it better if somebody could get me SportsCenter."

◎ 19 ◎

From the Global News Network
"It has been over a week since contact was lost with the *Prospector* spacecraft, the civilian expedition mounted by billionaire immigrants Max and Jasmine Jiang.

"The Prospector Foundation's mission control center has not only lost voice communication with the Jiangs, they have lost nearly all telemetry with the spacecraft. An active 'carrier wave,' indicating at least one ultra-high-frequency channel remains open, is their only indication that the spacecraft is in fact still there and somewhat functional. Without telemetry or voice communication, there is no way to know if the Jiangs are still alive.

"That in itself is enough to occupy the technicians in Palmdale. What has become even more troubling is the open radio channel is essentially a beacon that allows them to track the spacecraft's movement. Now due for a correction burn that would have taken them past Mars, something has altered their trajectory enough that there is now a high probability they will instead crash into the Red Planet.

"The American Space Force has dispatched their only crewed rescue spacecraft, the USS *Borman*, on a high-speed course that will intercept *Prospector* and save the Jiangs—assuming they are still alive."

The aggressive duty schedule they'd implemented to keep *Borman* running on a skeleton crew might have been exhausting if anyone had the time to realize how tired they were.

For Marshall, it had become an unexpected and exciting opportunity: For the first time, he was able to work at the pilot's station. Though it had come about by accident and absolute necessity, he relished every moment—even if it were only monitoring what the spacecraft had already been programmed to do. That was modern flying anyway: watch the machine fly itself and be prepared to intervene if it broke or tried to do something stupid.

He'd been rotating duties at the flight deck every twelve hours with Wylie, with occasional relief from Poole himself. As they'd drawn closer to their destination, that had happened more frequently: He and Wylie would have to set out with the rescue spacers aboard *Specter*, meaning they'd be doing the hard flying while leaving Poole and a couple of engineer's mates behind to mind the ship.

The tension between necessity and opportunity gnawed at him. Marshall was torn between the gravity of the task and his excitement for it. The anticipation had threatened to become all-consuming as the bright speck of RQ39 grew steadily larger—originally invisible against the background of stars, it had shone brighter than most after only a few days in transit.

They'd been traveling backward relative to their destination for days, keeping their engines pointed into the direction of travel until the time had come to decelerate and match orbits with *Prospector*. This had kept the ship and its asteroid companion out of view except from the cupola, which no one had much time to indulge themselves with. So those tantalizing views had represented only stolen moments taken from days packed with work. With the braking burn done, they'd turned *Borman* around to keep the smaller ship in view as they closed in.

Now it grew larger with each passing hour, first becoming a bright speck in the distance to now revealing its irregular, potato-like shape. The stark clarity of seeing it in airless space created an illusion that it might truly be that small, something he could reach out and grab were it not for the bright speck that now appeared near it: the still-silent *Prospector*. They'd pointed their high-gain antenna at it and began hailing it yesterday, and had so far only been answered with static.

The little bright speck hung there in the darkness like a distant ornament, a trinket waiting to be taken. Just as the asteroid they had come for grew increasingly larger as they closed in, the Jiang's distant spacecraft began to reveal its shape though it was still distant enough to remain stubbornly indistinct.

Marshall found himself spending far too much time gazing at it through the forward windows, having to force himself to bring his head inside and keep up his instrument scan. He was quickly finding the ship did a lot for itself, but he needed to be able to sense its pulse like a doctor hovering over a patient.

"Any change?"

Marshall turned to see Simon floating in through the connecting node, and was glad he'd just finished a scan—the first thing the captain asked for was a status report on his ship, and he expected details to be cited from memory.

"Relative velocity to target is ten meters per second, sir. We're due for another burn from the forward jets at the top of the hour, that'll take us down to six mps. Prop levels are—"

Simon held up a hand, stopping him short as he pulled himself into a nearby empty seat. "Not what I meant." He pointed out the window. "I'm asking about them."

Relieved, Marshall tried not to smile to himself. "Of course, sir."

Simon clapped him on the shoulder. "And lighten up a bit, Mister Hunter. Get the broomstick out of your sphincter."

"So that's why it hurts when I sit down."

"I didn't mean *all* the way out, son. You really are a chip off the old block."

"Sorry sir. Still not sure where the boundaries are."

"Eh, that's partly my fault. You just keep doing what you're doing, because you're doing fine. The only people on this boat who know we have some history are the XO and the master chief."

"That explains a lot," Marshall said, immediately wishing he hadn't. He must have been more fatigued than he thought. Still, it didn't seem to faze Simon—though not much did.

"You think the XO didn't want you here?"

"I did get that impression, yes sir."

He laughed. "Wicklund didn't have a problem with it. The chief was the one who was worried."

Marshall did a double take. "Seriously . . . sir?"

"Surprised?" Simon asked, looking amused. "It's because they're both damned good at their jobs. You'll find a lot of leadership is just about learning to play the role, especially when you don't feel like it. A good XO is *always* hard on junior officers, and a good chief is *always* there to mentor them."

"So the chief—?"

"Don't take it personally. He was more concerned about how it might look for me than he was about you. That's the other thing a good chief does: He keeps the new guys from making his skipper look bad." He gave Marshall a moment to digest that, then shot a glance up at the overhead. "So you haven't been up in the dome recently?"

Marshall gestured at the windows in front of him. "The view's pretty good here, sir."

"Maybe, but the optical telescope's up there and I want a better look at that ship." Simon pushed away with his fingertips and flew up into the cupola, motioning for Marshall to follow him. "Turn off the overhead lights on your way up."

He looked around the flight deck—should he be leaving it unoccupied? And why was he even questioning it when the captain had just invited him up into the dome? He made one last instrument scan, memorizing each reading before pushing out of his seat and floating up through the opening overhead. He remembered to snap off the ambient lighting, leaving the control deck dark but for the dim glow of instrument screens.

Marshall had deliberately refrained from coming up here, afraid he'd indulge himself too much and let some critical task escape his attention. As the protective shutters outside folded open like flower petals, he was reminded of why.

Simon had kept the cupola's interior lights off as well. He had pulled a compact Cassegrain telescope out of a storage locker and was setting it on a mount he'd unfolded from beneath the forward window. With the cabin dark there'd be no reflections to interfere with the view. Marshall held on to the opposite side with his fingertips as he absorbed it all.

The Sun hung off the ship's port side, its brilliance dimmed by electrostatic shades embedded in the windows, yet still washing out all but the brightest stars. Earth and Moon lay behind them, distinct but alarmingly distant. Marshall was able to cover both with a single outstretched hand.

Ahead was the lumpy gray mass of RQ39 and its tiny companion, *Prospector*. If Simon had any feelings about seeing their home world left so far behind, he was keeping them hidden while he was absorbed with aligning the telescope.

"Tally ho," he said, centering the view in the scope's wide-angle lens. He made a *tut-tut* sound and swapped out the eyepiece for one that would offer a closer look. As he adjusted the focus, Marshall thought he saw his shoulders sag. "It doesn't look good."

"How so, sir?"

"Hang tight a sec." Simon made sure the scope was tracking its target, slipped a CCD imager into the tube and captured some pictures before replacing it with the eyepiece. He checked that the image was still centered and motioned for Marshall to come look.

Without the atmospheric distortions of an earthbound telescope, the view should have been crystal clear. Through a thin cloud of vapor surrounding *Prospector*, he could make out the gray and white command and service module berthed to the silvery drum of a large habitat and logistics section. Solar wings and radiator panels extended like flower petals from its forward end. He was quite familiar with the layout, as it was almost identical to the cislunar cruise liners his father's company operated.

Beyond the cloud, larger shreds of the spacecraft tumbled about it. Marshall's heart sank. "Is that collision damage, then?"

"Atmospheric venting. Looks like they got holed all right," Simon agreed. "Their ground control didn't report anything indicating a tank was about to go. We'll have to get closer to see, but it looks like at least one panel of the service module's blown out."

"Assuming the service module's dead, could they be in the hab?"

"I've been thinking about that." Simon floated quietly for a time, staring out into the depths. He had too many memories from his own experience of being stranded in a crippled spacecraft in lunar orbit— it was the root of his distrust of inflatables, and this left him puzzled. They should've been fine in a "hard" hab unless it had been breached as well. He studied a schematic of *Prospector* on a nearby monitor, comparing it to one of the images he'd just captured. "It's possible since that's where the storm shelter is. But it has redundant systems, so they should have been able to communicate."

Marshall covered one eye, relaxing his dominant eye to try and tease out more details. "I can't see how many antennas were damaged."

"Assume anything on the service module's toast. That leaves the low-gain stuff on the hab."

"They'd still have two-way voice, then. Just no data."

"Exactly. I've seen this movie before," he sighed. "Better let your team know."

Marshall had assembled his small team in the wardroom. Their normal workspace, which had begun the journey locked down, well organized and sparkling clean, had become cluttered with emergency gear and spacesuits in varying stages of inspection. "I wish we had better news," Marshall began. He turned on the big monitor above the foldout table and pulled up the images Simon had taken earlier. To their credit, Rosado and Harper mostly kept their thoughts to themselves other than sharing some muted groans.

Prospector was severely damaged, perhaps fatally so. The images weren't any sharper than he remembered, though seeing them on a larger screen for the first time brought out details he hadn't noticed before.

A panel of the service module was indeed blown out, with the scorched frame and innards suggesting considerable heat before the resulting fire was quenched by vacuum—it had burned just as long as there was oxygen, so it had been fierce but short-lived. Through the haze of sublimated gases that had somehow escaped the conflagration lay a dangerous thicket of contorted alloys and splintered composites.

He pulled up *Prospector*'s schematic on the adjacent screen and rotated the image. "The blowout was on the Z-1 panel, which puts the debris field right in line with the CSM's hatch. That means we won't be able to make a direct approach with *Specter*, and I'm not about to send anyone outside through that cloud."

"Appreciate that, sir," Rosie said.

"Lieutenant Wylie will get us in position on the Z+1 side, close enough to hop across without full maneuvering packs."

"Untethered?" Rosie asked, though she already suspected the answer.

"We'll have our SAFER units activated, but yeah," Marshall said, almost apologetically. "Their command module has standard connections we can hook up to once we get there. We'll stay tethered to each other for the trip across just to be safe."

"*We*, sir?"

Marshall looked around the room. "I don't see who else can do this with you guys, Rosie. Chief Garver's qualified but Captain Poole's going to need him back here since Wylie's going to be chauffeuring us."

She nodded at the image of *Prospector* hidden behind the fog of debris. "You ready for this, sir? It could get dicey."

Marshall thought he knew where she was going. "Here's how I want this to work: I might be the on-scene commander, but you're the senior rescue spacer. I'm following your lead and trusting you guys to keep me out of trouble. Fair enough?"

She and Harper nodded their agreement. "Fair enough, sir."

He remembered once hearing that courage was being scared to death but saddling up anyway. "I'm counting on it."

Strapped into one of the quick-release harnesses next to Rosie in back of *Specter*, Marshall couldn't stop fidgeting with one leg of his suit. It didn't escape Rosie's notice, though nothing did on an EVA.

"You okay, sir?"

He grunted with frustration. "I think I cinched up my right leg too much. That whole side keeps pulling at me."

"Happens a lot in fitting," she said. "What seems fine in normal pressure all of a sudden doesn't in the actual environment. Most of us compensate by letting the adjustments out a half-inch or so."

"I did already. Thought I was being clever. Seemed like too much after my first couple of walks so I took out the slack." He stretched out his leg, kicking inside at the boot. "Must have been too much."

"You won't notice it once we're working outside, sir. At least not much. Next time let me know and I'll help you, okay?"

"Okay." The shuttle rocked as it detached from *Borman*.

"We're underway," Wylie called from up front. "ETA ten minutes."

The transit from *Borman* was straightforward enough: undock, clear the mothership, and make a quick burn to put them on a tangent that would take them clear of the debris obscuring

Prospector. As they circled the spacecraft, Wylie began recording what he saw through the heads-up display and relayed it back to the *Borman.*

Marshall unstrapped from the aft jump seat and made his way forward, hovering behind Wylie. It felt surreal, as if it were something he was watching on television: The little ship that had captured his imagination for the last few months now waited outside, not twenty meters away.

Wylie pointed at a dark spot on the service module. "Looks like our entry wound," he said, and keyed his mic. "*Borman* Actual, there's a hole in the Z+1 service panel, maybe a few centimeters wide. Really clean, too. I think that's the impact site."

"Copy that," Simon answered. "How's your approach from that side?"

"Clear. I can get them almost right up against the spacecraft."

"Understood, but I want you to back off and stay at safe maneuvering distance once you've dropped them off. Hunter, you up on freq?"

With his helmet already sealed, Marshall engaged his voice-activated suit radio. "Yes, sir?"

"I think Mr. Wylie has given us a pretty good bead on what happened to their spacecraft. Make boarding your priority, after the Jiangs are secure you can go inspect the entry damage. Stay on the Z+ side of the spacecraft, understood?"

"Aye, sir. Stay out of the wreckage."

"Good man. Actual out."

Wylie backed them in slowly and brought them to a stop within a meter of each other. When Marshall opened their outer door, *Prospector* was almost in arm's reach. He gestured for Rosie to take the lead and she jumped into action, reaching for their safety tether.

"Nice work, Lieutenant. I barely have to go outside."

"Just don't ding my spacecraft, Rosie. I can't afford the insurance."

Rosie smirked beneath her visor and answered Wylie with a quick double-click of her mic. She checked her connection then reached out to test Marshall's and Harper's, tugging at their waists. Without a word, she clipped the opposite end to a ring beneath *Prospector's* hatch. "Excursion team is secure. I'm going to give us some distance, sir."

"Copy."

She went through the opening feet first, keeping her arms against the rim and pushing against the other craft with her legs. The two spacecraft began to separate, falling away from each other slowly. She slipped her arms back outside and pushed away, the coils of her tether following behind. Harper floated out soon after. "You're next, sir."

Marshall pivoted into the opening and let himself be pulled through as his own line played out behind him. When it grew taut, the tension naturally turned him to face her. "Nice move, Rosie. Separates us without him having to use the RCS."

"Something we came up with on our own," she said, and pointed at *Prospector*'s closed hatch. "It'll also protect *Specter* when we open this tin can up. Who knows what'll come out of it?"

"Good point."

She called back to Wylie. "We're secure, sir. You can hail them again."

Two mic clicks, then Wylie's voice over the universal emergency frequency: "*Prospector, Prospector*, this is the USSF shuttle *Specter*. Comm check." He repeated it twice more, each time answered by hissing static. "No joy, Rosie."

"Understood. Thank you, sir." Rosie returned to their suit intercom. "Didn't think there would be, but we had to try," she explained. She banged on the hull and set her faceplate against it, listening for any vibrations transmitted up through it. She looked up at Marshall. "Could you head up to the hab and try the same thing, sir?"

"Got it." He pushed off, aiming for a handrail around the rim of the big logistics module overhead. After a minute of trying the same thing, he shook his head before realizing she couldn't see him. "Same here. Nobody's answering."

"Can you see anything through the portholes? Because I've got nothin' here."

Compared to the command module's big oval windows, the hab's small portholes were like trying to inspect the inside of a barrel looking through a garden hose. There was power but no obvious movement. "Lights are on but nobody's home. No movement, no signs of loose gear or debris either." *Better than the last spacecraft I boarded*, he thought.

"Crew cabin's dark," Harper said, shining her helmet lamp through one of the windows. "No movement, no response. That doesn't leave us many options."

He pulled against his tether to begin heading back to them. "Breach entry?"

"Afraid so, sir." Rosie removed a long-handled tool from her utility harness. "If you'll pull up their quick-reference guide, I'll do the dirty work."

"Got it." He tapped at a small display on his wrist where he'd already loaded *Prospector*'s emergency checklists. "First open the manual pressure equalization valve, staying clear of the adjacent purge vent. One-half clockwise turn."

She set the tool inside the valve fitting. "Opening the MPEV, one-half clockwise." She braced against a nearby handrail and pulled on the handle. Expecting a geyser of ice crystals to erupt from the purge vent beneath it, instead they saw nothing.

Marshall had been eyeing the cabin through a nearby window. There were no signs of venting atmosphere. "It opened, right?"

"Yes sir. No resistance. Just no air either."

"So they were already in vacuum."

"If they weren't, then venting the cabin into space sure would've gotten their attention," Rosie said. "What's that tell you, sir?"

"That the hab's either sealed off or also in vacuum. Otherwise there'd have been a lot more to vent."

"Bingo." They weren't giving up yet. She folded up the tool and slipped it back in her harness, then reached for the ratchet handle centered beneath the viewport. "That's funny—it's unlocked."

"That might explain things. Cabin must have vented when they got hit."

"Opening the spacecraft," she announced over their common frequency and waved for Marshall to stay put. "Clear?"

He kept his grip on the opposite railing. "Clear."

The hatch swung out easily. No random loose equipment spilled out into space. "Entering the vehicle."

"Copy that," Simon answered. "Keep me posted."

Rosie let go of the handrail and pulled herself in headfirst with Harper in trail. From outside, Marshall could see their helmet lamps light up the cabin. "We're in, sir. You're clear to enter."

"Right behind you," Marshall said, following them inside. He shut the hatch behind him.

In sharp contrast to the Stardust capsule, *Prospector's* command module was spotless. Everything was in its place: flight couches stowed, equipment bays latched shut, a single blinking blue light signaled the touchscreen control panel was waiting on standby and ready to be reactivated.

"Okay, this is weird," Rosie admitted. She floated down the docking tunnel, following a stream of light from the viewport on its far end. There was a small status panel nearby. "You were right, sir. Logistics and hab are under pressure, but I still can't see much."

"We need to get in there." Marshall held down the blinking standby button until the control screen blinked into life. "Here we go. Equalizing now." He soon found the pressure controls and air began flowing back into the cabin.

The small compartment pressurized quickly. Harper heaved its forward hatch open and Marshall watched her and Rosado disappear into the big logistics module. He moved into the docking tunnel to follow, waiting for their all clear to move ahead.

He was used to not hearing muck from Harper, but Rosie was uncharacteristically quiet. That didn't portend pleasant news. He took a deep breath, preparing himself for a gruesome scene and trying to clear his head of all the stories he'd read about the Jiang's expedition, all of the interviews he'd seen. He stared down the length of the tunnel, expecting to find the famous couple dead on the other side. He pushed ahead.

The hab and logistics module was easily eight meters deep and half as wide. The near end had been set up as their extended living space: pictures and small personal effects cluttered one wall in a similar manner as he'd seen aboard the *Borman*, with sleeping bags against the opposite wall, a widescreen monitor mounted to the overhead, and a folding table with seat restraints for a dining area.

The far end held their supplies: a tightly packed jumble of soft containers, mostly food, wedged behind an octagonal cargo netting that resembled a giant spiderweb. They'd looked to have gone through roughly half of their load, which would be right about on schedule.

Floating in front of that web was Rosie's spacesuited form, her back turned to him, staring into the half-empty logistics section. Harper continued inside, searching the nooks and crannies.

"Rosie?"

She turned silently, eyes wide and mouth agape in shock.

"Where are they?"

She blinked hard. "I don't know."

Marshall grabbed a nearby handhold, turning about to look for himself. "Where are they?" he repeated, more to himself than her.

"EVA Team," Simon cut in over their headsets with concern in his voice. "Report."

His eyes searched Rosie's. She simply shook her head in disbelief, again mouthing, "I don't know."

Marshall answered for them. "They're not here, sir." He said the words, but it felt as if it were coming from someone else.

"Say again, EVA One?"

Marshall collected himself and cleared his throat. "Actual, this is EVA One. Spacecraft is abandoned. I repeat, spacecraft is abandoned."

◎ 20 ◎

"What the hell?" Garver uncharacteristically blurted out. "How are they *not there*?"

Simon rubbed at his forehead. "You got me, Chief," he muttered. "This is a first."

Garver dug at his eyes with the heels of his hands. "Sorry for the outburst, skipper."

Simon waved it away and floated up into the cupola, staring at the abandoned spacecraft and wishing he had gravity just so he could indulge the feeling of collapsing into a chair. How did they just up and disappear? If they'd been holed by a meteoroid, where would they go? *Why* would they go anywhere?

They must have gone outside in hopes of repairing the damage and become separated from the spacecraft, he decided. That was the only thing that made sense. He keyed his mic. "Give me a bow-to-stern visual inside then inspect the exterior. I want to see that entry wound on their service module."

Simon took his binoculars from their mount and began searching *Prospector* for more clues. It had to be a repair gone wrong. Had to be. They must have taken a hit and decided to try and do something about it. He'd have done the same, but he'd also been at this for years with a crew of trained specialists who could work miracles under just about every rotten condition space could throw at them. He studied the debris field and imagined two rookies trying to effect repairs in that mess.

"Skipper?"

He shuddered at the idea and tried not to think about how that must have gone down.

"Captain Poole?"

Had one of them gotten tangled up in debris or ruptured their suit, and the other gone after them? Had something struck them both at once? There was a lot of jagged crap floating around out there. He decided to tell Marshall and Rosie to stay on the clear side of the ship—no sense risking them, especially with a skeleton crew...

"Captain!"

How long had he been lost in thought that Garver had raised his voice to get his attention? He tucked his legs and flipped, sticking his head down through the cupola opening. "What's up, Chief?"

"We may have something, sir. There's some electromagnetic energy coming from near RQ39. Infrared, occasionally into the microwave bands—UHF and EHF."

He turned back topside, instinctively swinging his binoculars over to the asteroid now several kilometers distant. That couldn't be... "Any chance its them?"

"Not unless they're carrying high-gain transmitters with them, sir."

Another spacecraft? He keyed the mic again. "EVA Team, Actual."

Marshall answered. "Go ahead, sir."

"Refresh my memory—weren't the Jiangs carrying some survey equipment or experiment packages to deploy here?"

"Affirmative, sir. They were going to place a remote-operated drill and an in situ resource unit, see what kind of raw materials they could harvest from it."

"Is that equipment still onboard?"

"Those packages were mounted to an external sled on the far end of the hab. They're both gone, sir."

That conformed to what Poole had seen through his binoculars. "*Specter*, Actual. Are you listening?"

"Aye, sir."

"What's your fuel state?"

"Bonus, sir. Ninety-two percent."

"How much delta-v do you need to go inspect RQ39?"

"Say again?"

"I need you to get eyes on that asteroid. We've detected some thermal and radio energy. Weak and intermittent, but it's there. Could be activity on the far side."

"You think our missing persons might be over there?"

"Only thing that makes sense," Poole said.

There was a delay while Wylie calculated their fuel. "Looks like five meters per second each way, figure another half-meter for station keeping. We've got plenty in the tanks for that, sir."

"Very well. Hunter, you hear that?"

"Aye, sir," Marshall answered for his team, already motioning Rosie and Harper to begin heading for the exit. "We're on our way back to *Specter* now."

With a quick tap against the translation controller, Wylie began pulling them away from *Prospector* as soon as Marshall closed the airlock. The abandoned spacecraft fell away quickly, spinning out of view as Wylie pitched around to align them for a short OMS burn. The little ship kicked for few seconds, adding velocity along its new vector. He motioned for the three to come forward, and pointed Marshall to the open copilot seat.

"We're not set up to scan the microwave or IR bands," he explained. "Rosie, I need you to manually frequency-hop the VHF and UHF radios. Listen for anything weird." He noticed the look she gave him. "Yeah, I know. *Everything* sounds weird out here. Listen up for anything that doesn't sound like cosmic background noise." He turned to Harper. "Nikki, maintain a listening watch on the emergency frequency. If they're out here then I don't want to miss them because we were chasing shadows."

They each plugged in spare headsets. "Sounds like a good plan, sir," Rosie said.

"Don't know if it's good, but it's the only plan we have right now."

The asteroid soon began to fill the windows.

"Nothing," Marshall said. "If they're out there, the mass is blocking their signal."

"Makes sense," Wylie said, frustrated with himself. "Should've held back, kept our distance while we flew around the back side."

"Spiral search pattern?" Marshall wondered. "If it's really them, we're just picking up random EM energy. We've already got an idea of where it's coming from. I think we'd have to get close no matter what."

"Grid search," Rosie said. "Pick apart this rock one square at a time until we home in on them. Now all we need's a map."

"Not like I have any clue what I'm doing," Marshall said, "but Rosie's right. We need a map, anything we can use to track our search pattern."

Harper pulled up an image of the asteroid. "We can at least start with quadrants and subdivide from there." She pointed out prominent shapes and features. "We identify some landmarks to set our boundaries and get after it."

The radio tuned to *Borman*'s frequency crackled once before going quiet as they passed into the asteroid's shadow.

"Radio blackout," Garver reported. "They're in shadow, sir."

Simon put down his binoculars. "Yeah, I just lost sight of them." He turned to Garver. "Then what's that tell us?"

Garver pulled at his chin, thinking. "That whatever we're looking for has to be on this side of the 'roid. Or it's a lot more energetic than just a drill and ISRU complex."

Simon pulled up his file on *Prospector*. "Any chance there's some components not accounted for?" he asked. "Did we miss a drone or remote-sensing satellite?"

Garver shook his head. "No sir. They deployed a couple of CubeSats to image it, simple cameras and magnetometers. Both have low IR signatures and their operating freqs are accounted for. This is different. Lots of EM radiation from that direction, sir. Like something just turned itself—"

Before he could finish, the master alarm began blaring and the caution and warning panel suddenly lit up like a Christmas tree. "Propellant alarm! Temperature and pressure warnings from tank two," Garver shouted from the control station.

"Any warnings from the coolant loops?"

"Negative, sir. Throughput's normal but the ducts alongside two are heating up."

"Purge valves?"

"Opened automatically, but delta-p is in the black band." The valves, meant to keep internal pressure from reaching dangerous levels, couldn't vent fast enough.

Simon unsnapped a covered switch to jettison the tank. "Number two is—"

Their world swirled around them as the big hydrogen tank exploded.

※ ※ ※

"I got nothing, sir." Rosie pulled off the headset and rubbed at her ear, her free hand cupped over the other. "Just background noise."

"No better here, sir," Harper said. "It's all static all across the spectrum. Nothing visual either."

"Wouldn't expect much different this far out," Wylie said, "not unless they have a signal beacon. Even if they did . . ." He trailed off, letting go of the thought.

Marshall had not been able to let go as easily. "It's been almost two weeks. If they've been out here that whole time, they're long dead. But if that radio noise wasn't them, where'd it come from?"

"Everything's in motion out here," Wylie reminded him as the darkened asteroid drifted past outside. "It was worth a look. We'll have line of sight back in a minute. I'm sure they had better luck."

"Report!" Simon shouted as he flew back down from the cupola.

"Engineering present and accounted for," a crewman called from his station. "We're both here on the command deck, sir."

Simon turned to look behind, finding two wide-eyed petty officers hanging on to their seats and struggling to make sense of the situation. "Can you give me powerplant status?"

One of the men held tightly to a pair of nearby handrails, fighting to read off figures and trends while the ship bucked like an angry bull beneath them. "Reactors went to safe mode, sir. Control rods fully engaged. Containment shells are intact."

He flew back up into the dome for a better look outside. They were rapidly becoming enveloped in a cloud of escaping gas. The Sun and RQ39 spun around them as their ship, knocked askew by the explosion, stumbled its way through a drunken spiral. The side-mounted hydrogen tank was split by a jagged wound that had opened up along its length, still venting propellant. Maneuvering thrusters pulsed wildly, automatically trying to compensate and right the ship.

"Shut down the RCS!" he shouted down into the flight deck. "Before we run out of gas!"

"Aye, shutting down," Garver called out as Simon flew back down into the command module. The bucking and heaving soon came to a stop, though the ship's tumble continued unabated.

"Nav platform may not be able to keep up with this, sir," Garver warned him. "Tank two is a goner. We need to lose it before we can get the ship under control."

"Roger that." Simon reached for the jettison switch.

Whatever they'd expected to see after they emerged from the asteroid's shadow, it wasn't this. The ship they had left behind was shrouded in a cloud of vapor, lazily tumbling through space. For a moment Marshall had thought they were looking at the similarly damaged *Prospector*.

"Holy shit," Rosie breathed.

"*Borman*," Wylie called, "*Borman*, this is *Specter*. How copy, over?"

He was answered by the pop and hiss of an empty channel. He repeated his call, and the radio crackled. "*Spec—*"

The four stared at each other as if one of them might have been able to discern an answer. The frequency sparked to life again. "...maintain...position."

"You're broken, *Borman*. Understand you want us to maintain position?"

The channel hissed, then came an emphatic reply: "Negative! Do not—"

"They lost antenna control," Marshall said, and pointed at the stricken ship. "Their signal cuts out as it rolls away."

"You're right," Wylie said, hearing the static rise and fall with *Borman*'s rotation. "Then we drop the UHF." He switched over his active channel to the rarely used high-frequency radio. "Never thought I'd need this out here. Hope they remembered to keep it on." He flicked the mic switch. "*Borman*, this is *Specter* on HF, button one."

They recoiled as the channel howled to life. It blessedly disappeared when someone spoke, though his voice was reedy from attenuation. The words came in a rush.

"*Specter, Borman*. Explosion in H_2 tank two."

"That sounds like Garver," Marshall said. "Is Sim—Captain Poole—okay?"

If anyone noticed his stumbling into use of the familiar, they ignored it. Wylie keyed the mic. "How's the CO?"

"Pissed," Garver said. "His orders are for you to stay clear. Danger close, repeat danger close."

Before he could ask anything else, they saw the damaged hydrogen tank separate from *Borman* and begin spiraling away.

Simon flinched, barely keeping his head from bouncing off a heaving bulkhead as he came down from the cupola. "Could be worse," he muttered.

"How's that, sir?" Garver asked coolly, trying to mask his tension.

Simon floated back down to strap into the pilot's seat. "If this was a movie, we'd have panels falling out of the overhead and all the avionics would be on fire. So we've got that going for us."

Garver laughed out loud. "Good thing they thought to put in circuit breakers."

"Yeah, awesome." One of the petty officers bit down on his lower lip as he continued fighting against their rolling and yawing. "How the hell are you laughing at anything right now?"

"Stress response," Garver said as he studied the fuel system's diagnostics, shooting a glance at Poole. "We've been in worse situations."

The petty officer glared back at him over his shoulder. "Yeah, I'm calling bullshit on that one, Master Chief."

"He's not kidding," Poole said, pulsing thrusters against the roll. "Remind me to tell you about the Sea of Okhotsk some time." The ship jerked hard as thrusters fought the escaping gas. "Let's just say that riding your boat down to crush depth is even scarier than being in a depressurizing spacecraft."

"I'll take your word on that, sir."

Poole tapped the controls again, more lightly and in the opposite direction. With another pulse to null that motion, the attitude indicator finally settled down. He blew out a long breath.

"Ship's stable," Garver reported. "Clear of the debris cloud."

Poole wiped his forehead with his ball cap. "How much RCS did we blow doing that?"

Garver checked the propellant totals. "Twenty percent, sir. And we vented a whole propellant cell. That leaves three cells in tank one."

Simon ground his jaw. "Tell me about our radio masts." Their antenna complex was adjacent to the propellant tanks.

Garver pulled up an interactive diagram of the comm and sensor module, much of it now in red. "The explosion took out our directional antennas. We can pick up HF and VHF if we're pointed at the source."

"We can still talk to *Specter*, right?"

Garver nodded affirmative. "We can relay our comms through their directional antenna. Limits us to S-band but it'll work. We'll have direct control once they're docked."

"Good. Clear them to approach the forward node, and make sure they get us external visuals. Get our people back in the barn ASAP."

"Copy that," Wylie answered. "We're heading to Waypoint One now. Tuning S-band radios to the common traffic freqs. Stand by." He gestured for Marshall to begin relaying *Borman*'s radio traffic through their antenna.

As he switched over frequencies, there was a high-pitched squeal as if an electronic being was clearing its throat. A computer-generated voice began a recorded recitation:

ATTENTION ALL TRESPASSERS, INTERLOPERS,
AND ENVIRONMENTAL RAPISTS:
   THIS PLANETOID AND ALL NATURAL RESOURCES
WITHIN IT HAVE BEEN DESIGNATED AS PROTEC-
TORATES OF THE PEOPLE'S SPACE LIBERATION
FRONT. EARTH HAS SUFFERED ENOUGH UNDER
CENTURIES OF NATIONALISTIC PROPERTY THEFT,
AND WE WILL NOT PERMIT FURTHER RAPING OF THE
ENVIRONMENT OF WORLDS THAT NO CORPORATION
HAS A RIGHT TO. AS NO ONE HAS RIGHTFUL CLAIM
TO PROPERTY PER THE OUTER SPACE TREATY OF
1969, WE THE PEOPLE OF EARTH ARE THEREFORE
THE SOLE ARBITERS OF ANY SPACE PROPERTY
DISPUTES. ANGLO-IMPERIALISM WILL NOT BE PER-
MITTED TO EXPAND BEYOND EARTH. THIS FREE
SPACE MANIFESTO APPLIES TO ALL NATURAL
WORLDS OF OUR SOLAR SYSTEM.

Marshall and Wylie stared at each other, dumbfounded, as the eerie computer-voiced "manifesto" began repeating itself. Wylie's eyes widened. "What in the actual hell was that?"

✺ 21 ✺

Poole had assembled his skeleton command staff—Lieutenant Wylie and Master Chief Garver—in the multipurpose wardroom, each in a pantomime of sitting with their feet slipped into restraints under the table. "First order of business," he said, pointing at Wylie. "How's Hunter's team doing?"

"They're secured in the 'lock, sir. They were out there a long time and it's going to take a while to rebalance their O_2 levels. We shouldn't plan on having them available for duty for another two hours."

"Make it four," he said, then, "scratch that. Eight. I want them fully rested and ready to go."

"Aye, sir," Wylie said warily, looking askance at Garver. They were in an all-hands situation and it wasn't like Poole to ease up when the pressure was on. He had something else in mind.

Poole eyed them both. "Gentlemen, I don't have to tell you we are in deep kimchee. We've lost most of our comms and half our remaining propellant. That severely limits our maneuvering space." He paused. "We don't have the delta-v to make our return schedule. I don't have to tell you what that means."

"It's going to be a long trip home," Wylie said dourly. "We're stuck with a simple Hohmann transfer that follows the Jiang's original trajectory before it all went sideways. I'm guessing the chief isn't going to paint a prettier picture." He looked at Garver, who'd been taking stock of their logistics.

"The lieutenant's right, sir," Garver said, though he knew Poole was well aware of exactly how screwed they were. "Water supplies can be stretched through the reclamation cycler, but we only have enough food rations for thirty days. That's assuming minimum caloric intake."

"We're on *Prospector*'s Mars flyby orbit," Wylie reminded them. "We won't make it half that far before we run out of food."

"That's why I've got Hunter's team resting up—it's going to get busy before it gets even busier. We're going to have to go back and salvage whatever we can from *Prospector*, dock with their hab and empty it out." He gave that a minute to sink in. "And that brings me around to my next topic: Gentlemen, why are we here?"

The lieutenant's brow furrowed, caught off guard. "Sir?"

Wylie might have been caught short, but Garver knew right away. "Search and rescue."

Poole snapped his fingers at Garver. "Bingo. We still have a mission, gents, which I intend to accomplish no matter what the consequences are for us. I don't know if there are enough rations over there to get us all the way home, but I'm damned certain there's enough to keep us going while we search for our spacefaring rock hounds."

Garver shifted uncomfortably, pursing his lips.

"Something on your mind, Chief?"

Garver lifted his eyes. "Sir, whoever broadcast that idiotic 'manifesto' is claiming responsibility. What happened to us looks a lot like what happened to *Prospector*. I'm at a loss as to how they managed it, but we have to consider hostile action."

"I'm not buying this Space Liberation Front or whatever the hell they're calling themselves," Poole said. "But I don't believe in coincidences, either. You can't tell me a bunch of space hippies were clever enough to pull off an op like this. They'd have to be clairvoyant."

"How's that, sir?"

"Lead times. They'd have had to launch it well ahead of *Prospector*, probably before they even announced their expedition. And I like to think we'd have noticed it."

"The Jiangs have been planning this for over two years," Wylie said. "Somebody with inside knowledge would've had to act long before they announced, then."

"Seems likely. It also seems likely that whoever is trying to deny access to resources out here has been thinking about it for a long time. Any asteroid that's a likely candidate for exploitable resources should be considered dangerous."

"They didn't come out and say so, did they?" Garver mused. "But they didn't have to."

Poole began ticking off points on his fingers. "They've declared asteroid and planetary resources off-limits for humans. And they're claiming credit for damaging two US spacecraft."

"One being a military vessel. They have to know that's an act of war," Wylie said, barely able to believe it himself.

Poole's fingers drummed the table, ever so slightly pushing him up against his restraints. "Been thinking about that, too." He stopped his drumming to wag a finger at both of them. "If I ever get the bright idea to go anywhere again without a full weapons loadout, feel free to mutiny my ass."

"You were trying to accomplish the mission, sir," Wylie said. "We had valid reasons to dump mass."

Poole was unconvinced. "If this were the surface Navy, even the Coast Guard, we wouldn't forget our first purpose."

Garver scratched at his beard. "That gets a little fuzzy out here, sir. They can bring along whatever they can fit inside. We don't have that luxury," he reminded him. "Fleet Ops approved your operational plan."

"That'll be the only thing that keeps my ass out of a sling if we get back," Poole said. "So here's my orders going forward: One, use *Specter*'s directional antenna to communicate with Fleet and advise them of our situation. Two, dock with *Prospector* and get a full inventory of their consumables. Get back to me on how far we can stretch them." He eyed them both. "Three—spin up the interceptors and charge the PDCs, even if you have to power down something else to do it. As of right now, we are at war. We just need to figure out with whom."

The distance between Earth and RQ39 meant that what soon became known as the "Free Space Manifesto" was received several minutes after Poole's crew first heard it, not long after Fleet Operations lost contact with the *Borman*.

That in itself had sent the Fleet Ops controllers into a scramble, something Roberta couldn't help but notice from her vantage point at the opposite end of the control room. She was easily distracted in "coast mode," passively watching as their newest X-37 was making its way up to geosynch.

WHAT'S UP? She'd texted a junior lieutenant she knew on the *Borman* control team. It was taking a huge chance with as busy as they'd all of sudden become, but he was a logistics guy which made her comfortably sure he wasn't getting his ass handed to him at that moment.

NOBODY KNOWS, he'd answered. E AND E SAID THERE WAS A TEMP AND PRESSURE SPIKE IN ONE OF THE H2 TANKS. THEN IT WENT DARK. THEY'RE NORDO.

She'd rolled back from her console to stare at the big status board on the far wall. It showed the position of every satellite, drone, and crewed spacecraft in the force, while *Borman* was so far out it was wasn't even on screen. "No radio," she exhaled. "Jeebus."

After the initial burst of activity, she watched the control team go dark in their own way. The lead controller and a couple of specialists were up and about, either answering questions from the brass or being pulled into one of the meeting rooms surrounding the control floor. She recognized a couple of new faces that had been hovering around the *Borman* team's consoles—the crewmembers sent back to save consumables so it could go on its grand interplanetary adventure. The rest of the team remained at their posts, hunched over their consoles, headsets pressed to their ears, each hoping to tease some data or a voice snippet out of the Great Big Nothing.

She couldn't imagine what that felt like, and didn't want to. She had her own drone now, with the occasional datalink glitch for sure, but they had always resolved quickly. Military pilots had spent decades refining the art of remotely controlling drones from opposite ends of the world, and adapting their techniques to space had been a natural leap.

It helped that the X-37s were smart enough to finish executing whatever their last commands had been if she momentarily lost contact with them. More importantly, there weren't humans aboard. No matter how much she might have loved her drones, she wasn't going out for drinks with them at the O club or popping in at their kid's birthday parties. It had become all too easy to forget how deadly serious their jobs were because she was having too much fun playing with some really expensive toys.

She hadn't been the only person in Fleet Ops feeling that way. Losing their flagship had immediately changed the mood in the Ops center. Calling it happy-go-lucky before was perhaps unfair, but it was the closest description she could think of. Spaceflight, even just pushing satellites around, was horrendously unforgiving of the slightest hint of incompetence. No one had the luxury of slacking off.

But this was different. Especially among the senior officers and NCOs, many of them Air Force and Navy transfers who'd seen actual combat, there was a quiet determination she'd not noticed before: not grim, not angry, though a little of both. She and the other junior officers found themselves unwittingly mimicking their senior's behavior. They were ready to stomp somebody's ass but had no idea who. Even without the *Borman*, they had ample resources. They just didn't have the first clue of where to aim them.

The intel analysts had their own ideas about this Space Liberation Front, though they'd quickly been sidelined by the DIA and CIA. Big Intel was on it, they'd been assured. That hadn't stopped them from their own sleuthing. She also knew nobody with half a brain seriously thought some kind of Greenpeace in Space had just showed up out of nowhere—which meant that was *exactly* what the suits in Washington were thinking.

Roberta drummed her fingers impatiently on her console, staring at the big red button on the control stick and wishing there was somebody she could just *shoot*, damn it. Caught up in her own thoughts and frustrations, she was surprised by a sudden commotion erupting from across the room. Shouting, hooting, some guys standing excitedly, others running for the outer office ring to alert the brass . . . had the balloon gone up? Do we finally have a targeting order?

She felt a strange commingling of disappointment, relief, and excitement when that didn't happen. It was the *Borman*, she'd learned, wounded but not dead yet. Unable to communicate on its own but still able to relay traffic through its shuttle. All hands accounted for, so at least she could rest easy that Marshall was okay.

Finally, she learned of their grim task ahead of raiding the Jiang's spacecraft for consumables on the outside chance there'd be enough to sustain them during what had just turned into a long trip home.

Her relief and excitement ebbed, replaced with a tension and dread that was becoming all too familiar. Alternating waves of adrenaline and serotonin coursed through her, competing for dominance and leaving her worn out and helpless to do anything about it.

Focus, she told herself. Her drone was coming up on its next burn to place it in geosynch, and she couldn't afford to become distracted. The day's space tasking order, or just "STO," had been simple: park the drone in orbit and await further orders. The equipment loadout in its cargo bay promised follow-on missions that were anything but simple: Hall thrusters, imagery packages, manipulator arms . . . they were planning a real party for somebody up there.

She tightened her grip on the ROV's controls, took a deep breath, and relaxed her grip. *Take care of your own bird*, she told herself.

Mating two disabled vehicles was difficult enough; maneuvering the larger of the two out of its own debris cloud and around that of the smaller ship had taken considerable skill and even more nerves. Marshall found himself flinching at every *ting* of something bouncing off the hull. Now that it was crucial for them to access all of *Prospector's* logistics, the collision risk had moved well down Poole's priority list. What he didn't say—and of this Marshall was convinced—was that no matter their condition upon returning home, alive or dead they were bringing back evidence of hostile actions beyond Earth orbit.

Marshall watched as Poole, again working from the cupola, expertly deployed their manipulator arm to grab the smaller ship and maneuver it onto their open berthing port. They were rewarded with the familiar, satisfying thud of docking rings locking together.

"Capture," Garver called up from the deck below. "All contact points are green."

"Very good." Poole left the arm in place. "Mr. Wylie, get us clear of this mess. I'll watch from here."

"Aye sir," he said from below. Thrusters fired along the length of the ship, gently moving the stack sideways and safely away from *Prospector's* floating detritus.

"Watch this." Poole pointed forward. "Just because there's no

atmosphere or gravity—okay, not really but you know what I mean—
that doesn't get us off the hook. Not everything is going to move at
the same rate. That's a lot of mass we just plugged onto our nose. It's
got its own inertia and I want to see how much flexion there is under
lateral thrust."

"Even though it's less mass than the node's certified for?"

"Not until I've seen it in person," Poole said, intently focused on
their new addition. He glanced down at the arm's control board for
any signs of excess mechanical feedback through its joints. "Little bit
of load on the first joint. Nothing to get too excited about." He kept
watching as thrusters fired along the opposite side, cancelling their
motion. There was some slight twisting—Marshall wasn't savvy
enough yet to know if it was a problem, but Poole didn't seem overly
concerned. "We're clear to maneuver," he announced tiredly to the
crew below. "Whenever that might be."

"I'll get to work, sir," Marshall said, and pushed away to float
down through the command module and into the forward node.

Prospector's logistics module felt a good bit more crowded now
that he was entering through its opposite end—opening the outer
hatch, he was greeted by a wall of tightly-wrapped packages. Each
was marked with a barcoded inventory number and labeled with its
contents, though in no more detail than "Meals-Day 121," as was the
first package he encountered.

Marshall recalled his knowledge of the expedition. They'd
planned on another six months for the return to Earth—one hundred
eighty days' worth of food for two people. Splitting it up amongst the
Borman's crew would make it sixty days' worth, maybe ninety if they
really stretched it. And there had to be some reserve, though he had
no idea how much. He made a mental note to dig into their mission
plans to find that out, and tried not to think about the fact that it still
might not be enough.

Being back inside what he had to properly call a *derelict*, now just
in shirtsleeves, he felt alarmingly exposed. Before, behind layers of
latex-impregnated fabric and polycarbonate glass, he'd been literally
insulated from the reality of it. Now it felt close. Vulnerable and real.
The little ship had a different smell than what he'd become used to,
and it made him feel like an intruder.

He couldn't place the scent, it being so far removed from his sole spacefaring experience so far. The air was pregnant with a sweet aroma that reminded him of his parents' backyard.

Lilacs. They'd installed filters that made their spaceborne home smell like a garden in springtime. When money was no object, why not do it if it was just going to be the two of them stuck in here for months?

He winced at the subtle reminder of the fact that they should have still been in here. It was like finding an abandoned cabin in the deep woods, filled with signs of life as if its owners should return any minute. He was Goldilocks, raiding the bear's porridge stash. He felt guilty picking through their belongings, even if they were only packages of freeze-dried food.

Accounting for each was going to take a while, too. He couldn't escape having to verify each item himself, but he could still give Captain Poole a first-look idea of what they had aboard.

He found a touchscreen control pad on the partition between the logistics and habitation sides of the module. If there were barcodes, then there ought to be an inventory list somewhere that would show what they had left in stores.

No luck. As he scrolled through its menu, he was rewarded with empty screens. It must have been dependent on the command module, which was mostly powered down. He moved into the CM and found the master cabin switch. It was on, but no lights or panel displays. He searched for the circuit breaker, and sure enough it had been popped open.

When he cycled the power back on, displays came to life. One in particular caught his eye: two blinking green lights on the biomonitor screen. It was looking for a signal, like a faithful dog waiting by the window for a glimpse of its owner returning home.

The persistence of this unfeeling technological sentinel shone a harsh light on his own dedication. Its silent devotion accused him: *I'm not giving up, why should you?*

It was too much. *Because we know they're dead and you're a stupid machine not sophisticated enough to figure that out,* he thought. Unable to avoid its accusatory glare, he angrily stabbed at the screen to turn it off. It blinked and went dark.

And then stubbornly came back to life with cursed persistence.

Would he have to disconnect the damned thing to avoid its presence? Each of the Jiang's biomonitor feeds displayed the well-known semicircular graphic signifying weak reception. Curious, he warily pressed one of the telemetry traces. STANDBY—SIGNAL PAUSED, it now read.

That couldn't be possible. Somehow, from somewhere, their suit monitors were still trying to transmit data.

He frantically pulled their ship's quick-reference handbook from a pocket in one of the folded-up seats and flipped to the "communications" tab. If the omnidirectional antennas couldn't find them, maybe the high-gain could.

⊚ 22 ⊚

While Marshall was supposed to be busy taking inventory on *Prospector*, Garver was on comm duty with Ops. It amounted to not much more than staying dialed in to their voice frequency with Ops and having to fuss with a headset while he was busy with other work—in particular, calculating exactly how few calories each of them could tolerate and remain halfway functional. It should have been simple math, but he couldn't balance the equation based on the food they'd brought with them.

He had his doubts about what they could scavenge from *Prospector* as well, unless Hunter found some secret stash of protein powder and vitamin supplements. Which, given its unique crew, could've been entirely possible. The Jiangs might have been insanely rich, but that didn't make them foolish. They'd come up the hard way, escaping real poverty to make it big in America. They showed the hallmarks of being careful, conservative planners. Maybe they'd built in enough reserves and redundancies in their own stores to save everyone's bacon.

It was tempting to poke his head into the docking tunnel, just to check on Hunter's progress, he told himself, but knowing it was really to hurry the kid up. There hadn't been a peep out of him since he'd disappeared into the bowels of *Prospector*'s logistics module. Garver looked down at the small loop of wire from his headset, jacked into the radio panel between the pilot's seats. If it had been longer, he'd have been in there taking inventory himself.

As if to chastise him for questioning his orders, that was the moment the channel lit up and a chime sounded to alert him to

219

incoming message traffic. "We copy your transmission, Ops. Ready to receive," he said. "Got a data packet for us?"

After nearly a minute's light delay, the voice on the other end returned. It was hesitant, uncertain. "Not exactly, *Borman*. This is a heads-up, you'll be receiving a text transmission relayed to us from the commandant."

"Say again? Understand we have incoming from the Pentagon?" Garver said, raising his voice and motioning for Poole's attention. By the time Poole arrived at his side, HQ replied.

"Affirmative, *Borman*. Relayed to them via the State Department. It's an offer of assistance from the Chinese spacecraft *Peng Fei*."

Their L1 station? Garver was skeptical. "Don't know what kind of assistance they can offer, Ops, but we'll take it." Garver made eye contact with Poole. The Earth-Moon L1 point was a cheap—in terms of fuel—jumping-off point for sending spacecraft farther into the solar system. Maybe they had a supply ship ready to shoot out in their direction?

Another minute passed. Uncertainty returned to the comm officer's voice. "Yeah, it kind of surprised us too, *Borman*. Fleet HQ advises they are standing by for Captain Poole once he's read their message."

"Copy," Garver said. "Stand by." He pulled up the message window and printed off a hard copy for Poole, who still preferred to get official traffic the old-fashioned way. In the meantime, he satisfied himself with reading the on-screen copy.

ATTENTION USS BORMAN//CAPT SIMON POOLE
FROM PRCS PENG FEI//COL LIU WANG SHU
WE HAVE RECEIVED WORD OF YOUR SITUATION AND OFFER OUR ASSISTANCE.
OUR NATION HAS BEEN AWARE OF THE PIRATE GROUP CALLING THEMSELVES THE "SPACE LIBERATION FRONT" AND HAVE BEEN CONCERNED ABOUT THEIR INTENTIONS FOR SOME TIME. IT IS TO OUR DEEP REGRET THAT YOUR FIRST KNOWLEDGE OF THESE BANDITS HAS COME AT SUCH HIGH COST. THE PEOPLE'S REPUBLIC OF CHINA WILL NOT ALLOW SUCH A BRAZEN ACT OF PIRACY TO STAND.
MY SHIP AND ITS CREW ARE AT YOUR SERVICE.

WE CAN RENDEZVOUS WITH YOUR VESSEL IN
SEVEN DAYS. PLEASE ADVISE IF YOU REQUIRE ANY
SPECIAL MEDICAL ASSISTANCE.
                          WITH KINDEST REGARDS,
          COLONEL LIU WANG SHU, COMMANDING

"Well," Poole breathed. "Didn't see that one coming."

"So *Peng Fei* isn't a propellant depot after all," Garver observed flatly.

"Clearly not." His eyes narrowed. "This is my shocked face, by the way."

"That always was a hell of a lot of tankage," Garver said. "Way more than they needed for lunar surface ops."

"I'd love to know what they're using for propulsion," Poole said, "preferably before they get here."

"Got to be nuclear, Skipper. Maybe electric, like VASIMR thrusters, but there's definitely a nuke plant running it."

"Agreed," Poole said. "I want to know how we missed this." He sighed. "Chief, your priorities just changed. We need Hunter to finish his inventory, but calorie intake isn't our concern anymore." He stared out the window, back toward the tiny blue marble of the distant Earth and the heretofore unknown Chinese deep-space vessel orbiting it. "I need all available information on this *Peng Fei* and her skipper. I want to know everything about her and the man running it. What modules did the Chinese use to build it, what kind of propellant is in those tanks, and more importantly, which PRC agency does it report to? Because it sure ain't their space agency."

"We're in a real fix, and they are offering help, sir," Garver said, having to point out the diplomatic angle. "We have to be careful about biting the hand that feeds us."

Poole looked annoyed, though he knew the chief was just offering the kind of contrarian advice he needed when his dander was up. "I know, Chief. And I'm not turning down a helping hand. I just want to know what's in the hand they're keeping behind their back."

Marshall was able to isolate and power up *Prospector*'s comm and datalink system, which wasn't what he'd been ordered to do but it wasn't exactly against orders either. If finding the Jiangs, alive or otherwise, was their ultimate mission out here then any reasonable action he took in pursuit of that goal was, by extension, within the scope of their orders.

When the directional antenna showed it was alive, he began slewing it to find the source of those weak biomonitor signals. It was simultaneously thrilling and somber—they were out there, waiting to be found, but he also knew they'd be long dead by now. He'd only be recovering their bodies.

Their suits were the only sign of life left. The thought crossed his mind that those suits must have had fantastic batteries, maybe solar rechargers built into the life-support packs.

It soon became obvious that he needed to trace out a search pattern that made sense. Just slewing the antenna around blindly would do nothing but waste time. He had to focus on which region of space they were most likely to be in.

That had to be RQ39, didn't it? It was the reason they came, after all, and they were supposed to have deployed a couple of surface experiments, both of which were missing. Wherever they were, the Jiangs should be too.

He rotated the antenna dish to face the asteroid, and was almost immediately rewarded with a solid green light on the biomonitor screen. So they were in the vicinity all right. Could they have been on the surface?

It would've made sense. That had been their intention; everyone had just assumed they never got there because of the wrecked spacecraft. What if they had? What if they'd been stranded on RQ39 after watching their home get blasted? To be standing there on a pile of space gravel, with Earth a *really* long way away, and seeing your only refuge, your only way home, torn apart . . .

The thought made him shudder.

That had to be where they were, given the evidence. Hell, the directional antenna was literally pointing at them even if was only somewhere on that big flying rock pile.

One question nagged at him: Why hadn't they tried to make it back to *Prospector*? At the time it would've been close enough, it was only over the intervening week that it had drifted far enough away in its own orbit to make returning impossible for their small emergency maneuvering packs.

He thought through what he knew of their EVA plan. The whole thing was a proof-of-concept experiment to see if humans could productively mine asteroids for resources in ways that robots couldn't. It had started with them deploying a pair of CubeSats a few days prior; in fact the little toaster-sized probes should have still been in orbit around RQ39. He made a mental note that they could be important later, if video from them could be retrieved.

The surface experiment package was externally mounted on its own sled, which included methane-powered maneuvering jets with enough propellant to take them to and from the surface. Its gravity was so low that they wouldn't even be landing, just floating above it. The only item that had to be mounted on the surface was the in situ resource unit so it could crack oxygen and hydrogen out of the regolith . . .

Oh my God.

His eyes darted back to the biomonitor screen. Did that steady green mean it was still getting live data, or was it just an open channel to two dead people? Their control center would know, but nothing was making it back to Palmdale after the explosion put the spacecraft in safe mode.

He stared at the green status bar, thinking through the implication. It just couldn't be. *They* couldn't be. Still alive, after this long? Even if the ISRU had supplied them with water and oxygen, their suits wouldn't protect them from radiation for that amount of time.

What must that have been like? They'd probably seen every-thing . . .

Then it all made sense.

He scrambled for the forward hatch, banging his head off a panel as he tumbled through their small command module. "*Sim—*" he began to shout, before catching himself. "Captain!" he stammered. "Captain Poole!"

Colonel Liu Wang Shu of the People's Liberation Aerospace Force made one final sweep of his quarters. He expected it would be some time before he returned, allowing himself to sleep for only a few hours at a time, and that he would accede to only when he was assured there would be no need for him to make critical decisions for his ship.

In truth there were very few decisions that weren't critical when operating such a complex spacecraft as the *Peng Fei*, whether in his eyes or those of his superiors in Beijing. He had campaigned mightily for a level of autonomy never before granted, shattering the long-established relationships between spacecraft and their ground control teams. While he understood the general staff's need to know where its capital ship was and where it was going at any time, no military vessel could function with every detail of its crew's activities planned and monitored to the degree he'd endured as a taikonaut aboard their Tiangong-3 station. At least not from the ground, he'd argued. There would be no aspect of their daily lives that didn't escape his notice. The general staff would have to trust him just as they would the command pilot of a strategic bomber, or the captain of a capital ship.

It had taken months of lazily orbiting Lagrange 1, the first region between Earth and Moon where the two bodies' gravity wells essentially cancelled each other's out. It was a highly desirable strategic location for a number of reasons, all centered on the fact that it took relatively little energy to reach and even less to depart in any direction they chose to move. That neither the Americans, Russians, or Europeans had not seen fit to establish even a perfunctory presence here was remarkable.

Or perhaps not. They were all locked into their own modes of thinking—and in the grubby Russians' case, strangled in the crib by a thieving government that had barely kept their economy above third-world levels. Though their research and development had been invaluable to his own nation's space program, they'd had no hope of funding such technology, being reliant on the rest of the world's table scraps. Pity for them, but the results of their early work now powered his own vessel.

The Anglos were constrained by their own bureaucratic inertia, the Europeans especially so, though the Americans could be annoyingly inventive. They were continually surprising, which made near-term planning a difficult exercise. Long-term, however, their government could be counted on to keep doing things the way they'd always been done. Upstart, troublesome businesses like Hammond Aero and SpaceX were another matter, but they at least weren't deploying armies on Earth or warships in cislunar space.

Peng Fei had been his country's answer to that. While it had its place as a waystation between Earth and Moon, it was far more than just a fuel depot. After years of steadily building its capability with successive small modifications, each delivered on launches from Earth as their cargo carriers stopped for propellant en route to the Moon, this great ship was ready to show itself to the world. That it would be on a mission of mercy to rescue its only serious challenger was indeed poetic: *Let your adversary first defeat himself.*

Liu pulled the worn leather-bound *Art of War* from beneath the elastic straps on his desk to reverentially place it in a drawer with the few other personal effects he'd brought with him. There was another precept of Sun's which he thought applied perfectly to this situation: *When seeking to determine the conditions for battle, with whom lie the advantages derived from Heaven and Earth?*

He chuckled to himself as he closed the small drawer: He was certain this would be the most unique application of that question yet.

There was a muted knock on the door of his sleep chamber—like most spacecraft, the commander's quarters were not much larger than the closets that sufficed as berthing for the other crewmen. Until they could find more efficient methods to build ships in orbit, mass and volume would always demand a steep price.

"It is t-minus ten minutes, Colonel."

He recognized Lieutenant Zhou's voice—young, serious, eager to please. "Thank you, Lieutenant," he said through the door. "I will be in the flight module shortly."

"Very good, sir."

Liu checked himself in the small mirror adjacent to his sleeping bag. His stiff, bristle-brush hair was clipped close, flecks of gray becoming more and more prevalent. He patted his eyes reflexively, as if working out remnants of sleep he hadn't had in hours. He pulled at his chin, ensuring he hadn't missed any stray whiskers.

His eyes swept the small stateroom one last time: nothing out of place, drawers and cabinets secure, sleeping bag tightly rolled up against the bulkhead. A small writing desk was folded into the opposite wall, beneath a personal TV monitor on standby and displaying the shield of the People's Liberation Aerospace Force. By his design, it looked almost as if no one lived there. No distracting family photos or personal mementos other than a single peony blossom pressed between glass plates, which his wife had plucked from her garden before he left Earth. It had no identifying markings, no hand-scribbled notes attached, no photograph to perhaps put it in context. Privacy aboard a spacecraft was scarce and something to be carefully cultivated. Being the only man aboard who knew its significance made it all the more meaningful.

Satisfied that his chamber was secure, he made his way through the short docking tunnel into the forward control module. It could comfortably hold four men at a time—one fourth of his crew—not including him. As the ship was about to depart its long-occupied halo orbit at L1 for interplanetary space, all four flight stations were occupied: two pilots, an engineer, and a weapons officer, in pairs facing what would be forward once the ship was under thrust. The pilots sat before two large triangular windows. Between the two pairs of consoles was a single, simple chair unfolded from the floor. Though it was supposed to be stowed to open up space, it never had been. The commander's chair was symbolic, it represented his command presence even during those rare periods when he was off duty.

He noted the command crew subtly tense up as he floated into the cabin. "As you were, gentlemen," he said before someone could announce his presence on deck. It was one of the very few departures from military customs he was willing to allow: In orbit, there was nothing more ridiculous or counterproductive than a small crew trying to snap to attention when there was no way for them to properly stand. It made for an odd combination of naval and air force courtesies—while the ship itself could be more closely compared to a naval vessel underway, the crew had to function more like a strategic bomber crew in flight and nobody snapped-to every time the aircraft commander left the cockpit. He suspected the *Borman's* crew would have been much the same had its captain not been such a dedicated naval officer in his former life. But then, there were undeniable parallels between this and the submarine service. They would see for themselves soon enough.

"Major Wu," he said as he strapped into his seat, "are we ready?"

The command pilot, and Liu's executive officer, turned to face him. "The ship is ready, sir, as is the crew. All off-duty crewmen are secure in their chambers. Control is awaiting your confirmation of final orders, sir." He tapped a screen on the pedestal between the pilot stations and a message appeared on a tablet attached to one of Liu's armrests. It did not waste words: CLEARED TO PROCEED.

"L1 departure approved," he said calmly. "Initiate terminal countdown at two minutes from injection node, as planned."

Wu entered a command into the flight computer and their new orbit path appeared on a large status screen mounted between the triangular windows. "Two minutes . . . mark. Countdown begun, sir." There were muffled bursts of control jets outside as the ship automatically adjusted its trim angle to keep them on a precise course.

"Beginning ignition cycle," the engineer, Lieutenant Zhou, reported. "Reactors will be at full capacity at T-zero, sir."

Liu imagined he could feel the ship gathering its full strength as distant turbopumps began whining, drawing propellant from the massive tanks behind the crew modules and into the manifolds. It would all come together to ignite in the plenum chambers at the precise moment to put them on the optimum minimum-time trajectory to intercept the *Borman*. Harnessing the ruthless efficiency of their nuclear engines with such exquisite precision was deeply satisfying. He suppressed a smile. *Ready or not, here we come*, as the Americans would say.

⊚ 23 ⊚

Marshall flew headfirst out of the node and into the command module, almost missing a handhold and managing to stop himself before tumbling into Poole and Garver.

"I didn't know taking inventory could be that exciting," Poole said bemusedly, looking over Garver's estimates. He adjusted a pair of reading glasses on his nose. "Find something interesting, Mister Hunter?"

"Them!" he blurted out. "I've found them!"

Poole peered at Marshall over his glasses, his interest piqued. "Clarify, please," he said, dispassionately projecting calm to get the young officer to settle down himself.

Marshall caught his breath. "I found the Jiangs."

Poole exchanged surprised looks with the chief, and Marshall noticed sideways glances from the other crewmembers. "Now you've got my interest. Where and how, Mister Hunter?"

"In their command module—I mean, I used the biomonitors to home in on their position. I powered up their module interface to access inventory logs, figured I could get through it faster. The biomonitor came on, I reset it, then it came back with faint telemetry—their suits are still transmitting data but it's really weak, sir. I used their directional antenna to get a bearing on them."

"And?"

Marshall tipped his head up toward the cupola, where RQ39 still loomed outside. "They're at the asteroid. With the ISRU and cargo sled gone, I think they're probably on it."

"But you couldn't pin them down with just one bearing," Poole

229

said, thinking out loud. "We'll need to get multiple bearings and triangulate."

"Do you know the frequencies their suit telemeters used?" Garver asked.

"Haven't found that yet, Chief."

Garver looked for Rosie, who'd been watching intently from the far side of the cabin. With a jerk of his thumb, she took off down the tunnel into *Prospector*. He looked back at Marshall. "It'll be faster to let her find it, sir." He glanced at Poole. "I suspect you'll be busy with other things soon."

"Damn straight he will," Poole said. "Get the shuttle prepped for departure ASAP. Once Rosie comes back with their suit frequencies, set your radios accordingly to get bearings on them." He raised his voice, drawing the crew's attention. "I know you're all a bunch of damned eavesdroppers, so let me make it simple: Mister Hunter here may have found our missing spacefarers. Before anybody gets their hopes up, at this point remember we are almost certainly recovering casualties."

Turning back to Marshall, he lowered his voice. "Now there's something you don't know about." He handed over the message printout.

Marshall's brow furrowed as he tried to digest it. "I...don't understand. China has an interplanetary spacecraft we didn't know about?"

"More correctly, we *did* know about it," Poole said. "We just thought it was a fuel depot."

He stared at the message, trying to recall what he knew about the *Peng Fei* and make sense of it. "Nobody in CIA or the Pentagon had a clue? How could they miss that?"

Poole regarded him with grim amusement as he took back the paper. "I'm just impressed that's your first thought and not 'Yippee, someone's coming to our rescue.' Makes me glad I kept you on the crew."

Marshall blushed. "There's that too, sir." He hadn't been looking forward to spending the next several months counting out all those meals and subsisting on a starvation diet.

"So what are your thoughts, Mister Hunter?"

Was the captain really asking him that? If he was, he might as well go with his gut...

"The Chinese lifted a lot of mass up to L1 over a couple of years to build it," he said slowly. "It was supposed to be a waystation for their lunar ops, but those never really got going, did they? Not to the extent they'd need a propellant depot that large. And if they put engines on it without us noticing, then what else is on it?"

"Meaning?" Poole prodded.

Marshall shrugged. "We've got weapons, we're just up front about it. They've already kept one big capability secret. There's got to be more they're not talking about."

Poole poked him in the chest with the rolled-up paper. "Very good, Mister Hunter. Maybe when you get back from your next trip you can help us figure that out."

With their departure burn complete, Liu saw to it that the *Peng Fei*'s crew fell back into their normal routine as it sped away from the Earth-Moon system. They had trained and rehearsed scenarios to the point where any contingency could be reacted to from memory. Now, it was vital that the men be either at their posts or resting, ensuring the ship ran smoothly now that their mission beyond Earth was underway.

Though he had hoped to someday be the first to do so, he could still be satisfied in the knowledge that the first people to escape cislunar space had indeed been Chinese even if they had been using American-made equipment. Whether the Jiangs still thought of themselves as Chinese mattered little to him—it was their heritage, as inescapable as the physical laws that defined their travels out here. It was a pity that they could not reconcile themselves to that reality, though they had to know the Party would not tolerate their insolence forever. They had already made a worldwide nuisance of themselves spouting insufferable lies about the supposed deprivations suffered by average citizens—as if they had experienced such oppression themselves!

They had finally found the limits of their own supposed freedom. Expatriates or not, they had gone too far for their own good, at long last running afoul of their birth nation's economic and security interests. As an officer of the People's aerospace forces, he could feel no sympathy for their plight. Leaving the confines of Earth's atmosphere and straying far from its gravity well exposed them to innumerable hazards, most instantly fatal. It was an environment not meant for humans, and it was only through meticulous preparation and exhaustive training that even the most superior specimens could hope to withstand an extended tenure in deep space. The thought of an average Americanized upper-class couple making such a jaunt filled him with disdain. What could they hope to accomplish other than survive? They accomplished nothing without the tireless work of hundreds of unheralded workers behind them, yet they achieved all the notoriety and amassed all the wealth.

It was the way of the world, Liu knew. His people had found a better way, one which the Jiangs had chosen to abandon. Not just abandon, he knew—they had actively opposed it from every vantage point they could take. And as their illicit fortunes had grown, they had found more ways to undermine his nation's unity. From speaking at universities, to mouthing their propaganda on news programs, to addressing foreign government assemblies, to ultimately financing those querulous little "nongovernmental organizations" that harassed and undermined the PRC . . . No, the corner of his soul that at one time might have felt concern for their plight was instead filled with contempt.

Their failures needed to be held up to the world as an example. Their disappearance had already shown the world how dangerous deep space was, and the crippled American vessel sent to their rescue only served as a punctuation of this fact. Never a place for the timid, it was certainly not a place for the foolhardy or the overly confident, which the Americans certainly were. Now, they'd tempted fate and needed rescue themselves. Fortunate for them that his ship was in a position to offer aid and assistance as the world watched in morbid fascination. Watch, and hopefully learn.

While used to being under constant scrutiny from military and party leaders, Liu was not accustomed to being in the public eye. Already known for being coldly efficient, he was compelled to see that his crew exceeded the already high standards he'd set for them.

He brought this merciless focus to bear on the mission plan and status report now laid out before him on the widescreen monitor in the command deck. Major Wu hovered behind him, feet slipped in floor restraints and hands clasped behind his back in a stiff parade-rest stance. This allowed him to surreptitiously worry at a fingernail, keeping his apprehension out of Liu's sight as he awaited questions from his commander.

"I see we are over two meters per second below our target velocity," Liu noted. "In one day's time. Why is this, Major Wu?"

"I am investigating this anomaly, sir. Our residuals after shutdown were within the lower bound of acceptable error, but clearly they have propagated more than anticipated."

"Clearly," Liu said. "And be careful about what you consider 'acceptable error,' Wu. What may be acceptable to the mission planners in their offices is not acceptable to us. There are no fuel farms, ocean currents, or jet streams out here to turn to our advantage. Every meter per second represents future opportunity to be lost or gained—ours or theirs. Is this understood?"

Wu lowered his head deferentially. "Of course, Colonel."

Studying the projections further, Liu decided to let him off the hook a bit. They had lost more velocity than planned but it could be made up with a correction burn soon. If main engine cutoff had indeed occurred almost at the exact second—which it had, he'd been there when it happened—then it left few alternatives. "Either our trajectory planning is in error or our mass budget has been miscalculated," he said, stroking his chin. He turned to Wu and lowered his voice enough that the rest of the command deck crew couldn't hear. "You know I don't like to guess, Wu. But since I am in a position to, I would speculate that it's the latter. We are carrying too much mass. Whether it is essential equipment, or our crewmen smuggled too much into their personal allowances, we may have to lose weight." He patted his flat stomach. "It's rather late to put the ship on a diet, correct?"

A slight smile from Wu. "Correct, sir." He eyed the connecting tunnel behind them, toward the aft modules. "If I may?"

Liu nodded his assent.

Wu cleared his throat. "I inspected each crew's personal equipment packages before launch, sir. If there is a gross error in that budget, I take full responsibility."

A thin smile crept across Liu's face, ending at his eyes. "But a gross error of that magnitude isn't likely, is it, Major?"

Wu continued. "It is not, sir. It is likely that our consumables inventory is in error, but much of that was predetermined on the ground. No, I believe it is one of two things: either density variations in our hydrogen and oxygen—"

"Which would be in our favor, over time," Liu interrupted.

"Yes sir, we'd have more propellant than budgeted," Wu agreed, "or Captain Huang's squad brought more equipment than they reported."

"That seems most likely to me as well, which in the end also redounds to our favor. Do not waste your valuable time with further investigation. Focus instead on correcting the shortfall with our next burn." Liu's eyes narrowed, though they signaled amusement. "One can never have too much fuel or ammunition."

Nick Lesko had been stuck with what little fare was available on the base hospital's limited television service, and with no internet he couldn't even stream from his own accounts. His phone was useless, as was the expensive laptop still sitting in its rad-shielded case by his bed. That thing could probably split atoms but it might as well have been a paperweight to him now.

He flicked through the same baker's-dozen channels, most following the same banal formula with only the faces changing. There was exactly one news station, but that at least meant the occasional sports programming so he could maybe catch up on some of the bets he'd laid before leaving Earth.

Lesko drummed his fingers impatiently. Not even two weeks yet, and it felt like a lifetime ago. There'd been too much work to do even without his contacts in Macau scrupulously monitoring every aspect of their preparations. He had no illusions that they hadn't also managed to plant an informant somewhere in Stardust's mission control team back in Cali.

If things had gone to plan, they'd have expected to hear from him by now. But things had most definitely not gone according to plan.

Why had he done it? There'd been a plan to eliminate the others after reentry, about which Lesko had his doubts—not that it couldn't have been done, but that it couldn't have been done without him somehow being connected to it. The alternative had seemed like an easy choice once it presented itself. "Natural causes" were always a better choice than an obvious hit if you had the opportunity.

But his sponsors had been fanatic about sticking to the plan. They always were. It was a trait he'd observed all across East Asia. They would want to know why he deviated from it, and how it had come to place him in an American military hospital.

He'd been wondering that himself. *I ain't no rocket scientist*, he told himself. *I didn't know it would cook our spacecraft*, though he vaguely remembered some dense blather from their trainers about cosmic radiation and something called the Van Halen belts.

Maybe he'd stumbled into the limits of his abilities, in which case he counted himself lucky to have realized it. *No more space adventures for me*, he decided. From now on, he would stick to machines on the ground.

He settled back into his bed, resigned to another repetitive cycle of news. Yet this time, their lead story piqued his interest:

"In what has become a rash of similar incidents, another communications satellite has 'disappeared' from sight. INDOSAT-21 is believed to still be functional, but its control center in Jakarta has been unable to send any commands or receive any information from the satellite. More worrisome for the region is this constitutes the bulk of their space-based information network. SinoComp Holdings of Macau has offered the use of its own satellites in order to plug what has become a considerable hole in the region's information network."

Carefully positioned for the camera in front of what Lesko assumed to be an Indonesian satellite antenna farm, the reporter droned on as colorful but mostly meaningless graphics followed.

So that's what their game was. There must have been a hell of a lot of money in cornering the developing world's communications networks. The bosses always withheld the full story and he'd have to figure out the big picture later, but that's how it went. If everybody knew the plan, somebody would eventually get pinched and bring down the whole shebang.

Lesko smiled to himself and reclined in his bed, patiently waiting for the sports report.

Roberta's first thought at using an Advanced Cryogenic Exploration (ACES) stage to put a new drone in geosynch was "overkill." It was a big stage for a relatively small payload, certainly smaller than the payloads the workhorse upper stage customarily moved back and forth from lunar orbit. The X-37's role was a "multimission space maneuvering vehicle" used in low to medium orbits. GEO was considerably higher at over thirty thousand kilometers, and the drone needed an extra boost to get there, but this was a mighty large kick. It was the highest they'd ever taken one of the spaceplanes, and the four-engine ACES would deliver it with nearly half of its propellant load left over. It had all seemed very wasteful until they got the first mission brief: close with and inspect the abandoned Stardust and the nearby SAMCOM-3 communications satellite.

That would require another small kick up to the graveyard orbit, another three hundred klicks higher. It would also require a little bit of orbit phasing, as the distance was enough to put them out of synch. They could use the Hall ion thruster package for station keeping around vulnerable satellites, but they'd still be hauling that hefty upper stage around.

It turned out they would need it for the *next* series of taskings. Once finished, they would be taking the new drone a third of the way around the world to the next assignment: another reportedly dead satellite at a different location in GEO. Given the amount of propellant that would be left over, she anticipated yet another burn and movement to a different longitude after that.

"What's bugging you?" Ivey asked from the flight station beside her.

"Reading the tea leaves in the propellant budget," she said, distracting herself with her work at the payload station. "Trying to figure out where they're sending us next. Why don't they just put it in the STO?" she wondered as she exercised the manipulator arms, cycling them through their full range of motion now that the drone's cargo doors were open. "Why keep us guessing? We can do a better job if we could plan ahead."

"Compartmentalization," Ivey said, mildly lecturing her as he flipped through the maneuver plan. "The probability of a secret being blown is directly proportional to how many people are in on it. They tell us what we need to know to accomplish the mission and that's it." He wore a sly grin. "But they forget we're all rocket scientists here. What information they do give helps me figure out what we're doing next. Look." He spread the printout of their maneuvering plan between them. "Here's the delta-v budget for this mission, with the margins we need to leave for the next mission."

Roberta stared at the numbers, struggling to discern their significance. "How does that tell you the next tasking?"

"Because I know how much we have to keep in reserve to deorbit at the end of all this. After this op, we'll have just enough in the tanks for two more before we lose ACES." He showed her a crude graph he'd drawn over a pocket map of Earth, with rough ellipses over two areas equally spaced around the equator. "These are the other two zones where satellites have started going dark. Phasing burns to reach each of them leaves just enough to deorbit afterward. The way we're configured, it makes sense that's where they send us next."

"Could be," she said. "But it could be a lot of things. Wouldn't this be a pretty short mission duration? These things usually stay up for months at a time."

"Depends on the mission." Another mischievous look flashed in his eyes. "And if I'm right, it'll be fun tweaking the planning cell. Those guys think they're smarter than everybody else here." He pointed at Roberta's console. "But don't let me distract you. How's your package?"

She fought the temptation to enjoin a double entendre and turned back to her console. "Manipulator arms checked out and stowed for maneuvering. Cameras are up and tracking." She clicked over to fill one of their shared screens with the visuals.

Ivey looked puzzled. "Blank screen. You sure it checked out?"

Roberta twirled a small joystick that controlled the cameras. "Yeah . . . yeah. Focus and color balance looked good inside the spacecraft."

"Sun didn't cross its field of view, did it? That'll throw the exposure off, send it into safe mode."

"No, I made sure to rotate it antisolar."

"Check your focal length," he said.

"It's set at infinity, right where it's supposed to be." She ran the camera through its full range of focus. "Yeah, it's correct. And it's pointed in the right direction." She swallowed nervously. "Infrared's blank, too."

Ivey checked his own instruments against hers. The X-37 was at the planned orbit and oriented correctly. Jacob's cameras should have been able to see their target by now. Instead, they were staring at a blank screen. The region of space where the abandoned Stardust and the SAMCOM-3 satellite should have been was empty.

☸ 24 ☸

The small cabin of the *Specter* shuttle was becoming as familiar to Marshall as his own quarters back aboard ship. He'd become as fastidious with it as his spacers had been with their suits, a fact he'd realized when he'd become annoyed with himself after finding switches misconfigured from their last excursion. It had taken an extra ten minutes to find and correct the problem after it had prevented him from powering up the little spacecraft.

And he was still mad at himself, checking and rechecking instruments and settings as they approached RQ39, determined not to waste any more time. Wylie might still be occupying the command seat, but he was leaving much of this sortie for Marshall to fly. The need to perform was not lost on him.

Rosie floated by the secondary control panel next to him, working the directional antenna to pinpoint the source of the mystery biomonitor signals. "A watched pot never boils, sir."

"How's that?"

She pointed at the cuff of his pressure suit. "You keep checking your watch. That means you're in a hurry, and pilots who get in a hurry tend to make mistakes. And since I'm not a pilot, that means I'm counting on you to not make mistakes. You're making me nervous, sir."

He looked away sheepishly. "Sorry. Just pissed off with myself."

She laughed. "Over a dead battery? That's why they keep spares on the charger, sir. You think you're the first pilot who forgot to isolate the backup bus?"

Marshall shot a glance toward Wylie up at the forward controls.

He hadn't mentioned it, which should tell him something. "I guess it is easy to miss."

"Wouldn't know, I'm not a pilot," she said, following his gaze. "But yeah, it happens a lot. Even to the salty ones."

Marshall nodded, silently wondering how long it would take him to get "salty."

"You're getting there, sir," Rosie said, reading his mind. "This run's been a steep learning curve. It's felt like a full six-month float and we've only been out for a couple of weeks."

The asteroid loomed large in their windows. Almost ten kilometers across, it was enough to have a perceptible, if weak, gravity field. Marshall pulsed their nose thrusters, parking them far enough away to keep from being drawn any closer. They hovered along its eastern limb while she listened on the biomonitor's frequency.

"Got it," she said. "Loud and clear, bearing two-nine-four, z minus three-zero degrees. Can you translate us port?"

"Stand by." First marking the bearing on a digital map of the asteroid, Marshall pushed against the control stick, goosing the starboard thrusters to move them in the opposite direction. The gray, pebbled surface passed slowly in front of them.

"Lost them," Rosie said as she tried turning the antenna to follow. "Can't keep up with the lateral motion."

After a few minutes, Marshall brought them to stop along RQ39's western limb. Rosie's eyes were shut in concentration as she gently tweaked the antenna controls, one hand keeping her headset pressed into her ear.

"Got it . . . got it! Zero-four-four, minus three-one degrees. I think we've got them, sir."

Marshall marked this new bearing on his kneeboard tablet, almost directly on top of the first. "It sure looks like it. Good work." He flicked his mic switch. "*Borman*, *Specter*. We've pinpointed their location. Request permission to proceed."

Poole answered quickly, no doubt following them from his perch in the cupola with his ever-present binoculars. "You're go for approach, *Specter*. Hold at fifty meters."

"You sure this is the spot?" They orbited alongside RQ39, holding at fifty meters directly above where they'd expected to find the Jiang's remains. "I don't see anything."

Rosie tuned the antenna while Nikki Harper looked out through the topside windows. "Signal's really strong here, sir. This has to be it. There's a heat source in the same vicinity too."

"That'd be their surface experiment package," he said, craning his neck and leaning farther into the window. "It was solar powered, those panels ought to make it easy to spot."

He backed the shuttle away, moving them farther out to expand their field of view. As he did, a glint of light coming from a depression in the regolith caught their attention.

"There!" Rosie exclaimed. "At your two o'clock, sir. Can you bring us overhead?"

Marshall nodded and gave the controls a gentle tap back. Thrusters kicked beneath them and they drifted up and right. A final kick left them floating above a boxy metallic framework beneath two black semicircular fans: the In Situ Resource Unit and its unfolded solar panels. A tangle of cables and hoses glimmered in the harsh sunlight, running from the unit and disappearing into the shadow of an overhang.

"That's their ISRU," Marshall said. "No sign of either of them, though. Maybe dust clinging to their suits blended them in against the surface. If it's anything like moondust—that stuff's supposed to get into everything."

"I don't know, sir," she said, leaning into the window herself. "I get the feeling this place isn't like the Moon, or anything else for that matter."

He turned to face her. "Ready to go investigate, then?"

"Walk on an asteroid?" she asked, for a moment forgetting why they were there. She exchanged looks with Harper. "Sorry, sir. I shouldn't be, well . . ."

He laid a gloved hand on an arm of her suit. "It's okay to be eager so long as we don't lose sight of why we're here. That's not something I worry about with you."

Marshall let her go first, keeping them parked above the Jiang's presumed EVA site. She pushed away from the shuttle's aft hatch and slowly floated across the gulf between them and the asteroid, feet first and trailing an extra tether behind her. When she made contact—"touching down" might be too strong a term in such feeble gravity—a cloud of gravel spread from beneath her feet and slowly settled back onto the surface. She bounced back herself slightly, having to give her maneuvering unit thrusters a tap to remain standing on the surface.

She'd been unusually silent for a while. "How's it going down there?" Marshall prompted.

"I guess that's one giant leap for me," she said. "It's weird, sir. Be careful when you come down." She dragged one foot across the surface. "You can't really walk on this, gravity's not nearly strong enough. Feels weird. It's not noticeable until it is, you know? It pulls at you just enough to be a nuisance. Standing's kind of on purpose if that makes sense. It's like you're in your own orbit, your feet are just touching the 'roid."

Which was exactly the truth, he thought. "What can you see?"

"Rocks." There was a crackle of static as she moved forward, suggesting some mild electrical discharge as she stirred up the regolith. "Lots of rocks. It's like the surface is covered with a blanket of loose gravel. Solid underneath, though."

"You aren't too far from their surface equipment. What can you see from there?"

"Heading there now," she said, and he watched her launch across the surface in one clean, continuous hop. "Using my MMU instead of trying to walk on this."

Rosie and Harper landed near the equipment setup, stirring up another cloud of gravel that stubbornly clung to her boots with static electricity. This was going to get real annoying real fast if they didn't figure out a way to compensate for it. She shook each foot, sending pebbles flying in all directions. "How do you read me, sir?" The crackling radio channel suggested the answer.

"Loud but broken. How me?"

"About the same. I'm going to limit movement to the MMU as much as possible."

"Makes sense. What's it look like down there?"

The resource extraction package was a short hop away: a square, open cage of aluminum alloys atop four legs set into the rock. Beneath it, a drill shaft was embedded in the surface. The cage held foil-wrapped storage tanks and mineral processors encased in their own composite shells. Its control box was sturdy and simple, built to function in harsh and unpredictable environments. It looked to be framed in high-strength plastic, cheap and more importantly nonconductive.

"ISRU's clean and pristine, sir." She lifted a protective cover beneath a row of status lights, all of them green. "It's drilled into the surface, looks like it's been running for a while." She whistled as she read off quantities. "Must have found a vein of subsurface ice, because it's been cracking a ton of oxygen and hydrogen."

"At least they'll have proved their hypothesis," Marshall said. "So this wasn't for nothing."

"Not sure where it's all going, though," she answered. There were umbilical lines leading away from the extractor into the nearby overhang she'd seen from overhead. "Weird."

She jumped up and flew over to the outcropping, using the MMU's jets to bring her back down in front of the opening. The lines led inside, behind a Mylar blanket draped over the opening. She pushed it aside to see the silhouettes of two pairs of boots lying atop a thin bed of gravel. She flicked on her helmet lamp, illuminating the inside of the little cavern they'd laid themselves to rest in. There they lay, two lifeless forms in dust-covered EVA suits, side by side beneath a rock overhang far from home.

Her heart sank. She'd come looking for them but hadn't really known what to expect when she found them. She waved for Nikki Harper to follow.

"Report." She must have been standing there for a while because he sounded anxious. For a boot officer, he'd been unusually patient so far.

"I've found them, sir. Stand by, please."

What must that have been like? she wondered. They'd come here fully expecting to die. What goes through a person's mind then?

Her mind went back to space survival and rescue school: "SEAL training with math." And it had been the toughest experience she'd ever faced. Between the physical and academic expectations, the washout rate had been on the order of ninety percent. The single worst exercise, or "training evolution" in typically anodyne mil-speak, had been the suit isolation drill: a full day, encased in an EVA suit, lying in a darkened vacuum chamber with steadily draining life support and no outside communication. It would be entirely up to the trainee to be in touch with their own body enough to stretch their consumables well beyond suit design limits, the goal being to survive until the lights and air came back on without having the safety crew come pull you out early.

The idea was to test the prospective rescue spacer's psychological limits in simulated deep-space isolation, on the theory that this could—in fact *would*—happen someday. "Somebody out there is going to be experiencing what may be the last day of their lives and it's up to you to pull them out of it. You will have to stay with them and keep them alive until you can both be rescued. The farther out people go, the higher probability of them getting into bad trouble."

It hadn't been the physically hardest part of training, but the combination of total isolation and dwindling resources had pushed her to her limits. She was in fact ready to push the big red "I quit" button just as the chamber's lights came back on.

Staring at the couple lying before her, she trembled. They hadn't had that luxury. They came here knowing this would become their graves. And there they lay, holding hands, together to the end.

She felt a catch in her throat. A tear welled up, sticking to her eye in the near-complete absence of gravity. Irritated, she shook her head to knock it free. It rippled out of her field of view, slowly traveling down to settle on her neck ring.

She unspooled a rescue tether from her utility harness to clip onto one of the lifeless forms. She brushed at a thin layer of dust just beneath the suit's chest pack and pulled at the D-ring connection.

As she pulled at the suit, a hand shot out and grabbed hers. Startled, she reflexively backed away. The light from her lamps fell on their helmets and she gasped as Max Jiang's eyes snapped open.

Oh my God.

Her eyes darted back and forth between the pair of helmeted faces before her. Max and Jasmine Jiang, after all this time, so far from home, were both alive.

"Alive!" she stammered, almost rolling back into Harper behind her, then checked to make sure her radio was still voice activated. Her normally cool, controlled voice stumbled over the words. "They're alive! We need a dust-off ASAP!"

⚜   ⚜   ⚜

Marshall moved the shuttle as close as he dared to the surface, flying formation with the asteroid over their position while they prepped the Jiangs for transport. This consisted of clumsily dragging each of them out from under their rocky shelter and into the open, where they could be tethered to each spacewalker and flown up to the waiting *Specter*.

"We're going to get you out of here," he heard her repeatedly say over the common emergency frequency. "Just stay with me." It was like a mantra and he wondered if she was doing it intentionally, whether for their sake or her own.

Looking down through his side window, he could see the bright yellow suits of his EVA team bouncing about as they prepped their evacuees, occasionally jetting above the surface with their maneuvering packs. "Keep clear," Rosie instructed firmly. "Minimum safe distances. I didn't come all this way to get blasted in the face by your MMU."

They wasted no time. Rosie had pulled both of them out from under their makeshift shelter while the shuttle maneuvered in closer. She and Harper each had one of the Jiangs harnessed to them, then to the safety tether leading back to *Specter*.

"You ready?"

"Ready," she said. "Evacuees are secure."

"*Specter* is stable. Bringing 'em up now."

Marshall kept the shuttle in position from the aft control station. He watched the safety lines go taut as first one limp form, then the next, lifted off the surface behind Rosie and Nikki. "Ten meters. Halfway there. Looking good, sir."

He was focused on their evacuees almost to the exclusion of everything else. The effect was startling; for a moment they were all he could see. He shook his head to clear it; this was not the time for tunnel vision. He checked the small auxiliary control panel: the ship remained stable relative to the surface and the inertia reel was taking up the slack as the Jiangs drifted toward him. Almost in reach.

He braced his feet in the floor restraints and reached out to slow them down as they drifted into the open hatch. He pulled them aboard, locking down the tether in its reel. "Both evacs are secure aboard. Need you guys back here ASAP."

"On the way," Rosie said, already heading for the equipment bay and the MMU mounts on either side of the aft hatchway. Having drilled this countless times, it was a matter of minutes for them to back their maneuvering packs into the mounts, lock them down, and glide through the open portal into *Specter*'s passenger cabin. She waited for her partner to go in first, then flew in herself and moved to pull the big outer door closed behind her. "EVA team secure aboard."

"Good work, guys. My spacecraft," Wylie called from up front as Marshall began pressurizing the cabin. "Hunter, stay there with your team. I'll fly us back."

Harper had already strapped Jasmine Jiang into a gurney mounted in the floor. Max Jiang floated beside her, still locked onto the inertia reel.

"What can I do to help?" Marshall asked.

Rosie slipped her feet into a pair of floor-mounted stirrups and moved to strap Max into the opposite gurney. Behind the glass of her faceplate, Marshall could see the concern clouding her eyes. "Don't know yet, sir. They're in bad shape." Still encased in her suit, she tore open the Velcro flap of her sleeve pocket and clumsily pulled out a pen light to shine in Max's eyes. "Eyes are sunken and dilated. He looks badly dehydrated."

"Same here," Nikki said of Jasmine. "We need to get them on IV fluids, stat."

"Agreed." Rosie eyed the pressurization panel, shedding her gloves and helmet even before it was in the green. "I can handle thin air," she said impatiently, anticipating Marshall's concern. "We coped with worse in survival and rescue school."

"Roger that," Harper said over her shoulder, not far behind in getting out of her suit. Marshall noticed they did not practice the same haste with their patients. As soon as the cabin pressure display went green, they were unlocking the Jiang's helmets and opening up their suits. Both pressed oxygen masks to their patient's faces.

She reached into Max Jiang's suit and pinched the skin of his chest, leaving a tent-like crest behind. "Piss-poor skin turgor. Let's get the fluids started." She turned to open the protective cover on an intravenous pump, then pulled a pair of shears from a pouch. She began cutting open an arm of Max's spacesuit. "It'll take too long to get them out," she explained to Marshall, and began probing Max's forearm before starting an IV line. With the suit open, he recoiled at the stench of accumulated body odor and a waste control garment that was well past saturation.

To her credit, Rosie seemed oblivious to it. "How're you doing over there?" she asked her partner.

"Blew a vein," Nikki muttered in frustration, "but I've got a good one now. Starting saline push." There was a faint electric hum as the IV pump started.

Rosie did the same, then pointed to a blue cabinet behind Marshall. "If you could, sir, there's some electrolytes in there. One each, please."

He hurriedly removed two squeeze bottles of a common sports drink, pushing one through the air to each medic. Rosie lifted the O₂ mask from Max Jiang's face and gently placed the straw in his mouth. "Can you take a drink for me?"

Jiang nodded weakly and closed his lips around the straw. She gave the bottle a little squeeze; a few stray globules of greenish-yellow juice floated free before he gulped the rest down. He coughed reflexively and Rosie put the mask back on. She checked to see that Jasmine had been able to drink as well. "That's real good, folks. We don't want to push too much too soon, enough to wet your whistles. Let's give these IVs time to work and you can have the rest. Deal?"

Max Jiang lifted his free arm in a weak thumbs up, then reached across for his wife's. They clasped hands, tears welling in their eyes. Rosie took a gauze pad and swabbed Max's away, motioning for Nikki to do the same for Jasmine. "You're going to be okay, Mr. Jiang," she said, looking to Marshall for affirmation. Crippled or not, going aboard *Borman* was a hell of a lot better than where they'd been and there was another ship on the way.

Marshall nodded, not so certain himself of China's motives with the *Peng Fei*. Part of him preferred to take his chances with diminished rations on a much longer return to Earth under their own power, but having two evacuees changed that calculus.

Looking at the frail bodies being cut away from their suits made him doubtful they could endure a long trip. Maybe they could snap back quickly with some food and fluids, but putting them on a limited diet for months seemed like an unacceptable risk. Ultimately that was up to Poole and he would base much of his decision on what his medics had to say, maybe even more so than the actual MDs back on Earth.

Marshall studied Max Jiang's face: jet black hair matted beneath his helmet and skullcap, eyes sunken from dehydration and starvation. Red blotches around his neck hinted at a bloom of friction sores beneath his cooling garment.

He laid a hand on Max's arm and they made eye contact for the first time. After months of following their expedition, watching every livestream, he was at long last face-to-face with a man he'd greatly admired. Weakened near to the point of death, his dark eyes still burned with determination. Marshall had no doubt it was this fiery spirit and inventiveness that had enabled them to survive almost two weeks in deep space in nothing but their EVA suits.

"I'm Ensign Hunter from the USS *Borman*," he began. "We'll be taking you aboard soon where you'll be under full medical care."

Jiang reached up to grip his hand, hoarsely whispering "thank you" beneath the mask. His strength was surprising, one more attribute which had kept them alive.

Marshall nodded silently, almost ashamed to reply. "That's not necessary, sir," he said. "This is what we do." *This is what we do.* It sounded self-aggrandizing: No worries, dear wayward traveler, just another day at work for us Guardians. It's our job, saving your asses from imminent death in the Big Empty.

Instinct told him it was best not to mention the *Peng Fei*'s impending arrival. Famously outspoken against their birth country's ruling party, they would not welcome the news of their rescuers.

❂ 25 ❂

Simon Poole waited just outside the medical module, purposefully staying out of the way while the Jiangs were maneuvered into hastily prepared EMS pods. They hadn't expected survivors, and therefore hadn't prepped the med bay other than to keep two sets of human remains on ice. He reminded himself to never again allow his crew to let their guard down like that ahead of a rescue op, or anything else for that matter.

Marshall and Rosie had quickly stripped out of their spacesuits back in the airlock and came up behind Poole. He regarded them briefly, as they were still in their cooling garments. It was a breach of procedure he'd address later. Right now he needed information. He nodded toward the Jiangs.

"So you found them in a cavern? Do I understand that right?"

"I wouldn't call it that, sir," Rosie said. "It was an overhang, maybe three meters across and a couple deep. It looks like they dug out part of it underneath, too, enough to fit their heads under, and piled up the regolith around the sides."

"Like a lean-to?"

"Exactly. They were dug in real good, sir. I took some quick readings after we prepped them for dust-off and they made themselves a nice little hasty radiation shelter."

"And they used the ISRU to crack oxygen out of the substrate," Poole marveled as he watched them lay in the EMS pods. "Hell of a way to prove the concept." He imagined they'd be anxious to get up and moving as soon as their bodies started to recover. "And a hell of a long time to be stuck in a suit."

"Almost two weeks," Marshall agreed. "I can't imagine what was going through their heads that whole time."

"That's what I want you to find out," Poole said. "You've been following them pretty closely, haven't you?"

Marshall did a double take. "Begging your pardon, sir—how would you know that?"

"Inductive reasoning. You have an abiding interest in humans exploring the planets, and they'd have been the first to see Mars in person." Poole smiled. "Plus there's not much soundproofing between berthing spaces. If there was any news about them, you were watching it."

"I'll make it a point to use earphones from now on, sir."

Poole waved it away. "You know more about those two than anybody else onboard. Once they're up and about, get me a full debrief. Keep it loose. Informal. The kind of questions you're probably itching to ask anyway."

"Like how'd they survive that long outside their spacecraft?"

"That, and why didn't they try to go back? It should've been close enough for them to reach, even after all of the crap hit the fan. What makes digging a hole on an asteroid seem like the better plan?"

Colonel Liu Wang Shu floated in his quarters, legs crossed tightly in a full lotus position that he found uniquely challenging in zero g. Once a person was limber enough, gravity helped the body's own weight maintain the position with little effort. It had taken some practice to achieve the same state in freefall. Now he freed his mind to enter a state of deep meditation, aided by the steady hum of the *Peng Fei*'s air circulators.

He envisioned their position in space as if he were flying it himself like an open-cockpit biplane, with bare hands and the seat of his pants. He could feel the power of their nuclear engine when it fired, its roar silenced by vacuum but hinted at in the steady rumble conveyed through its hardened crew modules, reverberating like an echo of distant thunder.

Liu visualized himself among the Sun and planets against the still backdrop of stars. He traveled along an invisible road defined by gravity and velocity, understood only by a system of elegant mathematics that had not so much been invented as discovered—

the universal language of nature itself, deciphered and available to anyone with the will to understand it. It defined his path among the cosmos and in a sense his own life. There was nothing in his mind that could not be defined by mathematics. Even his meditation could be described as such: equations of force and motion, tension and compression within the body, electrochemical reactions in the brain . . . even if leading to a heightened state of awareness, what some thought of as "projection," he believed could be described by natural processes. Which in turn meant mathematics. The act of solving complex equations was its own form of meditation; pages filled with differential equations were a form of poetry to those who chose to comprehend them.

His mind moved beyond its own position in space along a curved path, arriving at the crippled American ship named for one of its hero astronauts—common for their culture, whereas he had been pleased to see his vessel christened with something more imaginative and meaningful. It had been amusing to see the Americans and their western allies utterly fail to appreciate its connotation. He understood the liberal West's aversion to state disinformation, but was it propaganda when they chose to accept official explanations at face value for their own comfort's sake?

They had chosen defeat without realizing it, long before the battle was joined. A part of him was saddened that this was so often the case, though in the end that way saves more lives than it takes: It is best to let the enemy defeat himself.

While politicians—including generals—were often foolish, he always respected the tactical leaders he was matched against. Some were more inventive than others, but an honorable man, whether in charge of a ship or an infantry battalion, could be dangerous indeed.

Simon Poole had proven himself to be a dangerous man in both the American naval and space services, though he'd let his guard down for the sake of rescuing those troublesome Jiangs. Liu reminded himself that Poole's most consequential act had been chasing down a hijacked Orion spacecraft and arguably saving much of humanity in the process. And he'd done *that* as a civilian being paid to shepherd wealthy tourists around the Moon. He'd proven his survival skills and fighting sense—how would he respond now? That depended on how he perceived the root of his predicament, something Liu did not expect him to discern for himself. Therefore, expect the worst.

Liu paused, letting his mind take in the tactical picture at asteroid RQ39. The privateer spacecraft misleadingly named *Prospector* sat among a haze of its own wreckage, the crippled American warship nearby and in a similar predicament. Though still able to make way on its own power, losing most of its propellant had left it essentially stranded. They had no hope of return before its crew ran out of food. Had Poole chosen to keep his ship fully armed, would it have made a difference?

Liu smiled to himself: No, it would not have.

There was a knock on his door. Liu's mind withdrew from its deep contemplation. At first annoyed, he recognized the pattern of three brisk knocks on the door frame: Major Wu, with news.

Liu unfolded his legs, took a cleansing breath, and slid open the door. As expected, Wu hovered just outside in the corridor. "Yes, Major?"

"News from control," Wu said stiffly. "The Americans report they have found the Jiangs."

Liu lifted his eyebrows. "That is interesting," he said, "but hardly worth the interruption, Wu."

"Pardon me, sir, for not being more specific: They found them *alive.*"

His eyes narrowed. "I see."

Finding a misplaced spacecraft was not something Roberta McCall had ever seriously contemplated, and she didn't like it. Any other time it would have been an alarming curiosity, something left for the Ops planners to run down after so obviously screwing the pooch. That it happened while so many other satellites had been going dark all over the place put a decidedly different spin on things. Now she took a very personal interest in it, and was not about to leave it up to the intel weenies although she suspected they wouldn't ignore her this time.

After running so many successful ops against unfriendly sats, her teammates weren't used to having the opposing team pull one over on them. The tables were turned, and they took that personally. These weren't even state vehicles, unless you considered a South

American telecom consortium to be a state actor. And the privately contracted Stardust? That one was just weird. It should've been an easy target to run down, but its control center had lost contact days earlier.

That was something the intel group ought to have caught before the rendezvous, she fumed. Spacecraft rendezvous was no joke—if things weren't exactly where you expected them to be, bad things could happen. They went to great pains to avoid collisions in orbit, as vehicles had a way of sneaking up on you if you misjudged a rendezvous and lost sight of them.

That was ironically less of a problem for X-37 operators, as the camera suite mounted in the drone's cargo hold combined to give its operators an expansive, high-definition view. Roberta had already used them to sweep the area several times, slowly panning the cameras in a full circle around its axes. Nothing unexpected had turned up. Radiant dots in the distance could all be identified as previously cataloged satellites; conversely, no more in the vicinity had come up missing.

Word was the SAMCOM team had been annoyingly blasé about the loss of their satellite—it was near the end of its service life anyway. Their insurance company seemed a lot more interested in finding it. The Stardust people had been much more engaged, as orbital charters represented a considerable source of revenue and losing a spacecraft could seriously undermine their business. That particular concern was for the moment eclipsed by impatient inquiries from the government, as the fatalities onboard had invariably drawn the attention of the NTSB.

That all of this had missed the attention of the Space Control deltas in Huntsville and Vandenberg left her in a slow burn. Their Space Fence radar could track objects a few centimeters square *if* they passed over its antennas on Kwajalein and Ascension islands. That might work for the bulk of stuff in low and medium orbits, as everything worth worrying about would eventually cross their field of view. But GEO? The whole point of geostationary orbit was the *stationary* part. If a bird wasn't already parked within the antenna's sight, it wasn't going to be seen.

She'd learned it was a capability gap that had frustrated a lot of satellite jockeys for a long time, but maybe now the brass could be moved to do something about it. In the meantime, they were still left with a hole in space. It wasn't really her job to track down the missing targets, though she imagined this is what an F-22 driver would feel if flying an intercept mission only to find the target she'd been vectored to was gone. She'd be pissed off and wouldn't stop looking for it until either the CO or her fuel gauges said it was time to come home.

Fortunately, the CO hadn't waved her off and that ACES upper stage still had plenty of delta-v in the tanks—she hadn't even started using her onboard Hall thrusters yet, saving the more efficient but lower-thrust engines for later after ACES was discarded. The latest tasking order had left their vehicle out, so she had time on her hands. Those birds had to have gone somewhere, it was just a matter of how much they could do with the propellant each had aboard. SAMCOM couldn't do much more than descend to a lower orbit, where the Fence radars would eventually catch it. Assuming it hadn't, that left it somewhere in GEO.

Stardust was a different animal. Its controllers said it still had over 3.5 km/second of delta-v left in its tanks. That was enough to either go all the way to the Moon, deorbit for Earth, or anything in between. Probably not the Moon, she decided. She suspected it didn't have the nav program for that, and besides, what would be the point?

That left a lower orbit or reentry, which the Fence also should have caught. There was a lot of junk up there. Maybe it was as simple as they got lost in the noise?

Either way, it would've been maneuvering so its operators should have known what happened. That they didn't know had to mean somebody else did. Spacecraft don't just burn out of GEO on their own, particularly when the only surviving crewmember was back on Earth.

He was *here*, wasn't he? Hadn't they brought him home with those *Borman* crewmembers last week? Word was he was on some kind of quarantine at the base hospital. Sounded like a load of crap to her but it must have made sense to somebody.

She searched her memory for anyone she might have met from the provost's office, and picked up the phone.

⚙ 26 ⚙

Marshall had a long list of questions for Max and Jasmine Jiang, none of which he dared show in front of them. He tried to place himself in their position, and the last thing he'd want to see is some wet-behind-the-ears kid in a uniform hovering over him with a checklist and a clipboard. Instead, he'd taken care to break the list into manageable chunks that he could memorize and bring out during the natural course of conversation. They'd been through a trauma that he was still having trouble comprehending, and they'd need a soft touch.

He hadn't counted on Max Jiang. "You get me out of this, okay?" he stammered, pulling at his bed restraints. "I have to use the bathroom!"

"It's okay, Mr. Jiang," Marshall replied delicately. "You're on a catheter."

"I don't want that." Jiang grimaced. "It's most uncomfortable. You have me sedated?"

"We did, for the first day. You both needed rest and—"

"Then either get this tube out of me or give me more sedation. We have work to do, Mister—what is your name?"

"Ensign Marshall Hunter, sir," he said with an earnest smile. "We've met."

Jiang looked confused for a minute. "I'm sorry, we've never . . . oh. You mean, on the asteroid?"

"Yes sir. I was on the team that got you out."

Jiang shook his head angrily, clearing the cobwebs. "I know you must have questions, Ensign Hunter." He turned to face his wife in the bed opposite him, still asleep. He pawed uncomfortably at the tubes inserted at various places in his body. "But first, get these damned hoses out of me. And I suggest you do the same for my wife before she wakes up, or I promise you will wish you'd listened to me."

Marshall waved for Nikki. "Anything else?" he asked, hoping he didn't sound amused.

"Coffee," Jiang said tiredly. "For the love of God, coffee."

Marshall returned with two drinking bulbs of fluid, one black, one orange. He handed the orange bulb over first. "You have to drink this one first, sir. Coffee's a diuretic and your electrolyte balance is still on the low side."

"Of course it is," Jiang said somewhat resentfully as he took the juice. He probed at some sores along his arm, then hazarded a glance at his crotch. "The rash is even worse than I thought. After a month in those suits—"

Marshall looked embarrassed, hesitant to correct him. "Actually it was about half that, sir."

Jiang sucked on the juice, draining it in one long sip. "It felt like a month," he gasped at the end. "But what do I know? I broke my watch digging out our shelter." He reached for the coffee.

Marshall handed over the black bulb. "About that, sir. We do have questions about what happened out here, and we're curious as to how you both survived so long."

Jiang sipped on the coffee more slowly, savoring it. "Not bad for instant," he said offhand. "I should have thought to take some from our stores, though Jasmine would have probably stopped me. Diuretic, as you said."

"What made you decide to shelter on RQ39 instead of in your spacecraft?"

Jiang took another sip of coffee from the zero-g bulb. "We didn't see any alternative. Life support was gone. Our spacecraft had plenty of food and water, but no air to breathe. The ISRU at least gave us a chance to crack oxygen out of the regolith. We were quite pleased when it worked."

The man had a well-deserved reputation for understatement, Marshall thought. "I can imagine."

"Trust me, you can't." Jiang closed his eyes. "I have never been claustrophobic before. I am now." He opened them and fixed his gaze on Marshall. "Did you know we considered suicide?"

How would I? he thought. "No, I didn't," he said calmly. "Though I suppose it's understandable."

Jiang took a long, deep breath, as if rewinding the story in his mind. "We had fixed the in situ unit on the surface after studying the returns from our CubeSats," he began. "I was too focused on my surface machinery—we had already identified likely locations of subsurface ice. Then I heard Jasmine scream."

Concentrating on the ISRU's data, Max was startled by the shout from Jasmine. He snapped his head around and shot upright, dizzy from the sudden shift in his inner-ear fluids. "What is it?"

It wasn't his own movement confusing him. The ship was rocking and rolling, the hull thumping from thrusters trying to counteract.

"There . . ." she stammered in disbelief and pointed out a nearby window. "What is happening?"

He followed her gaze and saw a growing cloud of gas and debris outside. The ship had been rock steady in a common orbit with RQ39, now it slowly spun about its vertical axis as its shredded service module vented into space.

"*What is happening?*" she repeated, raising her voice to be heard over metallic groans from the docking tunnel, straining from the sudden torque.

"I don't . . ." He couldn't find the words. Who could possibly know what was happening? "Have you heard from Palmdale?"

"I haven't," she said quietly. She turned to the control panel, realizing that she should have done that first. "But we're losing oxygen and hydrogen, fast. Tank one is already gone."

He tapped the touchscreen panel. "Palmdale, this is *Prospector*," he called. "We have a situation."

He waited several seconds for their signal to reach Earth; in fact more than enough for it to return. His only answer was the steady hiss of an empty frequency, peppered with the occasional squeals and chirps of cosmic background noise.

"Palmdale, Palmdale. This is *Prospector*. Radio check, over." He counted ten seconds, then switched to the universal emergency frequency. "Mayday, Mayday, this is the spacecraft *Prospector*."

Another ten seconds, another empty frequency. He saw Jasmine still staring outside in disbelief. "You won't reach anyone," she said despairingly. "I can see the main antenna is gone."

"*Gone?*" He squinted outside, struggling to focus with middle-aged eyes. How could she see anything behind the thickening haze?

"Trust me, it's not there," she said, now pointing to the radio panel. "There's nothing to relay our signal."

Marshall glanced over his shoulder at Jasmine, still sleeping soundly beneath the restraints in her EMS pod, and tried to imagine her charging through a cloud of what used to be part of their spacecraft. "You made it back over there without getting your suits punctured. We didn't find any vacuum tape patches on either shell."

"A minor miracle," Max allowed. "One of many." He looked across at Jasmine. "My dear wife. Once she recovered from her initial shock, she was *on a mission*," he said, emphasizing each word. "She went into action. That's the businesswoman in her." He began chuckling until it degenerated into a hoarse cough. "I was just along for the ride."

Marshall eyed him skeptically. *That* seemed hard to believe.

Jasmine was already up in the supply module, tearing through stores while Max paged through the service module diagnostics. "You were right; I can't bring up any radios. Doesn't look like any telemetry is making it to Palmdale either."

"What about atmosphere?"

"It's gone," he said. "Both O_2 tanks are ruptured. The only air left is the command module's reentry supply."

"Ninety minutes?" she asked sharply, emerging from the docking tunnel with a bundle wrapped in Nomex cloth. She strapped it into her empty seat. "We may need it."

"May?" he wondered, looking around at their dead spacecraft.

"I know," she said, flying back up into the supply module. "There's no sense staying here. I'm getting us all the water we can carry."

Max did a double take. *And go where, exactly?* It took a second for him to realize her plan when she came back down with another bundle. "The ISRU?"

"Of course," she said. "It's working, isn't it?"

"It is," Max said. It had common fittings with their suit supply bottles . . . "Yes! We can extract oxygen from the substrate."

"We can't stay here, there's no air." She pointed outside to the asteroid. "And there's no food on that rock, but we can make our own air."

"We can take protein powder from the emergency locker, mix it with our drinking water."

"Yes," she agreed. "But we have to sure its fully dissolved so it doesn't clog our filler ports."

Max studied the bundles of supplies she'd brought down. "We'll need radiation protection." He opened the emergency locker behind their seats and pulled out two Mylar blankets. "We'll have to dig out the rest."

Jasmine looked through the open hatch, the universe outside spinning slowly as their craft tumbled. "Can you get this back under control?"

Max watched the twirling attitude indicator and their rapidly declining propellant. "I think we lost a propellant tank as well. The guidance platform has been trying to compensate. It burned through most of what's left." He pulled up a projection of their path through space. It now meandered off into a new direction. "We won't be able to come back here for long. It'll have drifted too far away."

"That's what I was afraid of." She checked the level of compressed nitrogen in her maneuvering pack. "We may not be able to risk a second trip."

Their suits were filthy with dust after hours of moving loose rock and digging beneath a nearby overhang to clear out a small cavern. Max stepped back to inspect his work with an odd satisfaction. "This will work," he said. "We have a nearly a foot of regolith around the entrance, and solid rock behind that." He draped one of the Mylar blankets across the opening, keeping it in place with more rocks. "This will help regulate temperature, so our suit batteries won't drain as fast."

"Will we be able to keep them charged from the ISRU?" Jasmine asked from inside their little cave, where she had been stacking nutrient packages and water bladders.

"That's my next job," Max said, holding up a bundle of cables he'd brought from *Prospector*. "I'll have to plug these into the stepdown transformer, then we can take turns recharging. We should alternate every two hours."

"What will we lose in the process?" she asked, coming out from behind the Mylar curtain.

"I haven't decided. We don't touch the oxygen processing plant, but that runs on too much voltage anyway. It will have to be a lower-powered system we can live without. That doesn't leave much."

"The spectrometer package," she suggested. "Or the telemetry relays."

"An easy decision, I think. We may yet be able to use the telemetry package."

"Good." She carefully sat on one of the larger rocks. It was more of an approximation of sitting, as the gravity was so low that any movement sent her floating away from her perch.

Max moved to join his wife, placing a steadying hand on her shoulder. "Your quick thinking saved us," he said. "You knew what we had to do right away, whereas I'd still be up there wasting valuable time, trying to fix the unfixable."

She stared up at the patch of black sky where the distant Earth hung. With the frenzy of reacting to the crisis now behind them, she slumped inside her bulky EVA suit. "No one can hear us, and who knows what Palmdale can see?" she said. "Saved us for what? What do we do now?"

Home was not much more than a bright blue speck in the distance. "What we've always done when nothing else made sense," he sighed, and took her gloved hand in his. "We pray."

"You guys worked fast under pressure," Marshall said. "That made all the difference."

Jiang nodded toward his sleeping wife. "And I give her all the credit. I was too absorbed with trying to fix what was broken. Thinking like an engineer. It took the hard-nosed businesswoman to realize that ship had sailed, as they say."

"She knew you were running out of time."

"Afraid," came a groggy voice behind him. "I was afraid."

Marshall turned to see Jasmine, eyes opening under still-heavy lids. "Mrs. Jiang. Can I get you anything?"

"A mimosa would be nice," she said with a weary grin.

Jasmine Jiang gratefully accepted the same electrolyte drink and coffee as her husband, along with Marshall's apologies for not having alcohol. "We're a military vessel, ma'am."

"Ah. I should have guessed from the short haircuts and extreme politeness." She took a sip of coffee and blissfully closed her eyes. "This will do fine, thank you, young man."

"Your husband was telling me about your experience on RQ39," Marshall said. "How you became marooned. You did an amazing job, ma'am."

"A skill I acquired in childhood," she said. "When you grow up in an uncertain world, you learn to prioritize quickly. Fear is a great motivator."

"I admire your clear thinking under pressure," Marshall said. "And begging your pardon, let me say how much I've admired you both. I've been following your expedition ever since you announced it last year." He blushed. "My friends think I've been a little obsessive. They're probably right. I just wish we could've met under different circumstances."

Jasmine reached for his hand. She felt cool, comforting, a woman in total control of herself. "Considering the alternative, I'm quite pleased with the circumstances." Tears began welling up in her eyes. Marshall handed her a quick-dry cloth.

Max Jiang pushed away from his bed and glided over to embrace his wife. Free from their spacesuits for the first time in nearly two weeks, they collapsed into each other with quiet sobs. Marshall turned away, embarrassed for what now felt like an intrusion.

Jasmine reached for him again as he moved away. "It's okay, young man. We need other people around us. We were alone for a very long time."

"I know," he said, trying to be soothing and hoping it didn't come off as condescending. He hadn't really had any practice at this. "We frankly expected you to be dead. It was a real shock to find your spacecraft empty."

Her eyes widened. "You were on *Prospector*?"

"I was . . . that is, we were. My team and I," Marshall explained.

"Did you see the other satellite, then?"

Marshall was confused. "You mean your CubeSats?"

"No. We saw another satellite after we had encamped on Malati. That's how we knew a rescue might be on the way."

Marshall played along. They had to have been delusional from fear at that point. "What kind of satellite?"

"Big enough to see from there," Max said. "It was dark. Conical, maybe cruciform. Big solar wings," he said, holding his arms out. "Are we still in orbit with Malati?"

"We are," he said. "Coplanar, specifically. Separation's increasing as we transit back to Earth."

"How soon can we return?" Jasmine asked, diverting them from Max's mystery satellite.

He looked down at the floor and wrung his hands, struggling with how to best explain their predicament. "I'm afraid that's complicated."

◎ 27 ◎

Marshall caught Rosie's attention as she hovered in the background behind the Jiangs. She excused herself and glided out of the module, turning down the corridor to head for the control deck.

Max's hand tightened around his wife's, drawing hers closer to him. "This ship looks to be capable enough. You made it out here in a tenth of the time it took us."

"We did," he acknowledged, "but our situation has changed. We don't have enough propellant for a high-energy return to Earth. Our current orbit—"

"Takes us around Mars," Max finished for him. "It has to if you're coplanar with ours, right?"

"That's correct," Marshall said. "We burned hard to get here fast then had to slow down to match orbits with your ship. In the end we're on the same vector as if we'd flown a Hohmann transfer. We just took a shortcut to get here."

"I don't understand," Jasmine said. "You can't take a similar shortcut home?"

Marshall struggled with how much to tell them, and sorely hoped Rosie had caught his hint to go get the skipper. "That had been our plan, yes. But I'm afraid—"

To his relief, Simon floated into the compartment and introduced himself. "I'm Simon Poole, commander of the *Borman*. And young Mr. Hunter here's correct, our plans have been forced to change."

"Forced?" Max's face contorted in a look that either showed concern or confusion, Marshall couldn't tell. "Forced how?"

Poole's lips drew tight. "There was an explosion in one of our

263

outboard hydrogen tanks and we were forced to jettison it. That took over half of our remaining propellant."

"This ship is nuclear-thermal, correct?" Jiang asked. "What's your specific impulse?"

"Eight hundred twenty seconds," Poole said, and held up his hands in caution. "I think I know where you're going, Mr. Jiang, but efficiency ain't everything. We do have enough to shave some time off the return trip, but that still relies on a Mars flyby to make up some of our lost delta-v, and we need enough in reserve for Earth capture at the end."

Jasmine read Poole's face. "That's not what concerns you, is it?"

"It's not." He decided to get right down to it. "We only laid up a month's worth of stores. Left our normal loadout behind, along with half our crew, to make the ship light enough for us to hightail it out here and get you home fast."

"What is your 'normal loadout'?" Max asked.

"Three month's rations for twelve crew, plus antisatellite weapons. We didn't see the need for those out here." Poole's mouth drew tight. "This may change my understanding of the tactical picture in the future."

Max Jiang was not military, but the irony wasn't lost on him. "Space has a way of challenging one's assumptions."

"It does," he fumed, then caught himself. "And I have some good news, but I must admit to mixed feelings about it." He explained the *Peng Fei*'s offer of assistance. "They're a little over a week out," he said when done.

The Jiangs did not appear as relieved as he'd expected. "What will happen to your vessel, Captain Poole?"

"We abandon it and hitch a ride home with the Chinese. Program the ship to execute the Mars flyby and Earth injection burns on its own, and we'll see it in another six months."

"You don't seem happy with that outcome, Captain."

"No skipper relishes the idea of abandoning ship," he said, eyes narrowing. "But I'm not sure I like the alternative, either—we take your rations for ourselves, transfer you to the *Peng Fei*, and fly our ship home."

The Jiangs looked at each other with alarm. "We would much prefer that you not do that, Captain."

✳ ✳ ✳

Liu Wang Shu hovered above a polar coordinate plot of their orbit relative to those of the *Borman* and asteroid RQ39. At his order, the control cabin had been kept dark since leaving Earth, "running red" with no illumination other than their red-tinted instrument screens. It had the practical effect of preserving the crew's night vision, but he was more concerned with its subtle psychological effect. It kept the command crew focused, a quality he could judge by their quiet seriousness whenever he entered the cabin. They were always professional, as he would tolerate nothing less, but the days of lazily orbiting Lagrange 1 had created a routine that threatened to become too comfortable.

They were transiting a region of space that radar surveys had revealed to be populated with an unusually high number of micrometeoroid threats. The small satellites the PLAF had deployed to catalog these navigational hazards could not mark all of them, so this made for a useful test of *Peng Fei*'s "clearance control" system.

There were a number of labeled vectors on the polar graph, each representing the location and direction of a known threat. Most were only a meter or less across, and knowing where they were offered an excellent opportunity to calibrate his ship's powerful search radar: Once the known quantities were accounted for, he could have much more confidence in anything else they may spot.

He opened up a file on one particular object that had been known for decades, and was pleased to see it would be in the vicinity.

"Captain Zhang."

A youngish pilot stiffened in his seat and turned to face his commander. "Yes sir?"

"Initiate a broad-spectrum sweep, relative bearings three-four-zero through zero-two-zero." They would clear a path along a forty-degree cone ahead of the ship's trajectory.

"As you wish, sir." The captain opened up a control menu on his touchscreen display and began spinning up the search radar. Within seconds, the big multifunction display mounted between the two pilots' windows was peppered with new objects, their details filling in and building upon each other with each successive pass of the phased-array radar. As they sped along, layers of detail built up quickly for the nearest objects. Soon, Liu had a clear picture of the space ahead of *Peng Fei* for several thousand kilometers. At their rate of travel, the picture shifted continuously. "No threats within our hazard avoidance cone, sir."

"Very good," Liu said, electronically tagging each new object and adding it to their catalog of potential navigation hazards. Liu was not a naval man, but he imagined this must be exactly like charting new passages along unfamiliar shores. He sent new directions to Zhang. "Now, please sweep this area."

"There is a return, sir," Zhang said with surprise. "It's small, perhaps three meters by two." Its outline appeared at the edge of their coverage and began resolving with more detail as they overtook it. Not a threat; it would pass well abeam to starboard.

"Can you acquire it visually, Mr. Zhang?"

"Yes sir. Allow me a moment to redirect the outboard telescope."

"Take your time, Captain." He gave the younger officer a moment to switch gears. "Please bring it up on the central monitor when you have it." He wanted the visual impact to be unmistakable. He watched the younger man's eyes widen as the image came into focus: originally cherry red, now baked by decades of unfiltered sunlight into a washed-out pink. Once-black rubber at its corners had likewise turned nearly white.

"It's a . . . *car*. Sir." And it was exactly what Liu had been looking for.

"Set condition Yellow," he ordered. "Target ahead, bearing zero-three-two, elevation plus four." When he tagged the object, a yellow box appeared around it on his polar plot and on the pilot's multifunction screen.

Without a word, Zhang motioned for his copilot to activate their offensive suite. New information appeared alongside the target; its range and bearing began constantly updating as they focused the radar on it. "Target is boxed, sir."

"Weapons free," Liu said. "Engage at your will, Captain."

"Yes sir. Activating penetrator missiles." Liu thought he saw a smile break across Zhang's face. The young captain carried himself with a square-jawed seriousness that Liu had always liked, and he was satisfied to finally see what the man took pleasure in: his job. "Weapon released."

There was a barely perceptible shudder beneath them as a missile was ejected from its tube and a replacement immediately locked into place. Liu watched as a tracking camera followed the missile. Had it not been guided by their radar, he would have quickly lost sight of it: Its solid rocket motor only burned for a few seconds, launching it toward its target. Puffs of gas erupted from its terminal guidance jets soon after.

Seconds later, there was a flash in the distance. "Impact!" Zhang said, uncharacteristically animated. Two boxes now appeared on the radar display. "Large fragments remaining, sir. Vectors have changed but they will still pass by starboard."

"Predicted range?"

Zhang paused as he studied the plot. "Within ten kilometers, sir."

Excellent opportunity, Liu thought. Just as he'd hoped for. "Engage with close-in defenses."

Zhang nodded and motioned again to his copilot, who punched in a quick command. A mechanical whirring noise echoed through the hull from outside. "Point-defense cannons are tracking both targets," he said, his hand moving toward a protected switch. "Selecting autofire." The computer-controlled guns would fire when they arrived at an optimal targeting solution.

"Hold your fire," Liu said. "Wait until they're abeam." A nearly head-on firing solution was relatively simple—he wanted to see how well they could engage a small target zipping past alongside. From the corner of his eye, he saw Zhang's hand freeze atop the switch cover. Good.

He still had to work quickly—the remaining shards of their target would slip by as fast as he could get the words out of his mouth. As soon as he began to order "weapons free," Zhang snapped the cover open and hit the autofire switch.

A muffled rattle coursed through the cabin as the electronically driven cannons fired a precisely calibrated cloud of slugs at each target. In seconds, each fragment disappeared, reduced to a cloud of shrapnel.

In terms of being a navigational hazard, they'd simply reduced a fair-sized obstacle into thousands of much smaller ones. They would eventually spread out, each presenting less of a risk over time, though they couldn't hope to catalog each tiny piece with its own orbital elements. Liu would mark the entire region as a "debris cluster" to be avoided.

In the meantime, he was quite pleased with their results. They had engaged a small, fast-moving object in a high-angle, off-axis shot and reduced it to confetti with a combination of missiles and point-defense guns. Whatever capabilities remained with the *Borman* would be no match. And what had been the permanent remnant of a famous early-century publicity stunt had been reduced to a cloud of plastic, rubber, and alloy fragments.

Marshall was baffled. "We're going to be out here for a long time on limited rations. You'd prefer to not get back to Earth ahead of us?"

"Not on a PRC vessel," Jasmine insisted, her husband nodding along with her.

Poole was noticeably less puzzled by their reluctance. "We'd have two of our rescue medics aboard with you," he offered nonetheless. "If that's what you're concerned about."

"We have the utmost confidence in your quality of care," Max said, "but that is not the root of our concern."

Marshall realized Poole was probing them, and he suspected the reason why. "You're worried about boarding a PRC ship, period."

Max crossed his arms. "Of course we are! We escaped the mainland two decades ago and haven't been back. We've been bothersome for them ever since. They don't want us back except to silence us."

"You're a very high-profile couple," Marshall said. "Do you really believe they'd harm you?"

"A place like that has lots of ways to silence dissenters without inflicting straight-up harm," Poole said. "They'll just invent some excuse to seize their passports and bank accounts while they put them up in a nice little country home. Give them all they could ever want except the freedom to live as they please."

"Or to leave," Max pointed out. "They'll parade us in front of state news cameras once in a while for what you call 'proof of life.' Just to show they're not complete monsters. But your captain is right, Mr. Hunter. If we return to Chinese soil, we will never be allowed to leave."

Poole frowned. "If you return to Earth on a PRC ship, they're definitely going to land you in China. But you're still naturalized Americans."

"And once we're under their control then none of that will matter. All bets are off, as you say. I can guarantee the moment we board will be the last time you lay eyes on us," Jasmine said gloomily. "No. We would rather take our chances with you, Captain."

Poole stroked his chin as he considered their options. "I'm not going to try and dissuade you. You are American citizens under our protection, which right now is still my responsibility. But you must understand we simply don't have the propellant for anything but a low-energy transfer that relies on a gravity assist from Mars. We'll be taking the long way home no matter what. Even raiding your stores, we'll barely have enough food for a minimum crew."

It was telling that with the most capable spacecraft yet fielded, it was ultimately limited not by its own fuel but by its human occupants. And deep space was notoriously absent of any food storage.

Marshall cleared his throat for their attention. "Mr. and Mrs. Jiang, if you could excuse us, there's something I need to discuss with the captain outside." He shot a glance toward the connecting tunnel.

Poole glided ahead of him into the corridor outside. "What's on your mind, Mr. Hunter?"

"My apologies, sir, but I didn't think this would be appropriate to bring up in front of civilians." He paused, not sure why he felt afraid to ask. "What if we just asked the Chinese for assistance?"

"You mean ask for some of their rations?" Poole eyed him skeptically. "I admire your optimism but I'm afraid I don't share it. You were right to bring that up in private, son."

"They must have already decided they have enough to take us on. If we can convince them to transfer those stores, add them to what we already have, it might close the loop. Wouldn't be the craziest request ever, would it sir?"

Poole thought about it. Any way to avoid abandoning ship was worth considering. A crooked smile creased his face. "Hell, I'm just irritated that I didn't think of it myself. Maybe I'm getting too cynical in my old age."

"As long as we're at it, what about propellant?" Marshall asked, stretching his luck. "Do we have common fittings?"

Poole shook his head. "That's where you risk being too clever by half, Mr. Hunter. Up until last week, intel thought the *Peng Fei* was a methane propellant depot. Now that we've seen them under power, the spectral signature confirms that's what they're burning."

"Whereas we use hydrogen."

"Much cleaner. It doesn't foul solid-core reactors. So what does that tell us about their propulsion?"

"We already know it's not chemical from the radiation signature. Either they don't care about carbon deposits, or they're using a different configuration."

"Trust me, nobody wants a dirty reactor core," Poole said. "My money's on gas-core, maybe a nuclear lightbulb."

"Then they're more advanced than anybody gave them credit for, sir," Marshall realized. "Given how quickly they moved all that mass out of L1, it would have to be something with a higher thrust-to-weight ratio than ours."

"Big, heavy, fast, and under PRC military control," Poole said, falling back into his natural skepticism. "I don't like that combination. I like it even less that we didn't see it coming. Too many people bought into their public relations."

Chief Garver emerged out of the darkened command deck at the far end of the corridor and pushed off into their direction. "FLASH traffic from Ops, skipper," he said, pulling up next to them and handing Poole a tablet.

Poole skimmed through the message. "This is time-stamped almost an hour ago," he said. "We can't download a flash message any faster?"

"Tactical comm's still offline, sir," Garver explained. "We have to route everything through *Specter*'s high-gain antenna. It doesn't have the bandwidth for a burst transmission."

Poole's scowl threatened to turn into a permanent feature. He went back to the top and read it over again. "Our friends on the Peng Fei did a little show of force. I'm sure it's all completely justified, above board, and clearly out of an abundance of caution. They even marked it as a navigational hazard." He looked up at Garver, gauging his reaction. "Do I sound like I'm ready for a promotion yet, Chief?"

"That level of blind naivete demands flag rank and a desk in the Pentagon, sir."

"Yeah, I figured you read this yourself." Poole handed the tablet to Marshall. "Your take, Mr. Hunter?"

Marshall read through the alert and accompanying intelligence analysis. "Pretty powerful search radar," he said, "even better targeting. They locked up multiple small, fast bogeys and took them out at once." He frowned, unconsciously mimicking his CO and earning a suppressed grin from Garver. "They used independently targeted interceptors and point-defense guns?" He looked up at Poole, eyes wide. "Holy shit. They blew up Musk's roadster?" he stammered. "Why would they do that?"

"Sending a message is my guess. This is why it pays to know your adversary," Poole growled. "First rule of space combat is whoever can take the first shot wins. And they don't care who's in the way."

◎ 28 ◎

"I appreciate your confidence, but I'm just a midlevel nobody," the senior lieutenant tried to explain. "The provost officer might politely listen to my theories, but in the end he's going to do what he wants."

Roberta sat calmly in the government-issue metal chair in front of the intelligence officer's government-issue metal desk, an Air Force hand-me-down like so much else of the Group HQ's offices. It was one more thing that made her grateful to work in the control center. "This is why Ops doesn't trust intel, Mike. If they took that attitude, spacecraft would get lost. People could get killed."

"Tell me about it." The young officer grew tired of pacing and sat behind his desk, instead drumming his fingers in frustration. "When are you going to figure out squadron- and group-level intel isn't that exciting, Roboto? It's not like they're out running ops in the field, deciphering secret messages and banging hot enemy agents. It's one way. You take the stuff that gets pushed down to us from the Wing and Pentagon and filter it for the unit COs. We don't generate intel, we interpret it."

"And the base provost doesn't have any illuminating thoughts on our new guest over in the hospital?"

"He's keeping them close if they do. Not that he'd tell us, even though the guy's in our house. Compartmentalization," he explained.

"Somebody's got to be interested in him because the whole 'medical observation' excuse is pretty thin," Roberta said. "If he's not already losing hair and skin from radiation poisoning, then he doesn't have it."

"Agreed," he said. "Poole's crew pushed to keep him in isolation but that's only going to hold up for so long. What's your angle?"

"You know about the op we're running in GEO, right?"

"The one where you lost the satellite and that Stardust spacecraft?"

"*Somebody* lost it," she said angrily, "but it wasn't us. We were on station, right where we were told to be. So how do two vehicles that big just disappear without us noticing?"

"Probably a gap in the radar fence," he groused. "It's great for anything that crosses its field of view, which is just about everything below eighty degrees inclination. Objects in GEO aren't moving relative to one another enough for a collision risk."

"Which is fine, until a GEO bird does something unexpected. Don't you find it odd that after everything that happened up there, they disappeared not long after we brought the only survivor home?"

"Lots of weird stuff happening up in geosynch these days," he agreed. "Seems like another satellite goes dark every day. Everything's going tits-up at once."

"Maybe their warranties all ran out," Roberta said, "or something else is going on. Those birds have high fault tolerances, multiple redundancies, and they're tested end-to-end several times over. *They. Don't. Break.* Not at this rate." She sucked on her bottom lip, suddenly hesitant to go further. "I don't believe in that many coincidences. Not after that Free Space Manifesto bullshit hit the networks. And I think this Lesko guy has something to do with it." It sounded ridiculous now that she said it. She was beginning to understand how hard it might be to share such theories with the brass.

The lieutenant's eyes darted back and forth as he considered his next words. "It gets better," he said, and pushed a tablet across the desk to her. "This just came across the industry news feed, hasn't even hit our message boards yet. Two helium-3 shipments didn't make their South Pacific drop zones."

Roberta took the tablet and skimmed the story. "Those things are like clockwork," she said. "Both launched from the Aristarchus catapult three days ago by TranSolar Mineral & Gas." Her brow wrinkled. "Isn't that owned by . . ."

"Max and Jasmine Jiang," he finished for her. "They're having a bad week."

✖ ✖ ✖

With reception still limited, the Jiangs didn't learn of it until several hours later with the daily data packet of news from Earth. Marshall wasn't surprised they were upset, though their reactions were still not what he expected.

Max's agitation grew as he thought through the problem. "This doesn't strike me as a simple equipment malfunction," he explained. "There are multiple fail-safes built into the catapult system. It's completely automated and runs a full diagnostic and calibration routine before every launch."

"It's timed with the Moon's orbital period, right?" Marshall asked. "So you only launch a few shipments a month?"

"Yes, timed so the pods all enter east of American Samoa. We have recovery barges rotating into the drop zone every month."

"You've never had a malfunction?"

"With the entry pods? Certainly. Early on, we had a number of problems with heat shields cracking from the launch acceleration. We still have the occasional parachute failure. But the catapult?" He shook his head emphatically. "Never. We can't risk having it miss and accidentally bombard Hawaii. It either works perfectly or not at all." He stared at the news story, thinking through the possibilities. "According to this, the catapult was within tolerance. I need to speak with our team in Samoa."

Marshall was apologetic. "I understand, sir, but our bandwidth is limited right now. We only have a few windows each day for nonoperational traffic."

"You may find the information useful, too," Jiang said, handing the tablet back to Marshall. "Those delivery pods all have transponder beacons, so we'd have known if it was a simple parachute failure. Likewise if they failed during entry interface. No, the shipments just disappeared somewhere between Aristarchus crater and Earth."

Something had to affect their trajectory, then. And the delivery pods didn't have any kind of independent maneuvering ability—once launched from the Moon, they followed an unflinching trajectory to their landing zone in the South Pacific. "They had to be diverted somehow," Marshall thought aloud. "How would that happen? Who would do that?"

"Who else in the world is experimenting with helium-3 fusion?" Jiang asked. "I believe you'll find it's a short list."

Marshall's eyes narrowed. "It's just us. The Chinese haven't been able to make it work, far as I know. Neither have the Europeans. The Russians can't afford it."

Jiang nodded slowly. "I'm no conspiracist, Mr. Hunter, but I'm also no Pollyanna. Today, helium-3 is valuable for experimentation. We mine it because we believe it will be a game changer someday. If I'm right, it could upset the entire world's energy industry."

"You're suggesting someone wants to prevent you from doing that?"

"If I sound paranoid," Jiang allowed, "recall we just survived two weeks inside of a cave we clawed out of an asteroid after our spacecraft exploded for no apparent reason. I'm entitled to sound paranoid."

"I'm not suggesting you are," Marshall said, backtracking. "But there are so many ways for machinery to fail unexpectedly out here. You're suggesting some unknown, outside actor interfered with your delivery pods."

"Perhaps more than that," Jiang said ominously. "Some previously unknown terrorist group is taking credit for damaging both our ships and claiming jurisdiction over solar system resources. There's entirely too much coincidence. Do you believe they're unrelated?"

"No one does," he admitted. "The question is who's financing it. One way or another, we'll find out."

"If that takes long enough, it will have become a moot question." Jiang pointed at RQ39 in the distance. "Asteroids like that are pots of gold in the sky just waiting to be exploited. They're brimming with rare-earth minerals, not to mention water ice. If we could find a way to put one in close reach, it would be like opening up a trillion-dollar mine overnight. Nobody's had those kinds of resources before."

"Of all the billionaires in the world," Marshall said, "you've been one of the few to see it that way. How many others do you think are coming around?"

Jiang's eyes darkened, as if confronting a threat. "Billionaires are nothing—imagine what you could do with a *trillion*. You could move entire markets just by adjusting your investment portfolio. Cripple whole industries with the right choice of words in a news broadcast."

"You could control entire countries by financing their debt," Marshall said.

Jiang nodded. "Or just buy the small ones outright."

"Economics is simply war by other means." Simon Poole sighed as he rubbed at his eyes, wiping out the sleep that beckoned him. He'd hardly left his place in the control module and couldn't remember the last time he'd seen the inside of his own quarters for anything more than a change of clothes and a quick nap. He was going to have do something to change that equation soon, he realized, especially with this latest insight from the Jiangs relayed via Ensign Marshall Hunter. "If your end goal is to dominate, there's lots more ways to do it these days than by overwhelming force."

"I think I follow you, sir," Marshall said. "That's what I can't figure out yet—is it all about money, or just for the sake of creating chaos? Because making other people's assets disappear doesn't do anything but hurt them."

"Sowing chaos among your adversaries can be a benefit all its own," Poole said. "Throw 'em off their game, get inside their decision loop—pick your cliché. Get them thinking about anything except what you're really up to."

"So all you need to do sometimes is just hurt the other guy?"

"Sometimes that's all you *can* do. Slow them down. They're not going to stop TranSolar from dominating the space-resource market; that ship sailed a long time ago. They're just the latest in a rash of vehicles going screwy. Have you seen the daily message boards on what's happening in GEO?"

Marshall recognized this was something of a test as to how well he was keeping up with the daily intel traffic from Fleet Ops. "Lots of comsats going dark, sir, and they can't all be attributed to last month's CME. And apparently there's now a hole in space where that Stardust we evac'ed used to be."

Poole continued to press him. "Do you think these events could be related?"

"It's a big sky," Marshall said. "But that they're all happening within days of each other? Hard to see that as coincidence, sir."

"There's a fine line between connecting the dots and joining the Tin Foil Hat Club," Poole said. "So to answer your question: I think it's about sowing chaos, and I don't think it's aimed specifically at the Jiangs. They just happened to be in the line of fire. Now the question becomes, who benefits from this?"

"I don't see how it benefits anyone. Why disrupt GEO?" Marshall wondered. "Why steal helium-3 shipments if you can't resell them?"

"Cislunar space was becoming the next great economic zone, and it just turned into the Wild West," Poole said, and made a sweeping gesture. "Nobody is going to do business there if they can't be assured their assets won't get swiped. And we—the US Marshals—just got taken out of the picture."

Marshall's eyes widened. "You think we were led into an ambush, sir?"

"Targets of opportunity at least," Poole said. "There's too many coincidences piling up. This is not the Bermuda Triangle of space. But tell me—who benefits from us not keeping space open?"

Marshall followed that line of thought and didn't like where it took him. Is this how wars started—when the people who could prevent it were barely able to discern what was unfolding around them? All he wanted to do was come up here and fly spacecraft, not have a front-row seat to the opening act of a global conflagration . . .

"You mentioned getting inside their decision loop, sir. Throwing something unexpected at them."

"I'm listening."

Marshall hesitated, but then it was the only card they could play right now. "We test the waters: ask the *Peng Fei* for the food and technical assistance we need to bring our ship home. How they respond could tell us a lot."

"I like the way you think," Poole said with a nod. "Do it."

The hushed atmosphere of *Peng Fei*'s control module abruptly ended with the blare of an unexpected alert message. Annoyed with having his concentration broken, Liu turned to Zhou at the flight engineer's station. "What is that alarm?"

The lieutenant reached over for the communications panel and muted the alarm. Of the six pack of digital radio dials in front of him, one was blinking steadily in amber. "Incoming transmission, sir. Unencrypted, on the universal emergency frequency."

That explained the alarm, Liu thought to himself. He made a mental note to have Zhou change its tone in the future. "Identifier?"

Zhou turned to him, eyes wide. "It's the Americans, sir. The *Borman*."

Liu arched an eyebrow. "How is your English, Lieutenant?"

Zhou waved his hand with an uncertain back-and-forth. "My academy grades were superior, sir. But I have not had the opportunity to exercise it in practice."

"Then there is no time like the present," Liu said, nodding at the blinking radio screen. "We are bound by international treaty to respond to any emergency call we may receive." His overtly formal tone was belied by the sardonic glint in his eyes. He gestured for Zhou to remove his headset. "Put it on speaker."

"As you wish, sir," Zhou said. He switched over to the still-blinking emergency channel and reached for a microphone. He spoke haltingly, keeping eye contact with his commander. "*Borman*, this is *Peng Fei*. We acknowledge your transmission. Over."

Still two days out, the light delay was a few seconds. The open frequency hissed and popped in the background before being replaced with a sharp crackle. "Good to hear you, *Peng Fei*. We understand you are inbound to our position, and we sure do appreciate the help. Be nice to have some company out here."

"Keeping it light," as the Americans liked to say, Liu thought. Nobody in their position should sound that damned happy. He motioned for Zhou to hand him the microphone as the rest of the command crew watched. "This is Colonel Liu Wang Shu. With whom am I speaking?"

Another handful of seconds, another crackle, and a relaxed drawl emerged from the static. "This is Captain Simon Poole. Pleased to make your acquaintance, Colonel Liu."

So he understood their naming conventions, at least. A surprising number of Westerners remained ignorant of that. How many times had he been called "Colonel Shu" by some overbearing American stooge? Should he play that game with them?

"Likewise, Captain Simon," he said, intentionally flubbing it. "What is your status? Over."

"We've seen better days to be honest, Colonel. We lost most of our comm suite with that drop-tank explosion. That's why we're stuck on the S-band. We're looking at a long trip back to Earth, longer than we made plans for. My crew was mighty happy to hear there's help on the way. Over."

"It is our pleasure to assist," Liu said coolly.

"Your offer to provide rations and other consumables is much appreciated, Colonel. The straight Hohmann orbit back to Earth will be a long trip but we should be able to manage it with your help."

Liu clicked the mic to acknowledge. "Stand by, *Borman*." He then left the frequency silent, turning the microphone over in his hand as he thought. Simon Poole had been an astronaut, but more importantly he'd been a nuclear-missile submarine commander before that. Which meant he was, as the Americans would say, "cagey." What would his motive be for reaching out to them now? Would being marooned this far from Earth make a man go against his nature? Did it mess with his psyche to such a degree that he would abandon good tactical sense? Or had their strategic plan succeeded, lulling even their most formidable adversaries into complacency? We were all one big, happy, spacefaring world now. The universe was more immense than any ocean on Earth, and we were all just as vulnerable. Or at least that was the image they'd worked to craft.

No, he decided. Poole was not the captain of a pleasure cruise. "Clever. He's probing us," Lie announced to the command crew. "This is why it is important to study your adversary, including his language. Simon Poole is from California, yet he is adopting an exaggerated 'country boy' accent. I suspect he wants us to believe he is relaxed. Unsuspecting." He eyed each of his officers. "We must never assume that."

As each nodded his understanding, Major Wu spoke for them. "What is our answer, Colonel?"

"Think he bought it?"

"Hell no, sir," Marshall said.

The chronometer ticked well past the time their signal would've taken to return. That meant Liu was thinking about it. Poole tapped his thumb on the microphone as he waited for a reply.

Liu's voice finally returned. "*Borman*, we believe there is a misunderstanding of our mission. We have been instructed to offer assistance by taking you and your crew aboard to provide a safe and swift return to Earth. We are not equipped to transfer any consumables. Over."

Poole eyed Marshall. "Note how they didn't say anything about our passengers? I don't think that was an oversight." He thought about his response and thumbed the mic. "This is *Borman* Actual," he said, reverting to terse military vernacular. It was time to lay out at least some of his cards, just to see how the other guy reacted. "Be advised, we have two evacuees from the US survey vessel *Prospector* aboard who require ongoing medical attention. Over." A bit of an exaggeration, but their reaction would tell him a lot.

There was a shorter pause before Liu came back. "We can arrange for appropriate medical attention pending our assessment of their condition. They will enjoy a standard of care commensurate with their status as Chinese nationals."

Poole pursed his lips. "So much for my acting career," he muttered, and pressed the mic. "All the same, Colonel, they are also naturalized American citizens. We are ultimately responsible for their care and safe return to United States soil. We are prepared to bring aboard additional medical supplies."

Liu's curt reply came immediately after the signal delay. "That will not be necessary, Captain. We can discuss particulars after rendezvous. *Peng Fei* out."

⚙ 29 ⚙

"We have a predicament, ladies and gents," Poole said to his small crew. At only half strength, their presence made the wardroom feel a lot more spacious than usual.

It hadn't escaped notice that the captain had pulled the compartment's hatch closed behind him, keeping the all-hands meeting private and out of the Jiang's hearing. He understood the need for secrecy, but they perhaps stood to lose more than anyone here. Marshall wondered if any of them would see the inside of this ship again after boarding the approaching *Peng Fei*. He was not concerned about their fate—there were no active hostilities between the US and the PRC, after all—but the Jiangs had legitimate reasons to fear them. The Chinese communists had shown themselves to not being above detaining troublesome expatriates when they were outside of their adopted country's jurisdiction.

"The PRC's roaming battlewagon will be rendezvousing with us in less than thirty-six hours. You all know we have enough propellant left for a Hohmann transfer to Earth, but it's a long trip and there's simply not enough food for all of us. We could stretch it with a skeleton crew; myself and maybe three others, assuming we use *Prospector*'s remaining stores."

Rosie raised a hand. "Sir, pardon my stupid question—so the rest of us would have to ride home on their spacecraft?"

"Affirmative."

She crossed her arms. "I have a hard time getting behind that idea, sir. Breaking up the crew is a bad idea."

"Abandoning ship could be a worse idea, Rosie," he said. "Even if we hand it off to ground to bring home."

"Begging your pardon again, sir, but would this calculus change if we were talking about a friendly vessel?"

Poole's eyes narrowed. "Of course it would. I don't trust them any further than I can spit. I would rather we all go on minimal rations and fly home together than split us up and see half of you stuck on a PRC vessel." He looked to Marshall, who had been given responsibility for their passengers.

"There's another wrinkle to this," Marshall began explaining. "The Jiangs. We can't put them on survival rats for that long."

"But they *want* to," Rosie interrupted, out of character. "They know the risks, sir."

"You need to think clearly, Petty Officer Rosado," Chief Garver said, his narrowed eyes and blunt tone checking her. "This isn't just an ethical question, there's a practical matter. I've inventoried *Prospector*'s stores and there simply isn't enough to go around, even counting their reserves. When Mr. Hunter says 'we can't,' he means it."

"And leaving them on a PRC vessel, beyond our influence, is tantamount to leaving them on that asteroid," Marshall finished, perhaps too dramatically but it accurately reflected his feelings. He noted Poole's eyebrows arch at his hyperbole, but he didn't correct him—which meant the skipper agreed. He drew in a breath. "I will volunteer to stay with them, sir."

"As I expected," Poole said. "I'll consider your offer if it comes to that. But I brought you all here because I want you thinking about alternatives." He planted his hands on his hips and drew his breath, ready to take a leap with them. "I don't believe in coincidence, and I don't think their hands are clean. But we are also under orders to accept whatever assistance is provided as a show of good faith and maintaining friendly relations."

He eyed the group. "Good. I see you all think that's a load of horseshit too." He swiped at the monitor in the bulkhead and pulled up long-range photos of the *Peng Fei*. "We need either more propellant or more rations. They have both. Question is, how do we avail ourselves of it?"

"Drive-plume spectrum confirmed they're burning methane, sir," Garver pointed out. "Carbon buildup from that stuff'll trash our reactors."

"Over time, yes," Poole acknowledged. "But we don't have the resources to crack it and extract hydrogen in the quantities we need. Regardless, we don't have common nozzle fittings and tank one doesn't have enough volume, even if we could transfer."

"But we do have common docking rings," Marshall said. "Could we use them as a booster?" He pointed at the *Peng Fei's* pair of enormous spherical propellant tanks. "It's a good bet they'd have the delta-v capability."

"That's my thinking," Poole said. "If we mate at both vehicles' forward nodes so we're aligned with their thrust axis, it could handle the load."

"We probably won't be able to use that ring ever again," Garver said. "We'll reach its lifetime load limit after the first push."

"Small potatoes, if it gets us home together," Poole said. "This ship's going to need work regardless."

"So how do we sell this to Liu? He didn't seem very accommodating."

Poole tugged at his chin. "That's the trick, isn't it? We still don't know his intentions, so we have to surmise how he benefits from this situation."

"We're out of the fight, before the fight even got started," Marshall said. "Before we even knew the PRC had this kind of capability." He tapped on the fuzzy digital image of *Peng Fei* leaving L1 under power, in a blaze of blue plasma. "We can deduce an awful lot about their performance from these images and their trajectory here: mass, specific impulse, propellant volume. This thing could easily cover territory beyond Mars, and quickly. Six months round trip to the asteroid belt."

"I'm more interested in all that hardware hanging off of it," Wylie said. "Those aren't fueling booms or sensor masts."

Poole nodded. "You're right. Their sensor suite's distributed all across the vehicle. Smart design but complicated in a spacecraft— you can't just upgrade it by berthing a new module, like ours. But you also can't take it out all at once."

"Like ours."

"Precisely. Liu's got eyes and ears all over this thing. And the rest of that hardware is just what it looks like: Missile mounts, point-defense guns, and an optical turret which I'm guessing is not a camera."

"Jeebus," Rosie said. "Did they forget the rail gun?"

"Not for lack of trying," Poole said. "Those things have to store a lot of energy to discharge at once, even more than this laser turret. With the problems their Navy's had deploying seagoing rail guns, I'm not surprised. Too much mass and trouble."

"It doesn't look as if mass is much of a problem for them, sir."

Poole studied the images and overlaid a 3-D wire-frame diagram that represented the Defense Intelligence Agency's best guess. "You're right. I suppose we should count ourselves lucky they haven't figured out warp drive yet." He scrolled down a table of equipment and capability estimates along the side of the screen. "They put this together over three years after at least a dozen Long March 10 launches. That nuclear lightbulb engine's a beast, too. They can move a hell of a lot of mass around the inner solar system with this setup."

"You believe they can boost us on our way, sir?"

"With delta-v to spare," Poole said. "Otherwise I wouldn't even propose it. I'm not interested in commandeering anyone's vehicles, and I'm sure as hell not letting them do the same to ours. I'm going to propose this as a mutually agreeable solution."

Rosie's face twisted in doubt. "What if he doesn't find it 'mutually agreeable,' sir?"

"We're going to test the waters gently. And if he doesn't like it, then we do something less than gently." Pooled glanced in Marshall's direction. "That's where you come in."

"Not sure what we can do, sir," Rosie said. "I'm a spacer, not a tactician."

"Good spacers are exactly the kind of people we're going to need, Petty Officer Rosado." He jerked his head aft, toward the medical module. "Along with people who speak fluent Mandarin Chinese."

"Retrofire initiated," Wu reported, though Liu did not need to hear his words to know. *Peng Fei* shuddered from the full force of its engines, a cluster of seven transparent quartz reaction chambers, each containing the nuclear inferno of a reaction that flashed the ship's methane propellant into plasma and channeled it through nozzles at the base of each chamber. The engine module itself resembled nothing so much as a cluster of incandescent torches clustered inside of a cement mixer.

With the fission reaction contained inside of its quartz chambers, the exhaust itself was not radioactive though it was fiercely energetic. Now turned about to point its engines at its destination, the big ship rode atop a fireball that blocked its view ahead. Mathematics drove them now, and they were confident they would decelerate to arrive at the precise point at the prescribed time. It was the beauty of orbital mechanics: One could navigate around the solar system with nothing but a good watch and a precise star reference.

It did serve to blind much of their sensor suite, however.

Marshall was on watch in the cupola, fighting sleep to keep his eyes trained on the point in space where they knew *Peng Fei* would have to appear. The sudden appearance of what for all the world looked like a new star in the sky was startling, even though he'd done the calculations to determine when and where to look for it. He knew it was less of the sight itself than the realization of *they're here*.

Marshall tapped out a quick, predetermined alert message to Poole. Within seconds, a shrill alarm blasted throughout the ship followed by his voice over the intercom. "General quarters, general quarters, all hands to action stations. This is not a drill."

Already in his EVA suit, Marshall flew out of the dome and down into the forward node, through the connecting tunnel and back into the *Specter* shuttle where the Jiangs waited patiently in fresh launch-and-entry suits recovered from *Prospector*. Not meant for spacewalks, the L&E suits would still protect them from vacuum and temperature swings. And they were in much better condition than the spacesuits the couple had survived in—Marshall doubted he could ever get them back into those things short of the threat of certain death. As it was, he felt guilty just flying into the shuttle, ordering "Visors down" as he grabbed his helmet from a storage rack and made one last check of the M55A2 space-rated carbine in its cradle beneath them: magazine loaded, chamber empty for safety. His freefall weapons quals had been a long time ago, and he tried not to think about what using it for real might be like.

As he strapped himself into the command pilot's seat for the first time, he looked back to see them both reluctantly locking down their faceplates. After their ordeal he desperately wished they could have left them up, but the threat of getting holed with what they were about to try was too great. *Hell of a way to do my first solo*, he thought.

With the shuttle already partially powered up, finishing the job had consisted of booting up the guidance platform and warming up the thrusters. "*Specter* is go," he called over the ship-to-ship frequency.

Garver answered him. "Copy that *Specter*, CO says you're cleared to undock."

"On our way," Marshall said. "Happy hunting, Chief."

Poole answered this time. "Just keep them out of harm's way, Hunter. We'll need them when this is over."

Marshall gave the mic two rapid clicks, signaling that he acknowledged his CO and that they were about to go silent. He made certain his radio transceiver was muted but the shuttle's intercom was still on. He turned to check that the Jiangs were still strapped safely in their seats. "Okay, folks, we're getting underway."

There was a muffled clattering as latches opened behind them, releasing the spring-loaded docking ring and pushing them away gently. He watched the *Borman* recede slowly behind them through a rear-view camera. Two quick flashes of light from the cupola signaled him that Poole had cleared them to maneuver. He pulsed thrusters and spun them about to face the ship as they slowly drifted away, back into the shadow of RQ39. The object that had sheltered them for so long would become their safe harbor in the coming hours.

Information coming into Fleet Ops had been scarce enough—when the *Specter* shuttle undocked and took its directional antenna with it, thus breaking its relay with the *Borman*, the panic this threw its ground controllers into was palpable from the drone stations on the opposite end of the darkened amphitheater. Roberta watched with interest as figures, silhouetted against their consoles, began frantically dancing about each other. One trotted off to a side office and was followed back out by a crop of fresh faces, all of them awkwardly navigating between the rows of chairs and control consoles.

"That's the detachment from *Borman*," Ivey pointed out. "They've been parked in here until their ride comes back in a few weeks."

She studied them. "Know anybody?"

"Not a one," Ivey said, then eyed her suspiciously. "What are you thinking, Roboto?"

"Something's up," she pointed out quietly, not wanting to wear her curiosity on her sleeve. She watched as Ivey scrolled through the Ops internal message board. It took him a few seconds longer than normal, a lag which she attributed to the sudden chaos over in Fleet Ops.

"*Borman* just went dark again," Ivey said. "They lost the whole stack this time, including the shuttle. No voice or data, like they just turned out the lights."

Roberta looked up at the tracking display on one of the big wall monitors. "That PRC ship's about to rendezvous. Bad time to lose comms."

Ivey followed her gaze, building a mental image of the tactical situation out at RQ39. *Peng Fei* was no doubt unaware, probably blind as a bat while in the middle of its braking burn. "Depends on your definition of bad timing."

At Ivey's insistence, he performed introductions as the senior of the two. "Excuse me, Commander?"

Wicklund turned slowly. Like the others she'd seen come down from duty in orbit, his movements were reserved, tentative, reacquiring the habits and reflexes of living in gravity. The man's face had the tan, weathered look of someone who had spent a great deal of time squinting into direct sunlight, like a pilot or spacecraft operator. His movements might have been slow, but his eyes were impatient as he regarded them both. "Yes, Lieutenant?"

"Begging your pardon, sir, but I understand you were on the *Borman*. We operate the X-37s and spend a lot of time watching what other satellites are up to."

"I would imagine you do," Wicklund said. "X-37's an impressive bird. But the more freedom of movement you have in orbit, the more you do have to pay attention to other equipment. Half our job up there is to keep the lanes clear."

Roberta kept her hands clasped behind her back, clenching and reclenching her fists to keep from bouncing out of her boots. Ivey placed a hand on her shoulder. "Ensign McCall here is especially good at that, sir. I've found she's got a real talent for pattern recognition."

"Is that right?" Wicklund asked, it being obvious this pair had some kind of agenda. He studied her for an uncomfortably long time before engaging. "I'm guessing there are some patterns you want me to recognize." He jerked his head toward the tactical display on the big wall monitors. "You both realize things are starting to get dicey up there?"

Ivey surreptitiously kicked Roberta's heel to spur her on. She handed Wicklund a tablet with preselected slides. "Yes sir, and I believe you'll find this relevant. This is a graphic depiction of all the satellite failures in geosynchronous orbit over the last two weeks."

Wicklund swiped through the graphs. "I'm aware it's a real mess up there. That flare roasted a lot of birds. What's your point?"

"Or it covered up a lot that were about to get neutralized anyway. Sir."

He looked up. "How so, Ensign?"

Roberta hoped the blush she felt wasn't showing. "The sats that went dark were clustered around two bands of longitude, 60 west and 100 east. In the beginning it looked like random distribution, but over time . . ."

Wicklund scrolled ahead. By the end, his eyebrows lifted a millimeter. "Not quite a bell curve, is it?"

"No sir," she agreed. "I think they've all been either hacked or whacked. But I don't know how."

He glanced over at Ivey. "You agree with her assessment, Lieutenant?"

"I do, sir. We've run this by the S-2 and the S-3—"

Wicklund held up a hand, stopping him. "But you couldn't sell this to your own chain of command, and now you're bringing this to me . . . why?"

"Their hands are full dealing with the *Borman* and that Chinese spacecraft. We haven't been able to get any traction with this, sir. There's something shifty going on up there, it's probably related to what's happening out at RQ39, and I think the civilian you rescued might be involved."

A look of scorn crossed Wicklund's face. "In that, you may be right. Lesko's a weaselly little shit; I've had my eye on him ever since we took him aboard. And you're definitely right about task saturation up at the decision-making levels, but they can't go chasing conspiracy theories while they're busy plugging leaks in the dike. They need hard evidence."

"Has anyone interrogated this Lesko character, sir?" Roberta asked.

"No," Wicklund sighed. "We were able to place him in the isolation ward for radiation exposure, at least that keeps him where we can find him until somebody decides to pay attention." He laughed to himself. "Word is he's going stir crazy from lack of connectivity."

"How's that, sir?"

"He's in nuclear medicine, probably the most heavily shielded floor of the hospital." He studied Roberta for a moment. "I'm guessing you're a classmate of Hunter's?"

"Yes sir."

"It shows."

"Not sure if I should take that as a compliment, sir."

"That makes two of us." Wicklund ran a hand through his salt-and-pepper hair. "There aren't many good things about being detached from my ship, but one is that I hold just enough rank to make myself a pain in the ass to the right people down here." He returned her tablet. "But all I'd be doing with this is restating your argument for you. I need more evidence."

Roberta's eyes darted between him and Ivey. "I have an idea."

◎ 30 ◎

Roberta McCall checked herself in a full-length mirror behind a ladies' restroom door inside Schriever's base hospital. She didn't typically care this much about her appearance—she certainly didn't typically wear so much makeup—but this would be a unique case. For the first time in her intel career, she was going on a field op. Not sanctioned, of course: No one in Group S-2 knew what she was up to. But after some background work and a few casual conversations with the medics and nurses on his floor, she didn't expect the target to respond to straight-ahead questions.

With this being a freelanced op, she had to be especially careful. Throwing on a pair of scrubs with a falsified ID to impersonate medical staff would be a quick route to a bad-conduct discharge, the "big chicken dinner." And she couldn't just sashay into his room in civilian clothes, that would raise too many questions among the others who'd be certain to recognize her.

So she'd visited a seamstress in town, one she remembered from last year after struggling into a dress for a friend's wedding. The little old lady had been an artist with fabrics, nipping and tucking until Roberta had come out the other side looking curvaceous enough that the bride barely recognized her and groomsmen were hitting on her. Glamming herself up had been fun at the time, but entirely too much work for her to make a habit of it. She didn't know how other girls tolerated it. Life was busy enough without adding more work.

This had managed to be even more so. The genius lady had managed to tweak a standard-issue women's flight suit into, well, she wasn't sure what to call it. It was still regulation, but when she tried it on . . . *damn*. It revealed curves she didn't know she had.

Roberta turned to one side and ran a hand along her hip, admiring herself. Maybe her friends were right, maybe she needed to get out more. But not in this—and as soon as she got what she needed, this was going straight back to the seamstress. She couldn't afford this look at work; nobody would ever take her seriously again.

She leaned into the mirror, checking her hair and makeup one last time, and tweaked the zipper of her jumpsuit down another half an inch. Just enough, she thought. *This had better work*.

She finished the look by donning her regulation brown leather flight crew jacket, which would serve to cover her up just long enough to keep from embarrassing the hell out of herself in front of anyone who might recognize her.

Satisfied with the final product, she slipped back out onto the nuclear medicine floor and headed for the isolation ward.

Nick Lesko numbly flipped through the channels on his room's TV for what felt like the hundredth time just this morning. No internet connectivity, so he couldn't even surf his favorite content sites. It was the usual collection of local news, mindless talk, cop show reruns, and obscure old movies that deserved to remain that way.

From the corner of his eye, he caught sight of a young woman in a tight-fitting charcoal gray jumpsuit as she flounced through the isolation ward door. He'd seen a few pretty nurses here, all of them strictly business. This one seemed different. She wore a mop of brown curls in a loose ponytail that bounced in synch with the rest of her body as she made her way through the ward and in . . . his direction? He couldn't be that lucky.

And yet, there she was, beaming a smile as she slid the glass door open. "Mr. Lesko?"

He sat upright and smoothed down his hospital gown, doing his best to look presentable. "That's me."

Her smile grew wider. "Awesome. Mind if I come in? I mean, if this isn't a bad time?"

He swept his hand in a welcoming gesture. *Like I have anything better to do.*

The bouncy young lady pulled a chair alongside his bed and sat close. "I'm Roberta," she said, extending her hand. He gladly took it, enjoying the touch of her handshake as it lingered just a second.

"I'm a liaison officer from Group staff. We haven't had the opportunity to check on you and so I wanted to see if there's anything we can do for you."

He fought the urge to chuckle at that. *Yeah, there's a lot you can do for me.* He pointed at the TV hung on the opposite wall. "You could improve the entertainment selection, for starters. Only one sports channel?"

"Oh, I'm so sorry to hear that," Roberta said. She reached for the remote, brushing his arm and making the hair stand up. "May I?"

"Go for it," he said. "You won't find much."

She scrolled through the channel menu and leaned in close. "I never knew that our selection was so limited. Everybody's so used to streaming that nobody uses cable anymore except hospitals and military bases."

"I wouldn't care, except that even my laptop's useless here."

A quizzical look crossed her exquisitely made-up face—she wore just enough to make things interesting without being trashy. Where did the military keep these women? Did they only roll them out for recruiting ads? "I don't understand," she said. "You can't use your laptop?"

"No internet access," he explained. "I'm cut off from the outside world."

Her lips glistened as she pursed them in thought. "I think I can help." She flitted her hands in a gesture of bewilderment. "This floor has a lot of crazy equipment and shielding in the walls that I don't begin to understand. They didn't offer you a portable hot spot?"

"Never mentioned it," he said. "You're the first person to explain that to me the whole time I've been here."

She touched his arm again, this time leaning forward for emphasis. It did not escape his notice. "Again, I am so sorry. It's a good thing I came down here to check on you, because we can certainly do something about that." She reached down into her bag and pulled out a small white cube. "Here, you can use mine for now." She wrote down the passcode on a notepad and tore it off for him.

"I can't—" he began.

"Sure you can," she said lightly. "You said it yourself, we've had you isolated for over a week. They wouldn't even let me come up here until they were sure you were safe for visitors."

"They think I'm radioactive," he grumbled. "I told them I'm not."

"You're not," she giggled. "But you do have to be careful, Mr. Lesko. I haven't been to space yet myself, but I know it can be dangerous."

"You have no idea," he said, feeling braggadocious. "Once is enough for me."

She leaned forward again, her hand on her chest. "I can only imagine, Mr. Lesko. They told me about what happened. You are lucky to be alive."

"Lucky." He laughed darkly. "Yeah. That was some luck." He opened up his laptop and typed in the code she'd given him. "That's it," he said, his mood improving as soon as he saw he was back online. "I'm part of the world again." He met her eyes. "Thank you."

"My pleasure," she said, and collected her things. She handed him another note. "This is my cell number. Let me know if you need anything."

"I'll do that." Lesko smiled. He'd definitely be calling.

"Great," Roberta beamed. "Now if you'll excuse me, Mr. Lesko. It was a pleasure meeting you but I do have more rounds to make."

She bounced out of the room just as she'd come in, but with an extra spring in her step as she checked her phone on the way out. Sure enough, Lesko had wasted no time using the hot spot she'd set up for him. She tapped an icon on her phone and activated the keystroke logger embedded in the small white cube now connecting him to the internet.

Having fresh access to the outside world after being removed from it for so long left Nick Lesko feeling giddy, like the first time he'd discovered the myriad treasures of the internet. It was too tempting to follow those rabbit trails, and likewise too important that he maintain his focus. He needed to know what was happening with their little project in orbit, what had those repurposed satellites been up to?

He reflexively looked over his shoulder, though there was of course no one to see what he was doing. Nothing but supply cabinets and monitoring equipment. The only window into his room was the sliding glass door. *It's supposed to be an "isolation ward," dumbass*, he reminded himself, and logged into the VPN his sponsors had created for their project. He watched as it synched itself to an encryption key running separately on his phone. It used to annoy him, how much memory their overcomplicated code ate up, but now he was relieved to have it. Who would have thought that he might someday need access from inside a military base?

In what was perhaps an unnecessary level of safety, the status monitoring program itself was disguised to look like an old PC game. But then, games had become so realistic that one would be hard pressed to find the difference unless they involved firing actual guns. Fortunately, Lesko didn't need fancy VR gear to manipulate this. It was a simple world map depicting coverage from each satellite they'd modified and used to hijack other satellites.

He was taken aback, now able to see the scope of their project illustrated so unambiguously. He let out a low whistle in appreciation—they hadn't been screwing around. No wonder they'd ridden him so hard.

A large portion of the world's geosynchronous communications and surveillance satellites had been either disabled or were effectively working for someone else. He wasn't sure who yet, and didn't really care, but turning a couple of old birds into roaming maintenance bots had been like unleashing a virus in orbit.

He scrolled through the roster of satellites, looking for the ones he was familiar with, and grew impatient. It was easier to just type in their names in the search bar. The first spacecraft he looked up was Stardust, and he breathed a sigh of relief. It was gone, deorbited. Good move, whoever had done it. What was that one he'd just heard about... Indo-something? He did a search and was rewarded with reams of data.

Roberta slid her tablet PC across the desk to Ivey. "He's in," she said, "partitioned behind a private network, which isn't surprising."

"So we can't see exactly what he's doing," Ivey said, disappointed.

"Except the keylogger tells us how to access his VPN and his encryption key for whatever he's running now." She smiled with satisfaction. "And it shows what he's searching for." She tapped on the screen, drawing his attention to the scrolling text being relayed to them from Lesko's computer inside the base hospital.

His eyes popped. "Those look familiar all right. INDOSAT, GULFSAT, NSTAR... it's like a who's who of disabled birds."

"I don't think they're disabled," Roberta said. "Their operators just can't see them anymore."

Ivey nodded and pushed the tablet back to her. "We've got to let the brass know. Come on."

"They've resurrected dormant comsats, modified them into maintenance drones, and turned them loose to hijack and repurpose other satellites. KH-13 was their grand prize. And they're using some high-grade encryption to cover their tracks," Roberta told her captain, Wicklund and Ivey at her side. She handed over a stack of transcripts. "The keylogger I left in Lesko's room recorded everything he's done since yesterday morning."

The senior intel officer flipped through the pages. "You figured all that out from this?"

Roberta nodded at the transcripts. "Not all of it, sir. A lot of that is outside of my expertise. But he's got a key generator running on his laptop, that's for certain."

"He's been busy," the captain agreed. "Hell, looking at the time stamps I don't know if he's even sleeping."

"Making up for lost time, sir," Roberta agreed. "We just can't see on what."

The captain eyed them each before landing back at her. "But you have your suspicions."

"He was working up in GEO at the same time we started seeing satellites go dark all over the place, sir. His crewmates are dead. And as soon as *Borman* broke orbit, we lost a Keyhole bird. Maybe I've watched too many movies but Lesko comes off as some kind of mob goon."

"What, like the Mafia? Everybody knows there is no Mafia," the captain deadpanned. "*Especially* in the casino business."

"That's what bugs me about this guy, sir. How does a casino fixer end up running a satellite repair team? What interest do they have?"

"His employer's listed in Macau," the captain said. "That right there raises all sorts of red flags for me." He put down the transcripts. "So now we can read at least some of their mail. What we don't know is who's on the other end. In the meantime, maybe you can get us in a position to look over their shoulders."

※　※　※

The X-37 had taken two days to sneak up on Necromancer and its KH-13 prisoner. The spaceplane hovered above the repurposed comsat, passively monitoring the electronic traffic passing between it and what Roberta assumed to be its operator. She couldn't determine direction, but the increasing delay between signals suggested it wasn't being controlled by a ground station on Earth. Its signals were being relayed from something much farther away.

That didn't leave many candidates, she knew, but that was something she had to keep between herself and her pilot. Jacob Ivey was deftly keeping their drone on station within a few meters of Keyhole and its metallic parasite. And from the drone's video feed, that's exactly what it looked like: an origami virus, its skeletal legs wrapped around the big spysat.

An alert flashed on her screen, and she pushed a new tasking order across the console to him. "New frag order. The one we've been waiting for."

Ivey read the order. "Cleared hot. About damned time," he said, flexing his hands around the controls. "You ready?"

"Born ready," she said, doing the same. "Let's take our bird back."

This close to their target, Ivey only dared use the slightest pulse of control jets to bring the X-37 almost on top of it. He stopped the drone within a meter of Necromancer. "You're up, Roboto."

Wearing a pair of 3-D goggles, Roberta carefully guided the drone's manipulator arm with a pair of hand controllers. She watched as the arm unfolded itself from the X-37's open cargo bay and reached for the first of Necromancer's four spindly legs.

She pressed a thumbwheel and a grappling claw opened up. "Okay. Be ready to move, this thing may not like it."

She pushed on the hand controllers. In orbit, the arm extended and its claw found the first leg. When she closed her fist, it in turn closed around the leg, severing it. "One down."

They waited for a reaction, expecting the satellite to try and evade. Either it wasn't that sophisticated, it was out of propellant (which she thought likely), or its controllers were at a disadvantage from light delay (which was just as likely).

"It's quiet," Ivey said. "I think you're good to go."

"Hell yes," Roberta said, and reached for the next leg.

By the time she made it to the last remaining leg, the parasite satellite's grip on KH-13 was tenuous enough that it took only minimal force to release. This time, she kept her grappler wrapped around it and turned to Ivey. "Now what?"

"Just got an update to the tasking order," he said. "Ready for some target practice?"

Her eyes widened. "Thought you'd never ask," she said. "Laser's charged."

"You're clear to release. Weapons free."

"Weapons free," Roberta repeated, and cut their captured satellite loose. "Separation point three meters per second." When it had drifted to a safe distance away from both their drone and the freshly liberated Keyhole, she thumbed a selector wheel atop her control stick. "Targeting the RCS tanks."

In orbit, an optical turret inside the X-37's cargo bay swiveled and locked onto Necromancer. There was a flash of green light from inside the turret, and soon after the parasite satellite's remaining propellant exploded.

She smiled with satisfaction. "Splash one."

⊛ 31 ⊛

It seemed to be a day for lost contacts. First the quantum datalink with their satellite controlling the American KH-13 had gone silent, and now the *Borman* was unresponsive as well. Lieutenant Zhou had been calling repeatedly and had so far received no answer. He confirmed once more that he was on the correct channel, the universal emergency frequency, and began repeating his mantra in precisely measured English. "Attention *Borman*, this is the People's Republic Spacecraft *Peng Fei*—"

Liu held up a hand. "You may cease, Lieutenant," he said. "What does our control center report?"

Major Wu answered for the command crew. He seemed hesitant. "They have no new information from the American control center in Colorado."

"That seems unlikely." Liu stared at the situation display above the flight station. "Our arrival is no surprise to them, and no doubt they've seen our drive plume. They know we're here." He tapped his fingers against the arm of his chair. "Wu, did Beijing confirm our new orbit parameters?"

"They did, Colonel. Main engine cutoff confirmed with no residuals. We are twenty kilometers from *Borman*'s keep-out sphere, closing at six meters per second."

That left them perhaps thirty minutes until they crossed the American's approach threshold; another hour and they'd be on top of them. This was no time to be out of communication. "That is enough to conduct terminal maneuvers with RCS thrusters," he decided. "Major Wu, bring us about, x-axis normal."

Major Wu slewed *Peng Fei* around, swinging the bulky ship about until its nose was pointed in their direction of travel. With a quick pulse of thrusters, he stopped them with the distant speck of the *Borman* centered in the forward windows.

The gray-white bulk of RQ39 loomed not far away, though Liu was much more enamored with the steadily approaching American ship. Exploration could wait; they first had to ensure their area of operations would be secure.

Slowly growing as they drew closer, the *Borman* still appeared indistinct. Compared to *Peng Fei*'s bulk, he'd expected to clearly see the American ship's dartlike profile clearly by now. That it was obscured concerned him—perhaps the damage was worse than he'd been led to believe?

He flicked a thumb controller by his chair and fine-tuned their approach, tweaking their pitch angle until the ship was centered in the docking camera's crosshairs. He zoomed in on the image until it became ragged with optical distortion. He backed off, but it remained indistinct. It was like looking at a toy encased in a snow globe. "Lieutenant Zhou, is that electronic noise?"

"No sir," Zhou said, confirming what his commander thought. "It appears to be debris from their tank explosion."

The cloud was following them in orbit, as these things tended to do with no atmosphere to disperse them. So they had not managed to even maneuver out of their own debris field?

It was both irritating and satisfying. The *Borman* was still obscured behind its own wreckage, and now it was out of contact as well. No doubt the Americans had not wanted to reveal the extent of their damage, and he couldn't blame them. He'd have done the same.

With no communications and a cloud of shrapnel to negotiate, it would be far too dangerous to attempt docking. Liu had kept his own EVA crew on standby, a team of six marines.

Liu pressed the intercom channel to their airlock node. "Captain Huang. Is your boarding party ready?"

"Ready, sir. All team members have completed pre-breathing and suit integrity checks. Weapons have been inspected and secured to their MMUs."

"Very good. Instruct your marines they should expect to find two civilians aboard; our intel reports they are most likely confined to the medical bay, multipurpose module P-3. They must be protected at all costs." He paused. "Even if it threatens your tactical advantage." He did not question Hu's professionalism, but he'd found young infantry officers could be overly aggressive.

"As you command, Colonel." Even over the intercom, Liu could hear the commando leader's begrudging tone.

"Ultimately it is they who have brought us here," Liu reminded him. "They are your mission objective, Huang. You take care of them, I will take care of the *Borman*."

"Ten klicks," Wylie reported from the pilot's station. He was pressed up against a forward window with a handheld optical rangefinder. "They're still hailing us, sir."

"As they should," Poole said from the observation dome. "I wouldn't want to come up on us in the blind."

"Pretty sure I don't like them coming up on us at all, sir," Garver said from behind him, in his EVA suit and pre-breathing through a mask. "She's a big bastard, ain't she?"

Poole answered with a grunt as he studied the PRC ship through his binoculars, judging what he saw against the constantly changing intel estimates. It reminded him of a club: forward pressurized modules and structural supports formed the handle, its cluster of massive propellant tanks the head. A sextet of radiator panels protruded like spikes from the bulky drum of the gas-core fission engine on its tail, completing the spacecraft's semblance of a blunt instrument.

Form follows function, Poole thought. A blunt instrument was exactly right. The spooks had clearly misjudged the PRC's true intentions—which was admittedly hard to do—but how had they missed that big cement-drum cluster of nuclear engines? It still glowed cherry red from its braking burn, casting a dull glow on the spherical tanks ahead of it.

Evaluating the other guy's capabilities was straightforward, guessing their intentions was a wholly different matter—that took a level of access and personal understanding that he doubted they possessed. One tended to superimpose one's own cultural proclivities onto the enemy. This made it hard to determine what they might really be up to; conversely it made it hard for them to do the same.

He recalled once meeting a PRC general who refused to believe that decades of American misadventures in the Middle East had not sprung from an intricately plotted conspiracy. He could not accept that it simply been a tragedy of errors, a series of bungled plans and missed opportunities instead of a sophisticated scheme hatched by forward-thinking leaders.

Poole laughed to himself: *Nobody* in Washington was forward thinking, unless you counted the next election cycle. It was hard for Americans to grasp the intricacies of a regime that planned for timelines measured in centuries. Freewheeling, unpredictable Americans had been giving hostile military leaders fits for centuries. Poole was happy to be counted among them.

It was hard to get inside of another person's head, especially when they were often pursuing wildly different goals. It was not so hard to understand the purpose of the ship he was now looking at. As it had rotated about to face them after decelerating into a common orbit, he realized their commander couldn't have planned it any better as a demonstration of force: After a few hours of watching their powerful gas-core fission engines on full display, he pirouetted his ship to face them, providing a slow-motion reveal of its full size and capability. No doubt much of its loadout was concealed, but what he could see was enough.

He handed the binoculars to Garver. "What do you think, Chief?"

Garver squinted into the eyepieces. "Like I said, Skipper—that thing's a beast. Figure she masses at least two hundred metric tons with full tanks." He adjusted the focus. "I count two forward missile racks, two lateral PDC turrets. Looks like that optical turret's connected to some beefy power conduits . . . it's gotta be a laser, sir. A telescope doesn't need to be jacked into a big capacitor bank like that."

"See the sensor masts?" Poole asked. Two trusses covered with antenna booms and radar panels extended from opposite sides of the superstructure, just aft of the pressurized modules.

"Phased-array radars, UHF and VHF antennas . . ." Garver's voice trailed off. "And a few things I don't recognize. What're those geodesic clusters on the end, sir?"

"Those disco-ball looking things?" Poole asked. "I was hoping you could tell me."

"They're either shells protecting directional antennas, or the surface geometry's the antenna itself. Lots of talk about them deploying quantum encryption, sir. Maybe that's what we're looking at."

Poole frowned. "If that's the case, we don't have a prayer of reading their mail."

"Hoping we don't need to, sir," Garver said. "I'd just as soon get our hands on their playbook."

"Me too. Time to get going, Chief," Poole said, more casually than he felt.

"Aye, sir." Garver pushed away to float down through the command deck and into the forward node.

Rosie and her team had likewise been pre-breathing from masks in the forward docking node. When they saw Garver emerge from the command deck and lock down the inner door, they knew it was finally time to put away their masks and lock down their visors. He watched as each spacer, without a word, switched over to their personal tanks and disconnected from the ship's oxygen supply.

"Report," Garver said tersely as he backed into his maneuvering pack by the outer door. The others were already locked into their backpacks, making the airlock node even more crowded than usual. They had already begun to unconsciously choreograph their movements inside the compartment: If one person turned left, the person behind him moved right, keeping out of the way.

"Suit checks complete. Outside is as clear as it's going to get," Rosie said. "We're ready, Chief."

Garver locked down his MMU, lifted his own carbine from a nearby weapons rack, and snapped it into a carrying plate on his chest pack. He looked each spacer in the eye one at a time, gauging their readiness for himself. In them he saw that unknowable mixture of tension, anticipation, and cold determination that he'd thought he would not see again. This was literally the last place he expected he'd ever have to prepare for a shipboard assault. *Never say never*, he thought to himself. He turned a dial to depressurize the airlock.

Poole's voice crackled over his radio earpiece. "Sentry team, comm check."

Garver let each spacer check in before doing so himself. "*Borman* Actual, this is Six."

"Copy, Six. You are go for EVA."

With one last look at his team, Garver opened the outer door. It fell open silently and the harsh, unfiltered light of the Sun flooded the compartment. He reached for the rim and pulled himself out into the void. He tapped his MMU controller and did a quick spin to check his thrusters and stability control before jetting off to the side, clearing the way for the rest of the team. Rosie was the last to emerge, and pulled the outer door shut behind her.

Garver led the team away from the ship, concealing them among the haze of debris surrounding the *Borman*.

At a young age in the mountains of Colorado, Marshall Hunter had learned a great deal about flying gliders from his father. He'd been unable to resist the urge to swoop along ridgelines, close enough to wave at hikers tackling the fourteeners. Flying so high yet so close to the ground had been the most exhilarating experience of his life until he'd learned to fly rocket planes.

Now that he was doing a little bit of each, it was unnerving. Piloting a spacecraft precariously close to what amounted to a free-flying mountain was different than skimming the Rockies in a glider. Its surface filled the shuttle's windows, almost in arm's reach. Too small to orbit, he was instead flying alongside RQ39, constantly making small adjustments as its weak gravity perturbed their common orbit just enough to threaten them. It was "lumpy" to boot, with mass concentrations that exerted stronger pulls in some areas.

His eyes kept darting back to the RCS gauges. He'd topped off from *Borman*'s tanks before departing but was having to expend more than he'd bargained for to keep formation with the asteroid. Moving farther out risked losing their cover, but it would save propellant. He hoped it would all be a moot point soon.

"Can you see them yet?" Max Jiang asked. They'd been surprisingly quiet despite having done nothing but float around the shuttle's small cabin for hours now.

"We're still below line of sight," Marshall explained, glancing at the chronometer on his panel. "It's not time for us to pop our heads up yet." They had worked out a communication schedule before departure based on the *Peng Fei*'s ETA. Marshall would pull away from his hiding place just far enough to pick up any signals from

Borman. If by radio, it meant Captain Poole was comfortable enough to talk in the open. If by light signals from the cupola, it meant something else that he preferred not to contemplate, which is why he did not expect to see his radio receivers come to life. "What frequency band did your CubeSats use?"

"VHF," Max said. "Very simple, adapted from aircraft radios."

Marshall frowned. These were spiking on the edge of the UHF band. "That's what I thought," he said. "I don't understand where this could be coming from."

He risked pulling farther away from the surface, just enough to give him room to turn and follow the directional antenna. He pivoted the shuttle's nose away from the surface, pointing it out into space. As the gravelly regolith moved out of view, a twinkle of light in the distance caught his eye. "What's that?"

Max and Jasmine floated up behind him, crowding against the other forward window. "Not one of our CubeSats," she said. "It's much too big."

"Is it a piece of debris?" Max wondered. "From one of our ships?"

"Not if it's emitting EM radiation," Marshall said. He squinted and leaned forward, straining to see details. "I think it's another spacecraft."

"That must be it!" Max exclaimed. "The one we told you about!"

Marshall eyed him, less skeptically now. Maybe they hadn't been hallucinating after all. "You might be right, Mr. Jiang. You say it was cruciform?"

"Yes, almost like a dagger. It narrowed at the nose. Two big wings near the tail, the wide end."

"And you thought it was surveying your ship after the service module exploded?"

Their eyes grew wide at the suspicion in his voice. "Might it be a scout of some kind?" Jasmine worried. "How could they have known to look for us here?"

"Pretty sure I don't have a clue," Marshall said. "We've been radio silent since yesterday and it's not like anybody had time to be looking for a ghost satellite. But there weren't any EM emissions to tip us off either..." His voice trailed off as he floated back into his seat, debating what to do next.

"Can it see us?"

Marshall didn't take his eyes off their mystery companion. "You know as much—scratch that, *more*—about that thing than I do."

"Then what do we do?" Max asked.

Marshall had been asking himself that very question. He had to assume it was somehow associated with the *Peng Fei*. If it was some kind of picket, then leaving their position would surely give them away. They had to remain hidden. "We lay low. If we can see it, then it can see us." He pulsed their thrusters, moving them back to the relative safety of the asteroid's surface clutter.

◈ 32 ◈

Nick Lesko by nature was not an inquisitive individual, at least not beyond the scope of whatever he happened to be working on at the moment. This was not to say he was incurious, it was that his mind was active if narrowly focused. It was a survival instinct he'd developed over decades of performing sensitive work for sometimes dangerous individuals—it was never good to be the guy who knew too much.

His recent isolation, in space and on the ground, had begun to change that. His need to be mentally occupied led him down paths he normally wouldn't have followed, whether out of disinterest or self-preservation.

Whether by necessity or accident, the control software they'd loaded on his laptop had provided a window into the full scope of the "project" he'd been hired for. And there was more, no doubt being controlled by someone else and partitioned from his piece of the pie. This he deduced from the news feeds he'd been following, searching for something to fill his mind besides the inane blather of daytime television.

Put simply, the space between Earth and Moon was getting dicey. Not only were all sorts of commercial satellites going dark, there were rumors that at least one high-priority US spy sat was out of contact. Putting the cherry on top, the military craft that rescued him, the one that was supposed to protect all this stuff in orbit, was now out of the picture.

So who profited from that? He wondered.

What most grabbed his attention was something that felt more personal. Lunar mining shipments which had been predictably arriving in their oceanic drop zones in a remote area of the South Pacific called Point Nemo were all of sudden not showing up in their drop zones. Someone was hacking and intercepting them—how? It would have to be early in their journey home. He'd learned enough to know that a small push one way in the beginning can lead to dramatic course changes at the end.

But it was what the news announcer had called that particular spot of ocean: the "spacecraft graveyard," the single point on the globe most distant from any land. That was supposed to have been their recovery zone after reentry. There would have been a trawler waiting to pick them out of the ocean, well clear of any prying eyes that might be interested in them.

A chill shot through him. Had it been intended to be more than just a spacecraft graveyard? He was supposed to eliminate his teammates with a carefully planned "accident" during recovery, but what if that itself had been a ruse? First rule of a conspiracy is to eliminate the low-level conspirators. So how "low-level" was Nicholas Lesko if this heist was as big as he now thought? Was that even the right way to think about it?

Disrupted lunar mining shipments, owned by the same billionaire couple who'd gone missing on their way to that crackpot flyby of Mars. And the American ship sent to look for them was now disabled itself, with a Chinese ship on its way to help.

He returned to the map and the concentration of hijacked satellites. Besides the fact that his sponsors were making a killing off it, someone had just made themselves a nice little surveillance network by hijacking other people's satellites—at least one of which had apparently belonged to the US military.

He hadn't given any thought to the regions their zombie sats were working in until now. South America and the Indian Ocean. Who gave a shit about either, really?

About ten minutes of internet sleuthing later, he had a good idea, both of Chinese strategic interests in both regions and their use of front companies in industries like telecom and banking to leverage their presence, so to speak.

Did that include holding companies run by casino operators in Macau? He decided it probably did. That explained the high-grade encryption and near-unlimited budget.

If a foreign government was involved, then just calling it a *heist* was thinking too small. What would the military call it?

An *operation*.

Lesko felt himself breaking into a sweat. He shut down the encryption key and snapped the laptop shut.

◎ 33 ◎

Poole's hand hovered over the radio as someone in precisely enunciated English continued calling for his attention, as had been happening for the last half hour. *I should feel a lot happier to be hearing a human voice out here.*

He turned to Wylie in the command pilot's seat next to him. "Think we should keep them waiting any longer?"

"Probably not, sir. They might think us rude." He was also tired of hearing the same phrase ceaselessly repeated over their radios, though he had to admire the discipline behind it.

"We can't have that, now can we?" Poole selected the shorter-range UHF and depressed the voice-activated mic switch. "PRCS *Peng Fei*, this is USS *Borman*. Nice to see you. We read you five by five. How copy?"

Whoever was on the radio sounded remarkably unaffected by finally having his calls answered. "Good day, *Borman*. We receive you loud and clear. Please stand by."

That meant they were putting the boss on the freq. The precise-enunciation guy was followed by someone whose English seemed much more seasoned, comfortable but not casual. "This is Colonel Liu Wang Shu of the People's Liberation Aerospace Force. With whom am I speaking?"

Poole felt a momentary tang of regret that he hadn't devoted more time to learning their language himself, though he might have if his time in uniform hadn't been interrupted for so long. *Too bad these weren't Russians*, he thought. He could've spoken the language and might have been a lot less suspicious of them. "Greetings, Colonel . . . Liu or Shu, you said?" he asked, knowing the answer.

"Liu," he answered. "Again, with whom am I speaking?"

Was there a hint of irritation there? Poole wondered. Every tell was helpful, though it could be hard to discern over the radio. Liu might be playing with him as well; Poole expected it in fact. "Colonel Liu, this is Captain Simon Poole, commanding officer of the *Borman*."

"Greetings, Captain Poole," Liu replied. None of that "Captain Simon" crap, then. That told him Liu wasn't playing around anymore and they could drop the Pidgin English routine. "We have been trying to make contact with you for some time. What is your spacecraft status?"

"We've seen better days," Poole said. "I regret the delay in answering your earlier transmissions, but we are having intermittent issues with our long-range comm. We've been limited to UHF line of sight."

"You were relaying communications through your shuttle's directional high-gain system, were you not?" No doubt they'd noticed *Specter* was missing.

"We were," Poole said. "We had to cut it loose. Long story." Which wasn't quite a lie, not that he cared.

"That is unfortunate," Liu said. "The debris cloud surrounding your vessel will make it too hazardous for us to dock. We will hold at the inner boundary of your approach zone and disembark a team to assist your crew in transferring to our vessel."

Poole pursed his lips. *Here we go.* "That won't be necessary, Colonel. We have a highly experienced crew of extravehicular specialists and we wouldn't want your people to risk transiting that debris field."

Liu didn't take long. "I'm afraid it will be necessary, Captain Poole. Our protocols require that our own specialists oversee any extravehicular activities in proximity to our vessel."

"I understand. They can just easily do that on the other side of the hazard zone." Poole adopted a casual tone. "If you folks can just sit tight, we can be on our way and nobody else needs to risk getting holed." He was counting on Liu's sense of subtlety to get the message across.

"We are confident that won't be a danger," Liu said calmly. "Captain Poole, prepare to receive our boarding party."

Poole flicked the voice switch off and turned to Wylie. "At least he's being honest."

Rosie watched with rising alarm as a string of six PRC spacers made their way across the gulf between the two ships in single file, carefully negotiating the close-in hazards that surrounded the *Borman* to arrive at its airlock.

She was concealed behind a large section of Mylar insulating foil, about ten meters away from Chief Garver, who had found his own piece. The other pair of spacers on their crew drifted another fifty or so meters away, likewise hidden behind pieces of what used to be a hydrogen tank. Each had used their MMUs to stabilize their personal piece of flotsam so that it was stationary relative to the ship, giving them a safe hide to watch from.

They were too far away to make out details of the other team, but the blocky gray and black protuberances jutting at right angles from each Chinese spacer's MMU were unmistakable. "Those look like weapons all right. You seeing this, Chief?" she whispered— unnecessary, but she felt reckless speaking out loud.

"Oh yeah." Garver said, and flicked on his helmet camera. "Now the skipper is, too."

"It's moving," Max said.

Marshall had only taken his eyes off the mystery satellite long enough to keep up his instrument scan and prevent them from scraping RQ39's surface. It hadn't been necessary to ask Max Jiang to help keep a lookout—he'd been glued to the other window the whole time while Jasmine sat brooding behind them.

Marshall pointed at the glowing blue exhaust from its tail. "Now we know how it gets around," he said. "Ion engines. Low thrust but very efficient. That thing can move about almost at will."

"It would have taken a long time to get out here, then," Max said, thinking through the mechanics of it. "How long do you suppose it's been waiting?"

Marshall watched it approach and silently pass by overhead. He raised *Specter* a few meters to ensure ground clearance and pivoted the shuttle about to keep it in sight. "If I had to guess—which I do— it's been here since before either one of us arrived."

"There wasn't anything in the catalog when we finalized the mission plan," Max said. "Nobody had surveyed RQ39 yet, that's why we came."

"That made it a very attractive side trip on your Mars flyby," Marshall said. "I remember reading about that a few times."

"They get it backwards all the time," Jasmine said crossly. "When Max worked out the orbital periods, it became clear that going to one would take us to the other. Nobody was going to invest in us flying to a barren rock in the sky, but you'd be amazed at how much capital flowed our way when we added Mars to the itinerary."

"It complicated the mission since we wanted to explore RQ39 for a while," Max said proudly. "We needed a larger upper stage for the velocity changes, but by that point money was not an issue."

The satellite sparkled in the sun as it emerged from RQ39's shadow, the glow of its ion engine diminished in the harsh light. Marshall dimmed the overhead windows to reduce glare as they studied it from afar.

It was dagger shaped just as they'd said, the body forming an elongated cone with a pair of what he assumed were either solar or radiator panels mounted on opposite sides of its tail, ahead of the ion engine grid.

The satellite turned to point its narrow snout in the direction of the *Borman* as it came to a stop behind a puff of thrusters. Marshall frowned. Whatever it was, he didn't care for strange satellites pointed at their ship. He gave the thrusters a kick and they began climbing away from the surface.

The Jiangs grew alarmed. "You're moving *closer*?"

"Four gomers, stacked at the outer door," Poole said, picking them up with an external camera. He pointed out their pattern on the video screen: The remaining two PRC crewmen stayed back to take up positions on either side. "Looks like two of them have MMUs and they're pulling two spacers each."

Wylie leaned in for a closer look. "Smart. That keeps the entry team nimble enough to get inside while a maneuvering element covers the exits. Wonder where they think we're going?" He smiled.

"They'll be wondering about more than that in a minute." Poole switched back to the UHF channel. "I have visual on your team,

Colonel Liu. Can you please explain why they're armed? That kind of thing might give a man the wrong idea."

"Please do not be alarmed, Captain. They do not present any danger to your crew or your ship. This is our common practice when boarding a different nation's vessel. It is just our 'SOP' as you would say."

"No danger," says the guy with guns pointed at us. "I wasn't aware you had much practice boarding other spacecraft, Colonel."

"There is always a first time, Captain. Rest assured our team has drilled this procedure many times. We have been expecting it to be necessary someday."

I'm sure they have. "Well then, I'm afraid we're going to have to decline your offer of assistance, Colonel. It's not American 'SOP' to allow armed agents of another country onto one of our vessels. It's just bad manners."

Marshall was able to get a much better look at the satellite as they drew closer. Holding back at five hundred meters, he could make out surface detail. One reason it had been hard to see before was the fact that it was nearly all black, as close to camouflage as could be achieved in space. It wasn't uniformly conical; the aft section was more barrel shaped and appeared to be the power module. That ion engine would need a lot of electricity, but this seemed like overkill. What looked like multiple capacitor banks surrounded the barrel behind the radiators; just ahead of them it was encircled by a ring of antenna and sensor blisters.

Max pointed at its large wings, folded out accordion style from either side. "Those aren't solar panels, are they?"

"Radiators," Marshall said, shaking his head as he studied it through the infrared filter of their docking camera. "Judging by the heat signature, it's nuclear powered."

"Can it see us from here?" Max asked nervously, never expecting he'd have wished to be so close to that asteroid ever again.

"Doubt it," Marshall said. "I can't see anything like optics or phased-array sensors. It's got a ton of antenna blisters, though. Somebody's controlling that thing." He pitched the nose down to pivot away from the satellite and switched on *Specter*'s rendezvous camera.

❊ ❊ ❊

The unexpected transmission from *Specter* was surprising enough, its video feed even more so.

"What the hell is that?" Poole switched over to the encrypted channel with *Specter*. "*Specter*, Actual on secure channel. What are you sending me here?"

Marshall's voice quavered as it was attenuated by the frequency scrambling. "Unknown... pointed... you... eastern horizon. We're... half klick abeam... enough to... line of sight."

"Stand by." Poole pushed out of his seat and flew up into the cupola. He spied a bright speck glittering near RQ39's eastern limb and reached for his trusty binoculars. "I see it." He whistled. "Mean looking sonofabitch."

"Can't see... shroud... nuke power... ion propulsion," Marshall said.

Poole filled in the blanks. "Ion engines, nuclear generator," he said for Wylie's benefit. "I'm checking out that shroud on its forward end now. Looks like optics."

"I'm not aware of anybody parking a telescope out here, sir," Wylie called from below.

"Way too overpowered for that," Poole agreed. "And nobody in his right mind's going to put a refractor into space. Too heavy and too complicated. That thing isn't for collecting light."

"PRC laser," Wylie concluded. "So we've got a nuke-pumped laser that gets around with ion engines pointed at us, a big-ass spaceship parked outside, and a squad of bad guys in armored spacesuits trying to bust in our front door. I've seen this movie before, sir."

"Me too," Poole muttered. "And I don't care for living out the sequel." He flew back down to the second pilot's station by Wylie and got back on the channel with Marshall. "*Specter*, be advised... it looks like that shroud's covering a laser turret. Thanks for the heads-up and lay low. Check in at thirty. Over."

"Copy check in... laying low. Out."

Marshall gave the translation controller a gentle tap, pushing them back down to RQ39's surface. From the corner of his eye, he could see relief wash over Max Jiang's face. Jasmine sat still behind them, strapped into her seat with her arms and legs crossed. It was a natural compensation against having her limbs float free, but something told Marshall that defensiveness might have been her natural state at home under gravity. She wasn't off-putting—if anything she'd been pleasant to him—but she carried herself with a natural dignity that became strictly no-nonsense when she sensed a threat, the counterbalance to Max's unbounded curiosity that had kept them alive.

"If it's a weapon, it's controlled by that PRC spacecraft," she announced.

Satisfied they were parked at a safe distance, Marshall turned to study her. "Why do you think that?" he asked. Focused on flying, he hadn't had enough time to consider it himself.

"If you didn't detect any electronic emissions, then it's not moving about of its own accord. Perhaps it's preprogrammed, but it seems more likely that an orbiting weapon would need to be under active control of someone," she explained. "Preferably someone close by."

"Within a fraction of a light-second," Marshall agreed. "I see your point." He thought back on their experience. "Can you go back over the time right before *Prospector*'s service module exploded?"

"It was all very sudden," Max interjected, "which is how I suppose these things happen. Everything's fine until they're not."

"We were both in the habitat module when it happened," Jasmine said. "There was no warning."

Max explained. "Once we were beyond a few light-seconds from Earth, we had set up the master alarm to sound if a life-critical system exceeded certain parameters. It gave us a buffer against the time delay with our support team."

"Your people back in Palmdale reported a rapid temperature and pressure spike. It would've probably tripped your alarm just as the tank was failing, too close for you to notice." Marshall thought about what had happened on *Borman*—a temperature spike, followed by rapidly rising pressure. The delta-p and delta-t warnings had sounded almost simultaneously before tank two went bang. He thought back to what he had seen of *Prospector*: an impact hole in the service module, and a large "exit wound" where their cryo tanks had been.

How clean had that impact hole been? He wondered, searching his memory. It might have been a meteoroid, but that didn't seem as likely anymore. Rapid heating did.

"We didn't get holed," he said, referring to both ships. "We got lased."

The Jiangs exchanged looks as the thought sunk in. It had been one thing to be marooned in deep space—at some level, they'd always known that danger lurked—but to think it had been by a deliberate, hostile act?

Jasmine was especially upset, it being her theory that this floating weapon was under PRC control. And now they were arriving in an orbiting fortress which no one who was supposed to pay attention to these matters seemed to know anything about. "Both our spacecraft have been crippled by hostile actors, and now those actors are coming to clean up the mess."

Marshall was having trouble believing it himself. How long had that hunter-killer sat been parked out here? It would've had to be launched well ahead of *Prospector*. "I don't doubt the Party's had it in for you two," he said, searching for an alternative explanation. "But enough to commit these kinds of resources? To risk a shooting war?"

Jasmine shook her head. "For all we know, RQ39 isn't the only Earth-crossing asteroid they've staked out. We might have just gotten in the way and offered them a convenient opportunity, as was bringing your spacecraft out to find us."

Marshall stared into space, mentally connecting the dots. "They're establishing territorial claims, like the South China Sea back in the teens."

"Which the West conveniently pretended wasn't a problem, until it became unavoidable. I suspect the same thing is happening here."

Max laid a hand on his arm. "She's correct. We don't know military strategy, but we do know our home country. I'm afraid there's no other way to see this."

"I'm curious, Mr. Hunter," she said in clipped tones, "what are you and your captain prepared to do about it?"

Marshall studied the glittering speck in his overhead window, wondering the same thing.

◎ 34 ◎

Studying the meager sensor returns on their latest visitor, Poole was coming to the same conclusions as the Jiangs. "It's got a hell of a heat signature," he said to Wylie. "Nuclear, for sure." He pointed out its many hot spots on the thermal image, which painted a surprisingly detailed image of the satellite. "Good thing, because the radar cross section's tiny."

"So not only did they park an H-K out here, they made it stealthy?" Wylie said. "Seems like overkill, sir. Stealth doesn't mean squat when you've got that big of an IR footprint." They could hide a spacecraft from radar, but the inability to dissipate heat without massive radiators guaranteed no spacecraft could hide for long.

"I've got my theories," Poole said. He switched on their more powerful fire-control radar, and the response was almost immediate.

"We've got lock . . . whoa," Wylie said. "Big burst of EM emissions there, Skipper."

"Not surprising," Poole said. "Wait for it . . ."

Wylie cursed when the return disappeared. "It's jamming us," he sighed. "Broke lock."

Poole waited to see if they could burn through, but the H-K was strobing their radar with false pulses in a jamming technique called "gate pulloff," used by aircraft to evade detection. It didn't make it invisible, but it did spoof the radar enough to keep it from locking on. And he was thankful Hunter had been smart enough to not try and paint the damn thing with his docking radar. The H-K seemed to "listen" passively across the EM spectrum and *Specter* would've been lit up like a Christmas tree if he'd turned on his radar. Broadcasting over a scrambled channel had been risky enough.

So was the thing piloted or autonomous? It was the difference between a drone and a droid. It was a long way from Earth; the signal delay implied some level of autonomy. But the "long way from Earth" part was what stuck in his mind . . . what was it doing here in the first place?

Poole chewed on his lip. "So, what have we learned here?"

"That stealth is still useful enough to defeat radar-guided weapons. Which all of ours are," Wylie said dejectedly, then caught himself. "Sorry, Skipper."

Poole gave him a weary smile. "Don't sweat it. I didn't think we'd need laser or IR-guided missiles out here. It was a rescue mission, remember? The only thing I thought we'd have to fight off out here was stray rocks."

"Who knew the PRC had staked a claim?" Wylie asked. "That's the real question, sir."

"Bingo." Poole jerked a thumb at the H-K in the distance. "That's obviously the mystery bird the Jiangs saw. It's not corporate espionage and it's not space pirates, it's a state actor. And I think we can rule out the Russians; they can barely afford to get their own weather satellites into orbit."

"Active control?"

Poole studied the infrared image. "Probably. My guess is it's limited autonomy, just to keep the EM traffic down and compensate for signal delay. Now that Beijing's Battlestar is in range, I'm betting they're in control. It's a force multiplier."

"We're boxed in good," Wylie said. "Spreading out the crew and getting the civilians clear was the right call."

"Damn straight it was," Poole said. "Now I have to figure out how to keep from stranding them."

"Entry team leader reports they are not opening their outer door, sir."

Liu shifted in his chair, unconsciously tightening his restraints in the expectation of action. He keyed his radio mic. "Captain Poole," he said calmly, "our team is standing by at your P-3 airlock. They are ready to enter at your discretion."

"Yeah, I'm still having a problem with the weapons thing there, Liu. I really need you to reconsider."

Liu caught one of his officers glancing at him from the corner of his eye, no doubt wondering how their commander would react. He kept his face a mask of stone, but for one small twitch from a corner of his mouth. "It is you who must reconsider, Captain." He gestured to Zhou.

Zhou nodded, complying with the command. "Laser is fully charged and tracking the target's main propellant tank, sir."

"Very good. Major Wu?"

Wu took a moment to activate their own fire-control radar. "Two interceptors are locked onto their propulsion section, sir."

Before Liu could say anything, Poole's voice boomed over the radio. "And what the hell are you doing locking weapons on my ship? You understand what that means, Colonel."

"I'm afraid it is you who have taken the first hostile action, Captain. You have already attempted to lock your own weapons on a People's Liberation Aerospace Force vehicle. That is still considered an act of war, and I am obligated to protect our national assets. Stand down, Captain Poole. This will be your only warning."

"He's not going to fire on us with his own troops out there?" Wylie asked hopefully.

"I'm not counting on his good nature," Poole said, checking his watch. "Sharpen your pencil, we're going to have do this the hard way." He switched radios to the secure channel. "*Specter*, Actual. Take notes, son, this is about to get complicated."

"Understood, Actual." Marshall switched off his radio and spun the shuttle about, pointing its docking collar—and lidar—at the *Borman*. He turned on the small transceiver as if they were attempting to rendezvous with it, and began relaying its range and bearing information to Poole as he did the same. "*About* to get complicated?" he muttered, and turned to face his passengers. "Faceplates down? Good. Switch to your personal tanks and disconnect from the cabin system. We're about to depressurize."

"Got 'em," Wylie said. "Range and bearing constant."

Poole nodded in acknowledgment; he first had to establish a baseline bearing and distance. "We've got to work fast here." He keyed the mic. "Looking good, *Specter*. We've got your position zeroed. Light 'em up."

Marshall answered with two rapid clicks and began turning to face the H-K.

"What are we doing?" Jasmine demanded. "We're making ourselves visible to that—whatever it is!"

Marshall turned to face her, genuine regret on his face. "Afraid you're right, ma'am. I'm also afraid we don't have a choice. You wanted to know if we're prepared to do something? This is it."

"Exposing ourselves is 'doing something'? How is that?"

He pointed at the H-K, now just a kilometer away. "We give it two targets to worry about while we light it up with our docking lidar. I feed that information to the *Borman* so they can use it to box in that killsat. We get one shot at this."

As the shuttle's laser-ranging data began to arrive, Wylie scribbled on graph paper atop the plotting board. Comparing the range and bearing from their own lidar data, pinpointing the H-K became a simple math problem. He began programming the solution into the control pad for one of their space-junk interceptors when the open frequency with *Peng Fei* came alive once more.

"Captain Poole, what is that vehicle I see out by our satellite?"

"That's our shuttle. We call it *Specter*. The name sounded cool, but really it's because it's kind of hard to spot. You may have noticed that."

"Your humor is becoming tiresome, Captain. You did not tell us there was another ship in the vicinity."

"You mean like that hunter-killer sat of yours?" Poole shot back. "*Specter* was on a survey sortie at RQ39 and was on its way back when it came across your big orbiting stealth laser." He shot a glance at Wylie, still checking his figures against the changing numbers. He spun a finger over his watch: *hurry up*. Perhaps it was unfair to expect a pilot to think like a sub driver launching a torpedo.

"Your shuttle is unacceptably close to our defensive platform. I am cautioning you to have them maintain a safe distance."

It was an absurd demand, which Poole used to both buy time and rhetorically plant his flag. "Did you just call that thing 'defensive,'

Liu? Because I'm curious what the PRC believes might need defending against out here. We have good reason to believe that weapon has been used against two American spacecraft, one being a military vessel. That, sir, is an act of war to which we will respond."

Wylie looked up triumphantly, if not somewhat surprised. "Interceptor one is programmed. We have a firing solution, sir."

A glint outside caught his attention; the H-K began slewing about, turning to face *Specter*. Poole's eyes narrowed to angry slits.

"Match bearings and shoot."

"Missile inbound!" Zhou exclaimed. "Sir, they've fired on us!"

"Confirm that, Lieutenant," Liu ordered calmly. He had not expected Poole to have acted so rashly. "Wu, activate the close-in weapons."

They were already standing by, it was a simple matter for Wu to activate their tracking program. "Point-defense guns are in free-fire mode, sir, tracking the target."

"Not firing?" Liu asked. "Zhou, have you confirmed that projectile?"

"Confirmed, sir. It's one of their meteoroid interceptors. They've targeted the laser platform, not us." Momentary confusion passed over Zhou's face. "I don't understand how . . . they're supposed to be radar guided," he said plaintively.

"The laser platform is being illuminated by infrared lidar," Wu interjected. "Two different sources," he said, consulting the satellite's status board. "Radar jamming is ineffective," he added unnecessarily.

"Is the laser tracking the inbound target?"

"Attempting to lock, sir. It's close in and moving fast," Zhou said, his voice raised as he attempted to take over control of the platform.

"Time to impact?"

"Imminent, sir."

The laser platform's ion engine did not have enough thrust to move it quickly enough to evade. Liu's mouth drew thin. "Very well." It was time to take the next step. He switched radio channels to the boarding team. "Captain, begin boarding operations. Take the *Borman*."

"Hang on!"

Marshall shut off his rendezvous sensors and began pulling clear as soon as he saw *Borman* release its missile. He turned away violently, kicking them in the pants with the OMS thrusters and zipping away from the H-K, the asteroid, and the opening salvo of what he hoped wasn't about to become World War III.

There was a flash of light outside. He waited for pinholes to appear at random, sunlight streaming into the cabin from multiple shrapnel wounds which never came. He turned to check on the Jiangs, both seemed to be okay. Neither they or his ship had been holed.

He turned about, pulsing the big OMS thrusters in the opposite direction to cancel their velocity. Both the *Borman* and *Peng Fei* swept into view, much farther away than he'd expected. How hard had he burned to get away? Near RQ39, a ball of incandescent gas expanded into space near the Chinese killsat.

"No joy!" he called back to *Borman*. "Repeat, no joy. They lased it, sir."

Poole barely heard his report as more pressing matters fought for his attention. A muffled grating sound echoed from the direction of the emergency bay, a pressurization alarm began blaring soon after.

"They've breached the outer door," Garver reported on their discrete channel. "Four boarders entering at the P-3 lock."

"Copy that," Poole said as he cut off the braying master alarm. "Are the two sentries keeping their positions?"

"Affirmative."

Poole switched over to their common frequency so his next command went out across their radio net. "All hands, prepare to repel boarders."

◎ 35 ◎

"Incoming missile destroyed, sir!" Zhou reported excitedly.

"Excellent work, Zhou," Liu said. If there were a time to give praise to build morale, now was it. "Is the platform recycling?"

"Affirmative, sir. Capacitor banks are recharging and the emitter is cooling," Zhou said with a self-assurance he hadn't displayed before. "It will be several minutes before it can discharge again."

Liu already knew that but indulged him for now; the young man had just taken direct control of their remote laser platform and successfully taken a snap shot that destroyed an imminent threat. He would be in line for a commendation when this was over. "Very good, Lieutenant. Make their shuttle your next target. It is a nuisance we do not need." He turned to Wu. "Activate the primary fire-control radar and target the *Borman*'s propulsion module. The time for gloved hands is past us. If Simon Poole does not hand over control of his ship to Captain Huang, then it will not leave this orbit."

A new alarm sounded in the control cabin, a shrill warbling tone. "Radar lock!" Wylie said. "They're painting us, sir."

Which Poole fully expected, but it was no less disturbing. "Spin up the PDCs."

"Damage control protocols?" Wylie asked, a procedure they had drilled repeatedly but whose possibility had always seemed remote, at least from hostile fire.

"Negative. Don't depressurize the habs yet," Poole commanded. He waited by the engineering station, watching the external camera feed from the port airlock. "I'll take care of that myself." He pressed the mic switch for his headset, calling to Garver on their secure channel. "Take them, Chief. We'll set up the others for you."

Garver answered with two rapid mic clicks. He and Rosie each lined up their sights on a PRC spacer, the ones with the bulky maneuvering packs taking stations above opposite sides of the med module. Crosshairs and range markers appeared in their visor, heads-up projections from the targeting lasers on the carbines mounted to their chest packs. Garver looked in her direction.

"I've got the guy on the right, Chief," she said, anticipating the question.

"I've got the left," Garver said, and checked a setting on his MMU. "Recoil compensation?"

"Active, Chief."

"Copy. Take the shot on three." Garver rested two fingers on the M55's big paddle trigger, an abomination to an earthbound marksman but a necessity for shooting in a bulky pressure suit with limited dexterity. He steadily increased pressure as he counted down. "One . . . two . . ."

On *three*, he felt the thump of recoil and the shot of compensating maneuvering jets push at his back. There was puff of fire as the caseless 10mm round erupted from the muzzle, almost immediately landing where the glowing crosshairs in Garver's visor sat: center of mass on a PRC spacewalker hovering about five meters to the left of their big P-3 airlock door. For a moment, Garver wondered if the guy would've considered himself lucky to be shot while parked just outside of the only emergency medical unit in this part of the solar system. Clouds of red and white mist erupted from the suited figure, spraying his vital fluids and oxygen in a bloody arc as he spun about from the impact.

To Garver's right, the other sentry was having perhaps even worse problems. Rosie had flinched, grabbing her trigger paddle with a hair too much force. Instead of a clean shot through her man's center of mass, the round had pierced his combined life-support and maneuvering pack. He was clearly still alive and in one piece, flailing for control as his MMU sent him tumbling. With one hard bounce against *Borman*'s hull, he went spiraling into space behind a cloud of violently expelled maneuvering gas.

"Rosie, report." It was Garver.

Rosie gritted her teeth and cursed. Her instinct was to go after him: She was a rescue spacer, not a shooter. What the hell was wrong with these people? Did they really think we were just going to let them take our ship? And what was the deal with that TIE fighter or whatever the hell it was they'd hidden at RQ39?

"*Rosado*," he said firmly.

"Right side is secure," she said, and swallowed hard. "Threat . . . neutralized."

"Left side secure," Garver said. "Stand by for action," he announced to the team.

Captain Huang checked his team inside *Borman*'s big emergency-receiving airlock, then began comparing the reality of it to his mental notes from their intelligence reports. While the ship's specifications were perfunctorily classified, much of it had been crafted from the kinds of multipurpose modules American contractors had spent years building for NASA. How they functioned and were connected was no mystery; how they were configured inside was another matter. It had taken some work to pry those secrets loose, but with so much American technology based on Chinese products he assumed prying those secrets loose had only taken marginally more work. What he had seen so far had been predicted accurately enough to confirm his suspicions.

He searched by the inner door and quickly found the cabin controls, a touch-screen system that should open up views of the rest of the ship. He navigated through its short menu using the English phrases he'd memorized, though so much of it was graphic that he'd had little need for them. Finding the environmental controls was easy, as was pinpointing their location relative to the rest of the pressurized modules. The door would be held in place by the nearly sea-level 14 psi air pressure. Stronger than any lock they could have devised, it was a smart move.

As he moved to vent the module ahead, clearing their way inside, a shout in his earpiece stopped him cold. It sounded like Chen. He would have corrected Chen for abandoning radio discipline but for hearing him exclaim what sounded like "ambush."

"Chen, report!" Huang called. "Specify your location!"

"Off structure, no control sir! We have taken enemy fire and they disabled my maneuvering pack!"

"Where is Sergeant Gao?"

"Unknown, sir." Chen gulped, as if trying to keep his stomach down. "I could only get a brief glimpse of him." He paused. "I apologize, Captain."

Huang immediately called for the other sentry. "Sergeant Gao, report!" he repeated, but there was no answer. He looked back at the remainder of his team, who had heard the entire exchange. The men were ready, he decided, and primed for a fight. They were about to get one.

"Charge weapons and prepare to board," he said. As they racked the bolts on their vacuum-proof QBZ bullpup-style carbines, he moved to clear their entry by depressurizing the rest of *Borman*.

Simon Poole locked down his helmet and made his way down the corridor, stopping in front of the medical bay. The inner airlock door at the far end was still closed, with a PRC breaching team on the other side. They could either pressurize the 'lock and get in, or vent the rest of the ship. That held the advantage of disabling or isolating the crew that they had to presume were still aboard; if he were a doorkicker for the bad guys, that's what he'd do.

He tapped an intercom control on his wrist, calling Wylie in the command deck. "You're still buttoned up, right?"

"Roger that, Skipper."

"Good. Stand by." He reached out for the med bay's door just as he saw a status light above the far hatch turn amber. Air whistled by him as the bay began to vent its atmosphere. *Here they come.*

Simon pulled the door shut along its sliding track and dogged down the latch, sealing off the rest of the ship for now. He watched a nearby environmental panel—it turned red, signifying the med bay was now in vacuum. He waited to see them open the inner door, giving them enough time to get it fully open.

He locked his feet beneath a restraint loop in the floor and took a deep breath, counting to three. He grabbed the latch and heaved it open.

Air exploded around him as the entire ship's atmosphere tried to vent at once through that single door. The med bay swirled in chaos as the PRC boarders scrambled for any handhold they could find before being swept back into space.

Poole slapped his mic switch as they tumbled out into the void. "Garver!" he shouted. "Weapons free!"

Muzzle flashes erupted from the surrounding debris cloud, giving away the team's positions. It was a risk they had to balance against trusting the enemy to not behave like an enemy, and that was a loser's bet. Their fire converged in a cloud of lead, turning the space outside the P-3 airlock door into a killing zone.

The howling wind subsided as the remainder of *Borman*'s atmosphere vented into space. Now in vacuum himself, Poole reached for the door to pull it shut and repressurize the ship. As he did, a gloved hand thrust out from behind it to grab him.

◎ 36 ◎

Marshall felt as if he'd swallowed a block of ice at the sight of the H-K platform turning toward them, still intact and no doubt building up another charge. He didn't know its specifics, but its heat signature was lighting up his IR sensors and a reactor that small wasn't capable of pumping out all that energy at once. Those big capacitor banks encircling it had to be storing power for its next shot. He didn't know how much time that bought them, but he'd take whatever he could get.

He knew the killsat's ion engine could get a lot more mileage out of its fuel than his own, but the problem with high specific impulse was that it typically delivered very low thrust, whereas the chemical rockets in *Specter*'s OMS could give him a hell of a kick from their hypergolic fuel.

So what? For a fleeting moment he was tempted to announce he had civilians on board. His mission had been to keep them out of harm's way, and in any other context that might have been the right thing to do. But this maniac driving *Peng Fei* didn't seem to care much about collateral damage—and if the Jiang's suspicions were right, he might even welcome it.

As the H-K's optical muzzle came about, he pulsed lateral thrusters to pivot them out of its line of sight. This would be a turning fight, and he had no weapons. All he could do was try to keep a step ahead of that thing's business end. His mouth suddenly felt dry, as if filled with cotton. He took a hasty drink from the tube in his helmet, flexed his hands and tightened his grip on the controls. *This is crazy, but waiting to get blasted is crazier.*

He gave the translation controller a tap forward, taking them closer to the H-K. He had to turn down his intercom volume to mute the Jiang's frantic protests.

With his feet still secured to the floor, for the moment Poole had the advantage. He instinctively recoiled and jerked back his arm, but whoever had grabbed him held his grip and came flying out into the corridor. He saw only a jumble of gray and black digital camo patterns flash by; his attacker had tucked himself into a ball and sprang off against the opposite wall, kicking his feet out and bringing his weapon to bear.

His EVA suit was skintight, a mechanical counterpressure garment like he'd seen the Marines use for their transatmospheric combat teams. Light armor protected the vital areas; his backpack and helmet were connected as one unit.

Poole kicked his feet free and launched himself toward his attacker, shocked that the man hadn't gotten off any rounds at him yet. He unslung his own M55 and raised it.

Huang had much practice controlling himself in unfamiliar environments; it was a principle of zero-g combat training that firm ground was wherever you could find it, no matter the orientation to what you thought was normal. The American habit of arranging spacecraft interiors along an octagonal profile had been used here, as he expected. He untucked himself and extended his limbs, slowing his rotation and giving them a surface to push against.

His enemy wore only a lightweight blaze-orange launch-and-entry suit, protecting him from vacuum but not for extravehicular use. Certainly not for a fight, though he found himself looking down the barrel of an American space-rated carbine just as he aimed his own. He did not intend to shoot; his orders were to commandeer the American spacecraft and keep it in operating condition. But with a weapon pointed at him, his training took over and he pressed the trigger.

He pressed harder. There was no travel, no break. Huang swore at himself and reached up with his thumb to disengage the safety. He knew it had switched off earlier; it must have been brushed and engaged when his team went flying back out of the airlock.

The man in orange flew toward him, also not firing his weapon.

Poole bellowed with rage as he sailed across the corridor, launching himself into the Chinese invader. He wrapped him up like a linebacker, driving them both into the bulkhead at the far end of the corridor.

They bounced off the hard wall, Poole briefly losing sight of his enemy. He hoped the other guy got the worst of it, but then he heard air hissing and noticed a hairline crack in his faceplate. He turned his head, searching, but was limited by his helmet's field of view. He pushed off with one foot to pivot and raised his weapon when a gray-camouflaged arm reached out and roughly brushed it aside. He felt an elbow drive into his side, sending him flying against the wall.

There was flash out of the corner of his eye.

Huang had only fired when he was absolutely certain of his target and reasonably certain his background didn't contain any critical systems that might react badly to a stray round.

They used fragmentation bullets anyway, technically illegal in warfare by the Geneva conventions but used in practice by nearly every law-enforcement organization across the world because they were effective and limited collateral damage. A jacketed round in this environment could have easily gone through a person and damaged something vital. And as he'd learned being attached to the PLAF, nearly every bulkhead and sidewall concealed *something* vital. Their spacecraft was packed to the rafters with plumbing, air ducts and electrical conduits; the Americans were no doubt the same and in fact had seemed to be less concerned with hardening their vehicle.

Blood sprayed from his target's leg; he saw him instinctively move to stanch the bleeding with his hands. Huang grabbed the man by his waist harness before he could shoulder his weapon, bringing him upright until they were face to face. He read the name badge Velcroed to his chest: S. POOLE.

He'd just wounded their commanding officer. If the ship's captain was defending their entry point alone, then where was the rest of the crew? For that matter, where were the traitors they were protecting? He already knew from news reports they were operating at minimum capacity. Some of them had been lying in wait outside; that's how they'd eliminated Chen and Guo. He'd have to own up to that failure later, during the after-action reports. At least one pilot was flying the shuttle; that left very few crewmen aboard here, and the Jiangs had to be with them.

Huang debated whether to kill him. On the battlefield, he wouldn't have wasted a moment debating it but at this point it would be an execution. An American field-grade officer would be a valuable prisoner. The heads-up displays in their helmets recorded everything and he had no idea how Liu or their superiors in Beijing would react. He was not ready to put his trust in selective editing later.

He'd already wasted too many seconds debating the matter. He angrily took Poole's weapon, spun him about, and shoved him up into the medical bay before sliding the inner hatch shut. He jammed the M55's barrel behind the locking lever to delay the inevitable return of the American EVA team still outside, assuming they weren't about to be preoccupied with saving their captain. Huang would simply use another exit.

He pushed away, flying toward the forward end of the corridor where he knew the command module would be. He kept his weapon at the ready, anticipating resistance. If anyone was left aboard, they had to be up there.

Huang made his way slowly forward, where he knew the command deck would be. He stopped at every node, clearing each compartment before moving on to the next. His confidence grew with each push ahead as it became clear there would be no resistance. The ship was empty but for its captain and perhaps one or two others. He would soon find out, as he arrived at the entryway to the command module.

It was a blind entry, its access tunnel from the main corridor not even two meters deep. But it was narrow, filled with electrical equipment racks as he recalled from the specs they'd acquired. Sensitive, so not likely to be something their own crew would want to shoot into. But it still created a chokepoint for him.

He looked around for anything to use as a diversion. The only spacecraft he'd ever served on was the *Peng Fei* and its Soyuz-derived craft used for ferrying back and forth from Earth. Colonel Liu had insisted on a clean, orderly interior, nothing like the tangles of straps and packages and cables he'd seen in American and Russian videos.

It seemed as if their spacecraft had been turned into orbiting storage closets.

Borman fared better, clearly subject to more disciplined leadership though still more chaotic than the strict order aboard *Peng Fei*. He found two large bundles strapped into a corner of the module, like seemingly everything else aboard. They were soft, extra uniforms perhaps? He pulled them free, placed them squarely in front of the entryway, and readied himself behind them with his weapon up and feeding the computer-generated sights in his helmet display.

He pushed the two bundles ahead, through the entry, and followed behind. A flash of gunfire confirmed his suspicion, as both bundles exploded in a cloud of shredded fabric.

Huang launched himself through the portal, weapon up and in the general direction of fire. He found one man, in an orange vacuum suit like Poole, sweeping the room with his carbine. He fought the urge to change positions and shift his fire, instead letting his own momentum do the work. He flew in sideways, holding his position and letting the confusion act as its own cover. He waited for his muzzle to cross his target and fired off a three-round burst.

His target spun about, scattering fragments of his shattered chest pack. He saw no blood, which told Huang that his fragmentation rounds had shredded the man's life-support controls. Ice crystals soon spewed from multiple holes as his life-giving air escaped into the vacuum, some of it red. So he had not escaped unscathed.

Huang needed this man alive, for the moment. He bounced off a bulkhead, back to the entryway, and dogged down the hatch. He soon heard air hissing around him as pressure returned.

Finding a foot restraint in the floor, Huang placed his other foot on the American's abdomen, pressing him against the sidewall. He raised his visor, keeping his weapon leveled at the man's chest. "I am Captain Huang of the People's Liberation Army. This vessel is now under our control."

The man lifted his own visor. "Wylie. Lieutenant, US Space Force," he coughed, "and you can't have it. Now that we've made introductions, *get the hell off of our ship*." His voice was hoarse, and Huang noticed blood escaping as he breathed: mostly internal injuries, then. Good.

"You are in no position to make those demands," Huang scoffed. "You have fired on military assets of the People's Republic of China."

"Pretty sure you shot first," Wylie gasped. "That's why you're here, right?" He wiped blood from the corner of his mouth and swallowed. "We lose a propellant tank far from home, and you show up to rescue us. Convenient. Or was that all just bullshit?"

Huang smiled thinly. "As you say, 'bullshit.'" He pressed in harder with his foot, keeping his weapon centered on Wylie's chest. "You are also harboring two traitors. Tell me, where are they?"

Still in vacuum and nursing a gunshot wound to his thigh, Poole sealed himself in the med bay. With any luck, the fight outside had gone in their favor and he'd find his crew making their way back inside soon. He'd lost comm with them during his scuffle and had not retuned his radios. He punched up the first channel with Garver's sentry team outside. "Six, this is Actual," he coughed. "Report."

Garver replied immediately. "Holding our position with three tangos down. Got them as they were flying out of the airlock. Quite the turkey shoot, sir."

"That's good. These guys are no joke, Chief." He coughed. "I just went a few rounds with one of them. He's somewhere forward, still an active threat."

Garver's tone changed. "What's your status, sir?"

Poole swallowed. No point in sugarcoating it. "Shot, Chief. Left thigh. I'm in the P-3 med bay, closed off from the ship."

He heard Garver mutter a curse. "You're still in vacuum? Did your auto-seal activate, sir?"

"Affirmative," Poole said. "Wouldn't be talking to you if it hadn't."

"Good point." The chief paused, no doubt signaling his team. "Okay, Skipper, we're Oscar Mike." *On the move.* "Sit tight."

Poole laughed, staring up into the open airlock. *Like I'm going anywhere.* He opened the secure VHF channel with Marshall aboard *Specter.* "*Specter*, this is Actual. Report."

Marshall wasn't sure how to answer that. They were unharmed, but they sure weren't safe, either. Every time he moved *Specter*, that damned H-K sat began slewing around. At the moment it was easy to evade, but he couldn't keep it up forever and the plan that was forming in his mind didn't seem like much of an improvement.

"Actual, *Specter*. We are maintaining close proximity with the H-K. It's maneuvering, trying to target us. I'm staying on its six but that won't last forever."

"Understood," Poole said. "How's your cargo?"

"Intact and functional." It was all he could say. Poole no doubt understood they couldn't be happy. "How's the fight at your end, sir?"

Poole gave him the shortest possible explanation. "Three tangos down, one to go. But he's in the CM and I'm stuck in medical with a GSW."

Marshall grimaced. The CO was wounded and a bad guy had taken the flight deck, which meant Wylie might already be dead. It was time to rebalance the equation. Any plan, no matter how crazy, was better than no plan.

He goosed thrusters one more time, moving beneath the killsat and matching its slow turn.

"What are you doing?" Jasmine demanded from behind him. "Because it looks like you're getting closer."

"That's precisely what I'm doing, ma'am," he said patiently. "We can't keep this up forever, and as soon as we pull away we're literally toast." He activated his landing systems.

A pilot himself, Max recognized what he was doing. "Are you trying to—*land* on that thing?"

"Something like that."

Poole noticed shadows crossing overhead, and looked up to see two of his crew fly in through the outer door, one by one.

Rosie, to no surprise, was the first one by his side. Without a word, she began maneuvering him over to a waiting bed that her partner folded out from a sidewall. She looked up impatiently at the remaining two spacers floating in as she strapped him into place. "We good to go?"

Garver was the last one in and slammed the outer hatch down behind him. He lifted the cover on a switch labeled EMERG REPRESS, and the sound of rushing air began building to a crescendo around them. "Go!" he said, watching the gauge climb to a safe level.

Rosie shucked off her helmet and gloves and began cutting away

Poole's already ruined launch-and-entry suit, its fabric giving way much more easily than the ballistic fibers of their EVA gear. She stopped at the auto-tourniquet's cuff and made sure it was still getting air before replacing it.

Poole watched her work from behind the full-face oxygen mask she'd given him, trying to judge his condition by her reactions. She caught Garver's eye, who floated over to his side while she prepared an injection.

"Chief."

"Skipper. You look like hell, sir."

"Feel like it." He turned to Rosado. "What's the verdict, Rosie?"

That she flinched at all told him it was grave—Rosado was the most dedicated rescue spacer he'd served with, and she gave up nothing when it came time to do the job. She glanced at Garver before turning back to him, examining his ruined limb beneath the auto-tourniquet.

"Sir . . . I'm sorry—"

Before demanding to know about what, he lifted his head to see for himself. Besides taking a bullet, most of his left leg had now been exposed to vacuum since his fight with that PRC officer. That had been, what, ten minutes ago? Poole frowned. The desiccated tissue of his exposed leg had become a grotesque palette of purples and blacks beneath the dried blood surrounding his entry wound. That there was no exit wound told him the bullet had fragmented inside his thigh— between dual traumas of gunshot wound and vacuum exposure, he knew what came next. The tourniquet alone had probably sealed that fate, even if it had kept him from bleeding out.

He reached for her hand, gripping it as strongly as he could as he met her eyes. "I know, Rosie. I trust you. Do what you have to."

"Aye, sir." She lifted a syringe to show him before inserting it with an IV line. "This is for the pain. Begin counting backwards from ten for me, sir." She motioned for a technician, out of sight, to begin setting up an isolation tent around him. This was going to be a real mess in zero-g.

"Screw that," he growled, mustering his strength. As he felt the cold rush of sedatives entering his bloodstream, he gave one last order to Garver. "Master Chief. Get that sonofabitch off of my ship."

The world faded from his view.

⟐ 37 ⟐

"What's your main gear span?" Max asked, guessing Marshall's intent.

"Twelve feet, three inches," Marshall said, reciting from memory a fact about *Specter*'s dimensions which he'd long wondered why he'd need it in the first place. "Height four feet, four inches." He'd had to look up the service manual for the amount of hydraulic pressure activating them; it would be enough.

"More than enough to straddle that satellite," Max said approvingly as he settled into the copilot's seat beside him. "What can I do?"

"Glad you asked." Marshall pointed at the radar altimeter. "Call out altitude—well, distance, but you know what I mean—inside of twenty feet."

"Feet," Max confirmed. "Not meters?"

"It's for landing," Marshall explained. "Everything's calibrated to Imperial."

"Just checking," he said, and finished strapping in. "What about the gear?"

Marshall thought about doing that himself but decided it was better to have a willing assistant who knew his way around a cockpit. He pointed at the gear handle. "Ever work one like that?" Because it did matter.

"Out to unlock, then down?" Max guessed.

"Exactly. Don't touch it until I say so."

Max held his hands up. "Your spacecraft."

Marshall smiled to himself. Max had flown multicrew airplanes

341

before, which was good to know. He'd make it a point to find out what types later, assuming they were around to talk about it. "This thing has skids, not main wheels. It was meant for landing on the lakebed at Edwards and they never got around to putting proper gear on it."

"Seems like an unfortunate oversight," Max said. "Until now." He looked out over the forward sill, at the big radiator wings. "You're going to snag those, aren't you?"

It was good to see the man's rekindled enthusiasm, and Marshall realized his new copilot was just delighted to be doing something proactive instead of being treated like precious cargo. "That's the idea."

"Why not just smash the laser itself?" Jasmine asked from behind them.

"I thought about that," Marshall said, "but that thing's had time to build up a charge. Getting in front of the optics would be suicide." He turned to face her. "I don't like this either, ma'am. Best case is this bird never lands on Earth again. But if we can do enough damage to those radiators, that thing becomes an expensive paperweight."

Colonel Liu Wang Shu had been watching the battle unfold from his perch in *Peng Fei*'s command module. An uncomfortable silence had taken over from the time Captain Huang reported their entry of *Borman*, during which he'd watched with alarm as his boarding team was picked off by fire from within the very debris cloud which obscured so much of their target.

Clever, he thought. Use your environment to your advantage. Was Poole a devotee of Sun, or Clausewitz? He was originally a Navy man, Liu remembered. He'd have been steeped in the views of Mahan and Rickover, which were not without merit, but this was a new theater of operations. He understood the Western temptation to think of space warfare in naval terms; entire subcultures had been devoted to "Starfleet" fantasies.

He knew the reality was different, *would be* different, in ways few had yet foreseen. There were similarities to be sure—there always would be—but the differences were profound. Limits to maneuver and endurance, the inability to hide heat signatures, the agonizingly long timeframes and supply lines . . . all combined to make space combat a theater as unique as air had been in the early twentieth century. The particulars might be wildly different, as a cruise missile was from a longbow, but the fundamentals would never change: Know your enemy, his capabilities, and your surroundings. Battles are won by first letting the enemy defeat himself.

Simon Poole was one of the original space warriors and he no doubt understood these concepts intuitively. Liu would not be surprised if he eventually composed a philosophical tome that would define this new arena of combat just as the American pilot John Boyd had for their Air Force.

If Liu permitted him to live.

Their weapons had been trained on the American ship the entire time. Had he not received the call from Huang, he would have ordered it destroyed.

"I have secured the primary objective and taken control of the *Borman*," Huang radioed.

"What about the secondary objective?" Liu demanded.

Huang paused. "The traitors are not aboard, sir."

"Could you not extract this information from the crew?"

"None are left to extract from, sir," Huang replied. "The only men left aboard were the captain and his command pilot."

"Then you do not have control yet, Captain," Liu cautioned him. There was a commotion behind him. He turned in irritation to Zhou. "What is the problem, Lieutenant?"

"Their shuttle, sir," Zhou said. "It has been evading the laser platform."

"As expected," Liu reminded him. "If your enemy has a maneuver element in play, you neutralize it. They will run out of propellant long before our gun emplacement does."

"Yes sir," Zhou agreed, "but it's closed the distance. It's inside the blackout zone."

Liu frowned and pulled up the feed from an external camera. The American shuttle was almost riding atop their orbiting cannon.

"We can target a PDC salvo, sir," Major Wu suggested. *Specter* now stood between the *Peng Fei* and its remote weapon, and would absorb all the rounds.

"No!" Liu barked as he realized the American's ploy. "That shuttle," he said, "holds our next objective. They removed the traitors, thinking that would keep them from harm."

"A reasonable assumption, sir," Wu said. "Shall we prepare our own shuttlecraft to retrieve them?"

Liu rubbed his chin as he considered the options. "Put Shenzou-1 on standby, but do not launch it. We have other means at our disposal. Perhaps their pilot can be persuaded."

An unfamiliar voice announced itself over the open unicom frequency. "Attention US spacecraft *Specter*. This is the PRC vessel *Peng Fei*. Please respond."

Marshall and Max exchanged curious looks, and he glanced back at Jasmine. She shook her head vigorously. Marshall ignored the radio calls as he approached the H-K satellite.

"*Specter*, this is *Peng Fei*. Your commander has been wounded and we have assumed control of the *Borman*. Respond or your ship will be fired upon."

"They'd do it, wouldn't they?" Marshall asked. "Even if it takes out one of their own vehicles?"

"You're the military man, not me," Max said. "But yes. The People's Army is ruthless if you stand in their way." He practically spat the words.

Jasmine maintained her regal composure, despite—or perhaps because of—her mounting alarm. Marshall saw it was an innate quality of hers: As the world went to hell around her, she grew stronger in the face of it. "The reason we left the mainland—the last straw, as you'd call it—was when a Party demolition crew destroyed our church"—she paused—"*during a service*. Lives mean nothing to them once they decide you're a great enough nuisance."

Her eyes pierced his, and he tried to imagine the scene: a building full of worshipers, and the walls start coming down around them. Driving the point home, a warning squealed in his ears—they were being painted by a fire-control radar. "I have to let them know," he said, apologetically.

"I understand," she said. "They won't care. It may even encourage them."

Marshall screwed his eyes shut, realizing his tactical error. *Damn it.* "We're a nuisance, all right." He had placed them squarely between *Peng Fei* and its remote gun emplacement. He reluctantly switched on his mic. "This is *Specter*. Hold your fire." He faced his passengers with a sorrowful look—he was supposed to protect them, but had made them unwitting combatants. "Be advised, there are civilians aboard."

A thin smile crept across Liu's face, ending at his eyes. "We have our confirmation," he said with satisfaction. "The traitors are on that shuttlecraft."

Wu stood ready at the tactical station. "Shall I proceed, sir?"

Liu held up a hand. "Negative, Wu. That is no longer necessary. Just keep the starboard PDC trained on them and stand by for new targeting." He picked up the microphone. "*Specter*, you are holding two of our citizens, both of whom are wanted for sedition. We are under orders to bring them safely back to the People's Republic of China. You are also operating in unacceptably close proximity to a valuable military asset. Disengage, or you will force us to fire."

"Guess that answers the question," Marshall said, and thumbed the mic switch by his side. "Can't do that, *Peng Fei*. Not as long as your goons are on our ship. I am in position to disable your killsat's coolant system; all I have to do is retract my landing skids. Evacuate *Borman* now."

The warbling radar alarm faded, replaced by a steady droning. "They're standing down?" Max asked in disbelief.

"Doubtful," Marshall and Jasmine said simultaneously. He turned to see her arch an eyebrow, somewhat amusedly. "That was a missile lock warning," Marshall explained. "They've still got close-in weapons trained on us."

"Can we cycle the gear fast enough?"

Marshall checked his limited sensor display, confirming the range to *Peng Fei* and doing the math in his head. He didn't know the specifics of their defensive weapons, but they all worked on the same principle: fling a precisely aimed cloud of steel at their target, typically an incoming missile. "Doesn't matter now. Just be ready for a rough ride."

Liu's voice returned. "In that case, *Specter*, we will target the *Borman* as well. I need not remind you that without it, our vessel is your only path back to Earth. Your intransigence will only add to your troubles."

If he only knew. Marshall took a deep breath. "Challenge accepted."

Garver climbed along a service handhold along the hull, moving as swiftly as he could between modules. He slowed down at the forward command module, not wanting to give himself away by creating any noise inside the now-pressurized cylinder. Whoever this gomer was, he'd sealed himself off inside and declared himself in control.

We'll see about that.

He checked his watch, synchronized with Powers who was approaching the same module from inside the connecting tunnel. They couldn't risk communicating but for brief microphone clicks, and Garver needed to be in position at the forward 'lock at the time they'd agreed on.

He was behind schedule—as usual in "EVA Time," *everything* took longer, especially when he was avoiding the external camera mounts. He stopped at the command module and checked his direction, avoiding the cupola or any open portholes, and pushed away. He tapped the controls of his maneuvering pack and a puff of compressed gas sent him jetting forward. After a few seconds he squeezed off a jet of gas in the opposite direction, coming to a stop abeam the forward airlock. The outer door was lightweight and opened easily. He slipped inside the chamber, careful to not bump against anything.

The inner door had a simple spin latch. He laid his hand on the crank and waited for his watch to count down. A single, long microphone click from Powers signaled he was in position on the other end of the module.

Thirty seconds.

"Captain Huang, what is your status?"

He looked around the control deck, still working to familiarize himself with its setup against the intelligence estimates he'd memorized. Much was as predicted, but there were just enough variances to slow him down though he'd managed to access an inventory list at their weapons console. "I'm examining their tables of equipment now, sir. They are mostly unarmed. The missile they fired at the laser platform was one of only two. Point-defense magazines are at fifty percent capacity."

"As expected, then," Liu said. "They left a great deal behind in their haste." He expected the Americans' future doctrine would prohibit such decisions, no matter the mass penalty. For now, it worked in his favor. "Can you disable their defensive weapons?"

Huang wasn't entirely certain he could. "Yes, Colonel. It is possible." It was as much equivocation as he dared allow.

"Then do so, and be prepared to evacuate on my order."

"Yes sir," Huang answered, just before his surroundings disappeared in a fog.

Two mic clicks had signaled Powers was about to vent the module. Garver watched the small porthole in the center of the hatch. Water vapor would condense immediately with the sudden pressure drop. When the window turned white, he cranked the latch over and sprang the inner door, flying into the command deck.

The mist dissipated as quickly as it had formed as the compartment emptied to vacuum. Garver swept the nearby corners with his weapon as he flew inside, angling for the overhead. Motion at the far end caught his eye—in the shadows, he saw two forms struggling with each other. It was a tangle of colors, the petty officer in his yellow EVA suit struggling with a figure in the same gray digital camo suit as they'd seen outside. There was a flash of silent gunfire, silhouetting one figure with his weapon raised.

No time to think, to sort out who was who—they were wrapped up in a tangle and he'd have to figure it out when he got there. Garver planted his feet against the forward bulkhead and pushed hard, flying across the open compartment and turning midair. He landed boots first against what he hoped was the enemy spacer, tearing their tangled limbs apart to send him flying down the darkened corridor.

Garver recoiled from the impact and bounced into the hatchway. He reached out to steady himself and brought his carbine up. Glowing crosshairs danced in his visor as he searched for his target and cursed. That camo pattern was damned near perfect in this environment.

Being Poole's "Chief of the Boat," Garver's advantage was that he knew every nook and cranny, every bulkhead and panel. And the lumpy gray mass moving across the overhead about ten meters away *definitely* didn't belong there.

He braced against the door frame, raised his muzzle until the crosshairs were centered and closed his fist around the pistol grip, pressing the trigger paddle for a three-round burst. Recoil thudded against his shoulder, the report carrying through the fabric of his suit like dull, distant thunder. The muzzle flash dazzled him.

Droplets of dark liquid and a fog of vapor erupted from where his shots landed. *Hope I didn't just shred a coolant line.* He trained his helmet lamp at the spot and found a figure in dark gray camo crumpled against the overhead. He pushed off slowly and came to a stop at a nearby handrail.

The dark liquid was blood, streaming from three separate entry wounds in his chest. The intricately woven fabric of his counterpressure suit had quickly unraveled, exposing him to vacuum. Garver reached up to pull the body level with him. Judging by the blank stare from the man's face, vacuum exposure was the least of his problems.

"Team, this is Six. One tango down. Repeat, one tango down." He left the PRC soldier and flew back to check on Powers. A single shot, through his faceplate of all places. Garver swallowed back against the bile rising in his throat. "And one KIA."

Liu's voice rose, reflecting his mounting irritation at their lack of progress. The longer this took, the more options the enemy could find to exploit. "Captain Huang, report!"

The channel was silent, as it had been for several minutes. "Do you have telemetry?" he asked of Wu.

"Negative, sir," his first officer replied somberly. "We have lost both biomonitor and visor imagery." He drew a breath. "I believe we must consider the captain to be neutralized."

"Neutralized," Liu repeated with disgust. As in, killed or captured. How had they done it? Regardless, he could no longer consider them to be in control of the American ship. Much as he would have preferred to avoid it—a clean victory being far preferable to a bloody one—they would be forced to escalate. "Target their remaining hydrogen tank, two missiles," he ordered.

◎ 38 ◎

Garver was just beginning to repressurize the crew decks when alarms blared and an angry buzzing sound stirred the hull. The PDCs had burst to life and he flew up into the cupola to see. Sure enough, two clouds of gas expanded into space perhaps a kilometer away as both missiles' remains clattered against the hull.

He slapped the nearby intercom switch, though with so few people left aboard he could've just as easily called Rosie directly. "General quarters, general quarters! Incoming fire! Secure your compartments!" Fragments from a defeated weapon were still moving fast and could do almost as much damage as the weapon itself, so he hastily closed the petals that shielded the cupola's ring of large windows. Hopefully one of the spacers could be spared from their emergency surgery on Poole to seal off the other modules.

The defensive guns had fired automatically, still on standby despite the PRC infantry's best efforts. The grunt he'd shot had been putzing around with the weapons console, and it was a good thing the controls hadn't been made too idiot-proof or they would've surely been sitting ducks. No doubt that had been the intent. And the skipper of that PRC ship had been smart enough to translate up as soon as it released weapons, getting out of the way before the inevitable defensive rounds came back downrange.

Offensive weapons required a little more of a personal touch. Garver activated the one missile they had left and targeted *Peng Fei*'s big cement-drum propulsion section—take out their power source and not only could they not shoot, they couldn't maneuver. It would even the odds.

349

The fire-control radar locked on quickly but was just as quickly jammed. They'd come ready to play, but Garver had marked their relative position and slaved the missile's guidance to that. One bearing was better than nothing. He pressed the firing switch and felt a mechanical thud as the missile was ejected from its magazine. "Missile away!" he announced on the intercom. "Brace for evasive action!"

He pushed off for the pilot's console and really wished they'd had an actual pilot left aboard.

Marshall watched the plumes of fire and clouds of gas erupt between the two ships, still many kilometers apart.

"Is that weapons fire?" Max asked, looking up through the rendezvous windows with him.

"Afraid so," Marshall said. He watched as *Peng Fei* began moving aggressively while the *Borman* seemed to lag. He motioned for Max to bring his focus back to the instrument panel. "Get ready. They're really not going to like this part."

"Neither am I," Jasmine said, gripping her seat.

Marshall made one last check of their position relative to the H-K and nodded to Max. "Cycle the gear."

Max pulled on the landing gear handle and slammed it down. There was a sickening groan of rending metal as the landing skids punched through the satellite's radiator wings. Ammonia coolant escaped in a continuous, fine mist into space. "Gear up," Max reported as he shoved the handle back into its detent. "One green, two amber."

As expected, Marshall thought. The nose gear was fine but the main skids were trashed.

Max suddenly pointed at a cloud of gas that had burped up from the *Peng Fei*, coming from the side of the ship facing them. "Did they just fire on us?"

"They sure did," Marshall said as he goosed the main thrusters. "Hang on!"

It looked like PDC fire; they didn't want to waste a missile on him while the *Borman* was still out there. He moved them swiftly away from the H-K satellite, which now sat dying as its own vital fluids escaped into space. With no coolant flowing between its powerplant and radiators, it would soon overheat and shut down.

Within seconds, a cloud of steel slugs meant for *Specter* instead shredded the killsat.

"We did it!" Max exulted, but Marshall wasn't convinced. They'd taken out one threat; a larger one remained and he had no weapons to bring to the fight. He angrily bit down on his lip: *That wasn't even the mission, genius.* He turned to study the Jiangs once more—if his mission was to keep them safe, had he just failed? What options did he have left?

The crew's delight at their defensive guns easily defeating *Borman*'s remaining missile was tempered by the loss of their hunter-killer. "Laser platform is—neutralized," Wu said solemnly. "Reactor is overheating and going into SCRAM mode, sir."

Liu clenched his fist and cursed silently. He would be held to account for the loss of a strategic asset, enemy action or not.

It was time to end this game. He could continue toying with the *Borman* and overwhelm them with missile fire. They would eventually exhaust their point-defense magazines, but it would be a messy affair that exposed his ship to more risk. If the *Borman* was to be destroyed, there were much cleaner ways to do it.

"Bring us about. Minus eighty degrees yaw, plus five degrees pitch," he ordered. "Energize the gauss cannon."

Marshall called frantically over the secure channel and was surprised when Garver answered. What he had to say was even more surprising.

"He's out? Right now?"

"Couldn't be avoided," Garver said. "They had to amputate. Rosie's with him but he's still under heavy sedation."

"Are you running the command deck solo, then?"

"Doing my best, sir. But you understand what this means."

Garver could be both subtle and painfully direct. "Affirmative, Chief." Marshall was now the ranking officer, whether or not he was physically aboard.

"What are your orders, sir?"

Before Marshall could wrap his mind around the enormity of what had just been put upon him, the unicom frequency barked to life.

※　※　※

"Attention, all American spacecraft. This is Colonel Liu Wang Shu. You have violated protected territory and attacked military assets of the People's Republic of China. You are hereby directed to stand down, surrender your vessel along with the fugitives from justice you harbor."

Before the Americans could demand to know what would happen if they didn't, Liu finished his message: "We have targeted the *Borman* with a one-hundred-fifty-millimeter, fifty-megajoule electromagnetic cannon." He then turned to his first officer. "Major Wu?"

"Gauss cannon is loaded and energized, targeted at RQ39's center of mass, sir."

Liu nodded with satisfaction, held up a finger and keyed the microphone. "Regardless of your intentions here, you have demonstrated yourselves to be opponents worthy of respect. I believe in offering my adversaries a choice, whenever possible, between life and death. An *informed* choice. In case you doubt our intentions, I shall provide you a demonstration."

He closed his fist.

"Firing," Wu said.

Being closest to the asteroid, Marshall and his passengers had a front-row seat to the devastation. There was no muzzle flash, no firebolt across space, no cloud of superheated gas and certainly no thunderous report; only a burst from *Peng Fei*'s aft thrusters to counteract the recoil. It was enough to show how much of a kick the magnetic gun had.

Within seconds there was a brilliant flash from the face of RQ39, almost dead center at what approximated the misshapen asteroid's equator. Fountains of ejecta, pulverized rock, exploded into space as if a volcano had suddenly erupted.

"Good lord," Max breathed. "Did they just fire a nuclear warhead?"

"No," Marshall said distractedly, doing the math. One hundred fifty millimeters was the size of a field artillery shell, and if propelled at enough velocity it wouldn't even need to be explosive. It only needed to be heavy and fast, and that round had just covered over twenty kilometers in about four seconds. "It's called a Gauss gun," he sighed. "It's a mass driver. It can hurl heavy projectiles extremely fast, over and over."

"And your—what—PDCs?" Jasmine asked. "They can't defeat it?"

"It's nothing like a missile," Marshall explained. "This would be like trying to shoot down an artillery round with a machine gun." He had no idea if she appreciated the absurd impossibility of that, but it was all he could think of.

In the distance, sunlight glinted off the Chinese ship. "They're firing again!" Max exclaimed.

"No," Marshall said, holding out a hand to steady him. "They're turning."

The unicom frequency squealed to life again. "This concludes our demonstration," Liu said with uncommon playfulness. He knew he had the upper hand; hell, he was holding *all* the cards. "Do not bother yourselves wondering what our regeneration time is, I assure you it is less than you would like. Particularly when it is operating at less than full capacity, which it was. If you do not stand down, we will be forced to fire at full charge against your vessel."

"Forced," Marshall scoffed. *Sure they would.*

Garver's voice came over the secure channel. "That thing's pointed right at us now, sir. What are your orders?"

Marshall screwed his eyes shut in frustration, forcing back a mounting headache as he racked his brain for a plan.

"We surrender, Chief."

◎ 39 ◎

"This is Ensign Marshall Hunter, acting commander of the American spacecraft *Borman*."

Liu recognized the voice. *Interesting*. "Ensign Hunter," he said with mocking surprise, "you are not aboard the *Borman*, I believe."

"You have a good memory, Colonel. I'm aboard our shuttle *Specter* with the Jiangs." A pause, as if the young man were working up the courage to go on. "On behalf of our—my—crew . . . we surrender. I am requesting rations and safe passage aboard your vessel to Earth."

It sounded as if he was choking on the words, Liu thought. That spoke well of him. "A wise choice, Ensign, which we are willing to accommodate. What is your current situation?"

"We took some damage from your point-defense rounds and our landing gear is damaged," he said, rubbing it in that he'd at least managed to take out their gun emplacement. "We still have maneuvering ability but do not have much delta-v left. Less than ten meters per second."

"Is that enough for you to rendezvous with our ship?" Liu asked, feeling magnanimous.

"Affirmative. Please advise the berthing port you wish us to use, and transmit your rendezvous and docking procedures."

Liu hesitated, and shot Wu a questioning look. "He will need that information, sir," the senior pilot advised him. "There is a significant collision risk without it."

"Very well," Liu said. "Prepare the information he needs and send it."

"One other thing," Marshall said. "We sustained some damage when we, well, rendezvoused with your satellite. I'm going to have to get outside to inspect our docking ring. That's going to delay us several hours."

Liu's lips drew thin, showing his mounting irritation. "You have done enough damage for one day, Ensign. I advise you to make haste."

Rosie ripped off her surgical gloves and shoved them into a biohazard container, angrily enough to almost take a layer of skin with them. "We're doing *what*?"

"You heard me," Garver said impatiently as he stripped out of his spacesuit. "The good young ensign doesn't see any other way that keeps us alive."

"What about you, Chief? Hunter's good people, but he's not salty. There's got to be a way out of this."

He took in the chaotic scene of the normally squared-away med bay—the complicated negative-pressure isolation tent could only do so much to contain the mess—and his eyes settled on an exhausted Rosie, still in her cooling garment and covered in Simon Poole's blood.

Emergency surgery in the field was trying enough for a paramedic; having done it in zero gravity on her CO must have left her drained in ways they'd never imagined. Or maybe it was her having taken a life for the first, hopefully only, time.

He turned to their commanding officer, still under sedation beneath the protective cocoon of an EMS pod. Submariner, then an astronaut, now some crazy combination of the two. Garver tried to draw on his own experience, put himself in the skipper's shoes. Poole could be insanely inventive. Would he have made the same call as Hunter?

"If there's an option he hasn't considered, I can't see it," he finally said. "Hunter said we should expect one of their Shenzou craft to arrive here after he's aboard *Peng Fei*. Let's get the docking node prepped for that. We'll worry about the rest later."

"Aye, Chief," Rosie said, and tiredly began to strip down to her underwear. It spoke volumes of their current state that in a confined space with three other men, no one seemed to pay any mind.

⸕　⸕　⸕

"Ugliest weld I've ever done in my life," Marshall said as he climbed back into the shuttle's cabin. He locked down the outer hatch and placed a vacuum torch back into the equipment locker. "Not that I've done many. None in space, for that matter."

"Will it hold up?" Jasmine asked. "You're certain this will be safe?"

"Sure, until it's not," Marshall said tiredly as he began repressurizing the cabin.

"I trust you," she said, "but you must understand. I would rather have you open that hatch and throw me into the vacuum than be imprisoned on a PRC ship. We'll eventually be just as dead."

"I'm really trying to keep it from coming to that," he said, and gestured at a tablet strapped to the control pedestal between the pilot seats. "Are you able to make sense of their specs, Mr. Jiang?"

The older man smiled. "I think we're well past that. It's Max, okay? And yes, my Mandarin is still perfect."

"Didn't mean that, but it'll be helpful. Sorry but I can't even read a Chinese menu. I'm going to have to lean on you two pretty hard."

"We have no choice but to help," Max said, and pulled up a list of procedures. "These are their rendezvous protocols, including terminal control frequencies and holding gates. And here"—he scrolled down to a vehicle diagram—"is the layout of their primary docking node." It held three docking ports in a T arrangement. "They want us to berth at portal one, the forward ring. Portals two and three each have a Shenzou-B docked to them. They are each capable of holding up to seven crew, and maintain a normal sea-level oxygen-nitrogen mixture at fourteen psi." He moved the image along with his fingers, tracing the ship's length. "At the far end, adjacent to the waste reclamation compartment, is the brig."

"They won't waste any time taking us there," Marshall said. "Nice how they thought to put it at the smelliest end of the ship." He took a deep breath. "Fourteen psi, huh? That's what I thought. Let's enjoy breathing without helmets for a bit longer. We might be in them for a while." He checked each of their fittings to make sure their suit bottles were replenishing from the shuttle's supply.

Marshall had piloted them into the *Peng Fei*'s approach zone slowly, unfamiliar with the hulking ship and not wanting to waste an ounce of precious propellant. Max sat beside him, following his movements while picking up everything he could about piloting the spacecraft. The controls he'd mastered for *Prospector* were much more intuitive compared to *Specter*, which Marshall called more "government issue." It had less glass, fewer touchscreens, more hardwired switches and buttons.

Marshall had first needed to program their automated docking sequence, translating the procedure from Mandarin with Max's help. The shuttle's lidar system was still working and would guide them into the docking target on *Peng Fei*'s forward node. As they glided silently toward the hulking Chinese ship, he let the flight-path director pulse thrusters to keep them on course.

"The biggest difference between this and flying an airplane is timing," Marshall explained. "Piloting a spacecraft ultimately depends on timing. We use the RCS to fine-tune our position and everything else comes down to hitting our burns at just the right second. A flight computer in a lot of ways is just a sophisticated countdown timer."

As the shuttle backed into *Peng Fei*'s forward docking ring, he made one final pass on the routine he'd programmed into the master flight computer and checked his watch against it. As he finished, the small text screen flashed a single prompt: EXECUTE?

Marshall entered the final command. "Yes, please."

The *Peng Fei*'s docking node was squared away, Marshall had to admit. Sparkling white, with no clutter nor a single piece of gear apparently out of place. A large red-and-yellow PRC flag dominated one side of the module while a portrait of the Party chairman adorned the other. Two unsmiling crewmen of the People's Liberation Aerospace Force stood on either side, their feet in floor restraints in front of the open Shenzou spacecraft. *SOP*, Marshall thought—keep the crew vehicles on standby when an unfamiliar spacecraft is berthing. You never knew when things might go sideways and the crew would have to bug out. He just wasn't used to seeing armed guards.

He moved aside so the Jiangs could emerge from the docking tunnel, the three of them still in their spacesuits. They each found nearby foot restraints and approximated standing as a wiry figure emerged from the opposite end. He pulled himself upright before

them, and while Marshall could not decipher the characters on his
name tape he recognized the three cherry-blossom insignia on the
epaulets of his jumpsuit.

Marshall cracked open his visor to speak. "Colonel Liu," he said
stiffly. "Ensign Marshall Hunter, US Space Force, Orbit Guard."

Liu grunted a brusque greeting and eyed them like a cat regarding
its kill. He'd seemed a lot more friendly on the radio. He nodded to
one of the guards—judging by the ranks on their collars they had to
be more than that, though right now Marshall could not think of
them as anything else—who presented him with three bundles of
clothing.

"You know what is happening here, Ensign Hunter," Liu said.
"Remove your spacesuits and put these on," he ordered. "You will be
escorted to our secure facility."

"I'm afraid we can't do that just yet," Marshall said nonchalantly.
He kept one hand on his visor. "We've been in a pure oxygen
environment at five psi since yesterday. We need a few hours to adjust
our gas mixture so we don't get decompression sickness. I'm
endangering myself just talking to you like this."

Liu glared at him. "Indeed you are. First you need time to inspect
your damaged spacecraft, now you need time to acclimate your
compromised bodies." He smiled thinly. "Is there anything *else* you
require, Ensign?"

One hand still on his visor, Marshall's eyes darted to the watch on
his wrist ring. "No sir," he said, looking at his companions. "Max and
I were just having that conversation—timing is everything in
spaceflight, right?" He slid his visor back down and took a deep
breath of pure oxygen.

"In your case, it has run out." Liu turned to one of the crewmen.
"Zhou, you will stay here with the Jiangs and manage their
acclimation to our atmosphere." He angrily snapped open Marshall's
visor. "You and I, however, have much to discuss. Perhaps a little
discomfort will encourage your cooperation."

Marshall ignored him, still eyeing his watch. "That's five."

Liu furrowed his brow. "Five?" What was this idiot going on about
now?

"Three," Marshall replied, then: "Two." He met Liu's eyes. "One."

The blast from *Specter* rocked the ship. A cloud of exploding hypergolics thundered out of the connecting tunnel, tearing the shuttle apart and opening them up to space. Marshall held his breath and slammed down his visor. He shoved Liu aside, the colonel's face a mask of shock as the ship's atmosphere emptied into the void.

Marshall sprang off the sidewall and dove into one of the adjacent tunnels, right behind the Jiangs. "Find me the flight manual!" he shouted over their suit intercom as he slammed the hatch shut behind them. He winced at the sharp pain in his elbows, already getting his first taste of the bends. He hurriedly double-checked his helmet lock and turned up his oxygen supply to burn the nitrogen out of his system.

The Shenzou-B layout was remarkably similar to the Russian's advanced Soyuz. "Geez, do they have to steal *everything*?" Marshall wondered aloud as he strapped himself into the center pilot's seat.

"The answer to that is *yes*," Max said, strapping into next to him as Jasmine settled into what was nominally the engineer's seat. "And right now, you should be grateful." He tapped a few commands into a touchscreen and the glass control panels flickered to life.

All of the information was in Mandarin, of course. "I can't read a damn thing," Marshall said. The pair of hand controllers and eight-ball attitude indicator in the center of the console were easily understood, and there was no time to rely on the Jiangs translating the rest for him. "You undock us, I'll pilot us out. Deal?"

"Deal," Max said, his fingers dancing across the screen as he searched for the right commands. "Ah, there we go. Emergency separation engaged."

A thud echoed through the little spacecraft as clamps unlocked and spring-loaded bolts pushed them away from the *Peng Fei*'s ruined docking node. As they pulled away, Jasmine activated a periscope mounted in the side of their flight module and trained it on the remains of *Specter*. The shuttle's tail had been torn open, exposing its cabin—and by extension, *Peng Fei*'s cabin—to space. Among the cloud of shredded alloys and composites, she counted at least three bodies in PRC uniforms. She and Max watched the scene in fascination and horror as Marshall pulsed thrusters, pushing them farther away. "I know we had to ride rockets to get this far," Jasmine said, "but to see that much explosive force ..."

"A little frightening, isn't it?" Marshall said.

"And in such a small ship," she said.

"Hypergolics are wicked. They'll deep fry your lungs when they're not exploding on contact. I hate the stuff."

"I suppose it has its uses." She shuddered. "After this, I don't intend to ever be out here again. It's not safe."

Marshall suspected that was intended for her husband as much as anything. "To be fair, those engines worked fine until I welded the thrust chambers shut." He found a radio panel and dialed in his ship's frequency. "Ahoy, *Borman*."

Colonel Liu Wang Shu gasped reflexively, his lungs violently emptied of air and unable to replace it. Numbing cold at first, he felt burning heat as the unfiltered Sun bore down on him in its full force as he fell into the void. The silence was like nothing he'd ever experienced, a complete absence of sound so utterly consuming that it was as a noise unto itself: The silent music of the planets eternally tracing their orbits. He could feel the raw scream in his throat, though he could not hear it.

His ship swirled past in his fading vision as he tumbled through space. *How odd to see it from here*, he thought. How few space travelers got to see their vessels like this—had any, in fact?

It was liberating in a sense, and would be quite the story could he ever tell it. So much to . . .

All became darkness.

❁ **40** ❁

Nick Lesko sat up in his bed when the glass door slid open. Hoping to have another visit from that bouncy brunette, he was sorely disappointed to see three men in suits walk in unannounced while a fourth stood outside, warning away any curious hospital staff. It became even more disappointing when they showed their badges.

"Nicholas Lesko?"

He nodded, eyeing them suspiciously. "Uh-huh."

"Agent Lang, FBI," the leader said, slipping his badge back into his chest pocket. "We have a few questions for you."

Lesko jutted his chin defiantly. "I got nothing to say. Not without my lawyer."

The three men exchanged jaded glances. "We were afraid you might feel that way." Lang loudly dragged a chair from across the room and sat, facing him. "We'll just get right to it. You're in deep shit, Mr. Lesko."

They stared at each other in silence. Lesko spread his hands in a "what do you want" gesture.

Lang rubbed at the bridge of his nose. "Very well. I get it, pleading the Fifth. That's of course your right. But you need to understand what you're being investigated for: espionage, for starters. Probably homicide, after NTSB finishes its investigation into the Stardust mishap. You're a smart guy. I don't have to explain what this means for you, do I?"

"I cooperate and you hide me out in some Nebraska backwater for the rest of my life. I don't, and you put me away for the rest of my life."

"Something like that, yes."

"You do what you gotta do, I ain't talking," Lesko said, weighing his options. The Feds thought they were in control, but what they didn't know was that there was no such thing as "witness protection" when it came to those pricks in Macau. If he talked, someone, somewhere, would find a way to get to him. If he couldn't stay on a military base forever, then the next safest place he could be was in a federal supermax prison.

No matter what he did, the rest of his life was going to suck. The question now was how much time did he have? He'd deal with the rest later.

"Permission to come aboard."

"Permission granted." Simon Poole floated up from the connecting tunnel and gripped Marshall's arm, a broad smile across his face. "Welcome home."

"Feels like it now, sir," Marshall said. "Never thought I'd be so glad to see this place." He kept his eyes fixed on Poole's face, on anything but his missing leg.

Poole didn't miss it. "Aw hell," he said, "have a look. Everybody's got to tear off the Band-Aid at some point."

"Yes sir, but..." Marshall said, "I mean...*damn*, sir. I don't know what to say."

"What is there to say? Hell, I can't wait to get back to Fleet Ops. I can hear it already: 'Peg Leg' Poole, the Space Pirate," he growled. "I should grow a beard and get a damned parrot to complete the look."

Marshall looked around the connecting corridor, surveying the damage. Patched bullet holes, stains that hadn't been completely removed, the medical bay closed off perhaps permanently, at least until they got back to Earth.

"It got sporty in here, as your Dad might say," Poole said, noticing him. "I watched him in zero-g combat once, you know. Never was something I wanted to try out myself. Kind of like one of those fight scenes in *The Matrix*, but without the trench coats and cartoon philosophy."

"Ship-to-ship isn't much more fun, sir. Standing next to a bomb that's about to go off is even less so."

"Technically that could be considered a war crime, you know. Faking surrender for a tactical advantage."

"Yes sir, I suppose some pencil-neck lawyer could see it that way. I doubt many of those types ever had a gun pointed at them."

"Of course you were *prepared* to surrender," Poole said, aping an officious bureaucratic tone, "but the Jiangs weren't obliged to go along with it. Changed their minds, did they?"

"They were pretty adamant, sir. And then my OMS went and malfunctioned like that . . ."

"Good thinking, by the way. You had a lot of people really cranked up here. 'Surrender is not in our creed' and all that. Not saying I'd have been any happier. Lucky for you I was sedated or I'd have found a way to personally come over there and knock some sense into you."

"I'd have been glad to have had you there, sir. Might have found a way out of it without blowing up *Specter*."

Poole put a hand on his shoulder and tapped his forehead with one finger. "You didn't hear me—I said *good thinking*. They caught us with our pants around our ankles, son. You found a way to zip up our fly without snagging our junk in it."

"An interesting metaphor, sir. But I don't think we're zipped up yet, are we?" They still had a long way back to Earth.

"Not yet, but we've got some ideas." Poole led him down the corridor, into the wardroom where Garver and Rosie waited with trays of their best freeze-dried, reconstituted steak. Four drinking bulbs full of golden-brown liquid were clipped to the table by each. Marshall picked up on the sharp scent of bourbon. "First, a toast."

There being no arguing with physics, they were still locked into a path home that included a Mars flyby, a six-month extension to their journey that no one had come prepared for. The following days were spent in a flurry of hops between *Borman* and the now-empty *Peng Fei* using their newly acquired shuttle, made flyable by the Jiangs' tireless translation of Shenzou's flight manual and liberal handwritten notes taped over every switch, lever, and circuit breaker.

"Looks like yet another packet of freeze-dried noodles," Marshall said as he sent another soft-sided package flying down an open corridor.

"Not bad." Max caught it in midair. "I recall you saying you couldn't even read a Chinese menu."

"He's a fast learner," Rosie said as she took the package from him, stuffing it into the Shenzou's forward module. "I think we're going to be thoroughly sick of this stuff by the time we get back."

"I can promise you will be," Max said. "Give me a good hot dog any time."

They spent two full days aboard the *Peng Fei*, raiding its pantry and—just as importantly—its computers. By the end of the week, when the synodic period dictated *Borman*'s departure window, they had emptied the ship of months' worth of food and absconded with hard drives full of information on the extent of PRC operations in cislunar space. There would be much to keep them occupied during the long journey home.

"Ensign McCall."

Perhaps having been a little too comfortable at her control station, Roberta sat up straight in her seat at hearing the Ops officer's voice behind her. She hastily checked her screens—nothing untoward in view, and the drone systems she was running were all working normally. So, not in trouble then. Not yet.

She stood, surprised to find him with Commander Wicklund in tow. "Yes sir?"

He began roughly. "I understand you've been doing a little freelancing, Ensign."

It was too bad Ivey was off today. She could use the backup. "I think I can explain, sir."

The Air Force colonel eyed her, then traded a look with Wicklund. "Can you? Because that would be interesting."

She swallowed. "Sir, I—"

The colonel held up a hand. "The less I know from you, the better. Wicklund here already briefed me."

Roberta looked at him quizzically.

"You think I'm going to just let you go around your chain of command, Ensign? It doesn't work that way."

"I don't understand . . ."

"We don't pay you to understand, McCall," the colonel said, jerking a thumb between himself and Wicklund. "That's our job."

She turned to Wicklund, perturbed. "You told him?"

"Hell yes I did, because it was brilliant and ballsy. Told him you deserved a commendation."

The colonel interjected. "Which I might have endorsed if I'd known beforehand. Lucky for you it worked. If it'd blown up in your face, we'd be having a different conversation."

"You pulled off a bit of an intelligence coup," Wicklund said, "which would've been great if you actually worked in the S-2 or investigative service."

"You did the right thing, but it embarrassed the wrong people," the colonel explained. "So no commendation medals for you, I'm afraid."

Roberta knitted her brow. "I wasn't looking for medals, sir. I was just trying to . . . well . . . defend my country and help my fellow Guardians." She knew it sounded corny as hell, and she didn't care.

The two senior officers exchanged looks. "No good deed goes unpunished, Ensign. In this case it ends with you being reassigned," the colonel said.

Roberta deflated. The drones had been fun while they lasted. "I understand, sir."

The colonel handed her a tablet. "Sometimes, recognition comes in unexpected forms."

Puzzled, she took the tablet. "I still don't understand . . ." she said, reading the orders. "I'm being assigned to your detachment, Commander Wicklund?"

"For now," he said, "until the *Borman* gets back. That should be enough time to get you up to speed and tie up any loose ends here on Earth." Wicklund gave her a wink. "Welcome aboard."

"Inmate 163922. Visitor."

Finally, Nick Lesko thought. His bloodsucking lawyer had decided to show up. He pulled himself up from the thin mattress atop the concrete bench that formed his bed and worked out the kinks in his back. With a loud buzz, the door to his cell slid open and a burly guard waited for him on the other side. Lesko ignored the man's name tag, didn't register his face as to him they were all the same. The guard's black and white uniforms were as ubiquitous as the prison's colorless milieu of concrete and steel; the only distinctions Lesko could make were by smell. This one smelled of mustard and onions, so it must have been after lunchtime.

The guard led him by the arm down a long corridor and around a corner to a series of small visitation cubicles, each partitioned from the outside by thick panes of shatter-resistant glass.

He'd only been here once before, the first time he'd met his scumbag lawyer. It had been a lot busier then. Lesko noticed right away there was no one else around. He looked to the guard, who pointed him to a cubicle at the end of the row. Behind him, the steel door shut with a thud.

As Lesko passed the last partition, he could see his visitor: young, well dressed, a slick of black hair pulled back from his head into a small, tight bun. Asian, and definitely not his lawyer. The man picked up the telephone receiver on his side of the glass, motioning for Lesko to do the same.

"Greetings, Mr. Lesko. We haven't met."

"We haven't," Lesko said suspiciously. "Who are you?"

"That is not important. But I bring a message from a mutual acquaintance."

Lesko's neck began to tingle. Behind him, the steel door thudded again. "Yeah? What message is that?"

The man remained silent, his eyes looking beyond Lesko. They were trying to intimidate him, and it was starting to piss him off. Where the hell was his lawyer when he needed him? "Guard—" Lesko began, and turned to look. Behind him, the guard had disappeared. In his place stood an orange-suited hulk, his coveralls barely containing his tree-trunk physique. A prong of coarsely formed metal glinted in his right hand.

For being so massive, he was shockingly fast. Lesko felt the blows, but didn't feel the blade sinking in until the third or fourth strike.

As he crumpled to the floor, vital fluids gushing from a half-dozen openings in his torso, Lesko stared up at the ceiling as the light faded around him. *A shank?* He'd expected them to be more subtle. *You do what you gotta do.*

◎ EPILOGUE ◎

Mars grew visibly larger by the minute as they approached from its night side. Mostly shrouded in darkness, its eastern limb glowed in burnt ocher as the Sun climbed over the horizon. Morning mists of carbon dioxide filled the lower plains while the massive Olympus Mons rose above the planet's thin atmosphere.

Marshall sat in the command pilot's seat, Captain Poole in the second pilot's seat beside him. Behind them, the Jiangs marveled at the passing planet from the cupola, furiously firing away with every camera they could fit up there. He hoped at least one picture would be of them with the red planet in the background; they deserved the indulgence.

The view from the dome would've been spectacular, but never in a million years did he think he'd get to see it from the pilot's seat. That was a thrill few could understand.

"Look at that," he said as more of Mars came into view. "I can't believe how fast it goes by."

"Life is like that," Poole said. "I know you're thinking about the planet, but still . . ."

"I think I know what you mean now, sir." He stared at the spectacle outside. "My first look at this was through my dad's telescope. It wasn't long after you guys came back from the Moon."

"Now *that* was a real shitshow," Poole drawled. "Nothing to do with your dad, believe it or not. I just about bought the farm there."

"A lot of us did," Marshall said, his voice trailing off. Memories of riding out the flood with his mother came back with a shiver. He pushed the thought from his mind, as he'd learned to do over the years: put it in a box where it belonged, lock it away, don't let it out. He focused on the planet outside. "I've wanted to go to Mars ever since. I can't explain it, I just always felt pulled to go like some people feel about climbing mountains. It's there and nobody knows much about it, so let's go." He sighed. "I just hope we get to come back."

"You never know where the fickle hand of fate will land, son." Poole smiled. "I got a message from your Aunt Penny." She wasn't technically his aunt, but Penny Stratton had been as close to his parents as Poole had been over the years. "She's back at NASA, heading up their human spaceflight division. You knew that, right?"

"I didn't. What did they do to convince her to quit flying missionaries around South America?"

"New deep-space project called Magellan, she said. Reusable and modular, based on this platform," Poole said, patting the glare shield. "They want to experiment with variable-impulse plasma engines, supposedly it can do this very trip in three months."

Marshall whistled. "That's serious." He eyed Poole. "Wait a minute . . . you're going to do it, aren't you?"

Poole patted the air where his leg used to be. "They're not going to let me stay, I can tell you that. This here is an express ticket to medical retirement." He laughed. "That'll be like my third retirement. I thought you had to be pro ball player to do that, but whatever."

"So the military won't let you command a ship, but NASA will?"

"I'm the flavor of the month, I guess. She wants somebody who knows his way around a spacecraft and a nuke plant."

Mars filled the windows now. Their flyby was already half over, yet this crowded out his attention. "I'm not sure what to say, sir. I hate to see you go."

Behind him, he heard Garver clear his throat. Had the chief been eavesdropping? "You do understand they still draw astronauts from active military, sir?"

Marshall's eyes darted between the two. This was more than just eavesdropping.

Poole placed a hand on his shoulder. "You're coming with me."

THE END

❀ NOTES AND ACKNOWLEDGMENTS ❀

Writing is simultaneously a solitary endeavor and one that should not be undertaken alone. There are a few people without whom I absolutely would not have made it this far, and they have my deepest gratitude:

My wife, Melissa, for her encouragement and steadfast belief in me. She has taken on more to allow me the freedom to write than any man could hope for.

The editorial team at Baen: Toni Weisskopf, Tony Daniel, and Christopher Ruocchio. They are blessings to work with and are all I could hope for in a publisher. I am still learning there is a fine balance between giving editorial advice and letting the writer run wild, and they consistently find it.

Further thanks go to fellow Citadel alumnus Randy "Komrade" Bresnik, retired Marine Corps aviator and NASA astronaut, for his insider's view of living and working in space.

Finally, Winchell Chung's Atomic Rockets website was invaluable. It is *the* one-stop shop for anyone trying to write believable science fiction. If you want to understand the peculiarities of space travel (and much of it is peculiar), there is no better place to start.

Now for some insight on where my head was while writing this:

Some readers may recognize similarities between my fictional *Prospector* Mars mission and Inspiration Mars, a private expedition promoted by original space tourist Dennis Tito. Ambitious but feasible, it would have departed Earth this year to send two people on a flyby of the red planet. I'm not in a position to judge how realistic an idea it might have been at the time, to me it just sounded like great story fodder.

A similar concept was studied during the Apollo days, which would have sent three astronauts on a flight around both Mars and Venus in a Skylab-type spacecraft. Neither project may have ever gotten off the ground but they certainly inspired me (puns intended).

As of this writing, the U.S. Space Force has only been around for a year. It will certainly be some time before we start seeing crewed spacecraft patrolling in orbit, though I do believe it will become necessary as civilian space travel becomes more commonplace. At the very least, there will eventually be a need for some kind of rescue capability.

My fictional Space Force rank structure may end up running afoul of reality, but in my defense Congress did pass a resolution in 2020 directing them to use naval ranks. I hold out hope that when the day comes for the USSF to field crewed spacecraft, they'll come around to the fact that naval ranks just sound right in that context. Think about it: Would you rather read about a spaceship colonel, or a spaceship *captain*?

Colonel Kirk, or Captain Kirk?

Lieutenant Colonel Adama, or Commander Adama?

General Ackbar or Admiral Ackbar? Hmm... Maybe when you get to flag rank it doesn't matter so much (*it's a trap!*).

The parallels I've drawn with Chinese military expansion in the Pacific should be obvious enough. Even though our little corner of the Solar System seems like it should be big enough for all nations to share, if deep space becomes a new economic sphere then we should expect there to be some "great power" competition over it. Bad actors will inevitably emerge and will have to be confronted; that seems to be the way things always go.

Hopefully I haven't mangled the very few Chinese translations attempted herein too terribly. My knowledge of Mandarin is limited to whatever I stumbled into online. Finding the name "Maleko" ("Pledged to Mars") was a happy accident and fit Max Jiang's character perfectly. *Peng Fei* ("Flight of the Roc") was another serendipitous find and sounded like a great name for a spaceborne battleship.

Readers may also recognize a common theme I touched on in *Frozen Orbit*, which is the need to expand our national economy into space. It may seem like too fantastic a goal, but trans-oceanic airline service was once an indulgence of the wealthy. Today that mode of travel is commonplace. Not only can normal people afford it, it supports an untold number of businesses while directly creating jobs for tens of thousands. Mine was one of them for many years.

I hope to see commercial spaceflight achieve the same status in my lifetime, if only so I may someday buy a ticket.